CRITICAL ACCLAIM FOR *DEADLY ALIBI*

'Curves I never saw coming' – ***For the Love of Books***

'You are not going to want to put it down' – **Jo Robertson, *My Chestnut Reading Tree***

'Of all the Steel books so far, this will be one that stays with me for a long time' – ***So Many Books, So Little Time***

CRITICAL ACCLAIM FOR *MURDER RING*

'A great murder mystery in its own right and highly recommended' – ***Fiction Is Stranger Than Fact***

'Smoothly professional fare from the always-consistent Russell' – ***Crime Time***

CRITICAL ACCLAIM FOR *KILLER PLAN*

'Her previous six novels featuring DI Geraldine Steel marked her out as a rare talent, and this seventh underlines it' – ***Daily Mail***

'I will be looking out for more from this author' – ***Nudge***

'A fast-paced police procedural and a compelling read' – ***Mystery People***

CRITICAL ACCLAIM FOR *FATAL ACT*

'A most intriguing and well executed mystery and... an engrossing read' – ***Shotsmag***

'The best yet from Leigh Russell – she keeps you guessing all the way through and leaves you wanting more' – ***Crime Book Club***

'Another fast-paced and complex mystery – a fabulous read' – ***Fiction Is Stranger Than Fact***

'Another corker of a book from Leigh Russell... Russell's talent for writing top-quality crime fiction just keeps on growing...' – ***Euro Crime***

'The plot is strong and the writing just flows with style and panache' – ***Goodread***

D0234852

CRITICAL ACCLAIM FOR *STOP DEAD*

'All the things a mystery should be, intriguing, enthralling, tense and utterly absorbing' – ***Best Crime Books***

'*Stop Dead* is taut and compelling, stylishly written with a deeply human voice' – **Peter James**

'A definite must read for crime thriller fans everywhere – 5*' – ***Newbooks Magazine***

'A well-written, a well-researched, and a well-constructed whodunnit. Highly recommended' – ***Mystery People***

'A whodunnit of the highest order. The tightly written plot kept me guessing all the way' – ***Crimesquad***

CRITICAL ACCLAIM FOR *DEATH BED*

'*Death Bed* is a marvellous entry in this highly acclaimed series' – ***Promoting Crime Fiction***

'An innovative and refreshing take on the psychological thriller' – ***Books Plus Food***

'A well-written, well-plotted crime novel with fantastic pace and lots of intrigue' – ***Bookersatz***

'*Death Bed* is her most exciting and well-written to date. And, as the others are superb, that is really saying something! 5*' – ***Euro Crime***

CRITICAL ACCLAIM FOR *DEAD END*

'All the ingredients combine to make a tense, clever police whodunnit' **– Marcel Berlins, *Times***

'I could not put this book down' – ***Newbooks Magazine***

'A brilliant talent in the thriller field' – **Jeffery Deaver**

'An encounter that will take readers into the darkest recesses of the human psyche' – ***Crime Time***

'Well written and chock full of surprises, this hard-hitting, edge-of-the seat instalment is yet another treat… Geraldine Steel looks set to become a household name. Highly recommended' – ***Euro Crime***

'Good, old-fashioned, heart-hammering police thriller… a no-frills delivery of pure excitement' – ***SAGA Magazine***

'A macabre read, full of enthralling characters and gruesome details which kept me glued from first page to last' – ***Crimesquad***

'*Dead End* was selected as a Best Fiction Book of 2012' – ***Miami Examiner***

CRITICAL ACCLAIM FOR *ROAD CLOSED*

'A well-written, soundly plotted, psychologically acute story' – **Marcel Berlins, *Times***

'Well-written and absorbing right from the get-go… with an exhilarating climax that you don't see coming' – ***Euro Crime***

'Leigh Russell does a good job of keeping her readers guessing. She also uses a deft hand developing her characters, especially the low-lifes… a good read' – ***San Francisco Book Review***

'*Road Closed* is a gripping, fast-paced read, pulling you in from the very first tense page and keeping you captivated right to the end with its refreshingly compelling and original narrative' – ***New York Journal of Books***

CRITICAL ACCLAIM FOR *CUT SHORT*

'*Cut Short* is a stylish, top-of-the-line crime tale, a seamless blending of psychological sophistication and gritty police procedure. And you're just plain going to love DI Geraldine Steel' – **Jeffery Deaver**

'Russell paints a careful and intriguing portrait of a small British community while developing a compassionate and complex heroine who's sure to win fans' – ***Publishers Weekly***

'An excellent debut' – ***Crime Time***

'Simply awesome! This debut novel by Leigh Russell will take your breath away' – ***Euro Crime***

'An excellent book…Truly a great start for new mystery author Leigh Russell' – ***New York Journal of Books***

'A sure-fire hit – a taut, slick, easy-to-read thriller' – ***Watford Observer***

'*Cut Short* is not a comfortable read, but it is a compelling and important one. Highly recommended' – ***Mystery Women***

Titles by Leigh Russell

Geraldine Steel Mysteries

Cut Short
Road Closed
Dead End
Death Bed
Stop Dead
Fatal Act
Killer Plan
Murder Ring
Deadly Alibi

Ian Peterson Murder Investigations

Cold Sacrifice
Race to Death
Blood Axe

Lucy Hall Mystery

Journey to Death
Girl in Danger
The Wrong Suspect

LEIGH RUSSELL

FATAL ACT

A DI GERALDINE STEEL MYSTERY

NO EXIT PRESS

First published in 2014 by No Exit Press,
an imprint of Oldcastle Books Ltd,
P.O.Box 394, Harpenden,
Herts, AL5 1XJ, UK

noexit.co.uk
@noexitpress

© Leigh Russell 2014

The right of Leigh Russell to be identified as the author of this work has been asserted in accordance with the Copyright, Designs and Patents Act 1988.

All rights reserved. No part of this book may be reproduced, stored in or introduced into a retrieval system, or transmitted, in any form or by any means (electronic, mechanical, photocopying, recording or otherwise) without the written permission of the publishers.

Any person who does any unauthorised act in relation to this publication may be liable to criminal prosecution and civil claims for damages.

A CIP catalogue record for this book is available from the British Library.

This is a work of fiction. Names, characters, places, and incidents either are the product of the author's imagination or are used fictitiously, and any resemblance to actual persons, living or dead, businesses, companies, events or locales is entirely coincidental.

ISBN
978-1-84344-204-2 (print)
978-1-84344-205-9 (epub)
978-1-84344-206-6 (kindle)
978-1-84344-207-3 (pdf)

4 6 8 10 9 7 5 3

Typeset by Avocet Typeset, Somerton, Somerset
in 10.5 on 12.3pt Times New Roman
Printed in Denmark by Nørhaven, Viborg

Dedicated to Michael, Jo, Phillipa and Phil

Acknowledgements

I would like to thank Dr Leonard Russell for his medical advice, my contacts on the police force for their time, my editor Keshini Naidoo for her unerring guidance, Alan Forster for his superb cover design, and Claire Watts, Alexandra Bolton and Jem Cook at No Exit Press for their constant help. Above all, I would like to record my gratitude to Ion Mills and Annette Crossland for their support and inspiration.

1

'AND DON'T EVEN THINK about following me. Did you hear me? I said, don't even think about following me!'

She slammed the door in his face. It was a chilly night, but going back for her coat would ruin her dramatic exit. As she crossed the driveway to her Porsche, a gust of wind whipped her hair into her eyes. Impatiently she brushed it away.

Turning the key in the ignition Anna waited, drumming painted finger nails on the wheel. She glanced in the mirror. The front door remained shut. The next time Piers lost his temper she was going to leave him for good. Right now she was sitting in her car at nearly two in the morning with nowhere to go. Her resolve wavered and she struggled not to cry, telling herself fiercely that she didn't need him. Clearly he wasn't rushing to follow her out of the house, but she was damned if she was going to slink back in straight away. He could stay there and stew for a while first. It struck her that he might be watching her out of the window as she sat on the drive with the engine idling. Spinning the wheel, she slammed her foot on the accelerator. The tyres squealed and she narrowly avoided hitting a black van parked at the end of the drive.

'Arsehole!' she shouted as she drove off down the road. 'You bloody arsehole!'

Drops of rain streaked the windscreen as she sped along. Once out of sight of the house she slowed down, aware that she was exceeding the speed limit. Driving cautiously, she kept to the main road for fear of losing her way. Without taking her eyes from the road, she rummaged in her bag and flung her mobile phone on the passenger seat, glancing down to check it was switched on. There were no messages. An oncoming car flashed its headlights and she swerved back onto her own side of the road, cursing out loud at the other driver in her fright.

'Fucking road hog!'

Her insults were pointless. No one could hear her. The rain was falling more heavily. Distracted by the rhythm of her windscreen wipers, she had to concentrate on the road glistening ahead of her in the soft light of the street lamps.

At first she was only vaguely aware of someone right on her tail.

'What the hell are you playing at? Do you want to get yourself killed?'

The other vehicle drew even closer and she swore again. He must have been off his head to approach so close. If she braked sharply, he wouldn't be able to avoid crashing straight into the back of her car.

'Back off, you moron, unless you want to get us both killed.'

Rattled, she put her foot down, but the other driver kept up. With perverse fury she braked suddenly. A flash of panic hit her as her tyres slid on the wet road. The van swerved, shooting onto the other side of the road where he slowed down to match her speed. Instead of overtaking or falling behind, he remained alongside her, keeping pace with her as she accelerated again.

Agitated, she wound her window down to shout at him, but the combined noise of their engines scotched any attempt to communicate. Through the window she glimpsed the driver leaning forward over his wheel, as though he fancied himself as a racing driver. Apart from their two vehicles racing along side by side the road was empty, but another car could come along at any time and crash headlong into either one of them. She eased off her accelerator and the other driver slowed down alongside her. She considered pulling into the kerb to let him go on ahead, but was afraid he might stop too. He was clearly crazy. As they neared a bend he braked and slipped back behind her to cruise along on her tail. He wasn't completely suicidal, then.

All she wanted to do now was get home safely. She drove slowly, looking out for a side road she could turn into. With luck she could slip away before her pursuer realised what she was doing. She passed a turning on the right, displaying a no entry sign. She braked abruptly. Her phone flew off the passenger seat. The van slowed down behind her. Worn out and stressed, she couldn't even remember why she had been so angry with Piers. It had been a stupid argument in the first place. She wished she was back at home, away from the road at night and its wildness. Leaning forward to retrieve her phone from the floor, she punched Piers' speed dial key. His phone rang, but there was no answer. She glanced in her mirror and glimpsed the other driver, his face a black mask in the darkness.

She flung her phone down on the seat again and switched on the radio. As soon as she could, she would turn round and head back home. Reaching a narrow side road she spun the wheel at the very last minute. Her front wheel hit the kerb. Her bumper must have skimmed the wall as she swung round, but she was past caring about the car. She grinned at the mirror. The street behind her was deserted. The side road was one way, wide enough for only one car to pass. Alongside it, a railing fenced off a small parkland. She kept going, hoping she wouldn't lose herself in a maze of one way streets. The road was too narrow for her to stop and check her sat nav but she guessed that if she went left and left again she would find Paddington Street, or else end up on Marylebone High Street. The rain was heavy now. The regular pattering of rain and the wipers swishing rapidly across the windscreen were making her drowsy. She turned a corner and gasped. A black van was racing towards her, driving the wrong way along the narrow one way street.

The van approached so fast she had no time to brake. The pavement was only inches wide. They were on a collision course. She heard herself screaming as the van careered towards her without slowing down. She couldn't see the other driver. Recovering herself, she slammed her foot on the brake, and tried to swerve. Her front tyre hit the kerb with such force that the front of her car slewed round, scraping along the wall, then swung round again. All she could do was grip the steering wheel helplessly while the car slid along. Before she could slow down, a splintering crash reverberated in her head and the whole car seemed to leap and twist in the air, jolting her bones painfully as it came to a standstill. The engine revved noisily. Her head exploded with a second impact. In the blackness, she wasn't sure if her eyes were open or closed. Salty blood filled her mouth, choking her. She knew she had to open the door and get out, but she couldn't move. Aware only of pain slicing through her head and the sound of rain drumming on the car, she lost consciousness.

2

BERN DIDN'T MIND working nights. The hour or two after the trains stopped running could be a real money-spinner. At any rate, it beat sitting in queues during the day. That was bad enough when he had an impatient passenger, but even worse was crawling through traffic to collect fares. It was a pity he was only allowed to clock up the miles, rather than charging by the hour. All things considered nights were better, as long as he avoided picking up drunks. It was almost three in the morning and he was making good time, bowling along the Marylebone Road. With a nice quiet fare in the back, he decided to follow an indirect route along back streets and notch up a few more quid on the clock. His passenger would be none the wiser, even if he knew the streets of London, which was unlikely. Bern could see him in the mirror, some swanky American sprawled in the back of the cab. Staying at The Dorchester Hotel, he could afford the extra. Probably wasn't even paying for it himself. Once this journey was over, Bern would call it a night.

It was lucky the one way streets were too narrow for anything faster than a slow crawl, because no one had thought to put out a reflective triangle to warn drivers the road was blocked by a Porsche convertible that had slammed straight into the wall. Bern managed to stop in time, but it was a close call. Ignoring complaints from his passenger, Bern climbed out of the cab, pulling his phone out of his pocket. Registering the condition of the Porsche, he regarded the smashed up vehicle warily, shouting into his phone as he walked. As he approached he realised there was a second vehicle involved in the crash, a black van that the Porsche had driven into. The poor bugger in the Porsche hadn't stood a chance. Neither of the drivers had. Shattered broken glass crunched beneath his feet although he trod carefully. He was reluctant to get too close but he couldn't turn back, even though it was almost impossible anyone could still be alive. The front of the Porsche was completely crushed. Bern had never seen anything like it.

Observing the driver of the Porsche in the shadowy interior of the car he stopped, uncertain what to do. Craning his neck to peer in through the cracked rear window, he saw the shape of a woman's head. He called out, but the driver didn't move. The front seat and dashboard were splattered with blood. He couldn't get close enough to the van to look inside it as the Porsche was blocking the road, but in any case he had seen enough. The interior of the Porsche was like a scene from a horror movie; blood everywhere. He turned away, wishing he hadn't looked so closely.

A voice in his ear was telling him the emergency services were on their way, and he was to stay where he was. He wanted to tell the woman on the phone that medical assistance was of no use to a dead driver whose blood was sprayed all over the dashboard, but he couldn't speak. His daughter was right. He was getting too old for this game. He had been on the point of retiring when Edie had unexpectedly died, so he had carried on. He couldn't sit at home by himself staring at the four walls, brooding over his bereavement after a forty year marriage. He had to get out of the house and do something. Driving was all he knew.

Feeling shaky, he returned to the cab where his passenger began shouting at him. There was nothing Bern could do but leave his hazard lights on and wait. He could hardly turn round in such a narrow roadway, and he wasn't about to reverse in the wrong direction along a one way road.

'What's the hold up here?'

'There's been an accident,' he explained, jerking his head in the direction of the two smashed up cars blocking the road.

'Well, can't you turn around? It's three o'clock in the morning for Christ's sake.'

'We can't just leave. There's been a fatal accident. There's nothing we can do for her, she's dead. The ambulance is on its way. Fat lot of good it's going to do her. You're not a doctor, I suppose –'

'Are you taking me to my hotel or not?' the fare interrupted. He clambered out of the cab. Well over six foot, he leaned over Bern as though spoiling for a fight.

'Yes, yes, I'll take you there just as soon as the emergency services get here. Look, there's no point getting shirty about it. This had nothing to do with me. Thc collision took place before we got here.'

His passenger glared at him.

'I want you to take me to my hotel now. I've got to be up early in the morning –'

'We've got to wait for the Old Bill.'

'Wait? Wait here? I don't think so.'

That was all Bern needed. So much for adding a few miles on the clock to earn an extra quid or two. He was driving around in the dark when most people were at home, and all he had to show for it was an irate customer and the memory of an accident which would probably give him nightmares. As if that wasn't enough for one night, he now had to wait for the police who would probably want a statement, holding him up even longer. He almost wished he had indeed reversed away and driven straight off when he had first seen the Porsche blocking his path. His real mistake had been to leave the main road in the first place. That was what happened when you tried to be clever. In the meantime the American continued grousing.

'Look, why don't you get back in the cab, mate? You're getting soaked out here.'

Grumbling, the passenger climbed back in and sat, arms folded, glaring. Bern shivered and pulled up the collar of his raincoat, hoping he wasn't going to catch a chill. He was definitely too old to be driving around at night.

At last the sound of a siren pierced the night air. A moment later, the blue flashing light of a police car came round the corner, followed by an ambulance. Bern was irrationally relieved to see a paramedic running towards the demolished Porsche. The driver was dead; it made no difference. But the image of her bloody face had become someone else's memory to expunge.

A policeman in uniform approached with an officious air. Noting down Bern's details, he asked him for a full account of what had happened. Bern gazed at him uncomfortably. All he wanted to do was to go home and sleep but he still had his fare, and the policeman was scowling at him. He was probably tired too. Bern answered his questions as helpfully as he could, but he had little to say.

'I didn't check the time but I must have arrived on the scene about a minute before I called 999. I just got out the cab to see what had happened, saw the state of the Porsche, and called up. That's all, really. I saw the vehicles and –' He broke off with a shrug. 'There was so much blood. It was horrible. I thought I ought to take a look, you know, in case there was someone still in the car, trapped maybe, and needing help urgently. But I could see she was past help.'

The police officer squinted suspiciously at him.

'How could you tell? That's for a medical officer to –'

'Take a look for yourself,' Bern cut in with a burst of annoyance, 'and then you tell me if you think anyone could survive with injuries like that. I'm telling you, it doesn't take any sort of medical training to see that woman's dead.'

Without warning he turned his head away and threw up, splashing the policeman's boots with flecks of vomit.

3

'I DON'T KNOW why we've been summoned to a hit and run,' Detective Sergeant Sam Haley grumbled by way of greeting. 'What's wrong with traffic?'

Her usually cheerful round face was twisted into a sour expression as she scowled up at the grey sky.

'Why didn't you ask the chief why we've been called out, if you're so keen to know?' Detective Inspector Geraldine Steel responded mildly.

She hoped her colleague might be able to tell her about the accident they had been summoned to investigate, but Sam shook her head.

'It's hardly the sort of question a lowly sergeant can ask.'

Geraldine acknowledged the remark with a rueful smile.

Their senior investigating officer, Reg Milton, had a tendency to regard questions as a challenge to his authority. In his defence, he was efficient in disseminating information promptly. When she had first arrived in London, Geraldine had found his authoritarian attitude abrasive. The longer she worked with him, the more strongly she suspected he was actually quite insecure beneath his arrogance. But Sam was right. Reg was not the kind of man to encourage informal questions. He was more comfortable issuing orders.

A light shower began to fall, dampening Geraldine's mood even further. Jumping into the driver's seat, Sam ran her fingers through her bleached blonde cropped hair, lifting it back into its customary spikes.

'It seems there's something suspicious,' Geraldine said as they drove off.

'It had better be bloody suspicious to get us out of bed at this ungodly hour on a Saturday morning.'

Geraldine couldn't help laughing.

'It's gone nine o'clock. It's hardly early.'

'It's nine now, but I've been up for nearly an hour. It's Saturday. I'd still be asleep if it wasn't for this bloody job.'

Up early to do some last minute shopping in preparation for her niece's visit that weekend, Geraldine had been secretly relieved to be summoned to work. Although she had only recently discovered that she had been adopted at birth, she had never felt close to her sister, Celia. Offering to spend time with her niece was Geraldine's way of making an effort to support her sister. Celia was taking a long time to come to terms with the loss of their mother who had died not long before Geraldine had relocated to London. Before Geraldine had moved, she had made a vague promise to have her niece to stay. She had been putting off fixing a date, but the invitation had somehow slipped out in an unguarded moment. To Geraldine's relief, Celia had sounded resigned rather than angry when Geraldine had called to postpone her niece's visit.

'So? What's so urgent we had to be called out in the middle of the night?' Sam repeated her question as they drove out of the car park.

Ignoring the exaggeration, Geraldine related what little she knew about the incident. A car had driven into a van. The damage to both vehicles had been out of all proportion to the speed indicated on the car's dashboard, where the speedometer had smashed on impact.

'So it's a car crash,' Sam replied. 'Big deal. Like I said, traffic should be dealing with it.'

'Yes, but they felt something wasn't right about it, so they called the Homicide Assessment Team out, and they also thought there was something wrong and so here we are, doing what we're paid to do. Someone died in that crash,' she added solemnly.

Sam grunted. Geraldine continued, hammering her point home. She was aware that she sounded pompous, but she didn't care.

What she had to say was more important than maintaining her image as a tough detective.

'Whatever time we're summoned makes no difference to the dead. Just because they have no voice doesn't mean they have no rights.'

'I know, I know, but this isn't a suspicious death, it's a car crash.'

'Well, let's wait and see what we find when we get there. We must have been called out for a reason.'

'A cock up, more like.'

The rain began to fall more heavily as they drove in silence the rest of the way.

Even on a Saturday morning the roads were congested as they approached central London and crawled along the Marylebone Road. Neither of them spoke. Sam stared ahead sullenly. Geraldine made no attempt to engage her in conversation, accepting that in her present mood the sergeant was best left alone. If Geraldine had been at home, she would have been tidying her spare bedroom in readiness for her niece's arrival. Celia would have been on the way to London. It would have been strange for Geraldine, not having her flat to herself, even if it was only for one night. She was surprised that her initial relief had turned to disappointment, now the visit had been cancelled. Forcing herself to focus on the task ahead, she ran through what little she knew about the incident so far.

At last they reached the entrance to Ashland Place, which was blocked by a police vehicle spanning the narrow side road. They had to park round the corner in Paddington Street.

'What happened exactly?' Geraldine asked as they entered the cordoned off area.

She felt her usual frisson of excitement, rapidly followed by a twinge of guilt because the summons meant there had been a fatality. Up ahead, a white Porsche had driven into a black van. From a distance, she surveyed the heap of crumpled metal and shattered glass, the mangled remains of two vehicles. A forensic canopy had been erected over the cars as protection from the rain that was now falling steadily. The highway glistened with rainbow patches of oil as she bent down to pull on blue overshoes before approaching the vehicles.

Beneath the canvas, white coated scene of crime officers were industriously measuring and photographing, collecting samples of glass and fabric. Apart from an occasional shout, the only sound was the muffled hum of traffic passing along the main road. Approaching the white car, she looked at its shattered front. The Porsche had slammed head first into a van, which had probably shunted it backwards. The car must have been travelling at speed because its front section had concertinaed, as though it was made of tin. The driver hadn't stood a chance.

'Someone's in there,' Sam muttered.

'Yes, someone's in there,' a scene of crime officer echoed, in a curiously hollow tone.

'What about the driver of the van?' Geraldine asked sharply.

No one answered.

Geraldine peered inside the Porsche. The air bag had been deflated to allow access to the dead woman seated at the wheel. Her face was covered in pools and rivulets of blood, making it difficult to distinguish what she looked like. From the little Geraldine could see of a turned up nose and neat chin, she thought the victim looked very young.

'Don't worry, we'll find out who did this to you,' she whispered under her breath to the dead woman.

She made her way along the narrow gap between the vehicles and the side wall of the building that bordered the road, to the front of the van. The side windows were intact, but the windscreen had been smashed. A scene of crime officer had the driver's door open and was examining the seat carefully.

'Was the van empty?' Geraldine asked. 'There can't have been anyone driving it. No one could've escaped unhurt from that,' she added, nodding to indicate the crash.

The scene of crime officer who was working on the interior of the van straightened up and shrugged.

'Yes, it's hard to see how anyone could have survived a collision like that. The Porsche must have been going at a cracking pace, although the speedometer was smashed in the crash and that indicates the vehicle was travelling at under twenty miles an hour. There's no sign of the other driver. We've searched the entire street in case he was somehow thrown clear, and managed to crawl away, but we've found nothing yet. The van must have been parked here, with no lights on, and the Porsche rammed straight into it. Which means she must have been doing more than twenty miles an hour to do this much damage. A lot more. We're getting the speedometer checked.'

'But what about the van? There must have been a driver at some point. Who's it registered to?'

The scene of crime officer shrugged.

'Somcone called Trevelyan. Your colleague over there has the details.'

Geraldine returned to the Porsche and stared at the blood spattered face of the victim for a moment before turning to look for Sam. The sergeant was talking to a uniformed officer standing by the cordon. Geraldine suspected Sam was happy to avoid viewing the victim.

'We're still checking the interior of the van,' a scene of crime officer replied, 'it'll take a while.' He frowned. 'But so far there's been no sign of any injured party. No blood stains. Nothing. The whole thing's weird, actually, because the van's facing the wrong way. It must have been parked here. Either that, or else a ghost was driving that van.'

He grinned as though he had cracked a joke. No one laughed.

It was all quite straightforward. No one sitting in the driver's seat of the van could have survived the crash. Someone had parked irresponsibly, the Porsche had come along travelling far too fast, and a woman was dead. With a sigh, Geraldine turned her attention back to the Porsche which had been shunted sideways across the street by the impact, so that the passenger door was almost flat against the wall. Only the driver's door was accessible. She leaned down to peer inside the car. There wasn't much to see from there, just the back of a head of long blonde hair soaked in blood like some ghastly lowlights.

'Don't touch anything,' the scene of crime officer warned.

'This isn't our first potential crime scene,' Geraldine snapped. The initial rush of adrenaline had faded and she felt exhausted.

Having studied the interior of the car, she went over and joined Sam who was still deep in conversation with a uniformed constable manning the cordon. He was gesticulating and seemed to be ranting about something, while Sam alternately nodded and shook her head.

'What was he going on about?' Geraldine asked, when she and Sam were on their way back to the car and the constable could no longer hear them.

'He was pissed off about some bloody reporter turning up earlier on, just before the Homicide Assessment Team arrived. It makes you sick, the way they exploit something like this, just for a story.'

'How did the reporter get here so quickly?'

'Apparently she was just round the corner. Aren't they always? Anyway, she heard the accident. It must have been an almighty crash, and she came running up hoping for a story. They sent her packing before she could get anywhere near the Porsche. Imagine if she'd got a picture and someone who knew the victim saw it! These people are vultures. They're shameless.'

Geraldine nodded.

'Still, it would have been useful to speak to her. She might have seen something.'

Sam shook her head.

'We can't have those bastards trampling around here one minute, and the next minute they're complaining the police are doing nothing about it, when they're the ones who contaminated the crime scene in the first place.'

'Did she say which paper she was with?'

'No. All the constable could tell me was that she was tall and busy poking her nose in where it wasn't wanted.'

'Oh well, never mind. She was probably a freelance reporter. The constable was right to send her packing, anyway.'

As they drove off, Geraldine continued airing some of the puzzling aspects of the accident.

'So what do you make of it all?' she asked at last, adding, 'we need to know when the van was left there.'

'It was the van driver's fault, really,' Sam agreed.

'The victim drove slap into him.'

'But he shouldn't have been parked there in the first place. A black van like that is hardly going to be easy to spot at night.'

'Could a collision like that havc been planned?' Geraldine asked. 'I mean, it's an odd place to leave a vehicle.'

After some discussion, they dismissed that idea. No one could have predicted that the Porsche would come round the corner too fast for the driver to stop.

There was nothing more to do but return to the station and find out as much as they could about the victim, and the owner of the black van.

'Well, that was a waste of time,' Sam said as they made their way back to the police station through slow moving Saturday traffic. 'Whoever summoned us was way off the mark. I don't think there was anything dodgy, unless you consider bad driving suspicious. It was just an accident.'

'What about the speedometer in the Porsche? Don't forget it showed the car was travelling far too slowly to cause that kind of damage.'

'So there was a fault with the speedometer. Big deal. Tell you what, why don't we stop for breakfast on the way?'

'Always thinking of your stomach,' Geraldine grumbled good-naturedly.

She wondered if Sam would have felt as hungry if she had seen the dead driver of the Porsche close up.

4

DETECTIVE INSPECTOR REG MILTON was observing the team assemble when Geraldine arrived. Although in some ways he was an effective leader, with his large frame and domineering personality, she wondered if she would be able to count on his support if she ever messed up. She was fairly sure he would always put his own career prospects first. He looked slowly around the room, sizing up his team. Despite greying hair and deep creases on his forehead, there was a sense of physical power in his broad shoulders and upright carriage, which was accentuated by his well-spoken voice. But if he was keen to get results solely to further his own career, that didn't really concern her. Reg had a reputation for running successful investigations. A young woman had died in a car accident because someone had been irresponsible enough to leave a black van blocking a narrow road at night without any lights on. All that mattered now was to identify the victim, establish the circumstances of her death, and track down whoever had left the van blocking a narrow one way street.

'It sounds like something out of Sherlock Holmes,' Sam whispered, when Reg referred to the case of the curious disappearance of the van driver.

'What's wrong with traffic?' a detective constable grumbled. 'If it's a hit and run, why the hell's it come to us? As if we haven't got enough to do.'

Sam raised her eyebrows at Geraldine who nodded. She was relieved that the sergeant had recovered her good spirits. In a vast and anonymous metropolis it was a comfort to be on friendly terms with her sergeant, especially as Geraldine hadn't been living in London for long enough to have met anyone outside work.

'This won't take long,' Reg went on briskly. 'But something's come up that we need to look into. At first sight it appears to be a clear cut case. A Porsche slammed head on into a stationary van that had been left parked in a narrow one way street, facing the wrong way. The driver of the Porsche was killed in the crash. It shouldn't have been beyond the wit of traffic to deal with it and we shouldn't have been involved at all, only the Homicide Assessment Team wanted to be sure there was nothing iffy about this accident.'

He looked around the room slowly.

'As I said, it looks straightforward. There was something wrong with the speedometer on the Porsche, so we're looking into that, and then we've just got to tie up a few loose ends and we'll be done.'

Turning his attention to the incident board, he pointed to the image of a woman's pale face. She had been cleaned up. While one side of her face was unblemished, the other was badly scratched from smashed glass. The detective chief inspector turned back to the assembled officers.

'This is the victim,' he said.

Geraldine studied the vaguely familiar face of a woman in her early twenties. She had dishevelled blonde hair and blue eyes. Apart from the ghastly pallor of her damaged face, she would have been beautiful. The inspector stuck some more images of the dead woman on the board and the assembled officers fell silent, watching.

'Even with an air bag the collision was almost certain to be fatal, according to the boys in traffic. The windscreen was shatter proof, but she suffered multiple lacerations to the side of her head and face, as you can see, caused by splinters of glass from the doors. It was some crash. She drove straight into a van at considerable speed, travelling along a narrow one-way street. She went into it head on. She didn't have a chance.'

He paused and glanced up at the incident board before referring to his notes.

'She was driving a white Porsche.'

He read out the registration number.

'Nice,' one of the uniformed officers remarked.

'Not any more,' Reg replied, showing an image of the crumpled front of the vehicle.

'The victim was a twenty-two year old white female called Anna Porter.'

He paused and the assembled officers looked appropriately subdued on hearing how young the victim was.

'Anna Porter?' one of the constables piped up suddenly, staring at the photo of the young woman's bloody face. 'I thought I recognised her. She's Dorothy in Down and Out, isn't she?'

'What's Down and Out?'

'It's a hit series on the TV. You must have heard of it.'

Reg gave a noncommittal grunt. Several of the younger officers muttered, recognising the actress.

'The key task is to question the driver who parked the other vehicle involved in this accident,' Reg added.

'Bloody idiot,' someone muttered.

He nodded at a sergeant who had been researching the vehicles. Anna had been driving her own white Porsche when she had crashed into a black van registered to a man called Piers Trevelyan.

'Anna and Piers lived at the same address,' the sergeant added and a murmur of interest rippled around the room.

'It's a crime of passion!' Sam whispered.

Geraldine smiled at her young colleague's enthusiasm.

'So,' the sergeant resumed. 'the victim was living with Piers. They'd been living together for about six months.'

'That seems to be fairly conclusive then,' Reg said complacently, 'let's go and pick up the boyfriend. See what he has to say for himself, and what his van was doing parked in Ashland Place just where Anna was driving.'

Geraldine scribbled down the address as the sergeant continued.

'Anna was an actress on the TV. Her boyfriend, Piers Trevelyan, is a big shot casting director, a well known figure in the film world by all accounts. He's worked with quite a few well known film stars, according to his website anyway. And this year he won a lifetime award for services to the British film industry.'

Reg listened, one eyebrow raised, as though sceptical about the information.

'There's one more thing. A business card was picked up from the floor of the car: Dinah Jedway, the victim's agent.'

'I can't believe that's Anna Porter,' someone commented, and a faint murmur ran round the room.

'She was so beautiful,' another voice agreed.

'I wonder what they're going to do on Down and Out now.'

'Come on then, let's sort this out,' Reg said firmly.

He sounded slightly agitated. The significance of the victim's identity wasn't lost on anyone in the room. The media was bound to go into a frenzy at the tragic death of a glamorous young celebrity. The police investigation would be a target for critics if they didn't wrap up the case quickly.

'We need to find out what Piers Trevelyan was doing, driving the wrong way along a one way street, and leaving his van parked there so dangerously,' Geraldine said.

'Just look at that,' a sergeant added, gesturing at a picture of the Porsche. 'It looks like she drove into a tank!'

Reg interrupted. 'The front of the van was smashed in. According to the traffic officers, there's no way anyone could have survived that impact.' He paused, frowning. 'But traffic can't believe the damage was as severe as that, if the van was stationary and the Porsche was only travelling at about twenty. They reckon it must have been travelling at least three times as fast as the speedometer indicated. That's what aroused their suspicion in the first place. They thought there might have been something odd about it, because the car had only just turned the corner.'

They all stared at the image of a smashed up black van displayed on the board, the front of the vehicle caved in.

'We need to find out what the hell happened,' Reg added.

It seemed he didn't quite believe it was a simple accident either.

Although there were no security cameras in the immediate vicinity of the accident, the side street was located off a busy main road in central London so there were plenty of cameras in the area. A team of detective constables was tasked with watching CCTV footage, tracking the journeys of the two vehicles and checking to see if there might have been any witnesses. Geraldine and Sam exchanged a complicit grin when they learned that their task was to find out what Piers had to say for himself.

'Put your feet up while we go out and do the real work,' Geraldine said with a laugh, although they all knew that CCTV evidence could be crucial. With a joke at the expense of the constables stuck at their desks watching grainy CCTV footage, Sam followed Geraldine out to the car.

5

Tall and lean, Piers was strikingly attractive rather than good looking. He had a tanned leathery complexion and dark grey hair, streaked with white above his temples. Piercing blue eyes and a pointed nose gave him the appearance of an elegant bird of prey, an impression reinforced by an air of watchfulness. He scrutinised Geraldine, as though sizing her up for a role. It was difficult to be sure of his age but he was well over fifty, probably into his sixties. He was casually dressed in dark jeans and black shirt. Clearly accustomed to dominating others, his self-assurance faltered when she introduced herself.

'It's Anna, isn't it?' he cried out theatrically, his eyes wide with apprehension. 'Something's happened to her. I knew it! Oh my God, poor Anna.'

Geraldine and Sam exchanged a glance. Neither of them had said anything about the accident.

'May we come in, Mr Trevelyan?'

'Yes, yes, of course.'

He glanced down at their shoes with a faint frown as though he was about to say something but thought better of it. Instead he turned and led them across real wood flooring into his study where the decor was stylish, if pretentious. The dark red walls were covered with framed signed photographs. Geraldine recognised a few faces from television, including a large one of Anna smiling archly at the camera. She sank into a plush green velvet armchair and explained as gently as she could that Anna had died in a car crash during the night. Piers dropped his face in his hands and sat for a few moments without speaking.

'Mr Trevelyan, can you tell us where you were between two and three this morning.'

His voice shook as he answered. He sounded slightly hysterical.

'Here, here. I was here. I was here all night.'

'Can anyone vouch for that?'

He shrugged.

'There was just Anna and me here.'

'What was your relationship with Anna?'

'Anna –'

His voice broke. He cleared his throat and resumed with an effort.

'Anna and I were living together.'

'The house is in your name.'

It wasn't a question.

'Yes, that's right. It's my house.'

'And Anna? What was the arrangement with her?'

'Arrangement? I'm sorry, I don't follow you. She lived here, with me. The house is mine. It's in my name. I pay the mortgage and she lives here, with me. I mean, she doesn't pay rent. She's my girlfriend –'

He broke off and stared at the floor, shaking his head slowly from side to side. Geraldine noted that he referred to his girlfriend in the present tense, suggesting he hadn't yet taken in the fact that Anna was dead, but she wasn't convinced that was significant. He was intelligent, and remained alert despite his apparent shock.

'Just to be clear, where were you between the hours of two and three last night?'

'Here. I was with Anna, until she went out.'

'What time did she leave the house?'

'I don't know. It was late. About one o'clock. Well after midnight anyway. It might have been closer to two.'

'Where did she go?'

Piers shrugged. 'How should I know? She just went out. For a drive.'

'Was that usual?'

Piers shifted uneasily in his chair. Geraldine waited. He was behaving erratically, but he had just learned his girlfriend was dead, and shock could affect people in unexpected ways.

'Usual? What do you mean, was it usual?' he prevaricated.

'Was it usual for Anna to go out on her own, so late at night?'

He seemed to be thinking. Geraldine repeated the question once more, adding, 'It's a simple question, Mr Trevelyan.'

'She went for a drive,' he said at last.

He looked old and confused.

'Had you had a row?'

He lowered his head and nodded wordlessly.

'Mr Trevelyan,' Geraldine spoke lightly. 'Can you tell us when you last drove your black van?'

Piers looked baffled.

'Your black van. When did you last drive it?'

'My van? I keep it outside. It's parked on the street. That's where I keep it. I hardly ever use it any more, but I hang on to it in case.'

'In case of what?'

'Oh, you know, moving stuff. I sometimes lend a hand, you know. Sets and props.'

'When did you last use the van?'

He shrugged.

'Two, three weeks ago. But it hasn't been out there for a few days.'

'What do you mean it hasn't been out there? Are you trying to tell us someone took it?' Geraldine asked. 'You didn't report it stolen.'

'No, not stolen. At least, not as far as I know.'

Geraldine frowned.

'Who else uses it?'

'Only my son, Zak. He sometimes borrows it.'

'Doesn't he ask you first?'

'Of course he's supposed to ask, but you know what kids are like, and he is my son. He knows I'd never refuse him anything.'

He dropped his head in his hands again, muttering Anna's name, but jerked upright when Geraldine told him the registration number of the other vehicle involved in the fatal accident.

'That's impossible,' he blurted out, his face white beneath its natural tan. 'There must be a mistake. That's the registration number of my van.'

'Yes. A black van registered in your name was parked in Ashland Place off Paddington Street last night. It had no lights on and Anna Porter drove into it and died in the crash.'

The accusation hung in the air between them, unspoken.

'Can you tell us what your van was doing in Paddington Street on Friday night?'

Sam was glaring impatiently at Geraldine who understood perfectly what the sergeant was thinking. The sequence of events appeared straightforward enough, and Sam couldn't understand why Geraldine was treating Piers so gently. Following an argument, Piers must have pursued his girlfriend out of the house. He had obviously driven after her, eventually abandoning his van, presumably after losing her. But she was still in the area, and had crashed into the van he had left. It sounded vaguely plausible, only Geraldine wasn't convinced the narrative stacked up. If he had been out pursuing Anna, or looking for her, he would have driven home when he lost her. If the van had broken down, he would have called for help. He was a member of the AA. Apart from such inconsistencies, he didn't strike Geraldine as a man who had been involved in a car crash. As far as she could see, he wasn't injured. He hadn't limped when he led them across the hall to his study, and his hands and face weren't even scratched. Before she decided to arrest him, she wanted to find out more about him.

'What did you argue about?'

He sighed.

'That was the last time I spoke to her.'

He raised a mournful face to stare straight ahead, unseeing. 'The last words we exchanged were spoken in anger. And it was all so stupid. Anna was nagging me to cast a friend of hers in a show I'm working on. He's useless, but they were at drama school together and she tried to convince me he's got what it takes.'

Geraldine nodded to show she was listening.

'I've seen him perform,' Piers continued. 'A good looking boy, but talentless. I can't give in to that sort of pressure. I have a reputation to consider. I'm always in demand, and do you know why? Because I'm bloody good at what I do. Everyone thinks casting's easy. Find a face that fits, make a few calls, set up a meeting, and the job's done. Well, I can tell you, it's not that easy. And you know what they say? You're only as good as your last job. That's what people remember. Cast a few duds and your career's over. I've seen it happen.'

He took a deep shuddering breath.

'Anyway, Anna threw a wobbly and buggered off. So I went to bed.'

'You went to bed?'

'Yes, I was shattered. I can't be running after her every time she throws a tantrum. I'm not as young as I was, and I get tired. Bloody tired. I had no idea where she'd gone, but I knew she'd be back soon enough –' He broke off, overwhelmed. 'That is, I thought she would.'

'Is there anyone who can vouch for your being here all night?' Geraldine insisted. 'Does anyone else live on the premises?'

He shook his head.

'No, it was just me and Anna. Just me now, I suppose.'

Piers protested vociferously about accompanying them to the station for a formal interview, until Geraldine pointed out that he had no choice.

'We'll leave him to stew overnight,' Geraldine muttered to Sam as they left the custody sergeant going through the rigmarole of questions.

'Why don't we just arrest him? They had a row, it was his van, he knew where she was, and he knew there were no witnesses if he followed her. He had the means and the opportunity, and he had a motive, so somehow he stage managed a crash. Maybe he didn't intend to actually kill her, but he did.' Sam paused. 'It was his van, for Christ's sake,' she added impatiently, when Geraldine didn't say anything. 'Surely you can see it had to be him?'

'Tell me how he could have climbed out of that van without any injuries and I'll accept he's guilty.'

'Someone must have managed it, so why not him?'

'Let's see what he has to say after he's been kicking his heels in there for a night. Right now, I want to check if the taxi driver who found the body saw anything.'

Geraldine found it hard to believe that Piers was responsible for Anna's death. That kind of immature road rage didn't seem in keeping with the debonair casting director.

'He must be three times older than her,' Sam said, as though his age made any difference.

'Being so much older than her doesn't make him a murderer!' Geraldine replied. 'We'll need a lot more than that to make this stick.'

'I can't see the problem,' Sam repeated.

'A clever man like Piers,' Geraldine mused, 'he seems like a wily old bugger, and a selfish one at that. Do you really think he would have risked his own life in such a clumsy attack?'

'I don't see how you can know that about him, wily and all that. I can't see the problem. It had to be him.'

Geraldine remained adamant.

'He would have to be an idiot to use his own van. They lived together. He would have had any number of opportunities to get rid of her, if that's what he wanted to do, without making himself such an obvious suspect. I just think he's cleverer than that. The whole thing points too clearly at him.'

Geraldine frowned. Something didn't add up about the car crash.

'We're missing something.'

She didn't think Piers would tell them what it was. But he wasn't the only person who regularly drove the black van.

6

THE DEAD WOMAN RESEMBLED someone wearing a half mask, one side of her face white and smooth, the other side criss-crossed with hundreds of small lacerations from the shattered glass of the car window. Individually insignificant, together they created a grotesque image, like a cracked egg shell. Geraldine wondered if the victim had been aware of their impact before she died. In a profession where looks were more important than skill, Geraldine hoped the dead girl had been spared the anguish of knowing she would be scarred for life if she had survived. She wondered if Anna's character would be written out of the television series, or if the producers had a list of lookalikes ready to step in if one of the actors had to drop out. It was a depressing reminder that no one was indispensable. But none of that was of any consequence to Anna now.

'There's more to this than meets the eye,' the pathologist said as soon as they entered the morgue.

Sam's eyes widened above her mask and Geraldine gave her a sympathetic glance before turning her attention to the corpse. Sam found autopsies difficult, and was often tetchy when they visited the morgue. Geraldine had never been badly affected in that way, except when she had once been unexpectedly confronted by the cadaver of a victim she had known while he was alive.

Geraldine had worked with Miles Fellowes on a previous case. Now, the young pathologist was almost rubbing his hands together with glee. His hazel eyes twinkled at her, making him look more like a mischievous sixth former than a qualified doctor. There would have been something macabre in his enjoyment of his work, had his enthusiasm not been so engaging. Like Geraldine, he was keen to press on. He turned to the body without pausing to greet the detectives, and launched straight into his commentary.

'This is an undernourished female in her early twenties. She's thin, borderline anorexic, but otherwise healthy. Reasonable muscle tone suggests she probably worked out, or at least took regular exercise. Now, to the effects of her fatal accident. Most obvious are the superficial injuries.'

He pointed to the scratches on the victim's face.

'There are multiple minor shallow incisions caused by broken glass from the side window of the car. Bruising to the thorax,' he gestured at a large dark area on the dead woman's chest and shoulder, 'and head trauma, all of which might have killed her, in conjunction with the shock of the impact, if she'd been left unattended for long enough.'

'He sounds as though he's reeling off a shopping list,' Sam grumbled.

Geraldine frowned at her and looked back at the body.

'What was the cause of death? We need to be specific.'

'Oh, we can be specific all right. The actual cause of death was this.'

He pointed to the back of the victim's neck and nodded to his assistant. Together they shifted the body onto its front. He pointed with one gloved finger to a deep gash on the nape of the victim's neck. The skin around the wound was bloodless, white.

'A sharp instrument passed through her neck, severing the spinal cord. That was what killed her. I mean, she would have died anyway, but this made certain.'

He grinned, as if to say, 'I've got your attention now, haven't I?'

Geraldine waited for him to continue.

'Yes, she would most probably have died from her other injuries – blood loss, head trauma – but that was what killed her all right.'

'It was bad luck that the glass happened to strike her in the back of the neck like that,' Geraldine said.

The pathologist gave a curious smile. 'It certainly would have been, if it had happened by chance.'

'Is there something you're not telling us?'

'Well,' he hesitated. 'The injury was inflicted with some force.' He paused. 'To the back of her neck.'

Geraldine frowned. She wasn't sure she understood the implication.

'A piece of flying glass?' she suggested.

'Coming from behind her, passing right through her head rest?'

They gazed at the wound in silence for a moment.

'The cut was effected with some force,' the pathologist repeated. 'It almost severed her head from her neck.'

'What are you telling us?'

'I'm not telling you anything. I'm just pointing out that it doesn't seem possible an injury like this was inflicted by a stray piece of glass. All the other lacerations make sense. They are what you'd expect from shattered bits of glass flying around, but this – this is different. How did a shard of glass find its way past her head rest to penetrate her flesh, cutting between the vertebrae? And –' he paused dramatically, 'where is it now? Having penetrated so deeply, it would have remained embedded in her neck. Even if it had somehow been dislodged, it would have fallen nearby. Yet scene of crime officers have found no trace of anything remotely in keeping with this wound. Whatever caused the injury seems to have vanished.'

'Along with the driver of the van,' Sam said.

Geraldine and Sam went straight from the mortuary to Zak Trevelyan's address in central London. He was studying set design at Central, the prestigious drama school in London that Anna had attended. They stopped outside a smart block of flats round the corner from Kings Cross station, just a few minutes' walk from his college.

Sam whistled. 'This must cost enough. I wonder who's paying the rent?'

'No one. Piers bought the flat, and his son's living in it rent free.'

'Oh my God. How the other half lives!'

'Come on, put your tongue back in and stop drooling.'

They rang the bell but there was no one in.

Driving along Gower Street, they passed the imposing entrance to the drama school. Sam raised her eyebrows.

'I wonder how he got to study at a place like that?'

'He could be a very talented set designer,' Geraldine replied with a smile.

Sam muttered about Zak being born with a silver spoon in his mouth.

'He still has to do the job.'

'Designing theatre sets?' Sam retorted scornfully.

'Come on, I daresay we'll find him at home if we call round early in the morning!'

Arriving back at the station, they went to see the team of detective constables who were checking security cameras in the roads leading to Ashland Place, under the supervision of a sergeant who greeted them with a shrug. He was a solidly built middle-aged officer, satisfied with his rank and the contribution he was able to make to the team.

'I'm no glory grabber,' he told Geraldine.

Coming from someone less contented, it might have sounded as if he was sniping at Geraldine for being ambitious. As it was, she understood he was simply stating a fact. She liked the sergeant. He joked that he had only joined the police because of his name.

'So, Bill, what have you got for us?' Geraldine asked as they entered the room.

There was an atmosphere of cheerful industry, with a row of constables all concentrating on screens. The sergeant shook his head.

'Don't tell us you haven't found anything. I was relying on you to knock this on the head for us by now.'

'Sorry, Geraldine. I'd have the idiot who left that van there cuffed and locked up, all ready for you, but –' He raised his pudgy hands in the air. 'We've studied the footage of the crash and you'll be very interested to know the Porsche didn't crash into a stationary van as we first thought. It was more complicated than that, because the van was travelling too.'

'The van was moving? Are you sure?'

'Yes. The van drove round the corner and accelerated towards the Porsche. The Porsche slammed on its brakes, but the two vehicles were too close to avoid an almighty collision.'

Geraldine was shocked. With both vehicles travelling towards each other the impact would have been intensified, which explained why the damage was so extensive.

'We need to know who was driving that van,' she said.

'We've gone through the five minutes immediately following the crash so far, but nothing's come up. The streets around are completely deserted from every angle. God only knows where the driver disappeared to.'

'Was he in the van when it crashed?'

'Well, we couldn't see anyone, but there must have been someone in the driver's seat. The van couldn't have driven itself round the corner and accelerated towards the Porsche. But it's impossible to see who's driving it. We've examined every frame. We'll carry on watching the scene until the taxi driver turns up –'

'Here he comes now,' one of the team called out. 'Seven minutes after the crash. The taxi's arrived.'

But there was still no sign of the van driver. He had simply vanished.

7

THE TAXI DRIVER WHO had reported the accident lived in a maisonette downstairs in a Victorian property off Ealing Broadway. The original narrow front garden had been paved over to provide off street parking for his taxi. There was barely space for another vehicle to park behind it. Two scrubby shrubs stood in pots on either side of a white front door. As they approached, they could see the paint was peeling on the door and window frames. Geraldine rang the bell and a few moments later a skinny dark-haired woman opened the door. She looked surprised when Geraldine asked for Bernard Hallam by name.

'Who are you?' she asked sharply. 'What do you want with him?'

Geraldine held up her warrant card and introduced herself.

'Oh, you're here about what happened on Friday night, are you? They said you might be back. My father was really shook up about it.' She sniffed disapprovingly, as though Geraldine was somehow responsible for the accident. 'What a terrible business that was, terrible. And no fit thing for a man his age to be dealing with when he should have been at home in bed.'

She was more concerned about her father than the fact that a woman had died in the crash.

'We'd like to have a word with Mr Hallam. Is he in?'

'Yes. He's taken a few days off, thank the lord. Well, come on in, if you must. He's here. Although why you need to come bothering him at home on a weekend is beyond me.'

'We won't keep him long.'

She took them into a neat little living room where a white-haired man sat hunched in an armchair, watching football. His daughter muted the television and he frowned.

'What are you doing, Rose, I was –'

'There's a police inspector here, dad. She wants to talk to you.'

He looked up and gave a tired smile. Geraldine sat down and declined tea.

'I'll leave you to it then,' Bernie's daughter said.

She stooped down and gave the top of his head a quick kiss before she went out, closing the door behind her.

Bernie kept his eyes on the television.

'It was a dreadful business,' he said by way of introduction. 'A dreadful business.'

'It must have been a shock to come across the accident like that,' Geraldine agreed.

'Well, I'm afraid there's not much I can tell you. A white Porsche had gone slap bang into a black van round the one way system. Crashed into it head on. It was the van driver's fault, going the wrong way. They must have been going at a hell of a speed. But of course you know that already. It was a hell of a crash, but that's all I know. I can't tell you anything about the victim. All I saw was the shape of a woman's head. I knew she was dead. I called the police straight away.'

Geraldine sat forward, her attention caught by a couple of his remarks.

'How did you know the driver was dead?'

'Well, I didn't know exactly, but the body wasn't moving and there was a hell of a lot of blood in the front of the car. In any case, stands to reason, no one could have survived that, could they? There was nothing I could have done about it, anyway,' he added defensively. 'I couldn't get at the body. And even if I had been able to, I wouldn't have known what to do. For all I knew the whole thing might have been about to blow. I did the only thing I could. I called the emergency services and kept away.'

Geraldine gave what she hoped was a reassuring smile.

'Mr Hallam, we're not here to question you about your actions. I'm sure you did what you thought was best at the time and, as you say, there wasn't much else you could have done.'

'Nothing, short of climbing in there myself, and I'm not a young man.'

Like Anna's boyfriend, Geraldine thought inconsequentially.

'You couldn't have done anything for her.'

'It was a woman in there, then, was it? I thought so.'

Geraldine nodded. Briefly she told him a few details about the victim.

'I want you to think very carefully before you answer my next question.'

He nodded solemnly.

'Did you see anyone in the van, or in the street, walking away from the accident? Anyone at all? Think carefully, please.'

He didn't pause to consider before answering.

'There was no one else there, only me.'

'I thought you had a passenger?'

'Well, yes, and him of course, but he was in the cab and hardly went near the crash.'

'Are you sure?'

'I didn't see or hear anyone.'

'One other question. You said you arrived on the scene after the accident took place?'

He nodded. 'That's right.'

'What made you say the vehicles drove into each other, head on?'

He looked round from the television with a puzzled frown.

'I saw them, same as you.'

'So the van could have been stationary when the Porsche went into it?'

The old man shook his head. 'I can't see how that could be possible.'

'Why not?'

'Well, given the extent of the damage – I suppose I just assumed both vehicles had been moving. I mean, I don't see how one car could have accelerated to such a speed over such a short distance to do that amount of damage.'

As they walked back to the car, they considered what the witness had told them.

'He seemed to know the van wasn't stationary, even though he claimed he wasn't there at the time,' Sam said.

'Yes. But then again, he's spent a lifetime driving. I suppose he must have a pretty shrewd understanding of what's likely in a collision.'

They agreed it was far-fetched to suppose the white-haired taxi driver could have been involved in the car crash, even though, by his own admission, he and his fare had been the only other people present.

'There might have been someone else there. Hallam must've been preoccupied by the sight of the crash, no doubt in a bit of a tizz. The other driver could have slipped away without Hallam noticing,' Sam said. 'He might have been hiding in the back of the van until the coast was clear.'

Geraldine shook her head in frustration. 'No one could have survived the crash intact. It's impossible that anyone could have been behind the wheel.'

Equally, it didn't make sense that the van driver could have survived to leave the scene without being spotted.

'Is it possible Bernard Hallam could have been driving the van himself?' Sam suggested.

'I don't see how he could have been. He was in his taxi.'

'That's what he told us. But what if that's not the whole story?'

They sat in the car and Sam outlined her theory. But she had to agree it was impossible for him to have left his taxi nearby, set the van off in the direction of the Porsche, then somehow jumped out before it really got up speed. He would have had to run off to collect his taxi and driven back round the corner to the scene of the accident in time to be first back on the scene to call the police. The theory would explain his presence at the scene, and account for any traces of his DNA in the van. All the same, it was impossible to believe the old man capable of achieving so superhuman a feat.

'And why?' Geraldine concluded. 'Why on earth would he have done it? And could he really have jumped out of a speeding van? I mean, really?'

'Could anyone? But apparently someone did.'

A sergeant had been investigating Bernard Hallam. They called the station to ask if he had anything to add to what they knew. He hadn't discovered any connection between the victim and the witness who had a clean record, and appeared to have been happily married for over forty years. Apart from the impossibility of his driving the van, he was an unlikely suspect.

As Geraldine was dismissing the theory as groundless, Sam latched onto it with enthusiasm.

'Perhaps he was stalking her.'

'Stalking her?'

'Yes! She was a well known TV actress, wasn't she? In Down and Out. The cast of these shows always have people stalking them, and his wife died less than a year ago, after a long marriage. He might have been suffering some sort of grief-crazed obsession with Anna as a reaction to his wife's death.'

Sam was getting excited about her theory. Geraldine thought about it for a few minutes, but it didn't seem possible.

'You were the one who didn't think Piers was guilty,' Sam reminded her. 'Someone must have been driving that van.'

Geraldine thought it quite likely someone had used Piers' van to throw the police off the scent by casting suspicion on its owner. With Piers so obvious a suspect, there would be no need for the police to look elsewhere for the other driver. Meanwhile, Piers had been alone at home, with no alibi.

'It's perverse to think Piers is innocent, just because it looks like he did it,' Sam had objected when Geraldine pointed that out. 'Surely that's exactly why we ought to be thinking he is guilty.'

'It's too neat.'

Sam had scowled at her.

'Come on then, let's go back in and speak to the taxi driver again, before it gets any later,' Geraldine said.

This time Hallam's daughter greeted them more aggressively.

'You again. What now? You've already spoken to him once tonight, and another policeman questioned him on Friday night.

How many more times do you want to speak to him? He's got nothing more to tell you.'

Still grumbling, she led them back to the living room where her father sat dozing in his chair.

'Dad, dad, they're here again. Dad!'

She shook his shoulder gently and he opened his eyes with a start.

'What? What?'

He caught sight of Geraldine standing in the doorway.

'Oh no, what now?'

He watched her through narrowed eyes as she took out her notebook.

'Writing it all down now, are you? Oh dear. Does this mean you'll be back again in half an hour with a video camera?'

He laughed nervously, trying to make a joke of their return visit. He was clearly feeling anxious.

'A few more questions, Mr Hallam, and then we'll leave you in peace. We'd like to know about your movements on Friday night before you reached Ashland Place.'

Hallam shifted into a more upright position.

'I've been doing night shifts. The roads aren't as busy –'

'He ought to retire, that's what he ought to be doing,' his daughter interrupted.

It sounded as though this was a familiar argument.

'Now then, Rose.'

She turned to Geraldine.

'Do you know how old he is?'

Geraldine ignored her.

'You reported the accident at five past three. Where were you between one and three on Friday night?'

'I was driving.'

He launched into a rambling account of his journey that night. He had spent about twenty minutes cruising around Central London before picking up a man from the Landmark Hotel. He had no idea who his fare was. All he could say was that his passenger was an American, a big man who had been quite belligerent when Bernie had stopped in Ashland Place.

'He kept on at me, telling me to take him to his hotel, as though nothing had happened.'

Geraldine was puzzled.

'You were taking your passenger from the Landmark Hotel near Baker Street to the Dorchester?'

Bernard nodded and fidgeted awkwardly on his chair when she leaned forward and asked why he had left the main road to drive round the one way system and along Ashland Place. With no hold up on the Marylebone Road, there was no reason for him to have made the detour.

'Why did you leave the main road?' she repeated.

He shrugged, and glanced uncomfortably at his daughter, mumbling something about traffic.

'You know we can check that. It'll all be recorded on cameras along the route.'

With a sigh, the taxi driver admitted he hadn't taken his fare a direct route to his hotel.

'He didn't know. He was American. It was only a few extra quid and it wouldn't have made any difference to him. At that time of night, he was lucky to get a cab at all.'

He turned to his daughter with an apologetic shrug.

'Everyone does it, Rose.'

'Oh dad. You could get into trouble –'

'Don't be stupid, Rose. I was tired, all right. I just wanted to make the journey count and then I was going to pack up for the night. He didn't care. He was loaded –'

'You don't know that,' Rose interrupted.

'I could tell. In any case, I don't suppose he was paying for it himself. It would all have been on expenses, so what difference did it make? Only then I drove into that accident. Jesus. I tell you what, I wish I had kept to the main road.'

'Serves you right,' his daughter retorted.

8

THEY DROVE BACK TO the station without talking much. It had been a long day and Geraldine was worn out. Sam was tired too and they parted as soon as they arrived at the station. It was gone nine and they still had to get home.

'See you tomorrow.'

'Good night.'

'Have a good evening.'

Geraldine nodded. As she turned away, she wondered whether Sam was also going home to put her feet up, or if she was planning to get changed and go out. It was Saturday evening, after all, and Sam was still in her early twenties.

Alone, Geraldine made her way back through the evening traffic. The streets in Islington were crowded with pedestrians. Gangs of young women tottered on absurdly high heels, dressed in flimsy fabric and fake fur. Couples sauntered hand in hand, studying menus as they passed the cafes and restaurants along Upper Street. Other people hurried by on their way to the station. Later the mood would deteriorate as growing numbers of drunken revellers wandered the streets, but for now there was an optimistic atmosphere, everyone intent on having a good night out. Her flat felt empty when she closed the front door and kicked off her shoes. It was a relief to shuffle into her slippers, but the silence which was usually welcoming felt somehow oppressive. The contrast to the bustling Saturday evening streets was stark.

Geraldine loved her flat. It was her own space. She could put her things wherever she wanted. Usually she stacked her small dishwasher as soon as she finished eating, but if she chose she could leave her dirty dishes in the sink without anyone criticising or nagging her. It was the same everywhere in the flat. Naturally quite tidy, there were times when she lazily left the place in a mess for days on end. To be fair, that usually happened when she was absorbed in an investigation and had neither the time nor the energy to bother with chores. But sometimes her solitude slipped into loneliness and she wished someone was there to greet her when she came home, someone else to put the kettle on, and ask her about her day. She tried not to think about her long term boyfriend, now married to someone else. It was a while since Mark had walked out on her and she rarely thought about him any more. But at times like this she couldn't help missing him.

After a quick shower she fixed herself a plate of pasta and settled down with a glass of Chianti to watch an old film on TCM. A good film generally succeeded in taking her mind off work, but this evening she wasn't distracted by the cleverly executed twists of a Hitchcock plot, nor did she lose herself in the skilfully built suspense. Her mind kept wandering back to the white-faced girl in the mortuary, barely twenty years old and brutally murdered on a London street not far from where Geraldine was relaxing at the end of the day. As the black and white drama played out on the screen, she pictured a figure leaning forward over the wheel of a van, driving towards Anna's Porsche. In her mind's eye she watched the two vehicles crash. As Anna lay injured, possibly dying, her assailant reached in through the window and sliced through her neck with a sharp piece of glass, to vanish moments before a taxi cruised into the street. All that was missing from the scene was the identity of the van driver, and the killer who had appeared so suddenly, and disappeared without trace. If Geraldine had been superstitious, she might have been tempted to suppose Anna had been attacked by a supernatural force. Not only had the ghostly driver crashed into Anna's car, he had mysteriously spirited her killer away. The whole scenario was impossible, like a teasing mystery film, only this story had actually happened, and there was no rational explanation for the strange series of events. The credits came up to tell her the film was over and she switched off the television with a sigh.

Before she climbed into bed, she took her mother's photograph out of a drawer. Since having it framed under protective glass, she had kept it on display beside her bed. She had only hidden it away because of Chloe's visit. The faded picture was the one memento she had of Milly Blake, the mother who had given her up for adoption at birth. Geraldine understood her mother's reasons for letting her go. At sixteen, and unmarried, she had wanted to give her baby a better chance in life than she could offer. On the face of it, Milly had been right to give up her baby. Geraldine had been raised in comfortable circumstances, by a caring family. After giving birth to a daughter, her adoptive mother had been unable to have any more children and the couple hadn't wanted their child, Celia, to be an only child. Even when her parents had divorced, Geraldine had been well looked after by her mother, and her father had continued to support them financially. Geraldine had no grounds for complaint. She had been brought up as though she was her parents' real daughter. But she wasn't. Her looks and character had been completely out of place in her new family. Despite all the material benefits of her upbringing, she had never felt at ease in her adoptive family.

Perhaps she would have fitted in more readily if she had known about her history all along, able to understand why she looked so different to the rest of her family. But her parents had never told her she was adopted. She had only learned about it on the death of her adoptive mother just over a year ago. Since then she had been ambivalent, desperate to meet her birth mother, yet afraid of the encounter. Until they met face to face, Geraldine could indulge in happy fantasies about their meeting, the instant rapport they would share, the immediate sense she would have of coming home. But the reality might prove very different. Her birth mother had left clear instructions with the adoption agency that she never wanted to meet her child. She still appeared not to want any contact with her. Geraldine had procrastinated over what to do for nearly a year. She didn't even know if her mother was still alive. Finally, she had resolved to find her mother and had traced her to an address in London. But when she arrived, trembling with hope, Milly had already moved away. The disappointment had been harsh. She was aware that she risked even more acute disappointment if she did succeed in finding her mother.

A wave of self pity turned to bitter anger against the mother who had abandoned her at birth. What right did she have to make a stranger of her own daughter? She thrust the photograph to the back of the drawer and slammed it shut. She didn't actually need to search for her mother. She had no relationship with her. Work filled her life. By the time she retired, she might be settled in a relationship, with a whole new family. The future was full of possibilities without her absentee mother. She didn't need to cling to a fantasy, and she couldn't afford to waste energy focusing on the wrong search. Not only was it important to seek justice for its own sake, but if Anna's killer wasn't stopped he might strike again. If tracing Geraldine's birth mother no longer seemed to matter, finding Anna's killer was growing more important with every passing day.

9

Piers was dishevelled and decidedly bad-tempered after his night in a cell. His greying hair was a mess, his face had lost its healthy colour, even his eyes looked dull and had developed ugly pouches from tiredness. He looked at least ten years older than when Geraldine had first seen him.

'What the hell is going on here?' he demanded, his voice taut and high-pitched with frustration. 'Where's my lawyer?'

His personal solicitor had been summoned and joined them as Geraldine was ushering the suspect into an interview room. Tall and suave, dressed in a sober suit, white shirt and dark tie, he wouldn't have looked out of place at a funeral.

Piers leapt out of his seat.

'Terry, at last! What the hell's going on? Surely they can't just keep me here without any reason –'

'I heard about Anna,' the solicitor said in a low voice as he took his seat beside his client. 'Sit down. I'm sorry, Piers. I never met her, of course, but it's a terrible shock all the same. Such a young girl. How are you?'

Piers shook his head vigorously.

'How the hell do you think I am? First Anna, now they want to lock me up. I was in a cell last night! That can't be legal.'

'Don't worry, Piers. We'll have you out of here in no time,' his solicitor assured him.

He sounded very confident.

'But have you heard about the van?' Piers muttered.

The solicitor hushed him.

'All in good time, Piers. Don't say anything. Leave this to me. I'll sort it out.'

'That's what I pay you for.'

'We'll soon have you out of here. They can't hold you.'

Geraldine interrupted their subdued exchange to go through the lengthy process of initiating the interview. On television this would be conducted in a matter of seconds. Real life formal police interviews weren't so quick and easy to set up. At last she finished the detailed introductory rigmarole, Piers had given his full name, the solicitor and attendant police officers had been announced, and they were ready to begin.

'Mr Trevelyan, can you tell me where you were between one and three on Saturday morning?'

He flung himself dramatically back in his chair, and ran his hands through his hair.

'Oh Jesus Christ, do we really have to go through this all over again? I've already answered that question. Check your notes, or did you forget to keep any?'

Geraldine kept her voice even. She stared directly at Piers.

'Mr Trevelyan, a young woman died on Friday night –'

'I'm painfully aware of that,' he interjected. 'Anna. My girlfriend. Some arsehole used my van to cause an accident that killed her. She's dead. This might be all in a day's work for you, but she was my girlfriend. I happened to love Anna, very much. So I'd like to go home and begin the process of grieving, in private.'

He stood up.

'Mr Trevelyan, please sit down. We haven't finished.'

'You may not have finished, but I have.'

'Piers –'

The solicitor put a restraining hand on Piers' arm and nodded at the chair, gesturing to him to sit down again.

'The police have to ask questions. The quicker we get through this interview, the sooner you'll be going home.'

He turned to Geraldine.

'My client is prepared to co-operate in any way he can to help you find the driver who is responsible for this accident.'

Geraldine inclined her head.

'Thank you.'

Piers shrugged his shoulders.

'Look, this has all been a huge shock. I don't want to seem unhelpful, but you have to accept there's nothing I can tell you about whoever was driving my van on Friday night. Do you think I wouldn't help you if I could? You think I don't care about what happened to Anna?' He took a deep shuddering breath. 'Someone must have stolen the van and driven her off the road. Presumably he was off his face on drugs. It was nothing to do with me.'

'The person who killed her was driving your van,' Geraldine pointed out.

'Well, I can't be responsible for whoever was driving my van, can I?'

'Unless it was you at the wheel.'

'Oh for goodness sake –'

'My client has already stated he was at home, in bed, at the time the accident occurred,' the solicitor reminded her.

He gave Piers a warning glance.

Geraldine turned to another line of questioning.

'You're telling us that a person or persons unknown stole your van from the street outside your house and followed Anna on Friday night. Can you think of anyone who might have done that?'

'A lot of maniacs might have stolen my van from the drive and followed her, just because of who she is – was. She drove men wild.'

'Was she being stalked?'

'God, yes, of course she was. Don't be naive. It goes with the territory. She was a good looking girl, a former glamour model. There were photos of her… She had plenty of fans, believe me, plenty of men ready to chance their luck.' He turned to his solicitor.

'Get me out of here, for God's sake. What the hell am I paying you for? Have you seen where I slept last night? Or rather where they kept me cooped up. I didn't get much sleep.'

Geraldine stared at the grey-haired man sitting across the table from her. He seemed more upset about his night in a cell than his girlfriend's death but she knew that grief affected people in strange ways and perhaps the truth hadn't yet sunk in. Piers turned back to her with a scowl.

'Let's try and apply some common sense to this, shall we? It seems pretty obvious what must have happened. Some crazy fan of hers found out where she lived. He watched her drive off. Seeing she was on her own, he thought he would seize his chance. He didn't want to lose her, so he broke into the van and followed her. He was pissed, or high, driving too fast, and ended up leaving the van in some godforsaken street where she was driving, and she crashed into it and that's what killed her. If that's not muddled thinking, I don't know what is. He smashed up both vehicles, killing the poor girl in the process. Realising he had destroyed his idol, he did a runner. Clearly he's insane. You should be out there looking for him, not sitting here with me. It wasn't my bad driving that killed her. How many times do I have to tell you? I wasn't there.'

He sat back in his chair and crossed his arms.

He looked irritated when Geraldine asked him if there was anything else he wanted to tell them. He glanced at his solicitor for an explanation. The brief just shrugged, as though to say he had no idea what Geraldine was talking about. Piers turned back to Geraldine.

'What do you mean, anything else? Her car was in a collision. She's dead.'

'Yes, her car was involved in a collision, but Anna didn't die as a result of the crash, not exactly. She was concussed, and badly injured, but that wasn't what killed her. Someone gave her a fatal injury after the vehicles collided. That was what killed her. This isn't a simple hit and run case, Mr Trevelyan.'

Piers looked perplexed. Already pale and drawn from lack of sleep, his face took on a greyish tinge. There was no mistaking his unease.

'So the van she drove into –'

'No, it wasn't like that. The van deliberately drove into her car.'

'What?'

'We've got it on CCTV. There's no question that this was

deliberate. Anna was murdered.'

'Murder? Anna was murdered? You're saying someone did this deliberately? But why? Who?'

Geraldine wasn't sure if he was shocked at hearing that his girlfriend had been murdered, or because the police had seen through a sophisticated attempt to disguise her death as a fatal traffic accident. At her side, Geraldine heard Sam sniff. She glanced around. She could imagine what her colleague was thinking: Piers worked in the world of acting; they couldn't take anything he said at face value. But Geraldine thought he was genuinely surprised. His solicitor meanwhile looked grave. He advised his client not to say anything. Ignoring his advice, Piers grew strident in his protestations.

'Mr Trevelyan, think carefully. Is there anyone who might have held a grudge against Anna, anyone who might have hated her enough to do this?'

'No one hated Anna,' he replied sternly. 'If you'd known her, you'd realise how ridiculous that question is.'

'Who did she mix with? Who were her friends?'

'Anna had no time for friends. She was a lead character in the series. You have no idea what that means. I don't think you have the faintest idea how time consuming the profession is, or how hard she worked. People like you think it's easy, appearing on television. Do you know how little time she was given to learn her lines, or the pressure she was under to deliver?'

'You mentioned someone she went to drama school with, the friend she asked you to cast in your latest project. Tell me about him.'

'There's nothing to tell. Dirk's a fool. He's the reason we argued in the first place. If it hadn't been for that idiot –'

'Why was she so keen for you to give him a part?'

Piers didn't answer. He stared stubbornly at his hands, frowning.

'What was their relationship?' Geraldine persisted, interested that he had clammed up so suddenly.

'There is no relationship, there wasn't, not since I met her.'

'And before that?'

'Before that they were together for a while, while they were students. It was all a long time ago and it never meant anything.'

Geraldine sat forward in her chair.

'Did it bother you that she remained friends with her ex?'

'They weren't friends, not exactly. They'd known each other at drama school, but they hadn't kept in touch, at least not until he wanted to use her to contact me. She was too innocent to understand what he was playing at. I've seen it all so many times before.'

'So you didn't mind her keeping in touch with an ex-boyfriend who was her own age?'

'His age didn't bother me. Why should it? Do you think someone of my stature would be threatened by a talentless young fool who thinks he has some divine right to be turned into a star? Anna was –'

Unexpectedly, he broke off and buried his face in his hands. His shoulders shook with silent tears. Geraldine was reassured by the sight of his distress. His calm reaction to the death of his girl friend had been unnaturally self-controlled until then.

10

ON SUNDAY MORNING, GERALDINE rang Zak's door bell. She had told Sam she wouldn't need her for this visit. If Piers' son had anything interesting to tell them, she would pursue that line of questioning with the sergeant beside her at the station. This was just an initial encounter. Zak had a key to the van that had killed Anna, and she felt a rush of adrenaline as a drowsy voice answered her summons. Every person associated with the case was a potential suspect. If she only kept looking for long enough, widening the circle of people she questioned, sooner or later she would come across the right person. If Senior Investigating Officer Reg Milton was right, they had already met him. The key to it all was recognising the killer when they found him.

'Who the hell is it? What do you want? It's Sunday morning.'

There was a very long pause after Geraldine introduced herself.

'What's that you said?' the voice asked at last.

Geraldine repeated her introduction.

'Can't you come back later or something? I'm not even up.'

'I'm afraid this can't wait.'

'What the hell. Oh, hang on then.'

There was some muffled swearing and then the voice asked her, very politely, if she wouldn't mind waiting for a moment. She guessed he wanted time to put on some clothes and stash whatever drugs he kept in his flat. Finally the buzzer sounded and she went in.

The accommodation was hardly what she would have expected of student digs. Piers had bought the flat as in investment, or perhaps as a liberal gift for his twenty-year-old son. Either way, Zak was living in a smart brand new one bedroomed flat in central London, a couple of minutes from Kings Cross station, and barely ten minutes' walk from his college. Geraldine felt a flicker of envy as the lift rose swiftly and silently, leaving her in a carpeted corridor that looked as though it had just been painted. She could imagine what Sam would have to say about it. Perhaps unconsciously Geraldine hadn't wanted to bring the sergeant to Zak's flat, because she suspected it might prejudice the sergeant against the young man. After all, he could hardly be reproached for taking advantage of his father's generosity. She wondered what his fellow students made of his good fortune. She guessed they were probably all keen to be friends with the son of an influential casting director. In terms of his living conditions and his career, Zak had certainly been lucky. She remembered Zak's powerful father, and wondered what price the boy had paid for his luxurious lifestyle.

Zak had inherited Piers' straight nose and high cheek bones, although his features were more delicate than his father's, and his complexion swarthy. He had enormous almond-shaped dark eyes and jet black hair that he wore down to his shoulders, with a long floppy fringe that he continuously flicked out of his eyes. If it hadn't been for his square chin, Geraldine might have mistaken him for a beautiful girl.

'You'd better come in and sit down,' he said, not ungraciously.

Geraldine looked around and hesitated, because there was nowhere to sit in the sparsely furnished room.

Along one wall, a tall wooden bookcase displayed a short row of hardback books and a few dog-eared paperbacks, a wilting spider plant, one framed photograph of a group of laughing young men, and an odd assortment of wooden boxes and pots that looked as though they might have been collected while he was travelling in the Far East, although he could have picked them up in Camden market. At one end of the room a table stood beneath the window, with a variety of art materials on it: paints, small pieces of wood, curling slips of coloured paper and a handful of pencils and paint brushes. There were more paint brushes in a glass jar on the floor beneath the window, and yet more in front of the book shelves.

Other than that, the floor was carelessly strewn with jeans and T-shirts, sneakers and newspapers, empty cigarette packets and beer bottles. A grey anorak had been thrown down beside a dying pot plant, and a few more books lay on the floor in no particular order. This was closer to Geraldine's preconception of a student flat, and nothing like the elegant public areas of the block.

Zak made no apology for the state of his room. Geraldine wasn't sure he even noticed how untidy the placc was. For a student of design, she thought it was a poor show, but she refrained from commenting. She wasn't his landlady, or his mother.

'Zak, your father tells us you have a key to his van?'

'What's the old tosser gone and done now?' he asked irreverently.

Geraldine resisted the temptation to remind him that 'the old tosser' was paying for Zak's expensive flat.

'Just answer the question, please.'

He took a step forward, his expression suddenly apprehensive.

'If my father's in any trouble –'

'Nothing that you need to be concerned about.'

'It's not just that I'm relying on him for the rent and all that, you know. I mean, I'm half way through my course, and – well, I'm under enough pressure, without having to worry about money on top of everything else. You probably think it's a doss, studying set design, but you've no idea how stressful it is. But the point is, well, he is my dad, and if he's in trouble, I mean, if there's anything I can do... ' He paused and passed his hand over his mouth, seeming embarrassed at having displayed his feelings. 'Not that he ever needs my help. So, what was it you wanted to know?'

Geraldine asked him about the van.

'My dad's van? With all his money, you'd think he'd just give it to me, wouldn't you? It's not as if I've got a car. He says I don't need one, living in London. Like he would know. We have to travel to Pimlico next week. And sometimes we're out rehearsing until quite late.'

He raised his fine eyebrows. Geraldine wondered if he plucked them, they were so neat. Sam had been right about one thing. Zak was spoiled. He was possibly the most spoiled youngster she had ever met. Yet for all that, he was somehow likeable. She could understand his father indulging him and wanting to look after him, especially if he felt he had to compensate his son for his mother's death. Although he was so young, she was conscious that Zak might also be a suspect. Beautiful people could be psychopaths, like anyone else, and narcissists were frequently callous.

'Your father told us you have a key to his van?'

'That's right. Dad gave it to me ages ago but he hardly ever lets me use it, so I don't know why he bothered.' He gave a sulky scowl.

He didn't seem particularly curious about why Geraldine had come to his flat on a Sunday morning to question him about his father's van.

'Where were you on Friday night?'

'Friday night? What? You mean the Friday that's just gone?'

'Yes.'

He frowned, thinking.

'I was out, in London.'

'What time?'

'What time are you talking about?'

'Where were you between one and two in the morning.'

'I was with Jackie and Ron on Friday.'

'Who are Jackie and Ron?'

'They're on the set design course with me. We spent the night together.'

'Here?'

'Hardly.' He giggled. 'Why on earth would we want to stay *here* all night? No, we went up town.'

'Where?'

He named a club in Leicester Square.

'What time was that?'

'I suppose we got there just before midnight, and it must have been about three when we left, maybe three thirty. It was after four when I got back here. Oh, it's all right,' he added with a grin, 'I wasn't needed on set yesterday.'

Geraldine wrote down the details of Zak's fellow students, Jackie and Ron, before she left. Zak showed her to the door without even asking the reason for her visit. One thing was sure, if he was guilty, he hid it well.

11

'THAT'S ALL WELL AND good, but that's just my point,' Geraldine protested.

She was standing in Reg's office, frowning at him across his desk.

'You think he's innocent because he's so obviously a suspect?' The detective chief inspector frowned. 'I'm sorry, Geraldine, but you've lost me. The man is obviously guilty –'

'No. We can't go jumping to conclusions like that.'

'Give me one good reason why you think he's innocent. And please don't tell me again it's because everything points to him. I'm not sure on what level that makes sense.'

Geraldine took a deep breath and tried to explain that it was precisely because Piers was so obviously in the frame that she didn't believe he had been driving the van when it crashed into Anna's Porsche.

'There are so many reasons why this doesn't feel right.'

'Doesn't feel right? Oh, Jesus. All right, Geraldine, give me just one of the reasons for this "feeling" because they seem to have escaped my notice while I've been busy studying the facts.'

Ignoring her senior officer's jibes, she continued.

'For a start, Piers would have been injured if he'd been driving the van on Friday night. He was given a thorough medical examination and the doctor found no sign of any injury.'

'He could have been lucky.'

'No sir, it's impossible.'

The detective chief inspector growled at her formal term of address, but she didn't stop to apologise. The habits she had acquired while working in Kent still crept up on her when she wasn't careful. Instead, she ploughed on with her argument.

'Secondly, there's no credible motive. Piers was the one with all the power in this relationship. He went from one young woman to another, picking them up, screwing them for a while, helping them with their careers, before discarding them and moving on to the next rising starlet.'

Reg was listening now.

'If she'd rejected him, or threatened to leave him, he might have reacted violently,' he suggested.

Geraldine nodded. The thought had crossed her mind. A man like Piers wouldn't have taken kindly to rejection. He was accustomed to being adulated. He certainly had a colourful history with women.

At forty he had married an eighteen-year-old starlet, Nicci Norman. He had left her after two years for another eighteen-year-old wannabe. Three years later he had married yet another young actress, Ella May Cooper. Their son Zak was born a year later, and it looked as though Piers might have settled down, but Ella had tragically drowned when they had been together for four years. By then in his early fifties, Piers had a series of young girlfriends, until he had remarried when he was fifty-five. His relationship with his third wife, Susan Pollander, another young actress, had lasted three years. At fifty-eight he had divorced for the second time, and after yet more brief relationships had been living with Anna for nearly a year, until her death.

'If he'd wanted to get rid of Anna, surely he would have just thrown her out, like all the others before her,' Geraldine said.

'Perhaps she wanted to leave him?'

'It's possible.'

'She was making a name for herself in this TV series, and might have thought she could make it without him. A man like Piers, used to being in control, might not have liked to have his position challenged, especially by a younger woman.'

Geraldine wondered if Reg was talking about himself.

'But she was on a short term contract, which gave him some control over her career. If she wanted to dump him, no doubt he would have wanted revenge, but think about it. He was influential enough to make sure she never worked again. He could finish her career with one phone call. She might have been idiotic enough to think she could be a success without his support, but he would have known better. He's not young, Reg. He's in his sixties. He knows the game and how to work it. Believe me, in this relationship he held all the cards. He might be a subtle and a cruel man, but I just don't believe he would have done something so crass as kill her.'

'You feel this, you don't believe that, he was holding the cards – this is mere speculation, Geraldine. Anna was brutally murdered by someone driving Piers' van. The man has no alibi, for Christ's sake.'

'That's another thing,' Geraldine jumped in. 'He's a clever man. He would never have done something so stupid and clumsy. Leaving his own van smashed up at the scene is tantamount to advertising the fact that he was responsible. Basically, someone drove into Anna's car. Why use Piers' van? It's almost irrelevant to the actual murder. Unless it was a double bluff.'

'I'm not sure what you're talking about, Geraldine. Clever men can behave stupidly. But this isn't a poker game. We're investigating a murder.'

Geraldine shook her head.

'All I'm saying is, why would Piers use his own van? Do you really think he would leave it like a calling card, putting himself in the frame? No one with any sense would do that, and he's intelligent. If he had wanted to kill her, he could have found a thousand ways to do it, without incriminating himself so blatantly.'

'You're right about one thing, Geraldine. He's incriminated himself. So go and arrest him before he has a chance to slip away.'

'But –'

Reg nodded at her.

'I think we've reached a decision here. Don't be blinded by this man's attractions,' he added sharply.

Geraldine turned on her heel and left without another word.

On her way back to her office, Geraldine checked with the team who had been contacting hospitals and doctors' surgeries. There was no sign of a patient showing injuries consistent with a recent car crash.

'Keep looking,' she snapped and the two constables looked up at her in surprise.

They didn't know she was still fuming about the detective chief inspector's insulting attitude. He was so keen to wrap up the case quickly, to further his own reputation, he had lost sight of what mattered.

'The driver of the van must have gone somewhere,' she told the constables crossly.

Her mood didn't improve when she reached her own door and heard Sam's voice raised in annoyance. Geraldine knew that the sergeant didn't get on with Nick Williams, the detective inspector who shared Geraldine's office. But Sam had to be careful. Nick was higher in rank than Sam. If she spoke out of turn, she could get herself in trouble for insolence towards a superior officer. Geraldine hadn't known Sam for long, but she trusted her and would be gutted to lose the sergeant over something so pointless as a clash with another inspector.

'Come on, Sam,' she announced loudly as she entered, as though she hadn't heard anything of the heated exchange that had been going on before she arrived. 'We're going to arrest Piers Trevelyan.'

Nick leaned back in his chair, placed his elbows on his desk and pressed the tips of his fingers together. He watched the two women with a faint smile on his face. He was clean shaven and his light brown hair was brushed straight back, accentuating his wide forehead. His right eye was permanently slightly closed, so that he looked as though he was winking, which reflected his general air of good humour. While she accepted that his occasional sexist comments could be interpreted as offensive rather than amusing, Geraldine still didn't understand why Sam was quite so antagonistic towards him. He was amiable enough, if a bit irritating, like an annoying older brother who cracked embarrassing jokes that weren't funny.

'Sam's been desperate to find you,' he drawled. 'She wouldn't tell me why.'

'It's not your case,' Sam muttered. 'I don't have to tell you anything about it. I came here to talk to Geraldine.'

She sounded like a sulky teenager. Geraldine suppressed a smile at her pettiness.

'Come on, then, we can discuss it on the way,' she said.

With a quick grin at Nick she left, with Sam at her heels.

Sam cheered up as soon as they left Geraldine's office.

'Where are we off to, did you say?'

'We're going to arrest Piers.'

'I thought that's what you said. But you didn't think he was guilty –'

'I still don't.'

'Then why –'

'Orders from above.'

Glimpsing Geraldine's irritated expression, Sam held her tongue and they drove in silence to Piers' house in Highgate.

Just as Geraldine was on the point of giving up, the door was opened by a raven-haired young woman dressed in a silk kimono.

'Is Mr Trevelyan in? I'm Detective Inspector Geraldine Steel.' As she was reaching into her pocket for her warrant card, Piers appeared in the hall behind the girl. He was wearing jeans and an open-necked shirt, which was untucked, and his feet were bare.

'What the hell is it with you people?' he growled.

'May we come in?'

'No you may not. Come on, Cheryl. Shut the door.'

He sounded sloshed. Ignoring his rebuff, Geraldine stepped inside. The woman looked as though she might burst into tears.

'What shall I do, Piers?'

'Aren't you going to introduce us to your new friend?' Sam asked.

'This is my sister,' he said, laughing very loudly and waving one hand in the air.

The woman's eyes widened in annoyance, but she didn't say anything.

Geraldine had heard enough. She still didn't believe Piers was guilty of murder, but she enjoyed asking him to accompany them to the police station once more. His girlfriend had been dead for two days and he was already consoling himself with her replacement. He stared levelly at her, suddenly sober.

'I'd like to phone my solicitor,' he said coldly.

'I'm sure you would. All in good time. But first things first, you're coming with us. You can make a call from the station. Unless you want it recorded that you resisted our invitation to come in for further questioning? Now I suggest you get some shoes on and come quietly.'

She turned to the shocked young woman who was staring desperately at Piers. Clearly neither of them was used to hearing him addressed in such peremptory tones.

'Get some clothes on and take yourself home. Mr Trevelyan won't be back for a while.'

'What's going on? Where are you taking him?'

'Oh, do shut up, Cheryl. Do what you're told – that's never been a problem before, has it? Just bugger off, there's a good girl.' He turned to Geraldine, his composure restored. 'I don't want to leave her running riot in my house while I'm away.'

'Nice to see you trust your sister,' Geraldine said.

12

BETHANY STUDIED HER FACE critically in the bathroom mirror. Not only was the surface of the mirror pitted and cloudy, but the light bulb above it had gone that morning so her face was only dimly lit from behind. It wasn't good enough, not today. She took her free standing mirror through to the living room and resumed her self-scrutiny in the daylight. Her older sister, who was only twenty-eight, already had a few grey hairs. The thought gave Bethany goose bumps. So far she'd had no problems, not on that score at least.

'I'm so going to dye my hair if I ever go grey,' she had told her sister. 'The very first grey hair I spot, that'll be it.'

'It's different for you. You have to take care of your appearance. You can't afford to look past it, not yet anyway.'

What her sister had said was true. Bethany wasn't naïve enough to believe that talent alone had got her this far. It had been a long struggle to get herself noticed as an actress, but at last she was through to the final audition for a role that would change her life – if she was cast.

'Next time I see you,' she whispered to her reflection, 'I'll be a star. A household name.'

Fluttering her eyelashes, she gave an alluring pout. She had always had faith in herself and it had worked so far – at least in her professional life. She had chosen her outfit with care: smart tight fitting black jeans and a short tailored jacket that showed off her trim figure. At her throat she wore a neat glass pendant suspended on a leather thong that Piers had given her. It had to be lucky, wearing a gift from a prominent casting director to an audition. With a final touch of eye make-up, she grabbed her coat and left.

As the gate swung closed behind her, she noticed a figure in a grey hood and sunglasses standing perfectly still on the opposite pavement. She wondered fleetingly why anyone would be wearing sunglasses on an overcast winter's day, as she worked out that she would arrive at least an hour early. All the same, she hurried along the street to the station and trotted down the stairs to the platform. It was as well to allow plenty of time for the journey. The trains could be unreliable. It was possible to work around planned engineering work, but there might be a points failure or an unexplained hold up, sometimes a person on the track. Bethany had once gone out with a train driver. Even after three months paid leave and counselling, he had never fully recovered from seeing a woman throw herself in front of his train. Bethany had agreed it was selfish to commit suicide in front of a stranger. Privately she thought that, in the unlikely event of her ever deciding to kill herself, she would definitely want an audience.

There were quite a few people waiting on the platform. Faces stared gloomily at the track, as if everyone was contemplating hurling themselves in front of the next train. Glancing round, Bethany was surprised to recognise the grey-hooded figure she had spotted on the pavement opposite her flat. Closer to the figure now, she could see the stranger was a woman. Beneath her hood she had blonde hair. Although she stood with hunched shoulders, the woman was still taller than many of her fellow travellers. As a drama graduate Bethany had been trained to be observant. She was almost positive it was the same person, in a grey hoodie and sunglasses. It was difficult to be sure behind the dark lenses, but again she had the impression the stranger was watching her. She cast the thought aside. It was just the audition making her jittery. Why on earth would anyone be interested in her? It was going to be different when she was famous. Right now, no one even knew who she was.

At last the train drew in. She found an end seat. Luckily it was one of the new rolling stock, which ran more smoothly than the bumpy old trains. Taking out a small mirror, she studied her face one last time. Everything had to be perfect today. She looked up as the train passed Wembley Stadium. At night the huge arch looked magical, lit up like the entrance to space. In the daylight it looked like the skeleton of an alien dinosaur. The day was chilly and she shivered as she left the station. She wished she had worn a warmer coat.

The audition passed in a whirl of adrenaline and excitement. She remembered her lines, which was always a relief, although it was impossible to tell how she was doing during her short performance. At least they all appeared to be listening. The producer remained aloof throughout, but Bethany was sufficiently experienced not to set any store by that. It could even be an encouraging sign. The casting director she had expected wasn't there. His replacement was friendly enough, and they all chatted briefly to her while she answered their questions in as relaxed a manner as she could. Yes, she was available for the whole of the run if the production was extended, or went on tour. It went without saying that she was willing to sacrifice anything else in her life for the duration of the show. She was shaking physically by the time she left the building, confident she had managed to keep her nerves hidden. Under the circumstances, she had acquitted herself well.

Reaching her flat, she thought she glimpsed a figure in a grey hood and sunglasses standing perfectly still between the street lamps on the other side of the road. She felt a flicker of unease before her door slammed shut and she leaned back against the wall, overwhelmed by the enormity of her day. The audition had gone well. That was all that mattered. Now she had to try and put it out of her mind. It might be a few weeks before she heard anything. Normally gregarious, she was relieved her flatmate was out. Lucy was bound to quiz her about the audition, and she didn't feel like talking. But as she was making a cup of tea her agent rang and forced her to relive the experience.

'Where are you?'

'I'm home.'

'That was quick. They didn't keep you hanging around then?'

'No, I got there early and they asked me to go straight in.'

'Good. That's always a good sign if they don't keep you hanging around.'

Bethany knew that was bullshit.

'So, how did it go?'

Bethany sighed. Now it was over, she didn't want to think about it.

'I don't know.'

She gave a brief account of what little she could remember of the audition.

'It went by in a blur, to be honest.'

'That's the adrenaline. It's not a bad thing. So, there were no surprises, then?'

'No.'

'That's good.'

Bethany scowled at the phone. Dinah's relentless optimism was wearing.

When she opened her bedroom window for a smoke, she noticed the figure was still there, standing motionless across the road. She turned away quickly, and hurried into the kitchen. It had been a strange day altogether. She was glad it was over and she had come through it without a hitch. Within a week, she might hear she had landed the part of a lifetime. The worst that could happen was that she wouldn't be cast, and she would have to continue the dreary round of auditions and waiting, auditions and waiting, until her lucky break came.

'I don't know how you put up with all the rejections,' her sister had said.

Bethany had just shrugged.

'I'm an optimist.'

It was true. She knew the future was going to turn out well for her. With her looks and talent, and her determination, how could she fail?

13

On Monday morning Geraldine overslept. She didn't stop for breakfast but set off straight away. There were warnings of severe weather conditions in Kent where she used to live. Her sister had sent her photos of her niece building a snowman. London meanwhile was cold, with a hard frost lacing the trees, although it was already February and hadn't yet snowed properly. She nipped into the canteen on her way up to her office. Of course there was a queue to pay. There always was when she was late. She wasn't bothered, aware that she faced a long morning of dull routine checking, looking for inconsistencies in statements made by Piers and his son, before they started formally interviewing their main suspect. Reg was convinced they had their killer safely locked up in a cell but Geraldine still wasn't sure Piers was guilty. Driving a van into his victim's car seemed such a stupid way to set about killing her.

'He's in the theatre,' Reg had said, waving one hand dismissively in the air, as though that explained everything. 'These people don't think like we do.'

Geraldine thought that was a feeble attempt to explain away something that didn't make sense. Always mindful that Reg was her senior officer, she kept her opinion to herself.

At half past nine the team was summoned for a briefing. Geraldine didn't expect to hear anything new. Reg would make encouraging noises and tell them to keep at it. She gazed around the room, nodding a greeting at her colleagues, most of whom looked as despondent as she was. Reg came in a few moments later. He looked stressed, his tie askew beneath his unshaven chin.

'We do have some news,' he announced in his pompous manner, 'although I'm not sure you're going to like it. Go on then.'

He nodded at a detective constable who had been speaking to the scene of crime officer team.

'The mechanics have been examining the Porsche and the van, and basically they've found something wrong with the van. The door was tampered with. Someone got in without a key and started the engine by fiddling around with the wiring. Whoever it was, they knew what they were doing.'

'So it was a professional job?'

'Well,' the constable hesitated, 'it could have been joy riders.'

'The point is,' Reg interrupted impatiently, 'anyone could have been driving that van when Anna was killed. It wasn't someone who had the keys to the van.'

There was a pause while they all considered the implications of this news.

'It must have been joy riders. Why would a professional car thief want to steal a clapped out old van like that?' a young constable asked.

'It can't have been just some random thief or joy rider,' Sam pointed out. 'It would be too much of a coincidence if that particular van, belonging to Piers, happened to drive into Anna's car somewhere up in London.'

'So do you think the van was stolen deliberately?' someone asked.

'It wasn't necessarily driven by someone who didn't have a key,' Geraldine said.

'Yes,' Reg agreed. 'Piers could have tampered with the van himself to throw us off the scent.'

'Whoever was driving the van on Friday night could have deliberately used it in order to frame the owner,' Geraldine pointed out.

'Yes, that's possible too,' Reg agreed. 'But it could equally have been Piers – or his son for that matter. One of them could easily have damaged the lock to make it look as though the van was driven by someone who didn't have a key.'

'Is that likely? It sounds a bit complicated,' someone said.

'All I'm saying is that the damaged lock on the van doesn't rule

Piers out,' Reg said, 'although it does open up other possibilities.'

He sounded irritated.

As Anna's boyfriend, Piers was the most obvious suspect. This new development only served to make things less clear. They were all interested to learn that more evidence had come to light in the van and was being examined, including a strand of long blonde hair which would probably turn out to have belonged to Anna.

'I think it's time to put pressure on the suspect,' Reg said and Geraldine nodded at Sam.

The interview didn't go well and ended inconclusively. Piers insisted he had been at home all night on Friday. He made the point that if he had wanted to kill Anna, he would have used a more reliable method.

'I lived with her. I could have despatched her in any number of ways –'

'What did you have in mind?'

'I didn't have anything "in mind", as you put it. I wasn't planning to do away with her at all. She was a wonderful girl and we were happy together –'

His voice cracked and he paused. Geraldine might have felt sorry for him if the black-haired girl hadn't been with him when they had picked him up the previous day. They had all known she wasn't his sister.

'All I'm saying is that if I *had* wanted to kill her, do you really think I would have attempted something so stupid as a car accident? Or even have staged some kind of fake accident so I could murder her and get away with it? The whole thing is preposterous, and frankly idiotic.'

After a frustrating morning, they let their suspect go. They had no evidence with which to hold him, and his solicitor was there, snapping at their heels. Geraldine returned to her desk and studied her file on Piers. They knew a lot about him. He had led a colourful life, with three marriages and a string of girlfriends. While he grew older, his companions remained in their early twenties. For all that his personal life had been so busy, officially he only had one son. Geraldine wondered how many other children he had fathered whose paternity had gone unrecorded. Piers was an attractive and charming man who took advantage of his position to meet and seduce aspiring young actresses. Geraldine wished she could find him guilty of murdering his girl friend. It would be a fitting end to his philandering. But however unsavoury a character he was, she didn't believe he would be crass enough to commit murder.

Geraldine had plenty of dull administrative tasks to complete. Instead she occupied herself delving into Piers' busy past, making detailed notes on each of his three wives, for future reference. She wasn't sure that any of them were relevant to the current case, but at this stage of the investigation no information could be discarded.

His first wife had been a student in Piers' class at drama school. She had been barely eighteen when they met, and not much older when she became his wife for a brief period. After the divorce, she had stayed with her second husband until her death at the age of fifty-two. Piers was in his mid-forties when he met his second young wife, on a production he was directing. They married as soon as the show closed, and a year later their son was born. That was the wife who had drowned. By the time he divorced his third wife he was nearing sixty, and he had been single ever since, dating a succession of young starlets. As far as Geraldine could discover, he had parted on good terms with his two ex-wives who had survived the marriages. Geraldine closed the document she had been studying and stood up and stretched. She had read enough about Piers for one day. Now she wanted to see what she could find out about Anna.

14

MOST PEOPLE WOULD BE at work now, their morning nearly over, stuck behind desks in monotonous nine to five jobs, watching the clock and waiting for lunch time. In a couple of hours they would all be back at their desks, yawning, watching the clock once again, this time waiting until it was time to go home. He lay in bed and grinned to himself, relishing his own good fortune. After a shower, he had returned to bed where he lay, stretching out his legs, enjoying the cool soft touch of silk sheets on his skin. He wouldn't get out of bed again that day until hunger forced him downstairs. With closed eyes, he allowed his thoughts to wander back through his memories. Everything brought him back to the van hurtling along a dark street, the deafening crash and eruption of shattered glass.

The possibility that Anna might survive the impact hadn't entered his calculations, but he hadn't lost his nerve on discovering she was still breathing. He never panicked. His training had drilled that response out of him. But he was thankful he had stopped to check she was dead. He might so easily have slipped away, leaving her unconscious but alive. That would have spoiled everything. As it was, he hadn't even stopped to think. With so many shards of glass to hand, it had taken no more than a second to finish the job. It was literally a stroke of genius. He shivered, remembering all the blood. He had been fairly well protected by the window frame. When he had reached in only his glove and sleeve had been drenched. Afterwards he had hidden his hand in his pocket and the blood had barely shown on his black sleeve in the darkness. A busybody police officer had nearly caught him red handed – quite literally – but he was quick thinking and the stupid plod had sent him away. It was a pity there was no one to share the joke. He had to be content to laugh about it by himself.

It was Monday. A whole weekend had passed since he had driven the Porsche off the road. He had been like a shadow, prowling in the night. It was hard to believe he had been there, despatching her with his own hands. It felt unreal, as though he had watched a character being murdered in a film. But he knew it had happened, just as he knew he would do it again. It was time for retribution. Now he had started there was no going back.

15

SHORTLY AFTER ANNA'S TWELFTH birthday, her mother had died of cancer. Now her father had lost his younger daughter as well, under circumstances if not more tragic, certainly more sudden. Albert Porter still lived in Acton, in the house where his two daughters had grown up. When his elder daughter's marriage had failed, she had returned to live with her father. Jane was four years older than Anna. Wondering if Jane would be at home with her father, Geraldine took a deep breath and rang the bell. She hoped she wouldn't find the bereaved father at home on his own and was relieved when a thin-faced woman opened the door. There was no mistaking the family resemblance.

Jane's eyes were red and puffy. Where Anna had been fashionably slender, her body toned and healthy-looking, Jane was gaunt, a skinny version of her attractive younger sister, as though all of Anna's features had been coarsened in her.

'We don't want any callers right now,' she said gruffly.

Geraldine hurriedly introduced herself before the door closed.

'A detective inspector?' Jane hesitated. 'What do you want with us?'

'Am I right in thinking you are Anna Porter's sister?'

'What if I am?'

'I'd like to ask you a few questions.'

'What sort of questions?'

'May I come in?'

'What's this about?'

'About your sister, Anna.'

'She's dead, isn't she? We went and saw her –' Her face puckered and she bit her lower lip while her eyes filled with tears. 'Anna's dead.'

Geraldine lowered her head. 'Yes. I'm sorry.'

'Then there's nothing more to say, is there? Except that we'd like to be able to bury her in peace.'

'I'm afraid that may not be possible, not yet.'

'What's that supposed to mean?'

Geraldine took a deep breath. She wasn't sure how Jane would react to what she was going to say.

'We're investigating the circumstances of Anna's death.'

'She died in a car crash, didn't she?'

'Yes, but –'

'But what?'

'Miss Porter – Jane, can I come in?'

'I don't understand. What do you want with us? We just want to be left alone.'

'Please.'

With a shrug, Jane gave a curt nod and led Geraldine into a drab front room where a grey-haired man sat hunched in a red armchair distractedly stroking a well-fed tabby cat that was curled up in his lap. The cat was purring loudly.

'Dad, there's a policewoman here.'

Mr Porter looked up dully and muttered a polite greeting. Had it not been for the tragedy that had struck the household, this might have been an ordinary Monday evening, with Mr Porter waiting for his daughter to dish up his dinner.

'Mr Porter, I'm very sorry about Anna.'

He shrugged and looked down at the cat.

Geraldine looked at Jane, who was hovering by the door, and then back at Mr Porter.

'We're investigating the possibility that your daughter's death may not have been an accident,' she said gently.

Anna's father gave no sign he had heard but, from the doorway, Geraldine heard Jane gasp. She glanced up. Jane was scowling.

'Can't you leave us alone?' she hissed. 'Haven't we been through enough? First we lost my mother, and now this –'

'Leave it, Jane,' her father interrupted softly. 'It's not her fault. She's just doing her job.'

He half rose to his feet, and gestured to Geraldine to take a seat. As he shifted, the cat slithered to the floor. It stalked out of the room with its tail held straight up in the air, brushing past Jane who was hovering in the doorway. Quietly, Geraldine explained that, unlikely as it seemed, there were grounds for suspecting the crash had not happened by accident. Anna's father looked baffled. Jane took a step forward. She went and perched on the arm of her father's chair, from where she reached out and put her hand on his sleeve. There was silence for a moment when Geraldine finished speaking. Then Mr Porter sat up. He sounded agitated.

'That's the most ridiculous thing I've ever heard. Why would anyone want to hurt Anna?'

Jane's response was more measured.

'Surely you can find out whose car drove into her.'

'Yes, we know the owner of the other vehicle,' Geraldine answered cautiously. 'But we haven't yet established who was driving it.' She paused. 'Can you think of anyone who might have wanted to harm Anna?'

'No, of course not!' Mr Porter snapped.

Geraldine turned to Jane.

'How about you?'

'Anna was a sweet girl,' she replied promptly, 'and popular, wasn't she, dad? Only a maniac would want to drive her off the road.'

'Oh, I don't think the person we're looking for is sane,' Geraldine agreed.

She questioned them further. It seemed that, when she went to drama school, Anna had lost touch with the childhood friends her family had known. Her class at drama school had been a close-knit group but Jane and her father hadn't met them. Jane shook her head.

'We only saw them on stage, in their shows –'

'Weird productions, most of them,' her father interrupted. 'I don't remember many of their names, but you can look them up on the website.'

'Did she have any particular friends?'

'Yes, there was that boyfriend, what was his name? Derek?'

'Dirk,' Jane corrected her father.

'Dirk, that's it.'

Geraldine asked about him, and they told her what little they knew.

Dirk and Anna had been in a relationship in her final year at drama school. Dirk was also an acting student, in the year below her.

'He seemed a pleasant enough boy,' Mr Porter said.

'He was a twit,' Jane chipped in.

'Yes, that's true, but he was harmless. At least he wasn't old enough to be her grandfather.'

Jane grunted. Clearly Anna's family had not approved of twenty-two-year-old Anna living with a man in his mid-sixties. Geraldine didn't blame them. Piers might not look or behave like a man in his sixties, but that didn't alter the reality.

Tired and dispirited, Geraldine made her way home. She didn't have a long distance to travel, but the traffic was heavy. Thoroughly disgruntled by the time she arrived back at her flat, she was ready for a shower and a glass of wine. Refreshed and out of her work clothes, she changed her mind about the drink and brewed herself a pot of tea instead. She was trying to decide whether to take the evening off or press on with researching Piers, his son, and Anna's ex-boyfriend, Dirk, when her phone rang. For an instant she thought it was Sam, but then she recognised the voice.

Geraldine could tell that Celia thought she was making an excuse when she said she couldn't talk just then because her dinner was burning on the hob. Undertaking to call Celia back as soon as she'd eaten, she rang off and turned her attention to the question of food. She was too tired to go out, and besides she would have to call Celia back soon. If her dinner really had been ready on the hob when they spoke, she had about half an hour to herself – an hour at the most.

Exactly one hour later, she picked up the phone and settled down to listen to Celia nattering about her weekend. Geraldine lounged on her sofa sipping a glass of Chianti. She had decided to spoil herself after all, since she wouldn't get much work done that evening now that she was on the phone to Celia. She smiled. For once, work could wait until the morning. She would only be going round in circles, driving herself crazy with incomplete pieces of information that made no sense whichever way she tried to put them together. She woke with a guilty start to the sound of Celia calling her name.

'Are you there?'

'Of course I'm here. You have my full attention,' she lied.

But her half-waking dreams had taken her to the scene of a car crash where a dying girl had been on the point of revealing the name of her killer.

16

GERALDINE TOOK THE NORTHERN line to Euston station. She crossed the busy main Euston Road, passing Euston Square station, and walked south, along Gower Street. It was mid-morning on Tuesday and the street was buzzing with traffic: private cars, taxis, and the occasional bus looming over the rest of the vehicles, while cyclists nipped along the kerb. Weaving through the traffic, they took their lives in their hands. The pavement was busy too. Most of the pedestrians hurrying along were young. Glancing into one of the London medical colleges on her way past, Geraldine saw rows of students sitting on a wide stone staircase, waiting for lectures. More people in their early twenties were waiting at the bus stop. She passed impressive old buildings and reached the drama school, housed in a high stone-fronted building. Entering through gleaming doors, she approached a young woman seated at a desk. Pretty, in a generic kind of way, the woman had a swinging brunette pony tail and heavily made-up blue eyes. She greeted Geraldine with a practised smile, displaying perfect teeth.

'I'm here to see a student called Dirk Goodbody.'

Geraldine waited while the receptionist checked through several schedules. The foyer looked as though it had just been painted, the wood flooring polished, chrome and glass windows gleaming in white walls.

Finally the receptionist looked up with a smile.

'Yes, he's on this site today, but I'm afraid you'll have to wait. He's in rehearsal.'

'I'd like to see him right now.' Geraldine held up her warrant card. 'We can have a quick chat here, or I can ask him to come to the police station, but that's some distance away and it means he'll be gone for the rest of the day.'

'But –'

'So perhaps a quick chat here would be best for everyone?'

It wasn't a question.

'Of course. He's in rehearsal room B7. That's up the stairs and turn left. It's the third door.'

'Thank you. Tell me,' Geraldine added, 'his name isn't really Goodbody, is it?'

The receptionist grinned. 'That's his stage name. He chose it. His real name's Dirk Goddard. The principal wasn't too sure about Goodbody, but at least it's memorable. And wait till you see him!' She handed Geraldine a laminated visitor's card. 'Here, you'll need this to swipe yourself in.'

Walking along the ground floor corridor, Geraldine passed a notice board covered with flyers about upcoming productions, information about auditions and printed schedules of rehearsal times. The stairs led to a second corridor. She found rehearsal room B7 easily and knocked on the wooden door. There was no answer. The corridor was very quiet. She knocked again, more loudly, before opening the door. A surreal scene greeted her. A row of figures stood very upright, dressed in black, their faces concealed behind black masks crowned with blond wigs. In front of them were two figures dressed in white, with white masks and black wigs. The pair in front were poised, arms raised, as though about to engage in stylised physical combat. No one moved as an irate elderly man turned round. He was squat and bald, and wore an outlandish loose jacket that flapped like a cape when he moved.

'This is a rehearsal!' he screeched, as though Geraldine was interrupting a life and death medical procedure. 'Leave the room!'

The old man's eyes bulged with fury as Geraldine stepped forward and held up her identity card.

'Is Dirk Goodbody here?' she demanded, doing her best to sound authoritative.

'Young woman, this is a rehearsal,' the old man shouted back at her across the room.

'I'm a police officer,' she began but he interrupted her.

'I don't care if you're the bloody Queen of England, you're

disturbing the rhythm of the performance. Please leave at once.'

'I'm conducting a murder investigation,' she interrupted him loudly, moving further into the room. 'If you obstruct me in the execution of my duties, you'll face criminal charges.' She turned to the assembled cast who had remained completely still throughout the exchange, like statues. 'Which of you is Dirk Goodbody?'

'Take a break,' the director growled, defeated. 'Ten minutes.'

Immediately the drama students relaxed their posture. Stretching their arms and legs and rotating their heads, they began chatting quietly amongst themselves. One of the white clad figures removed his wig and mask and bounded over to Geraldine. In his twenties, he was strikingly good-looking and seemed to be bursting with energy. Tall and sturdily built, he flicked his long blond fringe out of his eyes with a leonine shake of his head as he spoke.

'You wanted to see me?'

His voice was arresting, with an accent that smacked of Eton and Oxbridge. He smiled sadly at Geraldine, adding softly, 'I take it this is about Anna?'

As he leaned towards Geraldine and gazed into her eyes, she could imagine Piers resenting the young man's friendship with Anna.

'Were you and she very close?'

He shrugged his broad shoulders.

'I'm not sure what you mean by close. We were friends. But it's a small world and people like to gossip. Everyone knows everyone else. There are always connections. Some of the students here keep in touch with some of the graduates from Anna's year. A few of them are auditioning for a show Trevelyan's involved in casting. He's – he was – Anna's boyfriend –' He broke off and heaved a deep sigh. 'Well, people talk, you know how it is in this business.'

'No, I don't. Tell me.'

'Well, nothing's secret for long.'

'I guess it's the same in any organisation, wherever you have a lot of people working together.'

'You won't find anywhere quite like this business,' he assured her.

Geraldine wondered whether he could have killed Anna, perhaps motivated by jealousy. He was certainly strong enough to have despatched her with one blow.

'Is there somewhere we can talk?'

'It's not easy to have a private conversation here, but we could perch in a corner of the bar. Come on, I could do with a drink, seeing as we're on a break.'

Geraldine refrained from reminding him that she was actually working and he was being questioned in the course of a murder investigation. As a rule, people spoke more freely when they didn't feel under pressure. Once they were arrested and charged, the situation changed but for now he was under no obligation to answer her questions. If she scared him, he might clam up. So far she didn't think he had even realised she was checking him out as a potential suspect, although his nonchalance could be assumed. It was going to be hard establishing the truth from someone trained to lie about his identity.

No one else gave a second glance to the fit young man standing at the bar wearing only a skin tight white body stocking. Watching him out of the corner of her eye, Geraldine could see why the receptionist had grinned at his name. While Dirk bought himself a beer, Geraldine sat at a table in a corner of the bar and looked around a smartly decorated area, all white and chrome. A few young people were seated at a table on the far side of the room. At the bar a young boy with white blond hair was chatting to a tall skinny girl. There was an atmosphere of subdued activity, although nothing was happening. A few people were sitting around talking.

'Tell me about Anna,' Geraldine said when Dirk returned.

'Are you sure I can't get you a drink?'

'I'm fine, thank you.'

'Oh, of course, you're on duty.'

He nodded knowingly, as though they were somehow in cahoots. Geraldine stared blankly at him.

'Anna's a great girl,' he began cheerfully and then stopped, his eyes opening wide in an expression of shock which looked fake.

Geraldine watched the performance without commenting.

'Sorry,' he mumbled, 'it's so hard to take it in, that she's really dead.'

Geraldine didn't answer and was gratified to see that he looked unnerved by her silence. He took a gulp of his beer and wiped his lips on his sleeve.

'What do you want to know?' he asked at last, setting his glass down. 'She's dead, isn't she? Died in a car crash.'

'Who told you that?'

Hc shrugged. 'Everyone knows. It was in the papers. And, like I said, people talk.' He sighed. 'Poor Anna, she used to love seeing her name in the papers.'

'What was the nature of your relationship with the deceased?'

'Thc deceased,' he repeated solemnly. 'God, it sounds so final, doesn't it?' He sighed theatrically. 'We were friends. We were good friends.'

'Were you in a relationship with her?'

'You mean did we have sex? Yes. We got together in her last year here, when I was in my first year. She came straight here from school, but I went to uni first, and then I had a gap year.'

Growing expansive, Dirk told her about his trip to Africa, where he had spent time helping in an orphanage. He didn't appear to be deliberately trying to convince her he was a decent person, incapable of violence. He simply liked talking about himself. Finally he returned to the subject of the dead woman.

'Anna was two years ahead of me here, but I'm – I was – a year older than her. We got together in her last year. It was great. She was just lovely.' He sighed. 'We kind of drifted apart when she left.'

His face reddened slightly.

'Did you meet someone else?'

'Well, yes, there was – there is – someone else, as it happens.'

Geraldine couldn't imagine Dirk ever went for long without a girl in tow.

'And anyway she hooked up with her casting director soon after she graduated, which was lucky for me, because Trevelyan's a big cheese.'

'Why was that lucky for you?'

He looked surprised.

'Anna asked him to take a look at me.'

Despite all his studies and travels, there was only one topic that interested Dirk. He brought everything back to himself. He glanced at his phone and Geraldine pressed on, aware that she might not have much time.

'Where were you on Friday night between two and three in the morning?'

'What is all this? I mean, I know Anna's dead, but it was an accident, wasn't it? Why are you so interested all of a sudden? I mean, would you mind telling me what the hell's going on?'

He looked genuinely surprised when Geraldine explained that they were trying to establish the identity of the other driver involved in the accident.

'Can't you people tell that from the car registration? I'd like to help you get to the bottom of it, of course I would, but I really should be in a rehearsal right now. Other people depend on me to be there,' he added with conscious self-importance.

'We'll get done a lot faster if you just answer my questions. Where were you on Friday night between two and three in the morning?'

'Oh Jesus,' he broke off, frowning, as though it was an effort to remember. 'I was with my girlfriend, Megan. We'd had a busy day, so we went back to the flat, watched a film, went through my lines together, and crashed. I was with Megan all night.'

He gazed at Geraldine with a wide-eyed expression of innocence on his handsome face. Geraldine wrote down the name of his girl friend. She started to ask him about his friendship with Anna after she left the drama school, but just then a harassed-looking girl entered the bar and scanned the room. She was slightly plump, with long red hair. Her frown deepened when she saw them and she hurried over to tell Dirk everyone was waiting for him, and Wendel was going mental.

'He said ten minutes,' she reminded him plaintively.

Dirk looked at Geraldine anxiously. Then he turned back to the redhead.

'You go back up. Go on. Tell him I'm right behind you.'

The girl hesitated.

'Go!'

The girl obediently spun round and ran off.

Dirk sprang to his feet, towering over Geraldine as she sat at the table.

'I've got to get back to rehearsal. No one messes with Wendel. I'm in enough trouble as it is!'

'I'll see you again,' Geraldine muttered under her breath, as he hurried away.

17

THE ENVELOPE HAD BEEN delivered to the drama school by hand, addressed simply to Zak Trevelyan. With a burst of adrenaline he tore it open, trying to control his excitement. It was bound to be junk but, like all his fellow students, he was waiting for a lucky break. Although most of them didn't manage to find work until after they graduated, if at all, there were exceptions. Stories were passed around of students who were talent spotted and offered paid jobs before they had even completed their training. Some of the stories were true. He slipped a single sheet of paper out of the envelope and scanned it quickly. Like the envelope, the letter was typed. It was very short.

Hello Zak

It's a long time since we met. You won't remember me. You were just a baby when I saw you last. Your late mother was my sister. Perhaps I can take you out for dinner? Please give me a call on the number below and I hope we can spend some time together soon.

Darius (your uncle)

Zak wasn't sure whether to feel pleased or disappointed after reading it. He had always known that he had an uncle, but his father never talked about him and Zak had never asked. Reading the letter, he was curious to meet him. Besides, his uncle had offered to buy him dinner. It would be churlish to refuse. It wouldn't do any harm to meet the guy in a restaurant and find out what he was like. Plus he might talk about Zak's mother who had died when he was a baby. All Zak knew about her was that she had been beautiful and she had drowned. His father had been vague when questioned about her. Once Zak had pressed him, claiming he had a right to know. His father had snapped that he didn't want to talk about her.

The thin high-pitched voice that answered the phone could have belonged to a man or a woman.

'Hello?'

Zak hesitated. It might be his uncle on the line, but it could equally be a wife or girlfriend.

'I'd like to speak to Darius.'

'This is Darius. That must be Zak?'

'Yes. How did you know?'

'You sound like your mother.'

Zak was surprised. His mother had died seventeen years ago. A motorbike revved past on its way up the street and he missed what his uncle said next.

'What?'

'Can I take you out for dinner?'

'That would be great.'

They met at Garfunkel's in Tottenham Court Road. It wasn't very smart, but it was convenient. When Darius had asked him to suggest somewhere, Zak hadn't been able to think of anywhere else on the spur of the moment. It was just five minutes' walk from the college, and a safe choice as he didn't know his uncle. All the same, he was disappointed when his uncle agreed. But if the restaurant was second rate, the meeting wasn't. Zak recognised his uncle straight away. It came as a shock, because they were so alike, with identical straight black hair, dark eyes and olive skin, the same neat square chin and small mouth, and a similar lithe physique, like a Mediterranean James Bond. It was like looking at himself in twenty years' time, with short hair.

Zak was fond of his father, and grateful for his generosity, but Piers liked to talk, and he only had one subject: himself. Darius asked about Zak and seemed genuinely interested in hearing all about his nephew.

'I think what I'd really like to do, eventually, is direct,' he heard himself say, emboldened by his uncle's attention, and the wine that his uncle kept pouring.

'Then I'm sure that's what you'll do,' Darius said easily. 'You're clearly a very gifted young man. I can see that, and I've only just met you.'

Zak grinned. He was rather drunk, and his uncle's faith in him made him feel light headed. He wondered what he might achieve, if only his father would show the same confidence in his talent, but his father was always wrapped up in his own affairs. Zak felt an instant rapport with his uncle. After they parted, he found himself wondering if his mother had been anything like her brother.

The next time they met, Darius took him to a Turkish restaurant near Oxford Circus. They sat in a dimly lit corner of the large room and ate mezze and mixed grilled meats with salad. Zak drank far too much. He felt as though he had known his uncle all his life. He didn't mean to complain about his father, but Darius was so easy to talk to, he couldn't stop himself.

'It's not that he doesn't support me,' he qualified his grousing. 'I mean, he pays for me to be here, the rent and the fees and all that, so obviously he supports me. And he pays me a monthly allowance on top of all that.'

Darius nodded his approval. 'And so he should. You've got to eat.'

'But he makes me feel –'

He struggled to find the right word. Darius waited patiently.

'He makes me feel inferior.'

'Inferior?'

'Do you know what he said to me once? He said that when he was my age he was working on professional shows, and he learned his trade in the real world. It wasn't an accusation, or anything like that, but –'

'How insensitive.'

'He's not mean, or anything. It's just that he only ever thinks about himself.'

They ate in silence for a moment.

'Didn't you know my father? I mean, when they were married, when my mother was alive.'

'I met him, yes. He works in theatre, doesn't he?'

'Yes, and sometimes TV. He's a casting director.'

'Is he? I remembered he was involved in the industry somehow.'

'He's Piers Trevelyan.'

'Yes, I know his name. I just couldn't remember what he did.'

Zak was surprised. He thought everyone had heard of his father.

'He's very well known.'

'Oh, is he?'

Darius was offhand, clearly more interested in Zak than his father. Zak drained his glass of wine, feeling more and more relaxed and somehow optimistic. Darius was right. His father was insensitive. He wasn't that famous either, he just told everyone he was, and Zak had believed him.

Zak talked happily about his own work, his successes and disappointments, and his vision for the production he was currently designing, which was far and away his most ambitious project to date. He became very animated talking about it, and his uncle seemed to share his enthusiasm.

'That sounds brilliant. Someone's going to snap you up, once you graduate. With your talent and training you'll be in demand before long, I'm sure.'

As his uncle was paying the bill, Zak asked outright why Darius had waited so long before contacting him. A pained expression crossed his uncle's face.

'I should have been in touch sooner. I thought about you often, but I wasn't sure where you were living. You know how it is. Then I read in the paper about Piers' award – what was it?'

'The lifetime achievement award for his contribution to the British film industry? That one?'

'Yes, that's it. That reminded me of you, and then I read about that poor girl who died.'

'Anna Porter.'

'Yes. When I read about that in the papers, and saw your father's name again, I thought I really must get in touch and see that you were all right. I thought I owed it to Ella.'

'What was she like?'

'Oh, Ella was wonderful. An angel. A dark-haired angel. I don't suppose your father ever recovered from her loss. He never remarried, I suppose?'

'Well, yes, he did, actually. He's been married three times in all, and had more girlfriends than you could possibly imagine.' Zak gave an apologetic shrug. 'I guess he just loves women.'

'Or hates them,' his uncle added softly.

18

GERALDINE CHECKED THE NAME of Dirk's girlfriend in her notebook before wandering over to a wall of the bar where a series of black and white head shots were displayed. She browsed through them. All of the photographs were of young adults, most of them exceptionally good looking. The majority were smiling but a few wore expressions that were probably intended to look intriguing. There was only one student called Megan. Looking at heavily made-up eyes staring out of a round face, at first Geraldine didn't recognise the girl who had recalled Dirk to his rehearsal. Full cheeks and a snub nose gave her a childlike appearance, an impression highlighted by the anxious expression in her dark eyes. It was a pleasant face, nowhere near as pretty as most of the other girls, and lacking their confidence in front of the camera. Dirk Goodbody was on the wall too, grinning seductively. His expression was intimate and a trifle guilty, as though he had been caught out flirting with the photographer.

Geraldine returned to the foyer and asked the girl on reception about Dirk's girl friend, Megan Barron.

'Megan? You just missed her. She was here a minute ago but she's gone back to rehearsal. Can't it wait? Only they've already been disrupted once, and Wendel's in a real temper. Believe me, you wouldn't want to be around him when he's in a bad mood. He's a tyrant at the best of times, but a brilliant director. The students sweat blood in his productions. He gets the best out of them –'

'Can you tell me where Megan lives?'

The receptionist stiffened. Her tone became frosty.

'I'm not allowed to give out that kind of information.'

'That's OK, I shouldn't have put you on the spot like that.'

The girl smiled warily.

'It's not important, and you've been really helpful,' Geraldine added untruthfully.

The girl relaxed a little.

'If there's anything else you need to know –'

'No, that's fine.' Geraldine glanced around. 'It's a lovely place here. You wouldn't think it was so smart from the outside.'

They fell into chatting about the expensively kitted out site and the girl recommended that Geraldine take a walk around to the back of the building and see the entrance to the theatre.

'It's beautiful,' she said. 'All glass and white paintwork. Most other drama schools are run on a shoe string, and it shows. But some of our alumni are huge in the business.'

She reeled off a list of names, from serious Shakespearian actors to popular stars of film and television.

After a few minutes' chatting, Geraldine turned to leave.

'There is just one other thing,' she said, returning to the desk.

The girl grinned. 'I knew it, you're doing a Columbo on me.'

'A Columbo?'

'Yes. You know, that detective on the telly. My gran used to love him. First he lulled people into a sense of false security and then, when their guard was down, he'd slip in the real question, the one he'd been planning to ask all along.'

Geraldine laughed. 'I'm not that calculating,' she lied.

'Go on, then, try me.'

'I was only going to ask if it's true that Megan is living with Dirk Goodbody.'

'Oh yes.'

Clearly the girl wasn't averse to a little gossip. Geraldine leaned forward and listened intently, using all her skill at drawing information out of people without them realising. To begin with she didn't learn anything that she hadn't already known, but it was always useful to have her suspicions confirmed.

Dirk had moved into Megan's flat at the beginning of the year, when Megan's flatmate had gone to live with her boyfriend.

'The students tend to move around. Sometimes couples fall out or get together, and that can cause a bit of tension, but by and large everyone gets on and it all works out fine. It's important for them not to get too stressed about their personal lives, because it's a very demanding course.'

Geraldine grunted.

'No one realised straight away that Dirk and Megan were actually living together, not just flat sharing,' the girl added, lowering her voice to a conspiratorial whisper. 'She's besotted with him – can you blame her? But the relationship surprised us all.'

'Because – ?'

'No one thought she was his type. But –' she hesitated, 'what I'm going to tell you now is absolutely in confidence.'

Geraldine leaned further forward and nodded. What she heard came as no surprise. According to the receptionist, Dirk had continued seeing Anna, right up until her death.

'In a relationship with her, you mean? Not just friends?'

'Not just friends.'

'But what about Megan, and Piers Trevelyan?'

'What about them? Anna was living with Piers, but –' She shrugged. 'None of the students will tell you this to your face, but some of us thought Anna was playing a dangerous game. I mean, an actress messing a casting director around, and someone as powerful as Piers. She was asking for trouble.'

'Did Megan or Piers find out?'

The girl shrugged.

'Who knows? In any case, it's all water under the bridge now.'

The situation might have given Piers a motive for wanting to kill Anna, if the gossip was true. It might have driven Dirk to kill Anna, if she had decided to stop seeing him. As she walked away, Geraldine wondered whether Dirk had really been in a funk about his rehearsal, or if he had wanted to speak to Megan before Geraldine had a chance to question her about Friday night. He would probably have no trouble persuading Megan to lie to protect him. No doubt she was convinced of his innocence. Maybe she didn't even care. Infatuated women were hard to crack. But in covering for Dirk, she would also be providing herself with an alibi for Friday night. She was crazy about Dirk. He was still seeing Anna. Megan also had a powerful motive for wanting to be rid of Anna.

'That's two more possibilities, Dirk and Megan,' she told Reg.

'You're forgetting one thing,' Reg pointed out. 'It was Piers' van that killed her. If he found out Dirk was still seeing Anna, there's motive, opportunity and means handed to us on a plate. Why are we looking any further?'

19

MEGAN SCURRIED BACK UPSTAIRS without waiting for Dirk. He had told her to let the director know he was on his way, and she hurried to comply. It wasn't her fault Dirk hadn't returned straight away, but Wendel still growled at her until Dirk appeared.

'Have you forgotten what you're doing here?' the director bellowed as soon as Dirk stepped into the room. 'If you were out there in a real production in the real world,' he gestured towards the window, 'you'd be relegated to understudy by now. What the hell are you playing at? This is a rehearsal, not a fucking drop in session!'

'Sorry, Wendel, I had to talk to that detective.'

'I don't care if she was the Queen herself, this is a rehearsal. If you're not committed, then you can bugger off.'

The grey-haired director switched off his anger abruptly and the rehearsal resumed. Although they all knew his rage was only an act, there was a subdued sigh of relief around the room when he stopped yelling.

'You coming for a drink, Dirk?' another member of the cast asked when the rehearsal finally ended.

They were all relieved to have the evening off as Wendel was busy elsewhere.

'How about some chips?' someone suggested.

There was a general buzz of agreement in the group. Megan was hungry, but she had something more pressing on her mind. She grabbed Dirk's arm before he could answer.

'We might see you later,' she said, answering for him as well. 'Dirk and I are going over lines this evening.'

It was a convincing enough reason to forego socialising. Playing the lead, Dirk hadn't mastered his lines yet and they were opening in a couple of weeks.

Dirk began to laugh off her interruption.

'Later –'

She glared at him. Still clutching onto his arm, she dragged him towards the door.

'Come on, we can get something to eat on the way.'

'All right, I'm coming. Although I can't see what's so urgent.'

'You need to go through your lines.'

She was determined to get him home before tackling the subject of his wandering eye. All the way back on the train she hid her feelings but as soon as they were back in their flat she turned on him.

'Well?' she demanded, scowling, her hands on her hips.

'Well what?'

'What's going on?'

She stood with her arms folded, angry. For a second, Dirk was baffled. Realising what she was talking about, he wasn't sure whether to be angry or amused.

'Oh for fuck's sake, what is wrong with you? The woman was a police officer, Meg. She's investigating Anna's murder.'

Megan looked sceptical.

'What? Don't you believe me?'

'Of course I believe you,' she snapped, 'but why did she want to talk to you?'

'Look, you can go to the police station and ask her all about it, if you're so interested. I've had enough for one day. Are you going to fix something to eat or shall I go out? I'm starving.'

Megan wasn't sure if she was being unreasonable, but she couldn't back down now.

'So what did she want with you, then?'

Impatiently, Dirk explained that the detective was investigating the car crash where Anna had been killed.

'What do you mean, they're investigating it? I thought it was an accident. And what's it got to do with you?'

She glared at him suspiciously, while Dirk told her that the police wanted to trace the driver of the other vehicle involved in the crash.

'If you don't believe me, go to the police station and ask them yourself. For Christ's sake, Megan, what the hell's the matter with you? Do you really think I was having it off with Anna right under Piers' nose? I'm sick of your crazy suspicions. If I wanted to be with someone else, why the hell would I be here now?'

Megan wondered fleetingly if she was being insensitive. One of his ex-girlfriends had just been killed in a car crash. Instead of comforting him, she was pestering him with questions.

'I'm the one who should be upset,' he went on, with growing anger, 'not you. I've just lost a good friend, a friend who was going to help me get started. It could have been my lucky break. Chances like that don't come along every day. Without Anna to influence Piers, I'm back to square one, scrabbling around with everyone else, trying to get noticed. But you clearly don't give a stuff about my prospects. All you care about is yourself. It says a lot for our relationship. Maybe it's time we called it a day and moved on.'

Megan stared at him, aghast. Ending their relationship was the last thing she wanted. She burst into tears and he stopped his tirade against her.

'Don't cry,' he said quietly. 'Let's not argue. You must know how I feel about you.'

She wished she could trust him, but it was hard to believe he was really interested in her. Although she wasn't bad looking, of all the girls in her year at college she was easily the least attractive, constantly struggling with her weight, while Dirk was one of the best looking guys she had ever met. Like most of the girls in her year, she had developed a crush on him right from the first week of classes. No one had been surprised when he and Anna had started seeing one another. They had made a really good-looking couple.

After he and Anna split he had been out with a few of the other girls before moving in with Megan when her flat share had fallen through. They weren't officially a couple yet, but they were kind of together and she was biding her time. Once they graduated, she was determined to stay with him, whatever it took.

'I'm sorry,' she hiccupped. 'I've been a complete bitch. It's just that you always seemed to be so close to Anna. I know it's stupid to be jealous, but now –'

'Look, she's dead, so you can stop worrying. It was over between us a long time ago.'

Dirk bent down and kissed her, and she felt her legs go weak. After they made up, she was chuffed when he suggested they go out for a pizza and a bottle of wine that evening, just the two of them.

'What about your lines? Are you sure you don't want to run through them again?'

He still hadn't learned the whole part.

'They'll keep. Tonight I want to take my girl out.'

'I'll just change my top.'

'There's no need, you look great.'

Gazing into his beautiful blue eyes, she felt her face go red at the compliment.

Later, when they were lying in bed, chatting quietly, he raised himself up on one elbow and reached across to stroke her hair gently with his other hand. The tenderness of his gesture made her want to cry. She was disappointed when he began talking about Anna's accident.

'You know I told you the police are looking for the other driver?'

'What about it?'

He hesitated, still stroking her hair.

'The thing is –'

'Yes? What is the thing?' she asked, smiling.

'You know we used to be together for a while, me and her.'

He hesitated and she had the impression he was trying not to upset her again.

'What about it?' she prompted him gently. 'You can tell me.'

'The police are looking for someone who was involved in the accident that killed her.'

'Yes.'

'I think they suspect someone caused the accident deliberately.'

She turned her head and looked at the little hairs inside his nostrils, his soft lips and the stubbly hair roots on his firm chin.

'Murder, you mean?'

'I guess so.'

'Oh my God! Don't tell me they think you had anything to do with it.'

He sighed.

'Well, I am her ex, which could make me a suspect.'

'That's ridiculous.'

She sat up, indignant.

'Of course it's ridiculous. It's insane. But the inspector asked me straight out what I was doing on Friday night, when the accident happened. I'm scared, Meg.'

He reached out and took her hand in his. Her brow creased in a frown. She had gone away on Friday evening, visiting her parents for the weekend.

'Didn't you go out with the others on Friday?'

'We went for a drink and the others went up to Leicester Square but I was knackered, and –' he paused to kiss her, 'it wasn't the same without you.'

She felt a happy glow.

'I came back after one pint and was here about ten. When the inspector asked me where I was between two and three on Friday night, I said I was here –'

'Which you were.'

'With you.'

'What? Why did you say that?'

He took a deep breath and explained that he thought it best to have an alibi for the time of the accident. Of course he had nothing to hide, but once the police got hold of him they might question him endlessly.

'If it interrupts the rehearsal schedule, Wendel's going to fire me. He came that close today, I could feel it.'

Megan nodded. Wendel wasn't impressed that Dirk didn't know his lines yet.

'They can prove you weren't in the other car. They won't find your finger prints, or DNA, or anything. They can't arrest you without any proof.'

'That's true in theory, but do you trust the police? They're going to be desperate to get a conviction. And even if you're right, and they play it by the book, it would waste time, and interrupt rehearsals. This is the best part I've had. I can't afford to lose it.'

'But why did you say you were with me?'

'I don't know. I panicked. I couldn't think what else to say. I couldn't risk being thrown out of the play. You understand that, don't you?'

Megan considered.

'I thought I could rely on you of all people to understand how important this role is to me. It's a chance to showcase what I can do. And now I've lost my contact with Piers, I've got to think of my career. That has to come first.'

'If they find out you were lying –'

'But they won't,' he interrupted, 'not if you say you were here with me all Friday night.'

'You want me to lie to the police?'

'It's not exactly a lie,' he said. 'It's like you were here because I was here, thinking about you.'

She couldn't help smiling.

He leaned over and kissed her.

'I can't imagine they're ever going to check it out with you, but if they do it's simple. All you have to do is say we were here together on Friday night. They're never going to know any different, and it will save me being hassled by the police for telling them a lie. I might get in trouble, and for sure I'd lose my part.'

'Why did you do it?'

'I knew you'd be there for me,' he said simply. 'You won't let me down. I know I was stupid, it's easy enough to see with hindsight that I was daft to lie, but it's done now and I can't take it back. You won't let me down, will you? I need you, Megan.'

'You can rely on me,' she said, and he put his arms round her and kissed her again.

20

PIERS WAS IN A foul mood. He lay on his back trying to work out how everything could have gone so badly wrong. His life was spiralling out of control at breakneck speed. He felt dizzy just thinking about it. Only five days ago, everything had been going so well with Anna. He knew that couldn't last, but he hadn't expected his life to degenerate into bedlam overnight. He hadn't had time to even begin to cope with the horror of her death before the police began sniffing around. Now the papers had scented a story. Not content with raking over Anna's life, they had started spewing out whatever scandal they could dredge up from his past. Stretching out his arm, he knocked a glass of whisky off his bedside table. He watched the damp patch spread on the carpet, inhaling its sharp smell, before reaching for the bottle. He raised it to his lips. The door bell rang and he ignored it, but it rang again and again. The caller was certainly persistent. If it was that bloody police officer again, he was going to tell her exactly what he thought of being hounded like this in his own home.

Cheryl was standing on the door step looking peeved, but although he had kept her waiting for ages she didn't complain.

'What do you want?'

He knew what she wanted. What they all wanted. When he was younger he had enjoyed exercising power over young women like her. It was like picking cherries off a tree. But he was getting old. Apart from all his recent trouble, he had begun to feel his age lately. The women he screwed had once been young enough to be his daughters. Now they could be his grandchildren. The thought was no longer comfortable. Staring at Cheryl's large blue eyes, he wondered what the hell he had seen in her with her nose job, dyed black hair and fake tits. Nothing about these youngsters was natural. He couldn't understand it. They didn't need to mess with their looks. They were young and beautiful. He was the one who ought to be worrying about his appearance. But their adulation had nothing to do with him as a person. They pursued him because of what he could do for their careers. Since Anna had been a hit in Down and Out, more women than ever had clamoured to attract his attention in any way they could. Anna had claimed to find it amusing, but he was bored of unwanted attention from strangers.

Cheryl stood on the doorstep shivering, but he didn't invite her in.

'What do you want?' he repeated.

'You asked me – you invited me round –'

'Did I?'

He frowned. The last time she had been round he had been unceremoniously dragged away by the police for questioning. She was bad luck. She had phoned him several times since his return home, but he had no recollection of having invited her round again.

'You said you wanted to see me,' she reminded him reproachfully.

If he had, he must have been drunk.

He felt like slapping her. Did she really expect him to welcome her into his home at a time like this? As if his life wasn't complicated enough without another pathetic hanger-on driving him nuts.

'My girlfriend's just been murdered,' he said bluntly. 'Bugger off.'

Her expression softened. 'You shouldn't be alone right now.'

'You think I'm better off fucking a slag like you?'

She recoiled as though he really had slapped her. He tried not to laugh but he couldn't help himself. She looked so startled.

'Listen, kid, I'm pissed. I want to be alone. Go away.' He paused, gazing at her speculatively. 'How old are you?'

'Twenty.'

He really was old enough to be her grandfather. Did she imagine it would make him feel better spending time with a kid like her?

'Come on then, if you're coming in,' he said. 'Don't stand on the doorstep all night.'

As soon as they were inside the house he regretted his impulse. He didn't want her there. The sight of her in his hall made his skin crawl. He didn't want her anywhere near him. But the stupid bitch had trotted in behind him and was offering to look after him.

'I'll make you a nice cup of tea,' she fussed.

For answer, he raised the whisky he was still clutching and swung it in the air between them. He took a long swig from the bottle before offering it to her.

'Drink,' he urged. 'Go on. Drink.'

She hesitated and he saw fear in her eyes. In his satisfaction, he felt his tension slip away. It served her right. She should be afraid. He hadn't wanted her to come round. He had told her to leave him alone, but she had refused to listen to him. Now she would have to take what was coming to her. He wasn't sure what he was going to do to her, but if she didn't like it that was her look out. She should have listened when he told her to go away.

'I've never drunk whisky,' she protested, adding coyly that she was 'a white wine girl.'

Her derisory attempt to sound sophisticated made him laugh. She smiled nervously, intimidated by his amusement which she didn't understand.

'Go on, you might like it,' he insisted, holding the bottle right up to her face.

'I don't think I will.'

'How will you ever find out what you like if you're afraid to try anything new? You can't live your whole life scared of everything.'

Stung, she took the bottle and drank.

'Steady on,' he cried out, grabbing the bottle back. 'You don't have to finish the lot. It's not bloody lemonade.'

Giggling, she staggered sideways. Her inebriation was infectious.

'Come on,' he said, 'let's go and have a smoke. Forget about our troubles for a few hours.'

She nodded. Clutching onto the banister, bent double because she was giggling uncontrollably, she followed him unsteadily up the stairs.

'You're not going to hurt me, are you?' she asked when they reached the top.

'That depends on you,' he replied.

She shook her head, too pissed to ask what he meant.

21

On Wednesday morning, Geraldine was irritated to see a small gang of reporters gathered outside the gates to the complex where the Murder Investigation Team worked. At first sight they could have been any group of people chatting in the street but she recognised one of them, a pushy woman in a bright green raincoat, and a closer look revealed a couple of cameras. As Geraldine slowed down to turn into the gate, a journalist bent down to yell through her window.

'Anything to tell us on Anna Porter?'

'Have you arrested anyone yet?' another voice shouted.

Geraldine stared resolutely straight ahead. It was an annoying start to the day.

It was obvious a high profile actress like Anna would be newsworthy. She appeared on television almost every day in a popular soap. Just about everyone in the country would be aware of her untimely death. It was all over the media. What was worrying was that they were already baying for an arrest, when the official police position remained steadfast: the young woman had died in an accident. It wasn't clear whether the reporters at the gate had been enquiring about an arrest for dangerous driving, or if the media had already gathered that a murder investigation was under way. She hoped not. It would mean even more pressure on them to come up with a quick result.

'You look cheerful,' Nick greeted her as she stomped into the office and chucked her bag on the floor.

'Bloody reporters,' she grumbled.

'Don't tell me they're pestering you already? Someone was quick off the mark.' He groaned sympathetically. 'Your victim died bang in the middle of her fifteen minutes of fame. Everyone's talking about it. How could they not be hyping themselves up, all wanting to be first to break the next episode in this new soap?'

'Yes, but how did they get on to the fact that we were involved? Why aren't they pestering the transport police? Who the hell told them we're looking into it?'

'God knows how these reporters get hold of their information. Some people say they inhale it into their blood stream just by standing near you.'

He grinned, holding up his arms in a cross formation, as though warding off a vampire.

Ignoring his frivolity, Geraldine marched off to look for Sam. She found her young colleague in the canteen. Geraldine sat down and blew on her mug of coffee, making a hole in the froth.

'What do you say to doing a little job today?'

'I've already got a job, thanks.'

'I'm serious. Listen.'

Carefully Geraldine outlined her plan for Sam to hang around the bar area in the drama school, picking up information about Dirk, and anyone else who had been associated with the victim. Geraldine couldn't carry out the investigative task herself as she had already visited the drama school as a detective inspector. In any case, she suspected the students would chat more freely to someone closer to their own age.

'No problem,' Sam said cheerfully.

'You'll have to be circumspect,' Geraldine warned her. 'Don't do anything that might come back on us. We can't afford to look underhand.'

'Even if we are.'

'We're legitimately looking for information.'

'By lying our way into the students' confidence.'

'No. That's where you have to be careful.'

'Don't worry,' Sam smiled. 'Everything will be implied. They can draw their own conclusions, and I'm sure they will. They're all publicity whores. They'll be falling over themselves to tell me what they know, just in case they're making contact with a journalist. I won't say a word of a lie, they'll fool themselves into believing I'm a reporter. Mum's the word.'

She winked at Geraldine who laughed.

Not for the first time, she thought how fortunate she was to be working with such an intelligent colleague. Not every officer would have been so quick on the uptake. Geraldine had been lucky with both her sergeants so far. Sam wasn't as steady as the sergeant Geraldine had worked with in her previous post. No one could replace Ian Peterson. But Sam was a decent officer nevertheless.

'See you back here at lunch time,' she said, and returned to her office.

She would have much preferred to be out and about, gathering information, instead of sitting at her desk reviewing paperwork, but there was no help for it. She couldn't conceal her identity at the drama school and Sam could. All Geraldine could do now was wait for the sergeant to return and hope she would come back with some useful leads.

Geraldine waited with growing impatience. She had resisted the urge to phone Sam, trusting that the longer the sergeant was out, the more chance there was that she would return with some helpful information. Geraldine spent most of her working life waiting, for scene of crime officer findings, for medical reports, for results of DNA tests, for witnesses to turn up… But years of experience didn't make her impatience any easier to control. It was late afternoon by the time Sam returned to the station.

'I hope this is worth the wait,' Geraldine said.

'It is.'

Sam took out her notebook. Masquerading as a reporter had given her the opportunity to jot things down. It helped that she didn't look like a typical police officer. With her cropped white blonde hair, faded jeans and multiple ear piercings she couldn't have dressed more appropriately for the part she had been playing.

'Did anyone ask who you were?'

Sam shook her head.

'Nope. I told the guy behind the bar – perfectly truthfully – I wanted to learn all about the time Anna spent at the academy. I didn't even mention her death, so no one seemed to connect me with the police investigation.'

'Clever,' Geraldine admitted.

Anna had been in a relationship with Dirk during her final year as a student.

'I know that.'

'Goodbody,' Sam added. 'Surely that can't be his real name. But what a dick, if he chose that as his professional name, unless he's funding his way through college by working as an escort. Did you see him?'

She whistled.

'Don't tell me you were attracted to him?'

Sam laughed.

'If I was straight, I'd have been after his details like a shot.'

'So, did you find out anything we don't already know?'

'Plenty.'

According to student gossip Dirk and Anna had carried on seeing each other while he was living with Megan, after Anna had moved in with Piers. The new relationships were a matter of expediency for them both. Sam's information tied in with what Geraldine had heard, and with Piers' claim that Anna had been trying to persuade him to cast Dirk in a leading role. Meanwhile Dirk's new girlfriend, Megan, had given him somewhere to live, and had allowed him to remain friends with Anna without arousing Piers' suspicion.

'All of which strengthens the case against Piers,' Sam concluded. 'A crime of passion committed in a jealous rage when he discovered Anna was still seeing the handsome young Dirk.'

'What about Megan?' Geraldine asked. 'Could she be the one to have snapped and plotted a clever murder that put someone else in the frame?'

Leaving Sam to write up her report, Geraldine set off to speak to Megan.

22

Megan and Dirk lived in a back street in Wood Green. Although it wasn't close to the college, it was only about half an hour's journey to Gower Street. Their rooms weren't far from the tube station so Geraldine took the tube to Wood Green. It was a case of travelling into central London in order to travel out again, but it meant she could read through Sam's report on Megan on the train.

The front door to the property was black, the paintwork faded and flaky. Geraldine crossed the narrow strip of front yard, which could hardly be called a garden. It appeared to have been paved over a long time ago, as the flagstones were cracked and chipped. Other than a few scrubby weeds poking up between the slabs, the yard was empty: no plants in pots, no garbage, no old bicycles or bottles, only two large rubbish bins on the side of the yard furthest from the front door. There were four bells with names attached: Flat 1 Khan, Flat 2 Barron, Flat 3 Rivers, Flat 4 Silver. The bell to number 2 felt greasy. Geraldine tensed slightly as she touched it. There were four flats in a two storey building so there must be two flats to a floor. With no mechanism for buzzing visitors in, the upstairs residents would have to come down from the first floor to answer the front door.

After a couple of minutes the door was opened by the plump girl she had seen summoning Dirk to his rehearsal the day before. He had sent the girl away before Geraldine could speak to her. Geraldine wondered whether he had wanted an opportunity to persuade Megan to give him an alibi before the police questioned her. The girl drew back and began to close the door.

'He's not up yet.'

Swiftly, Geraldine slipped one foot across the threshold and pressed her shoulder against the door. She spoke lightly, smiling reassuringly all the while.

'It's you I wanted to speak to, Megan.'

'Me?'

The girl blinked in surprise, but there was no mistaking the fear on her face. The knuckles of her left hand whitened where she was clinging to the edge of the door, and her lips trembled. She took an involuntary step back, enabling Geraldine to edge forward until she was standing firmly in the doorway.

'You are Megan Barron, aren't you?'

Geraldine knew she was correct, but the girl hesitated before admitting to her name.

'What – what do you want with me?'

'I'd just like to ask you a few questions.'

'Me? What do you want with me?'

'Can I come in?'

'No, that's not a good idea, not right now.'

'What's wrong with us talking right now?'

'I told you, Dirk's asleep. He's bound to hear us talking.'

'Do you have something to say that you don't want him to hear?'

'I've got no secrets from Dirk.'

'So then it's not a problem if he hears us talking.'

'I just told you, he's asleep. If we go up and talk in the flat, we're bound to wake him up.'

Geraldine took a step forward.

'We can talk here, very quietly. This won't take long, Megan. Or is there a problem with you talking to me?'

'No, no, there's no problem!' Megan gulped. 'What do you want to know?'

She glanced over her shoulder and Geraldine wondered whether she was afraid of the police, or of being overheard by her boyfriend if she said the wrong thing.

'Where were you Friday night?'

'Here. I was here.'

'Alone?'

'No, no. I was with Dirk.'

'He was here too?'

'Yes.'

She was squirming now. It must have occurred to her that Geraldine might know she was lying. There could be witnesses to prove Dirk hadn't been at home that night.

'At least, I think we were here on Friday night.'

'You're not sure then?'

'Yes, yes, I'm sure. We were here, together, all night.'

'He couldn't have slipped out without your knowing?'

'No. That's not possible. I'm a very light sleeper.'

Having committed herself to her story, Megan became increasingly credible in her lie. She sounded quite confident now as she repeated her claim that they had been in the flat, together, all Friday night.

'Would you be prepared to swear to that in a court?'

'A court? What? Yes, yes, of course I would.'

And why not? She had already repeated it to a police inspector.

Geraldine stared at the round-faced girl. Megan had recovered her composure and was returning the gaze with sullen resolution. After a faltering start, she wasn't going to be as easy to break down as Geraldine had hoped. She considered telling Megan that Dirk had still been seeing Anna until she died, but decided to keep that in reserve. For now, she simply thanked Megan and retreated onto the path. Megan tried to hide her relief, but it was clear that she was struggling to suppress a grin.

'Is that it, then?' she asked, making no move now to close the door.

'For now.'

Megan became reckless in her relief.

'I'd ask you in,' she said, 'only Dirk's still asleep.'

As though his name was a cue for him to step out of the wings, Dirk appeared in the hallway behind Megan.

'What the hell's going on?' he demanded, rubbing his eyes and yawning.

He was dressed only in boxers and vest but seemed quite unselfconscious about his appearance. If Geraldine had been a man with a body like his, she might have enjoyed showing it off. Catching sight of Geraldine, he glared at her.

'What the hell's she doing here?' he demanded in a theatrical undertone.

'She's just going,' Megan assured him.

'What's she doing here?' he repeated.

Megan shrugged wretchedly. Geraldine waited, curious to see the interaction between them. Dirk looked irritated, while Megan's surly face softened on seeing him. When he spoke angrily, she cowered like a dog that expected to be beaten.

'You said she's off?' he muttered.

'Yes.'

Dirk turned to Geraldine and flashed a warm smile.

'Megan says you're leaving, but surely you've only just arrived? I must say, it's good to see the forces of law and order hard at work,' he added heartily, without a hint of irony in his voice. 'I take it this is about poor Anna? Is there anything we can do to help?'

'You've already been more than helpful, both of you,' she replied.

As the front door was closing behind her, Geraldine caught a glimpse of Megan's anxious face. She tried to imagine their conversation. Dirk would probably round on Megan in fury. Or he might be reassuring his nervous girlfriend, exhorting her to stick to her story.

Geraldine sighed. If only she could see through brick walls, hear what people were saying out of earshot, her job would be so much easier. She didn't believe Megan's claim that she had spent Friday night with her boyfriend, but it wouldn't be easy to persuade Megan to tell the truth now that she had committed herself to her lie. Not only was she set on protecting Dirk, but she would have to admit she had lied to Geraldine if she changed her account of Friday night. Still pondering about how far Megan might be prepared to perjure herself to defend Dirk, Geraldine made her way back to her office.

Since he had been living with Anna, and his van had been involved in the accident, Reg wanted Piers arrested and formally charged with Anna's murder. If nothing else, they had enough to hold him for a while and stop the media baying for an arrest.

'It's time we sorted this out,' he told Geraldine.

'We don't know he did it.'

'What makes you so sure he didn't? Have you got anything to go on, other than your gut feeling?'

Geraldine was about to protest, but Reg went on before she could speak again.

'Look, I know you've got reservations, but the chances are he's guilty, and if he isn't, then perhaps arresting him will jog his memory and he'll come up with something to help us establish whoever was driving his van that night.'

'Without keys,' Geraldine reminded her superior gently. 'It could have been anyone.'

Reg grunted. They both knew they were going round in circles.

Geraldine suspected the detective chief inspector was under pressure to come up with an arrest, but he was paid to deal with that. She wished he wouldn't try and pass the stress on to her. There was no reason to rush to arrest the first possible suspect. If they were wrong, they would end up having to release him anyway, and they would have given an innocent man a hard time. Still, they had little else to go on. Nearly a week had passed since the murder. They had put out an appeal for witnesses to come forward, including the reporter who had tried to view the crash before the scene of crime officers arrived. So far no one had been in touch.

'The public want us to protect them, but they don't work with us,' she grumbled as she made her way back along the corridor to her own office. 'We're not bloody magicians.'

23

When Piers woke up his head was pounding. It was dark outside. Squinting at his watch in the half-light he was surprised to see that it was half past nine on Thursday evening. It was a long time since he had lost twenty-four hours in a drunken binge. Everything in his life was spinning out of control. Considering what he had been through with Anna, it was hardly surprising he had lost track of time. He felt rather than saw that he was sprawling on his bed, wearing only a shirt.

'It's Thursday,' he said out loud.

Someone moaned near his feet. Realising he wasn't alone, he looked down in surprise.

A girl was lying across the foot of the bed. She raised her head and he saw her face peering up at him from beneath a mess of black hair. The sheets were crumpled and her face was smeared with black make-up.

'What the hell happened to you?'

'You did, Piers. You and your bloody whisky.'

Whisky. He stared around wildly. A bottle was gleaming on his bedside table. He reached out, but it was empty. With a sudden roar of rage he chucked it straight at the girl's head. She ducked and the bottle hit her a glancing blow as it skimmed past her.

She let out a shrill yelp and clambered onto her knees, covering her face with her hands. Seeing her pale naked body he tried to remember what had happened before he lost consciousness, but his mind was a blank. She should never have come there. All he wanted was to be left in peace. With renewed anger he leapt off the bed and saw the bottle lying on its side on the carpet. He stooped to retrieve it, feeling its cold weight in his grasp. Too late the girl understood his intention and scrambled off the bed in a panic, screaming at him to stop. But he couldn't stop now. He didn't want to stop. Women were the cause of all his problems. For so long he had believed he was getting his way with them, when all the time they had been exploiting him, every one of them playing him for a mug. It was payback time.

He must have spoken aloud because she interrupted his reverie.

'What are you talking about, payback time?'

She was yanking on her jeans, hopping about on one foot while she backed away from him towards the door.

'Oh no you don't,' he cried.

Lunging forwards, he grasped her by the hair and spun her round onto the bed. She was shrieking again so he slapped her face, hard. It was his house. He hadn't invited her in. He didn't have to listen to her racket.

'Shut the fuck up, you prick teaser, or I'm really going to hurt you.'

She curled up in a ball, facing away from him, quivering and whimpering softly. He stared at her scrawny back, each vertebra clearly sculpted on the flesh, and thought he was going to puke. He had no idea what he was doing. Releasing his grip on her hair, he sat down heavily beside her and watched her skinny back shake with silent sobs.

'Do me a favour and get the fuck out of here,' he said at last.

He felt drained of energy. When she sat up, her hair fell back from her face exposing an irregular dark stain on her cheek. At first he thought it was her make-up. Then he saw it was a large bruise. He wondered if he had done that to her and realised with a cold shiver that he really didn't care. He thought he ought to show some concern. The last thing he wanted was for her to go running to the police to accuse him of assault. The smug detective inspector would rub her hands with glee at being handed proof he was violent. In her twisted mind, it would only be a short step from there to a murder charge.

'Are you all right?' he asked.

The girl didn't answer but sat on the bed, shaking.

'Are you all right?' he repeated

'No. No I'm not. You nearly fucking killed me.'

'Jesus, don't say that. It was the drink.'

He forced himself to speak gently although his heart was pounding. 'I've been under unbearable pressure lately. I warned you not to come in. I knew I was too drunk to cope. The last thing I'd ever want to do is hurt you. Cheryl, you must know what you mean to me.'

He had no idea what he was talking about. He just wanted her to go away and not cause him any trouble.

'Get away from me!'

'Calm down. No one's going to hurt you.'

He threw himself onto his knees on the floor in front of her, hoping she was too stupid to realise it was all an act. Under normal circumstances he wouldn't have given a toss what she thought, or how badly he hurt her. But the police suspected him of murdering Anna. He had to protect his image.

'You must know I really care about you, Cheryl. You're special. I've got great plans for you, for your career –'

'You told the police I was your sister.'

'I said that to protect you. From gossip. How can I help to build your career if people know you're my girlfriend? No one would take you seriously as an actor. They'd say you only got the part because I'm sleeping with you. I saw what that did to Anna,' he lied. 'But I know you can make it on your talent. And I can help you.'

He wasn't sure that made any sense at all. On the contrary, he seemed to be contradicting himself. But the girl was listening intently, her face no longer twisted in fear.

'What plans?'

He suppressed a smile because the crisis had passed.

'I'm too tired to talk about it now. Why don't you go home, and I'll call you in a few days, when all this fuss with the police has blown over, and we can pick up where we left off, before it all started?'

At last he was alone. With a sigh of relief, he fetched a new bottle of whisky and settled down in bed alone. It was safer that way. Women caused him no end of trouble.

24

Although Megan would never have admitted it openly, she knew Dirk was unfaithful. She tried not to speculate about where he went at night. She knew that if he ever suspected her of checking up on him, their relationship would be over. Dirk had chosen her. He wanted to be with her, but he was weak. With so many girls throwing themselves at him, she accepted that he didn't always manage to resist their wiles. She clung to the hope that, when they left college, everything would change. They would live together without other students around to lead him astray.

At the moment she suspected he was screwing a married woman, because he was so secretive about what he was up to. He regularly stayed out on Friday nights. She didn't believe him when he said he went out drinking with his mates and stayed with a guy who had a spare room.

'I just want to know who these mates of yours are,' she had protested. 'It's not unreasonable. What if I need to get in touch with you?'

'What could you have to say that was so urgent it couldn't wait till the next day?'

'Things happen,' she had answered miserably.

They both knew she was right to be suspicious, but he refused to give in to her nagging. Eventually he had gone on the attack.

'If you don't trust me, we might as well forget the whole thing. I'll move out tomorrow, if that's what you want.'

'No, of course not. I don't like the idea of you staying out all night, that's all. I worry about you.'

'So you're my jailor now, or is it my mother?'

'I can't help worrying when you don't come home. What if something's happened to you?'

'Oh for goodness' sake! Stop obsessing about what can go wrong, will you? It's doing my head in, the way you go on and on.'

Megan tried to put his furtive affair out of her mind, but it was hard.

She was pleased when she was cast in the same production as Dirk. They had often rehearsed in different venues in the past, but for this show they travelled into college together and were able to hang out together in their breaks, although Dirk spent more time in rehearsals than she did, as he had a lead role. Megan only appeared in the chorus, with her face covered. She did her best to conceal her disappointment at playing such an insignificant part. The trouble was, there were too many girls chasing too few parts. But it could have been worse. At least she was spending more time with Dirk.

She sat in the bar waiting for him, gazing at his photo on the wall. After about twenty minutes, a few other members of the cast wandered into the bar.

'You waiting for Dirk? He's still with Wendel and James,' one of them told Megan. 'They'll be a while yet, I expect. Once Wendel gets going, he doesn't stop.'

They smiled at one another. Wendel was one of a number of ancient directors the academy wheeled out of retirement to work with the students. In his day, he had been highly regarded, working with some of the most prominent names in the profession. The general consensus among the students was that he was past it. One problem with old, retired directors, was that they weren't in any hurry to finish for the day. Megan sighed. She could be stuck waiting there for another couple of hours. It was stupid not to go home, but she stayed, waiting for Dirk.

She watched another girl saunter up to the bar, her slim hips gyrating as she moved. Bethany had graduated from the acting course the previous year. Those who had left often remained friends with existing students, and still visited the bar when they were in London. Megan gazed enviously at her long thin legs, perfect in jeans, and her bohemian red flowery top. Turning round, Bethany spotted Megan and sauntered over to join her.

'How's it going?' Megan asked.

'I just had a recall! TV!'

'No!'

'Yes!'

'Oh my God, well done.'

'Yes, well, I haven't got the part yet.'

Megan trotted out the usual platitudes about how encouraging it was even to be called back for a second audition. It meant someone was seriously considering casting Bethany.

They chatted for a while about people they knew.

'Wendel's a right pain to work with,' Bethany said firmly. 'I'm so glad I'm not with you lot. He's horrible, and he doesn't even try to help anyone once they leave. How many people have actually worked with him after they graduate?'

Bethany paused, as though waiting for an answer. Megan shrugged.

'It's not easy to get anything' she replied at last. 'There's so much competition –'

'Some people manage. It helps if you're well connected, of course.'

The conversation naturally drifted on to Anna and her sudden death, the circumstances of which had been playing on Megan's mind ever since the police had begun to show an interest in Dirk.

'Yes, I know Anna's dead,' Bethany interrupted Megan. 'It's so sad. But look what Piers did for her before she died.'

'Screwing her, you mean?'

'No, I mean landing her a role in Down and Out. How awesome is that?'

Bethany's face lit up as she mentioned the show.

'So are you going after him yourself now?'

'Piers doesn't like girls who throw themselves at him,' Bethany responded primly. 'In any case, you know what they're saying about him.'

She lowered her voice. Instinctively, Megan leaned forward so she could hear.

'They're saying he's been arrested.'

'Who? Piers?'

'Yes, Piers. Who else? That's who we're talking about.'

Bethany glanced round the room. Satisfied no one was sitting close enough to eavesdrop, she continued in hushed tones.

'They're saying he's been arrested for murder!'

'Murder?'

'Shh. Keep it down. They think he murdered Anna!'

'Who does?'

'The police.'

'How do you know?'

Bethany shrugged and waved one ringed hand in the air.

'People, you know. It's what everyone's saying.'

'I thought it was a car accident.'

'Yes, but they're saying Piers deliberately drove her off the road. Of course Piers says he's not bothered.'

'Do you think he did it?'

'I don't know. But I made sure I got something out of it, just in case.'

Megan was silent, registering the familiar way Bethany referred to the casting director, and how she claimed to know what he liked. A rumour had been going around the college that Bethany had been seeing Piers while he was still living with Anna. Megan suspected it might be true. If it was, she hoped Anna hadn't known about it, and that her death had at least spared her that humiliation.

'Anyway, at least you're free of her now,' Bethany added cryptically.

'What do you mean, I'm free of her?'

Bethany gave a dismissive shrug.

'Oh come on, don't act all innocent. You must have known what was going on between them. Don't try to tell me you didn't know about it.'

Megan didn't answer. She had known all along that Anna had continued screwing Dirk after she had moved in with Piers. It wasn't hard to work out why. Piers was in a position to introduce her to influential contacts, leading to parts that otherwise she would only have been able to dream about. How else would she have landed a lead in a popular television soap, straight out of drama school? Piers wasn't unattractive, but he was old. Dirk could do nothing to further her career, but any woman would be happy to get her hands on him. Beautiful Anna had decided to have her cake and eat it and, for a while, she had managed it.

'If Piers had discovered she was having an affair, he would have thrown her out, and serve her right,' Megan said, trying to mask the bitterness she was feeling. 'He wouldn't have killed her. Honestly, the lies and gossip that fly around this place would keep the tabloids busy all year.'

'Don't knock the tabloids. They're on our side, mostly. And I'm not lying,' Bethany retorted. 'I thought you knew.'

'I know Dirk wouldn't have gone on seeing Anna once she moved in with Piers, and even she wouldn't have been crazy enough to risk her career like that. It's just bullshit.'

'I'm only saying –'

'Spreading rumours about other people. You've got no reason to assume they were still carrying on. It's all lies.'

Megan hoped she wasn't trying too hard to pretend she had been oblivious to Dirk's affair with Anna.

'No it's not. And anyway, Piers didn't give a monkey's.'

'What do you mean?'

Bethany gave a smug smile.

'He didn't exactly believe in monogamy.'

'How do you know?'

'Pillow talk.'

Megan frowned, not sure if she understood correctly.

'You mean – you and Piers – ?'

Bethany tapped the side of her cute nose and winked.

'Guess who's got an audition for Down and Out next Wednesday?'

'I don't believe it! Shagging that decrepit old geezer to get an audition. You're shameless!'

Bethany laughed.

'I hope so,' she replied, 'I do hope so! But honestly, Megan,' she went on, suddenly serious, 'you must have known Dirk and Anna were still seeing each other?'

Her tone suggested she thought Megan must have been an idiot if she hadn't seen what was going on. Megan turned away and took a gulp of her drink. She didn't trust herself to speak calmly. One thing was for sure. That bitch Anna wouldn't be bothering Dirk again. Megan smiled grimly and took a gulp of her beer – a silent toast to eliminating any competition for Dirk's attention.

25

GERALDINE AND SAM WALKED along a wide path and down a short staircase that led to a terrace in front of an imposing house. The bell rang loudly and a buzzer sounded for Geraldine to announce herself. Before she could speak, the gleaming white front door flew open. Zak stood framed in the entrance, slender and willowy. Dressed in black jeans and a black T-shirt, there was something theatrical in his appearance. Geraldine wondered if Piers ever opened his own front door. A puzzled frown crossed Zak's refined features, as though he recognised Geraldine but couldn't place where they had met. The furrows on his brow deepened when she jogged his memory. At her side she was aware of Sam tensing as he grumbled audibly about a bad penny.

'Is your father in?'

'What if he is? What do you want with him?'

For answer, Geraldine took a step forward. After a second's hesitation, Zak stepped aside. He looked sulky. Geraldine saw that his hands were trembling. He was scared. She recalled his reliance on his father to pay his rent, and no doubt his college fees. But more than his financial dependence was the emotional attachment of a young boy to his only parent. If Piers went to prison, at nineteen Zak would receive no support from social services. For the first time in his life he would be forced to cope on his own.

They followed Zak into a plush study where Piers was reclining in an armchair, a newspaper folded on his lap. He opened his eyes but didn't stand up. Running an elegant hand through his grey hair, he asked whether they had made any progress with their investigation. Sam glanced at Geraldine, who began the standard announcement.

'Piers Trevelyan, I'm arresting you –'

'No!'

Zak sprang forward with an anguished cry. Like an actor in a Victorian melodrama he struck an aggressive pose, standing in front of his father with his arms crossed, glaring fiercely at Geraldine.

'Leave my father alone! You will not take him!'

Geraldine looked away to stop herself smiling at his histrionics, while he launched into a tirade against the police in general, and Geraldine in particular. His voice rose to a screech.

'Why are you hounding him? Can't you see he's grieving. Leave him in peace.'

Ignoring the young man, Geraldine stepped to one side so she could see the suspect who was sitting quietly in his chair, watching her, as she read him his rights.

'This is ridiculous!' Zak burst out. 'My father never lifted a finger against Anna. Why would he? Look at him. He's an old man.'

Piers reacted to that, scowling up at his son and growling, 'Less of the old.'

The boy carried on, regardless. 'He's devastated about what happened to Anna. It wasn't him. They were living together for Christ's sake. He cared about her. He loved her. He would never have hurt her. Go away and talk to Anthony, and stop wasting your time harassing a helpless old man.'

Piers rose to his feet in one swift motion and sighed.

'Put a sock in it, Zak.'

'Anthony?' Geraldine repeated. 'Who's Anthony?'

'If anybody did her in, it was him,' Zak insisted.

'Did her in?' his father echoed, wrinkling his nose as though he had just encountered a bad smell. 'Really, Zak. What an expression!'

Not for the first time, Geraldine had the feeling she had stumbled onto a stage, or a film set.

'Who's Anthony?' she asked again.

'My son is referring to my next door neighbour, Anthony

Garnett,' Piers answered frostily. 'There's some history between us. But it has no bearing on Anna's death.'

Geraldine turned back to Zak.

'Why did you say your father's neighbour might have wanted to harm Anna?'

Piers sat down again with a sigh, while Zak launched into a rambling account of a row between Anna and their neighbour. It had kicked off soon after she had moved in with Piers. There was enough off street parking outside the house for several cars, but when Piers left his car there Anna had preferred to park in the street.

'Why?' Geraldine asked.

'She didn't like driving in reverse. It's true of a lot of women,' Piers said dismissively.

One Sunday morning when Zak was visiting his father, he had witnessed an incensed Garnett run down his drive, gesticulating at Anna and yelling at her for parking her Porsche outside his house. When Anna had retorted that she had as much right as anyone else to park on a public highway, he had told her in no uncertain terms to park outside her own house, and had threatened to call the police. In response, Anna had jumped in her car and roared away without a backward glance.

After that, it seemed relations between the two households had deteriorated further.

'Tell them, dad,' Zak urged his father, 'tell them everything.'

Piers explained that Garnett had made several angry phone calls to the police, complaining about noise, overgrown trees and other neighbourly issues. A couple of times a uniformed constable had shown up and gone through the motions of speaking to Piers, but nothing was ever done. The police weren't interested, and the feud rumbled on unresolved. Geraldine listened patiently to Piers' account of these hostilities.

'We'll look into it,' she said when he finished.

Disputes between neighbours were commonplace. They rarely led to murder. But it might make sense of Anna being attacked while she was out driving in her Porsche, which seemed to be the focus of the neighbour's fury.

With Piers back in the custody suite waiting for his brief, Geraldine and Sam discussed what Zak had told them. They agreed it was possible Garnett had been so overcome with rage that he had taken Piers' van and rammed it into Anna, on a crazy impulse. He might have seen it as a way to get Piers into trouble, while he smashed up Anna's Porsche. Geraldine asked Sam to look into the history of Garnett's dispute with Anna, and check if he had form. If they discovered Garnett had ever been accused of any kind of violent assault, they might consider him a possible suspect.

'Imagine if he's been had up for attempted murder!' Sam whispered. 'This could be it, Geraldine. We could be on the point of wrapping it up.'

Geraldine smiled. Although it was sometimes misplaced, she apprcciated her sergeant's enthusiasm. She hoped fervently that Sam was right. Meanwhile, Piers was in the custody suite, and they had work to do.

26

REG MILTON DECIDED TO interview Piers himself.

'He'll find it more difficult to stand up to a man.'

Geraldine doubted if Reg's badgering style would intimidate this suspect. If anything, she suspected the director would have been more likely to let his guard down to a woman. Nevertheless, for once she was happy to finish her day's work and leave on time. This was the first evening she had taken off in six days, and she was planning a quiet evening in, with a long soak in the bath followed by an early night or perhaps a film on the television. Sometimes it helped to take a short break when she was finding herself bogged down in an investigation. If she could empty her head of the suspects, she might be able to think more clearly in the morning. So she was irritated when her mobile rang shortly before she reached home.

Expecting to speak to Celia, she was pleasantly surprised to hear the voice of her former colleague, Ian Peterson. He invited her to meet up for a drink one evening, if she had time. There was something uncharacteristically strained in her old friend's voice. On impulse, Geraldine said she was free that evening. If she had been at home in her slippers, she wouldn't have considered going out again. As it was, she was still in the car and could easily turn round and head off to Kent. In light traffic she might get there in an hour and a half.

'But I can't get there for a couple of hours.'

'Perfect!'

He sounded so pleased, she was swept along with his eagerness and agreed to meet him later on, without stopping to think how tired she was. A moment before, she had been desperate to get home and put her feet up. Now she was heading off to Kent for a drink. It was daft. After she hung up, she couldn't believe she had agreed to drive all that way to see him. But she had said she would go, and she wouldn't let him down.

They met in a quiet pub they used to frequent when they had worked together in the Kent constabulary. Ian was standing at the bar watching the door, as though uncertain whether she would turn up. His expression changed as soon as he saw her. His face broke into a grin. Geraldine had thought he had sounded strained on the phone, an impression borne out by his appearance. He looked older than when she had last seen him, and very tired. There were small pouches under his eyes, as though he hadn't been sleeping, and his bulky shoulders drooped in the posture of an older man. She wondered if he had been ill as she returned his smile, and joined him at the bar. He ordered her a drink without pausing to ask her what she wanted. There was a comfort in such undemanding familiarity.

'We'll just make it a quick one,' he said as they sat down, 'or I'll be in trouble.'

He laughed loudly.

Geraldine sat beside him. Close up, she was even more shocked than she had been on first catching sight of him from the door.

'Are you keeping well?' he asked, scrutinising her face in his turn. 'How's London treating you? Are they looking after you there?'

He barked a rapid series of questions. She understood he didn't want to talk about himself.

'Enough about me,' she said at last. 'What about you?'

'I'm fine,' he replied, although she could see that wasn't true.

'How's married life?'

He shrugged and took a gulp of his pint before answering that it was fine. It would be insensitive to tell him she didn't believe him.

'But let's not talk about me,' he went on quickly. 'You're the one who's getting on with your life and doing something exciting. Tell me all about London.'

There was a wistfulness in his expression that she couldn't fail to notice.

She leaned towards him.

'Ian, what's wrong?'

'Well, my new DI's a shit.'

'I'm a hard act to follow,' she laughed.

He didn't join in her laughter. Instead he glanced nervously at his watch.

'I can't stay long,' he muttered, 'or I'll get it in the neck.'

Geraldine understood that Ian hadn't told his wife about their meeting. Bev had been unnecessarily suspicious of the intimacy that had arisen between them when they had been working together. It wasn't unusual for two officers on the same team to develop an instinctive mutual understanding. She watched him when he went back over to the bar for just one more pint, the way his head hung forwards.

'How's Bev?' she asked directly when he returned with two beers.

His smile didn't reach his tired eyes.

'Bev's great.'

She wondered if he realised she knew he was lying.

'Ian, what's wrong?'

'Nothing.'

She didn't press him, although he looked so miserable it was almost unbearable. When she had worked with him he had always been robustly cheerful. She was struck by a sudden impulse to comfort him, like a child, and pulled herself up sharply. He had probably just had a row with his wife. Whatever the reason for his miserable mood, it was none of her business, unless he chose to share it with her.

They talked about London, and life back in Kent, for a while, but she couldn't help feeling concerned.

'You know you can always talk to me – about anything you want. We are friends as well as ex-colleagues,' she hazarded at last, unable to ignore his despondency any longer. She didn't add that he was the closest friend she had.

He didn't answer.

'Have you got time for another one?' she asked.

He looked at his watch and shook his head.

'I'd better go.'

Hurriedly he gulped down the last of his pint and stood up.

'We must do this again soon. It was really good to see you.'

He placed his hand on her shoulder for a second before he left. With an irrepressible pang she watched him slip away without a backward glance, hurrying back to his wife. After he had gone she sat quite still for a moment, remembering the pressure of his hand on her shoulder. It was a long time since a man had touched her.

At last she stood up, and set off on the long drive back to her empty flat.

27

LEAVING THE POLICE STATION the following morning, Piers issued a stream of futile threats.

'You'll be hearing from my lawyer,' he fumed, pointing an accusatory finger at the officer in charge. 'You haven't heard the end of this yet.'

The custody sergeant took no notice. He had heard tirades like that many times over. They both knew it was just so much hot air.

'I'll be talking to the media about my wrongful arrest,' he blustered.

'You have that right, sir,' the sergeant responded stolidly.

Two hours later, showered and pristine, Piers was sitting at home savouring the aroma of freshly ground coffee. No one brewed coffee as well as Maria. He had found his dumpy little housekeeper over ten years ago on a film set where she had been working as a cleaner. Observing how industrious she was he had recruited her to work for him, and she had been with him ever since, progressing from cleaning to running the entire household. Now she was in charge of a cleaner who came in two mornings a week.

His morning cafetiere was one of the things Piers had missed most when he had been banged up. The memory of that night still made him feel sick. He wondered how anyone could survive being locked up, night after night, in a bare cell stinking of piss and antiseptic. It was disgraceful that a man in his position should be subjected to such barbaric treatment. He shuddered at the memory. Glancing at one of the tabloids, he set his cup carefully down on the table and stared at a grainy picture of Bethany hanging onto his arm under a headline: 'In Bed with Suspected Killer.' Piers swore aloud. The little cow had got wind of his visit to the police station, and blabbed to the papers. Everyone must have read about it by now. The police had released him, but he remained a suspect in a murder investigation.

He could hardly bear to read what the paper had published about him. His face twisted in disgust as he read what Bethany had said. With a sigh, he helped himself to another cup of coffee before reading through the article again, slowly.

'When glamour model and actress, Bethany Marsden (22), was seduced by an older man, she had no idea he would soon be helping the police with an enquiry into the death of another one of his conquests. Blonde bombshell Bethany said, 'I was shocked when I heard the police wanted to talk to him. I had no idea Piers was two timing me.'

'60-year-old Piers Trevelyan is being questioned by the police as part of an ongoing investigation into the brutal murder of Anna Porter (20), star of the small screen, playing the part of Dorothy in Down and Out.'

Piers slapped the paper down on the table, making the crumbs on his plate jump. The reporter described Bethany as a 'glamour model and actress'. That was as good as calling her a sex worker. His frown relaxed slightly. At least the paper had knocked four years off his age. As for the lying bitch who had sold her story, that kind of tawdry publicity would do her no favours. Once his name was cleared no one in the industry would touch her. She had branded herself as toxic. All the same, her name was on the front page of the papers. By the time his innocence was established a lot of people would have forgotten the details of the case, but they would remember her name. All in all, the article was likely to further her career, unless he stepped in to scupper it. He bit thoughtfully into a slice of brown toast, planning how to make sure she never worked again.

The shrilling of his mobile phone startled him out of his reverie.

'Dad?'

'Hello Zak.'

'Dad, have you seen the papers?'

Zak's agitation had a calming effect on Piers.

'Yes.'

'Is that all you can say?'

'It answers the question.'

'Hardly. Have you seen the crap they're printing about you?'

'Yes.'

'Dad!'

'Anna's dead. I have no control over what the papers say about it. Now control yourself and don't make a drama out of the situation.'

'They're saying you killed her –'

'Because she was driven into by a van belonging to me. But I'm not the only person who had a key to the van.'

'What's that supposed to mean? Are you trying to frighten me now? Because you know that hasn't worked since I was in short trousers. You don't scare me.'

'Oh, grow up, for Christ's sake. I'm warning you. You do know they're going to come after you once they've finished with me. You need to be prepared, that's all I'm saying. You know what these reporters are like, not to mention the police.'

'What are we going to do?'

'Nothing. There's nothing we can do other than tell them the truth, that we had nothing to do with Anna's death. But whatever you do, don't say a word to the papers. Anything you say will be misquoted or twisted to big up their "story".'

'But –'

'Ignore it, Zak. All this will soon blow over, believe me.'

'How can I ignore it? Everyone's going to see the papers. They'll all be talking about it. How will I be able to look anyone in the eye ever again?'

'Stop that, Zak. Calm down.'

Piers felt a wave of resentment. After all he had done for his son, the boy was concerned only about the impact of his father's problems on his own life.

'But what am I supposed to do now?' the boy was burbling.

'Carry on with your life. There's nothing else you can do. And stop fussing. This will all die down soon enough. It's of no consequence. Believe me, son, I've had far worse stories circulated about me, all lies, and no one even remembers them a week later. It's just part of the media circus. And anyway, this isn't about you. It's about me. Stop behaving like a hysterical narcissist and grow up for fuck's sake.'

Having issued that piece of fatherly advice, Piers hung up.

28

PIERS' NEIGHBOUR WAS A prosperous solicitor who worked for the London office of an international law firm, which was located near Baker Street. Leaving the station, Geraldine made her way north, away from Regents Park. The pavements were crowded and traffic crawled along the busy roads. After walking for about ten minutes she reached Marylebone House, a tall brick and glass block of offices. The woman on the central reception desk directed her to the fourth floor where she found Garnett's secretary in a small smart office. The secretary looked up enquiringly as Geraldine entered the room.

'I'm here to see Mr Garnett.'

'Anthony or Gerald?'

'Anthony.'

'Do you have an appointment?'

Geraldine explained she had telephoned earlier and showed her identity card. With a perfunctory nod the secretary asked her to take a seat.

'Mr Garnett will see you soon,' she added politely, as though Geraldine was a client.

Anthony was a portly man in his mid-fifties. His greying hair was thinning on top, white above his small flat ears. He looked a model of respectability in a pin-striped suit, crisp white shirt and sober tie. He sat very upright, diminutive behind his large polished wooden desk, and greeted Geraldine in a formal tone.

'How can I be of assistance?'

He raised his eyebrows when she explained the reason for her visit.

'My next door neighbour?' he repeated. He sounded faintly exasperated. 'What has he been saying about me now? Frankly I'm surprised at the police, spending so much time on what is essentially a disagreement between neighbours. I take it you are aware there's a long running dispute between us, and I've had occasion to lodge a complaint on more than one occasion about the behaviour of his latest companion. His late companion, I should say. Do you know she was almost the same age as his own son?'

'It's about the death of Anna Porter that I wanted to speak to you.'

Garnett's expression grew more solemn.

'Oh yes, I heard about her accident. It was in all the papers.' He leaned forward confidentially. 'I had no idea she was such a celebrity.'

'What do you know about her?'

'Only what I read in the papers, and what I saw for myself. I don't like to insult the dead, but the truth is the girl had no idea how to behave, and precious few morals. Of course that was her affair, but when she turned up in the street at all hours, drunk and making a terrible din, that was no longer a private issue. And then she had the gall to complain because I happened to see her from my bedroom window when she was sunbathing naked in their back garden. She was on display there, I could hardly miss seeing her when I looked out. But the worst aspect of her antisocial behaviour was that she regularly parked her car right outside my house.'

'I'm not here to enquire about your disagreements with your neighbours,' Geraldine interrupted quietly.

'What then? Only I have a lot of work –'

He glanced down at the file on his desk and tapped it with a plump manicured finger.

'I'm investigating Anna's death.'

'As I said, I don't like to speak badly of the dead. And it was certainly a tragedy. What a terrible waste of a young life.'

'Mr Garnett, I work for homicide and serious crime command.' In case he hadn't registered the significance of her words she added, 'We don't investigate accidents.'

His expression didn't alter. He carried on speaking in an even, matter-of-fact tone. Like Geraldine, he was accustomed to dealing with human atrocities.

'So you're telling me the girl's death wasn't an accident?'

She nodded.

'She was murdered, eh? I can't say I'm terribly surprised. Shocked, of course, but not overly surprised, I'm afraid.'

'What do you mean?'

'I assume you've come to tell me Piers ran her down. Well, that doesn't come as a surprise. That's all I'm saying.'

'What makes you think he's a suspect?'

The lawyer raised his eyes to meet hers. 'Correct me if I'm wrong. I thought it was generally the husband, or the boyfriend, in these cases. God knows, she gave him reason enough to want to be rid of her, but not to kill her.'

'What reason?' Geraldine asked. 'You said she gave him enough reason to want to be rid of her. What did you mean by that, exactly?'

The lawyer hesitated before speaking.

'I don't like to malign the girl, now she's dead, but the truth will come out anyway. A young man used to visit her when Piers wasn't around.'

'Could it have been his son?'

'No. I know Zak. He's very dark. This was a blond chap who went to see her when Piers was out. I saw him leaving the house quite a few times.'

Geraldine thought of Dirk Goodbody.

'Could this visitor have been a friend of hers?'

Garnett gave a short laugh.

'He was more than a friend. I saw them kissing in the garden.'

'I believe actors kiss a lot.'

'Not like this.'

'Can you be more specific?'

'Do I have to spell it out? They were kissing on the lips, and his hands were all over her. This was a sexually active relationship she was carrying on behind Piers' back. It wasn't only the kissing. There was something furtive about the way he skulked off down the street, as though he didn't want to be seen.'

'Are you sure?'

'Positive.'

It wasn't an easy exchange. The lawyer grew tetchy as the questioning progressed. At some point he realised that he might be a suspect himself, and became reserved. Geraldine was constantly aware of the need to be careful, both in what she asked, and in her manner. He would be the first to lodge a complaint if she overstepped her authority, and he would be sure to follow the correct procedures.

'Are you accusing me of murder?' he asked her point blank at one point.

She denied it as convincingly as she could.

She felt drained by the time she left Marylebone House. It was sunny outside and she realised she had been too preoccupied by the investigation to enjoy the recent spell of good weather. On a whim she walked past the station and on down Baker Street, passing the London Underground Lost Property office, the Sherlock Holmes museum, and a few cafes, and on into Regents Park. Ahead of her a lake glistened. White and brown ducks scudded around and a few swans glided lazily on the water. She turned right and crossed a wide bridge. To her right, at the water's edge, a heron stood motionless, as though suspended in time. The peace of the scene overwhelmed her and she stood spellbound. As the daylight faded, the air grew chilly. People sauntering along the paths, chatting and laughing, began to walk more quickly. There were only a few people left on benches, staring at the lake. Leaving the park, she made her way slowly back to her empty flat, wondering what she was doing with her life.

29

A RECENT GRADUATE FROM their drama school was performing in a production at the studio theatre in the Barbican. When one of her classmates offered Bethany a ticket, she agreed at once. She had nothing else planned for the evening. The set was sparse, the production edgy. While they were manoeuvring their way to the exit, the other girl said she was going to wait and congratulate her friend. Bethany didn't want to hang around. She hadn't known the actor very well, and in any case the theatre was stuffy and she had a slight headache, probably brought on by the stress of waiting to hear about her audition. It was possible she would have a second recall. She might be asked to read with other members of the cast with very little notice, and she couldn't afford to look burned out if the call came.

'Tell him it was fantastic and he was brilliant!' she gushed before leaving her friend in the foyer.

The play had been oppressive but her threatened headache disappeared outside in the cool air, and her spirits lifted. It was a pleasant evening, mild and fresh. It wasn't late, so instead of taking the train from Barbican station, which was just across the road, she decided to walk to Chancery Lane. It was less than a mile away. From there she could catch the Central line straight back to Mile End, where she lived. She could have saved herself a walk by taking the train at Barbican station but, apart from the added hassle of changing trains at a busy station, she fancied walking along the bridge that spanned the main road.

She went South and turned right at the roundabout, heading down Newgate Street to Holborn Viaduct which would take her right over the top of Farringdon Street. This was the real purpose of her walk. She had seen the Victorian road bridge from below, with its carved stone pillars, ornate decorative cast iron ramparts, old-fashioned street lamps, and statues set on high plinths. Stone dragons or griffins – she wasn't sure which – dominated the wrought ironwork. She hadn't been able to see the statues clearly from below, and wanted to walk across the top of the road bridge to take a look at them close up. Her anticipation grew as she approached the bridge and saw larger than life statues illuminated in the glow of huge round lamps.

As she strode along the pavement, she could hear other people scurrying behind her. She hurried on to the roundabout, ignoring a homeless man slumped in a doorway, a mangy dog at his side. The lace on one of her trainers was loose. Crouching down to tie it up properly, her attention was caught by a figure in a grey hood who stopped at exactly the same time as she did and stood a few paces behind her, as though waiting for something. It reminded her of the tall woman who had appeared to be following her on the way to her audition. Momentarily shocked, Bethany froze. The stranger pulled a phone from her pocket, and began talking. Rebuking herself for her stupidity, Bethany straightened up and glanced over her shoulder. The hooded figure had disappeared. Reassured, she turned and continued on her way. Nothing had happened, yet the incident had unnerved her. She walked faster.

Reaching the bridge, she glanced behind her and felt a shiver of fear. This time there could be no doubt. A grey figure was walking along the pavement, head lowered, a few paces behind her. She couldn't make out the face, couldn't tell if it was a man or a woman, but she could see sunglasses gleaming beneath the hood. That was odd at this time of night. It was enough to convince Bethany she was being followed by the same person she had spotted watching her from the street outside her flat. She knew this was something celebrities had to suffer. Although she wasn't exactly well known yet, she had played some major roles in productions at drama school. Anyone could have seen her on stage. She felt sick, remembering one scene where she had stripped down to her underwear. It must be a crazy fan stalking her.

Whether the stranger was curious to find out about her life, or just wanted to feel close to her, the whole idea gave her the creeps. Knowing that her pursuer knew where she lived, she shuddered. With a brief flash of anger she was tempted to turn round and confront her stalker, but apart from cars zooming past, the street was deserted. It could be dangerous to engage with a fanatical admirer who might turn violent. Bethany glanced around. They were alone together on a busy London street at night. No one would notice if Bethany was suddenly knifed and slumped to the pavement, bleeding to death. If anyone did pass by, they would assume she was drunk, or homeless. The truth might not emerge for days.

Her breath came in shallow gasps. All her senses were alert. Tingling with adrenaline, she could feel her heart beating. It was dark, but the road was well lit. She hurried along the bridge without even glancing up at the statues, no longer interested in the intricate ironwork. She didn't pause in her stride to look down over the parapet at the busy road far below. All she wanted to do was reach the station quickly, go home and lock the door. She hoped her flatmate would be in. Cars roared under the bridge, but other than vehicles on the road below, the Viaduct was deserted. Apart from a crazy stalker who had followed her all the way from the Barbican, she was alone. She tried calling her boyfriend, but he didn't answer. She considered running into the road and flagging down a car but when she looked back over her shoulder, there was no one behind her.

She breathed freely again, dizzy with relief. Her legs felt wobbly and she blinked to clear her blurred vision. She was glad there was no one else there to witness how she had allowed her fears to get the better of her. She didn't have a stalker. No one was following her. It was coincidence that she had recently happened to see two, maybe more, people in grey hoodies. It was hardly an unusual kind of jacket. One day, when she was famous, she might find herself the object of unwanted attention, but that time hadn't yet come.

There was no alarming sound of footsteps on the pavement behind her, no warning whiff of sweat or damp clothes, no sinister voice hissing unexpectedly in her ear; only a gentle touch on her throat. Before she had registered what was happening, the pressure tightened around her neck with a fierce burning sensation. She heard herself choking as she gasped for breath. Frantically her fingers scratched at her skin, as she scrabbled to loosen the strap around her neck. Fighting to breathe, she was hardly aware of falling to the pavement. By the time the strap loosened, she had already given up the struggle to breathe.

30

After eating at a Vietnamese restaurant off Tottenham Court Road, the five friends took the Central line to Chancery Lane station. On the way they enjoyed the attention they attracted. Some of their fellow passengers leered openly at them, others were more discreet in their observation. The friends sniggered when an old woman sitting opposite them glared at them, her face twisted in disapproval at their short skirts and skimpy tops.

'Cheer up, grandma! Didn't you never go out on a hen night?' Lia shouted over her shoulder as they bundled off the train.

Standing beside her friend, Kirsty screwed up her nose at the tangy smell of her friend's breath, a mixture of spices and alcohol.

The other girls weren't interested in the old woman's disapproval. They had just discovered how far they had to walk to reach the club.

'It's only half a mile,' Kirsty reassured them as they left the station.

'Half a mile!' Stephanie protested. 'In these heels!'

'You're going to be dancing in those heels when we get there,' Kirsty laughed.

'Catch me,' Stephanie replied.

The other girls batted her with their wands, screeching.

'It's Kirsty's night. If she says dance, you dance.'

Stephanie squealed as she defended herself from their fluffy prodding.

'Some angels you lot are! Bugger off, Lia, you'll break my wings.'

A couple of young men walking towards them whistled and called out, their words lost in the roar of traffic. The girls screeched in mock indignation. One of the men ogled Kirsty's L-plates as he passed her.

'Want a few lessons, sweetheart?'

'She's getting married in the morning,' Lia shrieked, and the rest of the girls joined in a wild chorus.

'Blimey, we're not even drunk yet,' Stephanie said as they teetered along in their heels, giggling.

'Speak for yourself.'

Laughing and nattering, Kirsty led them along the main road and on to Holborn Viaduct. The others looked around curiously.

'Where are you taking us?'

'Yes, where are we going?'

They passed a huge statue raised up on a plinth at the side of the road. Kirsty leaned across a low stone parapet and gazed out past the ornate metal railing. Her companions paused to catch their breath and adjust their costumes.

'Look, just look,' she said, 'look down there. It's like flying!'

'Not the state my wings are in,' Stephanie grumbled.

Far below them traffic thundered past along the Farringdon Road.

'Makes me dizzy,' Lia said. 'I don't know how you can bear to look down there.'

She turned away from the railings and walked on a few steps.

All at once she stopped in her tracks. As her companions stared down over the railing, chatting and laughing excitedly, a high-pitched scream cut across the hum of traffic. The others turned to look at Lia.

'What the hell – ?' Kirsty began.

She stopped speaking as Lia swung round and ran over to her friends. She was shaking visibly, and they could see she was trying to talk.

'Oh my God, she's having a stroke!' Kirsty cried out.

They clustered in front of her, all talking at once.

'Lia, Lia, what's wrong?'

'Lia, pull yourself together.'

'Lia, Lia, speak to me!'

The stricken girl covered her mouth with one hand, gesturing wildly at the ground with the other. They looked down where she was pointing.

'What is it?'

'What the fuck is that?'

The passing glare of a car's headlights illuminated a figure lying on the pavement. They fell silent. A woman's face was staring up at them from the ground. In the shadowy light of the street lamps her complexion appeared bluish in colour. By themselves her blackish lips might have identified her as a Goth, but with bloodshot eyes she looked more like a character from a horror film.

'It's a mask,' Kirsty whispered. 'Her face is blue –'

'What's she doing there?'

'Must be drunk.'

'Or stoned.'

'Look at her eyes… '

'This is really freaking me out.'

'Do you think we should do something?'

They spoke in hushed tones, shocked by the sight of a stranger lying motionless at their feet.

Trainee nurse Stephanie stepped forward and stooped down to examine the figure.

'It's a woman,' she said briskly, 'probably dead. Can you all step back so I can get some light here?'

It wasn't a question. Automatically, her friends obeyed the authority in her voice. Lia began to cry. Kirsty watched Stephanie kneel down beside the prone figure, turn her head to one side, and listen to the woman's chest. Sitting back on her heels, she reached out her hand, frowning as she disturbed the woman's clothing to examine her neck. Finally she spoke.

'You'd better call the police.'

Kirsty's hands were shaking as she pulled out her phone.

'Shouldn't we call an ambulance?' one of the girls piped up.

'It's too late for that,' Stephanie answered.

'How do you know? You can't be sure.'

'Do you want to come over here and see if you can find any signs of life?'

Kirsty dialled the emergency services and asked for the police. It felt awkward saying she and her friends had found a dead body on the street. She had to repeat her message before the woman at the other end of the phone seemed to understand what she was saying.

'Of course I'm sure,' she snapped.

It was beginning to sink in that her hen night was ruined.

'We're standing right here. We know when someone's dead. That is, my friend Stephanie does. She's a nurse, or at least she will be soon. Anyway, she knows what she's doing and she said this woman is dead.'

Her voice rose in panic. She seemed to calm down as she listened again. When she spoke again she sounded impatient.

'I've no idea who she is. We just found her. I don't know what happened. We just found her here, dead.'

She hung up abruptly and burst out crying.

'It's my hen night,' she wailed. 'Everyone will be there.'

While Kirsty had been talking on the phone, Lia had continued to sob quietly. Stephanie meanwhile had been observing the body. Having established the woman was dead, she was careful not to touch her again.

'There's definitely something not right about this,' Stephanie announced quietly.

Taking no notice of Lia, who was moaning about wanting to throw up, Kirsty moved closer to Stephanie to hear what she was saying. The body gave off a stale smell. Even Kirsty was interested, her disappointment forgotten in her curiosity about the dead woman.

'What do you mean?'

'Look.'

Stephanie pointed first to the swollen tongue in the dead woman's open mouth, and then to a dark brown ring that encircled her neck. On either side of it was a band, lighter in colour but still clearly visible. It looked as though something had been tied around her neck so tightly it had cut into her flesh.

'Oh my God,' Kirsty whispered, as she glimpsed the significance of the weal round the woman's neck.

'Something stopped her breathing,' Stephanie said.

'Or someone,' Kirsty added.

31

GERALDINE WENT INTO WORK early the next morning, as usual. In London the roads could be unexpectedly congested at any time, but this Saturday morning her journey was relatively fast. Her easy drive didn't improve her mood. The senior crime command centre was already humming with quiet activity. After checking her emails, she made her way along the corridor to find Sam who had a team of constables still looking for the missing van driver.

'He must be somewhere,' Sam insisted. Trying to appear decisive, she sounded plaintive. 'People don't just disappear into thin air.'

Most of the team were convinced it must have been Piers, his son's alibi having checked out. No one could explain how he could have been driving the van and escaped from the crash alive. In the absence of any other information, they were working on the assumption that whoever had been driving the van had also committed the murder.

'It seems highly unlikely that someone else appeared on the scene after the crash and killed Anna,' Reg pointed out, 'but we need to keep an open mind.'

'You mean two people might have disappeared?' Sam said.

The team were busy contacting every hospital and doctor's surgery within a hundred mile radius, on the assumption that the van driver couldn't possibly have escaped unhurt. If that drew a blank, they would widen their search area.

'Whoever was driving that van must have been injured in the crash,' Sam argued. 'He's going to be needing medical attention soon, if he hasn't already checked into a hospital or consulted a doctor. No one's seen him yet, but it can't be much longer before he shows himself. We're alerting every doctor and nurse who might have come in contact with a patient whose injuries could fit with our accident, and all the undertakers as well. It's a massive undertaking, which –'

'Which I'm sure you're carrying out thoroughly and efficiently,' Geraldine finished the sentence for her.

Sam gave Geraldine a grateful smile. Seeing that the sergeant looked exhausted, Geraldine suggested they go for a coffee.

'Have you had breakfast yet?'

Sam shook her head and they went to the canteen where Geraldine insisted her colleague have a full breakfast. As she tucked into egg and beans on toast, she filled Geraldine in on their progress so far. The search had found several possible suspects who had turned up at accident and emergency departments in London hospitals displaying injuries consistent with serious car accidents. One by one they had been ruled out, after raising the hopes of the team. None of them could feasibly have been driving Piers' van between two and three on the night of the accident.

Geraldine agreed that it was impossible for the driver to have walked away unharmed. She actually found it hard to believe anyone could have escaped from the van alive, after such a serious accident. What had happened seemed impossible. The driver had not only survived, but had left the scene without being noticed or picked up on any CCTV film in the area. There were no shots of the van itself from the security camera covering that stretch of road. Only the back of the Porsche was visible, coming to an abrupt halt when the van hit it. The film was grainy and fuzzy, but helpful in pinpointing the time of the accident.

With the van out of the sightline of the camera, it might have been possible for the driver to clamber out without being caught on film. But Bernard had driven up in his taxi just seven minutes after the accident took place, and was positive he hadn't seen anyone leave the street where the crash took place. Sam's constables had scrutinised CCTV film from both ends of Ashland Place. No one had left the narrow street in the seven minutes before the taxi drew up, or in the subsequent five minutes before the first uniformed police arrived, and no one had opened a door or window in the walls on either side of the road. There was no way the van driver could have walked away without being spotted. Yet he had.

Back at her desk, Geraldine was fed up. She had spent a whole week working in vain. She had checked through CCTV which had already been watched by a team of constables, studied Bernard Hallam's statement for the tenth time, and gone over reports produced by scene of crime officers who had found no trace of the vanished driver. Expert car mechanics had discovered no evidence the van had been modified, and were adamant it couldn't have driven into the Porsche without someone at the wheel. Rereading the post mortem report didn't help. The investigation seemed to have hit a brick wall. All they could do was wait and hope a doctor or undertaker would come forward with information. On a previous case Sam had told Geraldine the team had complained that she distrusted other people. They said she found it impossible to delegate any work to others, and was determined to control every aspect of the case herself. In this instance no one had so much as raised an eyebrow about her going over what they had done, they were all so keen for someone to discover a lead to the van driver.

With nothing new to do, and too dispirited to read through statements once more, the only sensible course was take a break and prepare to start again fresh. Ten minutes later she was sitting in the canteen with a half eaten bun and a mug of coffee, barely conscious of the food she was eating. Meanwhile her mind continued to race, thinking about Piers, his son, his neighbour, as well as the young stud, Dirk, and his new girlfriend. Somewhere in their statements there must be a clue to the identity of the killer. She was both irritated and relieved when Nick came over.

'Mind if I join you?'

She gave a noncommittal grunt. She could hardly tell him to leave her alone.

In some ways she was glad of the distraction.

'You look down in the dumps,' he commented cheerfully.

She was tempted to retort, 'Just because I couldn't tell you not to sit here, doesn't mean I want to talk to you.' Instead she merely shrugged.

'What's on your mind?' he asked again.

Geraldine gazed into his irregular eyes that seemed to be winking back at her. One strand of his light brown hair had flopped forwards over his wide forehead. Together with his striped scarf and sports jacket, she thought it gave him the appearance of having just stepped off a film set. Everything seemed to remind her of the theatrical people she was investigating.

'What's up?' he repeated.

It was actually quite pleasant to be able to discuss the investigation with someone who would understand her frustrations without being directly involved in the case. With a sigh, she told him about the murder.

'Yes, I heard about it. The disappearing driver. Some people get all the interesting cases. So, we've got one actress, and two men. That sounds like a recipe for trouble to begin with. Or the start of a bad joke. Is that the key?'

'The key?'

'She was sleeping with both of them, wasn't she? That sounds like a recipe for trouble.'

'Yes, although that's hardly unusual. No, the real conundrum is how the killer managed to slip away without being seen. That's what needs attention.'

'You look like you could do with a bit of attention yourself,' Nick said. 'How about a spot of supper tonight? My treat.'

Before Geraldine could think what to say, her phone rang. Her heart raced at the thought that a lead might have been discovered, but the call wasn't from a colleague. Instead, she was disappointed to hear her sister's voice.

'How's your investigation coming along?'

'Lots of hard work to be done,' Geraldine replied, forcing herself to sound cheerful. With a nod to Nick to indicate she had to take the call, she stood up and left the table.

'How about you? What's your news? And how's Chloe?'

'She's still disappointed you let her down –'

'You know I couldn't help it.'

'Yes, that's all very well, but she's a child … '

With solemn assurances that she would make it up to her niece, Geraldine made her escape from the second tricky conversation in as many minutes. She and Celia had grown up together, but they couldn't be more different. Sometimes she felt they had grown up on different planets, and not under the same roof at all. In the meantime, she was grateful that Celia's call had rescued her from a slightly awkward situation with Nick.

Although she hadn't enjoyed defending herself from her sister's criticism, after she hung up she felt more lonely than ever, her sense of helplessness almost a physical ache. Returning to her office, she tried not to speculate that Nick's invitation might have signified something more than a casual encounter with a colleague. Knowing he was married, she had never really given him much thought, although he was undoubtedly attractive, friendly and attentive. She wondered if he had made a similar advance to Sam, and if that was the real reason the sergeant found him so objectionable.

She didn't hear Nick enter the office until she was startled by his voice close to her ear.

'How about this evening, then?'

She turned and saw him leaning over her, his hand on the back of her chair in a proprietorial gesture.

'You're married,' she blurted out.

Nick took a step back and smiled sadly. 'Married, but separated.'

'You mean you don't live together?'

'We're still in the same house, but –'

'Don't tell me, your wife doesn't understand you.' She turned away from him, aware that she had sounded bitter.

When he repeated his suggestion, she replied that she was working. She regretted her curt response as soon as she had spoken. It was a while since she had last enjoyed some male attention. If he really was separated from his wife, it would be a shame for her to reject his advances. He might be lonely too. On the other hand, she and Nick worked together. They shared an office. On balance, it would be stupid to risk going out with him. Stifling a sigh, she turned her attention back to the investigation. She wondered if the driver who had killed Anna was also sitting at home, fretting over what he had done, and waiting for the police to arrive on his doorstep, or if it had been a calculated murder and he was congratulating himself for getting away with it.

32

THERE WAS A BUZZ of anticipation around the major incident room where they had all gathered in the afternoon. Everyone sensed that something new had come up, although no one seemed to know what it was. In the meantime, they speculated as they waited for Reg who had summoned them, only to keep them waiting. Geraldine wondered if that was a deliberate strategy to assert his authority. She wouldn't have put it past him. Outwardly brash, with apparent confidence to consult his colleagues, she found it irritating that he made a point of allowing her to voice her opinion, but never seemed to take her views seriously. It would be less patronising not to invite her opinion at all.

'I don't know why we had to drop everything and rush here just to hang around waiting,' Sam muttered.

Sam was disgruntled, but Geraldine knew the sergeant wasn't really put out. As for Geraldine, she welcomed the demands her job made on her time. What could be more important than protecting the public, possibly saving lives? Work gave her life meaning and purpose. With no love life, and a strained relationship with her sister, there was no one who cared deeply about her. If Geraldine's life ended prematurely, Celia's grief would be fleeting. Geraldine's adoptive mother was dead, and for all she knew, her birth mother was dead too. As an adult Geraldine had been devastated to learn about her history, and shocked that her adoptive mother had never told her the truth. The social worker attached to the case had warned her from the start that her birth mother didn't want to meet her. Whichever way she turned, she met with rejection. If it was hard not to care, it was harder still to care. Even if her birth mother was alive, and Geraldine succeeded in tracking her down, there was no guarantee Milly Blake would change her mind and agree to meet her.

'He could at least have been on time,' Sam was saying.

Geraldine turned to the young sergeant and smiled. Sam gave a resigned grin and ran her hands through blonde hair which stuck up in spiky tufts. Before she could say anything else, the detective chief inspector entered the room. He strode purposefully to the white board where he displayed a picture of a girl's face. It was difficult to be sure, but Geraldine thought she looked about twenty. Her features were regular and well-proportioned. She would have been pretty, but her skin was tinged with blue, her lips looked black, and her eyes were red and puffy. Geraldine had a feeling she had seen her before, but she couldn't remember where.

'A girl has been found.'

Reg didn't need to add that the girl was dead.

'She was discovered last night on Holborn Viaduct, on the A40, where it crosses Farringdon Road.'

He turned and pointed to a red weal on the dead girl's throat.

'You can see the ligature marks where she was strangled.'

'The bridge is in Holborn Viaduct,' a constable pointed out. 'Why is this coming to us?'

'We're already working on a case,' someone else agreed.

'As if we haven't got enough to do,' another voice added.

'It may be nothing to do with the case we're working on, but this victim, Bethany Marsden, recently graduated from the drama school where Anna Porter trained.' He tapped the board as he said the name. 'It's a close community. She would have known Anna. They were in the same year at the drama school. Bethany also worked with Piers Trevelyan, our main suspect.'

'Of course,' Geraldine muttered.

'What's that?' Reg asked sharply, as though he thought Geraldine was challenging him for naming Piers as a suspect.

'It's just that I thought I recognised her. When you said her name, I remembered I'd seen her photo on the drama school website.'

'I would expect a detective of your rank to be able to recognise faces,' Reg snapped.

'She looked a little different on the website,' Geraldine retorted, stung by the contempt in his voice. 'Her face wasn't black and blue, for a start, and she'd combed her hair for the photograph.'

She stopped talking abruptly, careful to keep her expression blank. Inside, she was seething at the harshness of his rebuke. It would have irritated her if he had addressed her like that in private. In front of her colleagues it was humiliating.

Reg turned his attention back to the image of the dead girl with her messed up face. Geraldine swallowed her pride and focused her attention on the victim's face, as though staring at the photograph would somehow reveal her killer's identity. She wondered if everyone else on the team was thinking the same as her. Piers had been living with Anna, who was now dead. He was known to have a penchant for pretty young girls. Bethany had been very attractive, before her face had turned blue and bloated.

'The body was discovered by a group of girls out on a hen night.'

'Great!' Sam muttered. 'I'm sure they were all sober and observant witnesses.'

'Fortunately one of them's a nurse,' Reg replied. 'The officers who arrived first on the scene managed to get a reasonably sensible statement out of her, although they were all drunk. The other girls were too hysterical to make much sense at the time, but we'll need to speak to all of them, in case any of them noticed anything.'

He pulled another image onto the screen, of a tabloid newspaper report. 'In Bed with Suspected Killer' the headline screamed. Reg read aloud: 'When glamour model and actress, Bethany Marsden (22), was seduced by an older man, she had no idea he would soon be helping the police with an enquiry into the death of another one of his conquests. Blonde bombshell Bethany said, "I was shocked when I heard the police wanted to talk to him. I had no idea Piers was two timing me."'

He glared around the room.

'It seems the tabloids knew more about Piers' affairs than we managed to discover.'

'Perhaps because we can't just make things up,' someone muttered.

'It can't be coincidence that she was sleeping with Piers as well,' Reg went on.

Even Geraldine didn't challenge the implied accusation. They were all chastened by the revelation that Piers had allegedly been conducting an affair they knew nothing about, an affair with a second young actress who had been killed.

With work to be done, and tasks to be allocated, the mood in the incident room grew frenetic. Geraldine and Sam were sent to check out the crime scene, after which they were going to speak to the victim's family. The witnesses who had discovered the body had already been questioned. Walking to the car, they discussed the value of speaking to them again. On balance they decided it might be worth finding out what the nurse could tell them. The other witnesses were probably going to be a waste of time. Neither of them mentioned Reg's rebuke as they drove to the crime scene. The detective chief inspector's manner no longer seemed important as they went to view the corpse of a dead woman for the second time in eight days.

33

THE A40 WAS CLOSED off at either end of the bridge. They slowed down at the cordon and Geraldine held up her warrant card. A uniformed constable waved them through and they drove up onto the bridge where a white forensic tent was in place. For the second time in eight days they put on white forensic suits and blue plastic overshoes. Geraldine gave Sam a sympathetic grimace. At least Bethany had only been dead for a matter of hours, during which time she had been lying out in the fresh air, so the smell was damp rather than putrid as they entered the tent. Even so, Geraldine was aware of the strain in her colleague's eyes and the tension in her shoulders, as she prepared to view the young woman's corpse.

The images that had been sent through to the station did little to prepare them for the ghastly sight on the ground in front of them. The dead girl's clothes had been neatly cut open all the way down her front to allow the pathologist to conduct a preliminary examination on site. Geraldine had worked with the pathologist before and knew better than to press him for information before he was ready to give his report. Miles was smart but young, and he could be irritatingly immature. The more urgently she questioned him, the more evasive his answers were likely to be. Forcing herself to wait patiently, she watched his deft slim fingers moving rapidly, his face puckered in concentration as he probed and measured. At last he looked up from his work and shook his head.

'I'm afraid she's dead, inspector,' he announced solemnly, his blue eyes sparkling with amusement.

'Show some respect, for Christ's sake,' Sam mumbled under her breath.

Geraldine grinned at the pathologist kneeling beside the body. She didn't object to his light hearted tone. Everyone developed their own way of dealing with the horrors they faced. She had no doubt he would adopt an appropriate tone if the victim's family were present. In the meantime, he had developed personal mechanisms for coping.

'Very useful,' she replied. 'Can you tell us anything else?'

'She was in her late teens, early twenties –'

'Twenty-two,' Sam interjected.

'Good muscle tone,' Miles continued, with a nod at Sam for her interruption. 'I'm guessing she was a dancer or something like that. Not a gymnast or a ballet dancer, but she was fit.' He tapped the dead girl's flat stomach. 'All muscle. If she wasn't a dancer of some sort, she was certainly an exercise junkie.'

His hand moved up the torso and came to rest lightly on the dead girl's chest.

'She had fake breasts.'

He poked at one of them and grimaced.

'Might as well be made of rubber. She wasn't malnourished, but was probably under weight, like so many of these young women are these days. Not anorexic exactly, but probably suffering from a subclinical eating disorder.'

He paused. When Geraldine didn't answer, he pulled at the girl's hair, separating it out on her crown.

'Her hair wasn't naturally blonde.'

Miles heaved himself up onto his feet and dusted his knees with the backs of his hands.

'I've finished here,' he announced cheerfully. 'You can take her away now. I'll do a full post mortem first thing in the morning.'

Two men stepped forward to remove the body.

'Just a minute,' Geraldine stopped him. 'Is there evidence of any other injuries, apart from the neck wound which presumably killed her?'

Miles frowned at the question.

'Cause of death was strangulation. You can see the ligature wounds for yourself. Something like a thin leather strap was placed around her neck and pulled or twisted so tightly that –' He broke off with a slight shrug. 'Well, you can see the results for yourselves. As far as I can tell, there were no other significant injuries. The knees have minor bruising, probably caused by her fall, and there are scrape marks on her palms where she might have put her hands out as she went down. Apart from that, there are no obvious signs of sexual assault, or any other injuries occurring before she was strangled. It doesn't look as though she was sexually active before she died, but I'll be able to tell you more about that when I've got her back to the mortuary. There's a limit to what I can do out here.'

'Of course.'

They were all silent, contemplating the body. Even the faint hum of traffic in the distance seemed to stop for a moment. Geraldine stood perfectly still, transported to another place and time in her mind. If it hadn't been for her fake breasts, the dead woman could have resembled a child as she lay flat on her back, her limbs outstretched. For a crazy instant, Geraldine imagined she was standing watch over a sleeping child. No longer part of an investigation in a forensic tent, she was back in her flat and Chloe had come to stay. Only the figure on the ground wasn't a child, and she wasn't sleeping. Until a few hours ago she had been a living, breathing woman, younger than Geraldine, looking forward to a long life. Now her future had been savagely snatched away.

There was a gust of cold air, accompanied by the sounds of footsteps and muted voices. The scene of crime officers stopped what they were doing and watched in silence as the body was lifted up and carried outside to a waiting van. A faint sigh seemed to flutter around the forensic tent before they settled back to work, with quietly determined faces. Geraldine stood on for a few minutes, studying the scene and gazing at the ground around the site where the body had lain. It was pointless. There was nothing there that the scene of crime officers wouldn't spot in their close scrutiny of the area. Meanwhile the forensic pathologist was calmly packing his instruments into a large bag. Geraldine turned to Sam and gave her a nod. Together they walked across to the exit, and slipped out onto the bridge.

Geraldine stood still for a few seconds, gazing down at the street below.

'What are we waiting for?' Sam asked impatiently. 'I thought we were leaving.'

'We are.'

But Geraldine knew she would be taking the image of a blue-faced young woman with her in her mind, knew too that the memory would haunt her until they found her killer. Bethany had clearly taken so much trouble over her appearance while she was alive, it was almost unbearably sad to remember her with distorted features and discoloured complexion.

34

SAM CLAIMED THE SIGHT of one carved up young woman was enough for her in one week. She made a joke of it, but Geraldine couldn't help worrying about her young sergeant. Sam would have to toughen up if she wanted to stick with a career in homicide. It might even be better for her to work in fraud, but Geraldine was reluctant to suggest a move that would mean losing her. In the meantime, there was no reason why Sam should have to view every post mortem. It meant Geraldine couldn't discuss the medical findings in the car with her colleague on the way back to the station, but it could be useful to mull over what she had seen by herself. It was an uncomfortable thought that her own leniency might not actually be helpful to Sam in the long run. Nevertheless, she had assured Sam it was fine for her to stay behind while Geraldine went to the mortuary alone.

Miles reported his conclusions rapidly.

'It's pretty straightforward this time. My guess is that someone came up behind her, grabbed hold of a leather strap she was wearing round her neck, and –'

He drew his hand swiftly across his own throat to indicate the victim had been strangled, rolling his eyes as he did so. Geraldine suppressed a smile at his comical expression.

'Did you say she was wearing a leather strap round her neck?'

The pathologist held up a bag containing a black leather cord.

'This was inside her shirt.'

Geraldine had seen such necklaces before.

'Do you think she was wearing it before she was attacked?'

'Probably, because it wouldn't have been easy for someone to come up behind her and throw the cord round her neck without her noticing what was going on. If that happened, I would expect to find some evidence of defence wounds from where she tried to stop her attacker getting the cord in place round her neck. On the other hand, if she was already wearing the necklace, it would have been relatively easy for someone to sneak up behind her, seize hold of it and tighten it quickly enough for his victim to lose consciousness before she had a chance to react. There are no defence injuries on her arms or hands, and little sign of a struggle, which suggests she was taken by surprise and it was all over very quickly.'

He looked down at the body. Once again Geraldine was struck by how young the dead girl looked. With her beautiful blue face, she resembled a cartoon character, a fantasy princess from a different world.

'She doesn't appear to have put up much resistance, if any. There's no sign of a struggle. My guess is she was taken completely by surprise, by a very efficient killer.'

'You seem to be doing a lot of guesswork,' Geraldine grumbled.

'Well, I'm sorry. I'll try to be there to film it next time.'

Riled, he ran quickly through the injuries.

'The cause of death is exactly how it looks. Asphyxiation by strangulation with a cord round her neck.'

'Why is she so blue?'

'The blue tinge is caused by cyanosis. Severe hypoxia – lack of oxygen – induces this blue discolouration of the skin. It happens with asphyxiation. There is some evidence that she tried to prevent the cord being tightened, but it was already too late. There are scratch marks on her neck, and I found flakes of skin under her finger nails. We'll need to run DNA tests, but I'm guessing – that is, the likelihood is – that it's her own skin under her nails, scraped away when she tried to prevent the cord from tightening round her neck.'

Miles confirmed that the dead girl had not been subjected to a sexual assault. Geraldine felt relieved, although it made no difference to Bethany now.

'Let's hope that some of the traces of skin cells under her nails belonged to someone else,' he said.

Geraldine left, instructing him to contact her if he had any further information for her. He could call her at any time.

Back at the station Reg was talking to Sam and the team of constables who had been watching CCTV footage.

'Well, look again.' Reg sounded annoyed. 'People don't just disappear into thin air. Whoever killed her must be there on the film somewhere. Find him.'

'Still banging on about Anna's missing killer?' Geraldine muttered.

'No,' Sam answered in an undertone so no one else could hear, least of all Reg. 'He's not talking about Anna. This is Bethany's killer he's on about.'

'Don't tell me her killer vanished without trace as well,' Geraldine said. 'This isn't *Star Trek*. Beam me up, Scotty.'

She was joking, but Sam looked serious.

Reg scowled at Geraldine who dropped her eyes. He must have heard her quip. It wasn't even funny. Sam explained to Geraldine that a couple of constables had been studying CCTV film along the Holborn Viaduct in both directions. More officers had been studying film of the stairs leading from Holborn Viaduct to the street below, trying to gain sight of the killer leaving the scene. So far none of them had seen anyone leaving the bridge on foot, and no car had stopped on or near the bridge. Bethany's killer seemed to have vanished from the bridge as mysteriously as Anna's had from the car crash.

'The method of killing is completely different,' the detective chief inspector pointed out in his clipped voice. 'So presumably we're looking at different killers, but –' he paused, frowning. 'We can't ignore the fact that both victims were involved with one man, Piers Trevelyan.'

'And in both cases the killer vanished impossibly,' Geraldine added. 'Who the hell are we dealing with?'

No one answered.

Reg glared at her as though she was somehow responsible for the cases proving so tricky. He was never comfortable unless he felt in control of a situation. Confusion made him angry, and he hated anything that threatened to undermine morale and consequently his authority over the team. But the facts remained.

'It makes no sense,' Geraldine said.

'Then we just have to work harder, and sort out this mess,' Reg growled.

He stomped from the room and the business of the day resumed in an atmosphere of quiet industry.

35

It was easy to see Bethany had inherited her good looks from her mother. Now middle-aged and running to fat, she must have been stunning when she was young. Her present appearance wasn't improved by her eyes, which were puffy and swollen from crying. She stared blankly as Geraldine introduced herself.

'We've done it,' she replied, without moving to close the door. 'It's done.'

'I'm sorry? What's done?'

'We've been to identify her – we've seen it –'

She faltered, unable to complete the sentence, while her expression remained wooden. Geraldine guessed she must be sedated.

'Mrs Marsden, I'm here to ask you a few questions about Bethany.'

'What for? She's not coming back.'

'We don't believe your daughter's death was an accident.'

'I know that. I saw her.'

After a momentary flash of anguish the grieving woman's eyes glazed over once more. Geraldine pressed on.

'We need to find out who's responsible for Bethany's death.'

Mrs Marsden shrugged.

'What's the point now? She's dead. Nothing's going to bring her back.'

Geraldine sighed. This was so difficult.

'Is your husband in?'

'Gary? Huh. You'll be wasting your time talking to him.'

Despite her dismissal, she opened the door and gestured for Geraldine to enter.

The living room was crammed: three armchairs, a two-seater settee, several footstools, every spare inch of the carpet hidden beneath occasional tables covered with china dogs, small bunches of silk flowers, glass ornaments, paper weights, and framed photographs, mostly of the dead girl. Among the assortment of colourful chintz furniture, flowery curtains and gaudy ornaments, at first Geraldine didn't notice an elderly man hunched in an armchair. He didn't stir when they walked in. Only when his wife called his name loudly did he raise his head. Seeing his face, Geraldine realised he was not as old as his bowed posture and white hair had led her to suppose, no more than sixty.

'Mr Marsden?'

His eyes slid past her to gaze helplessly at his wife.

'Gary,' she called him again, in a very loud voice. Geraldine wondered if he was deaf. 'Gary, there's someone here to see you.'

'Both of you,' Geraldine added. 'I'm here to speak to you both.'

Mrs Marsden dropped on to the sofa as though the effort of inviting Geraldine in had sapped her energy. Geraldine perched on an armchair and cleared her throat.

'I'm so sorry for your loss.'

Neither of them answered.

'I'm sure you are as keen as we are to discover who carried out this terrible attack on your daughter.'

Bethany's mother dropped her head in her hands and wept silently. Her father didn't respond.

Geraldine decided she would have to be blunter. She turned to the woman.

'Mrs Marsden, I'm sure you want to help us find Bethany's killer, and bring him to justice.'

'I told you, didn't I?'

'What?'

'I said there's no point in talking to Gary. You can't get much sense out of him at the best of times and now – since we lost Bethany – it's like he's –'

She broke off with a helpless gesture, raising her eyebrows.

'Of course the doctor's put him on something. Both of us. It's supposed to help, but look at him.' She sighed. 'It's no life.'

Geraldine muttered some sympathetic platitude about time, before guiding the conversation back to the investigation. At least Mrs Marsden seemed to know what was going on.

'What can you tell me about Bethany's friends, the company she kept?'

'Friends?'

'Did she have any particular friends?'

'A boyfriend, you mean?'

'That would be a good place to start.'

Geraldine was surprised to see Mrs Marsden break into a smile.

'Bethany always had a few admirers in tow.'

'Not always youngsters,' her husband chipped in unexpectedly.

'That's true enough,' his wife agreed. 'I was just the same when I was a girl. Lots of boys.'

She sighed again, briefly transported away from the painful present. Geraldine waited.

'Not like Bethany though,' she resumed, sombre again. 'She went for older men.'

She paused again, a distant look in her eyes.

'Older men?' Geraldine prompted her quietly.

Mrs Marsden glanced over at her husband who had sunk back into his lethargy and was no longer paying attention.

'Yes. There was that Piers bloke. Do you remember him, Gary?'

Mr Marsden grunted.

'We only met him once, after one of her shows at the drama school. He'd been directing her. He was a smooth talker. But you wouldn't trust him as far as you could throw him. Bethany seemed really smitten with him but the next minute it was someone else, that dark-haired chap. Do you remember him, Gary?' She clearly wasn't expecting a reply because she continued without pausing. 'At least he wasn't as old as Piers, but still too old for her.'

'What was his name?'

She shook her head.

'I don't know. Was it David? No, it's gone. There were so many.

He wasn't anyone special. But nice enough.'

'Can you describe him?'

She screwed up her face with the effort of remembering.

'I saw him once, although we never met as such. He was outside, in his car, waiting for her. He had dark hair, and looked very handsome, Italian or Spanish, I'd say. And he must have been fit, because Bethany said he was a –'

Mr Marsden sat upright quite suddenly and looked around as though he was waking up.

'That's enough, Margery,' he said firmly. 'Enough.'

'He doesn't like talking about her,' Mrs Marsden mumbled. 'You'd better go. I don't want to upset him.'

On the doorstep, Geraldine tried one more time.

'You were about to say something about Bethany's last boyfriend?'

'Who?'

'The man she was seeing after Piers Trevelyan?'

Mrs Marsden looked confused.

'Piers? Yes, there was a man called Piers. He was much older than her.'

'And after that?'

'I never met anyone else after that, no more boyfriends.' She sighed and her expression grew distant again. 'I used to have so many young men after me. You wouldn't think it to look at me now.'

She started to close the door. Geraldine spoke quickly.

'Can you tell me anything else about Bethany? Did she seem worried?'

'Worried? Bethany? No, Bethany wasn't a worrier.'

'Well, if you think of anything else, please let me know.'

She thrust a card at Mrs Marsden before the door closed. It was unlikely she would keep it, if she even remembered Geraldine's visit. There was no point in returning for at least a week. By then the bereaved parents might have recovered from their initial shock. Geraldine understood doctors might consider it necessary to prescribe sedatives in such cases, but she wished they wouldn't issue drugs that dulled the thoughts and memories of people who might hold vital information. It didn't help the investigation.

36

NICK WAS OUT ON Monday morning. Sam sat down in Geraldine's office while they went over possible links between the two victims. Both were in their early twenties, female and blonde. They were both involved with Piers, who was still under suspicion. He had probably been in relationships with them at the same time. Apart from that, they had studied together at drama school where they would have had many friends and acquaintances in common.

'Two friends, similar in appearance and experience, both killed at around the same time. This is not a coincidence, however much Reg bangs on about car accidents not being the same as garrotting.'

'But don't multiple homicides usually follow similar patterns?' Sam asked.

'Not necessarily. The killer could be hoping we won't make the connection between the victims.'

'But the victims knew each other. They studied together and they were screwing the same man, for Christ's sake. How much more closely could they be connected?'

'Or,' Geraldine continued, ignoring Sam's interruption, 'perhaps the killer was just using whatever came to hand.'

She paused. Everything about Anna's death pointed at Piers whose van had been used in the accident, although they hadn't yet established he had been driving it at the time. The van had driven directly into the path of Anna's oncoming car and she hadn't stood a chance. Whoever had been driving the van must have been following her. Bethany's death on the other hand could have been spontaneous, the killer taking advantage of the leather thong around her neck to throttle her, but it was also possible she had been followed from the theatre she had visited that evening.

Apart from the question of whether both victims might have been pursued prior to their deaths, the manner of killing was different in just about every detail. But even that didn't mean that a different person had been responsible for each murder. Geraldine decided to confront Piers about his relationships with both victims. He appeared amused by her accusation.

'First of all, if you believe everything that's written about me in the papers, you're a fool, if you'll pardon my bluntness. Secondly, Inspector, I'm over sixty. Do you really think I'd be carrying on with two women at the same time? I loved Anna,' he added solemnly. 'I know she was young, but I was hoping she'd stay with me. I genuinely loved her. As for Bethany, I directed her once at college, but that was the extent of our relationship. I barely knew the girl.'

Geraldine wasn't sure whether to believe him or not. But his reference to his age could be an unconscious allusion to the young man who had been involved with Anna. Despatching Sam to quiz Dirk about Bethany, she went to look into another connection between the two victims: the drama school.

The college was only a few minutes walk from Euston Square station, and parking wasn't easy, being so central. It made more sense to take the tube. Geraldine didn't have to wait long for a train, and was soon walking along Gower Street to the main entrance to the college. She explained the reason for her visit and a young girl on reception led her upstairs to a quiet office where a round-faced middle-aged woman was chatting on the phone. She looked up and nodded when the receptionist rapped on the open door.

'Try not to worry about it, Lucy,' she said briskly into the phone and hung up. 'What is it?'

'There's a detective here to see you.'

Gesturing to Geraldine to take a seat, she introduced herself as Sue.

'I look after the students' welfare, help them when they have trouble finding accommodation, and generally lend a listening ear when there are problems. Some of them are only eighteen, and away from home for the first time, and London can be a daunting place if you're not used to life in a city. But I'm guessing it's not any of our current students you want to talk about, although we are keeping a close eye on Dirk just now.'

'Dirk is Anna's ex-boyfriend?' Geraldine asked, although she knew the answer.

'Yes. He seems fine but he's rehearsing a play about a suicide, and he's playing the brother of the dead girl. They're not the same thing of course, murder and suicide, but even so, we're keeping an eye on him. Megan's been great.'

'Megan?'

'Dirk's girlfriend. It's no secret that he and Anna split up soon after she graduated, when she met Piers. Of course she'd met him before, he comes here as a visiting director.'

'I thought he was a casting director?'

'Yes, that's his work. But they all like directing here. It gives them freedom to experiment.'

Sue was clearly knowledgeable about all the students in her care. Geraldine asked her about Dirk.

'What would you like to know?' Sue hedged. 'He's a real sweetheart. A bit of a lad, with an eye for a pretty girl.' She smiled.

Geraldine was silent, thinking that she had heard the same words used about Piers. Then again, with so many pretty girls studying acting, perhaps it was hardly surprising. For all she knew, it could be shorthand for establishing that a man was straight, in the entertainment world.

'Dirk was living with Anna for about six months, I think, maybe longer, before she left here. And then not long after that we heard she'd been cast in Down and Out. It was a great boost for us, of course, having one of our students land such a high profile role so soon after graduating. Poor Anna, she could have been –' She broke off with a sigh. 'She was a brilliant talent. Such a loss.'

Cautiously, Geraldine asked if Dirk and Anna had remained on good terms after she left. Sue's brows lowered.

'On good terms? I should think so. Why wouldn't they? The students here are a close knit bunch and very supportive of each other, even if they aren't in the same year group. There are so few of them, you see. And it's a hard life, so they tend to stick together. They bond, you see. It happens every year.'

'Dirk wouldn't have been upset when she left him for a successful older man?'

Geraldine was surprised when Sue broke into a smile.

'Good lord no. He would have been delighted for her. We all were. So you're thinking he might have killed her out of jealousy?'

Her smile broadened, as though Geraldine had said something amusing.

'We keep our melodramas for the stage, Inspector. Relationships breaking up is just part of the way of life for young actors, I'm afraid. He might not have been very happy about it, on a personal level, but he would have been pleased for her. And he certainly wasn't pining for her.'

Sue was clearly protective of her students' reputations. Nevertheless, Geraldine thought she was probably a reliable witness.

'What about Dirk and Bethany?' she asked.

Sue shook her head. 'He didn't make out with all the girls,' she said. 'I'm sure I would have known if there was anything going on between Dirk and Bethany.'

'What about Piers and Bethany?' Geraldine pressed her, although she could sense that Sue was beginning to worry she had already been indiscreet.

'I saw that story in the paper,' she said sharply. 'We get used to the tabloids here. To be honest, the real scandal is how they get away with the stories they invent. Piers was with Anna,' she concluded firmly.

'So Piers wasn't in a relationship with Bethany while Anna was living with him?'

Sue stared at Geraldine sternly. 'I suggest you ignore the tittle tattle in the tabloids, and concentrate on your work, as we do on ours. Now, if you'll excuse me, Inspector, I have work to do.'

37

It wasn't apparent how tall the principal of the drama school was until he stood up to greet her, an imposing figure on his feet. He looked about sixty, slender and grey-haired. His lips curled into a slow smile, and he intoned his speech like a dirge, while his grey eyes remained wary. Geraldine wondered whether he always spoke like that, or if he felt this was an appropriate way to conduct an interview about a dead student. He formed a stark contrast to the woman who looked after the students' welfare. Between her and the principal, the students appeared to be in safe hands. Except that two of them were dead.

'How can I help?' he asked as she sat down.

'Mr Ellory –'

He held up an elegant white hand.

'Everyone calls me William.'

'William, I need to know everything you can tell us about Anna and Bethany.'

His expression grew even more solemn than before.

'It goes without saying that I'll help you in any way I can. This was a terrible tragedy for two very talented young women. They both had brilliant careers ahead of them. You must know that Anna was already carving out a name for herself on television. And Bethany –'

Once again Geraldine felt as though he was preparing a funeral speech, or perhaps reprising the announcement he had made to the other students. He must have spoken to them about what had happened.

'It would have been terrible for anyone,' she interjected softly.

'Indeed it would.'

He inclined his greying head without saying anything else.

'Is there anything you can think of that might help us to discover who is responsible for their deaths?'

William sat forward in his chair and stared straight at Geraldine, his grey eyes steely.

'Do you mean to say you don't know who did this? I heard Piers Trevelyan had been arrested, but I suspected that was unfounded rumour.'

'He's been helping us with our enquiries,' Geraldine said cautiously.

'It's no secret he was living with Anna, or rather she had moved in with him. But I don't believe for one minute he could have killed anyone. It's a ludicrous idea. I've known Piers for a long time. He's a huge talent, and he could be temperamental, unreasonable even. It's not uncommon with creative people. We learn to manage them here, and we teach them to manage themselves.' He inhaled deeply. 'I thought you had this all sewn up and had come here for witness corroboration. Although what we'd have been able to tell you I can't imagine.'

As briefly as she could, Geraldine explained that Piers was being questioned.

'But you're going to let him go? Only we have a production coming up that he'll be directing, and we need to know the situation. Are you going to arrest him?'

For answer, Geraldine repeated her earlier enquiry.

'Well, we'll do everything we can, of course. The college is open to you – ask Sue for a key card for the duration of your investigation, so you can come in and out of the building freely. And you must question anyone who might be able to help. I'll announce to the students to come to you with any information. Perhaps I can post a contact number on the board? It's only accessible to those with swipe cards. We're very careful with security. We have a lot of very expensive equipment here. I would just ask that you respect our rehearsals where possible. Our students work on a tight schedule and missing a single rehearsal can impact on a production, especially where a lead is involved.'

He paused. Geraldine waited.

'I think that covers everything,' he said finally, rising to his feet. 'And I should stress that Anna and Bethany both graduated last year. Of course we continue to care about our alumni – we're a very close knit community here. But they were no longer enrolled with us when all this happened.'

'Is there nothing more you can tell us?' Geraldine asked, without standing up. 'You must have known both the girls very well.'

'Indeed, I know all my students,' he replied, sitting down again.

He talked for a while about how talented both the victims had been. Geraldine listened patiently as his formal oratory slipped into personal reminiscence.

'Anna was always so earnest about her work, and so ambitious! We all thought she was one to watch, and we were right. She was the first in her year to get an agent, the first to be cast on television, and –'

He broke off, gazing helplessly at Geraldine. They both knew what he was thinking.

'Bethany was a different kettle of fish altogether. Anna was the ingénue, the romantic lead that Bethany aspired to emulate, but her talents lay in comedy, although she hadn't yet realised it.'

He stopped. Once again Geraldine could guess what must be going through his mind.

'They were so young!' he broke out suddenly.

'You must have worked very closely with them,' Geraldine said after a pause. 'We know they were both involved with Piers, but other than that, did they have any particular boyfriend in common, or did they have any enemies? Someone who was jealous perhaps? Were there any odd characters among the students or staff while they were both here?' She paused. 'Is there anything you can think of that might help us? Anything at all. Were you aware of anyone who might have wished to harm these girls?'

It was difficult to pose the question tactfully, but important to ask.

'Is there anyone I suspect might have committed these dreadful murders, you mean?'

He shook his head emphatically.

'We get some characters here that you might think of as quirky, eccentric, but actors aren't as unconventional as you might think.'

'Yes, I'm sure they're just like everyone else –'

'Yes and no. Our students are dedicated to their work.'

He was dithering, uncertain what to say, trotting out stock phrases he must have used thousands of times before.

'Anna had a boyfriend called Dirk,' Geraldine prompted him.

'Dirk was in the year below Anna. He's still here. I can summon him if you wish to speak to him, but I really don't know that he'd be able to add anything –'

Geraldine told him she had already spoken to Dirk.

'Was there anyone else? Bethany's mother mentioned a dark-haired man.'

'That would be Marco. He and Bethany were an item but they split up in their final year. A lot of relationships founder then. It's the pressure. They feel they have to focus exclusively on their careers.' He sighed again. 'They all knew each other, Anna, Dirk, Bethany and Marco. We had such hopes… I'm afraid Marco's a sensitive boy. He'll be terribly upset about what happened. Sue will tell you where you can contact him. She keeps in touch with everyone. And now, if you'll excuse me, I need to go and watch a rehearsal. I promised some of the students.'

He stood up.

'You might think we're putting the students under unnecessary pressure here, but they thrive on the regime. Believe me, if they don't, they won't cope long in the industry. People outside the profession have no idea how demanding acting is, or how dangerous it can be.'

'Dangerous?'

He launched into a brief diatribe about the implications of

health and safety regulations on stage fighting. Geraldine could see this wasn't going to shed any light on the investigation. The dangers she was dealing with were real.

38

A GROUP OF GIRLS came forward, claiming to have been friends with Bethany. Geraldine spoke first to her flatmate, Lucy, a tall, skinny girl with white blonde hair, pale skin and blue eyes so large they looked unreal. She was almost incredibly beautiful, in an ethereal way. Geraldine remembered her face from the photographs displayed on the wall in the college bar. As Lucy sat down in the small rehearsal room being used as an interview room, Geraldine saw that her white legs were shaking. She fidgeted constantly with her hands, alternately interlocking her fingers tightly and releasing them.

'Please don't be nervous, Lucy. There's no need. I just want to ask you a few questions about Bethany. You were sharing a flat with her, weren't you?'

'Yes,' Lucy whispered. 'We've been sharing a flat since last year. Bethany graduated in July but she said she might stay on – that is – we talked about it – it all depended on where she was.'

'Where she was?'

'Yes, you know. Wherever she found work. She was thinking of going to America – Hollywood –'

Geraldine wasn't very surprised when Lucy began snivelling. She waited a moment for her to regain control of herself before she resumed questioning her.

'What can you tell me about Bethany?'

'We were friends. Bethany was –' her lower lip trembled. 'I wanted to be like her. And now –'

Tears sparkled in her beautiful eyes.

'What was she like?'

Lucy paused for a moment, considering.

'Bethany was all right,' she said at last.

'All right?' Geraldine prompted her. 'In what way?'

'If you'd met her, you'd know what I mean. She was a strong character. She knew where she was going, what she wanted to do with her life. I mean, I'd be a nervous wreck before an audition,' Lucy explained earnestly, 'but she knew how to handle herself.'

Geraldine could well believe that Lucy would be anxious about auditions. The principal had said the successful students thrived under pressure. Lucy didn't seem very robust, but perhaps her looks would carry her through the tough world of the entertainment industry.

'How did she seem just before she died? Was she worried about anything?'

Lucy smiled wistfully.

'Bethany didn't worry about anything. She was always positive. She was waiting to hear about a really important audition she'd had, about a week ago. They said they'd call her. That doesn't mean anything, but I think she was pretty hopeful. That's what she was like, always expecting the best. She'll never know if she got the part now, will she?'

'So there was nothing particular on her mind, as far as you were aware?' Geraldine asked quickly, before Lucy could start crying again.

'Only the audition. It was a really big deal, a TV role. A casting like that can be a career maker, you know.'

'I can imagine.'

Lucy seemed to have been in awe of Bethany, who had been the dominant character in their living arrangements. Lucy freely admitted she would be at sea without her. Bethany had organised paying the bills, fixing the washing machine, and making sure they had milk in the fridge, and food in the cupboards. Lucy was keen to tell Geraldine all about her experience of living with Bethany, but nothing she volunteered was of any help to the investigation.

'It wasn't that she made a big deal out of taking responsibility for the place, she just did it.'

It was a casual aside when Lucy mentioned that Bethany had a part-time job in a pub. She seemed surprised when Geraldine was interested to know the details.

'In a murder investigation any information might be significant,' Geraldine told her, and Lucy started to sob.

'It sounds so dreadful, a murder investigation,' she mumbled.

'What about boyfriends?' Geraldine asked, when Lucy had calmed down.

'There was Marco. I think they'd just split up again. It was difficult to be sure, because they were always breaking up and getting back together. I think they enjoyed the drama. Just being together wasn't exciting enough for them. They were both thrill junkies.'

'What do you mean?'

Lucy shrugged.

'I don't think Bethany was scared of anything. Marco used to say she was a daredevil. And he was right. She was always looking for excitement.'

'Were she and Marco happy together?'

'Who knows? They argued a lot, but it was more point scoring than anything. I don't think they were ever really angry with each other. They just used to bicker and break up and then they'd get back together again. I think Marco wanted Bethany to move in with him but she said she liked her independence.'

Geraldine watched Lucy closely as she asked whether it was true Bethany had been seeing someone else.

'You mean that story about an affair with Piers?' Lucy gave a sad smile. 'There were always stories going around, but if she *was* seeing him, she was very discreet about it.'

'She told a reporter.'

'I don't believe she said any of that. You can't believe everything you read in the papers. Was that story attributed to a particular journalist?'

Geraldine confirmed it hadn't been published under any journalist's name.

'Though I wouldn't put it past Beth to have made the story up herself,' Lucy added. 'She would have done anything to get herself noticed.'

'Including having an affair with Piers,' Geraldine thought. She refrained from saying it aloud.

'What can you tell me about Marco?'

'Marco? He's really nice, and he's fit. But he's got a terrible temper. He says he gets it from his Italian mother.' She smiled. 'He says he's passionate, but he's really bad-tempered. But he didn't kill her,' she added quickly.

'What makes you say that?'

'I mean, he's got a temper, but he's not violent. And he was bonkers about Bethany. He wanted her to live with him, and in any case he's not the sort of guy who would do that. Kill someone, I mean. He's a decent guy. He's just a bit fiery, that's all I meant.'

'What about Dirk?'

'Dirk? He's with Megan, although they're a bit secretive about it. And before that he was seeing Anna.'

'What about Dirk and Bethany?'

'No. They were never an item. I don't think this has anything to do with Dirk.'

'Thank you, Lucy. You've been very helpful. Here's my card in case you think of anything else.'

The other girls had little to add to Lucy's statement. Not one of Bethany's classmates was prepared to say a bad word about her, and they all denied any knowledge of an affair she had been having.

'She had a boyfriend,' they all said.

They were all so generous in their praise, Geraldine wasn't sure she found their testimony completely credible.

'There must have been someone she didn't get on with,' she said to each girl in turn, but they all returned the same answer. It seemed that Bethany had been both popular and universally admired, and she had only been seeing Marco all the time she had been at the college.

Marco had classic Mediterranean good looks, with raven black hair and eyes as dark as Geraldine's own. Understandably subdued by what had happened, his voice remained flat and devoid of emotion to begin with, but his eyes betrayed his distress from the moment he entered the room. Geraldine kept her questions carefully low key. Nevertheless it wasn't long before Marco lost control.

'I'm sorry,' he muttered, wiping away tears sliding down his cheeks, 'I loved her. She was –' He broke off and dropped his head in his hands. 'I can't believe she's gone.'

'Marco, think carefully before you answer. Was Bethany worried about anything recently?'

'What?'

'Did you notice anything different about her lately?'

'No. What kind of thing are you talking about?'

'Anything different.'

'No. She was fine. She'd just had an audition and was feeling so hopeful –' His voice broke with emotion. 'She was always so positive, so sure everything was going to work out for her. She was headed for great things, you know. Everyone said so.'

He looked up with a suspicious scowl.

'What's this about? What's all the questions for? We were told Bethany was mugged. So what's this all about? How would anyone here know what happened? She was by herself when she was killed. You need to get out there and find out who did it. They should be locked up.'

Gently Geraldine explained they suspected Bethany's death wasn't an accident. Marco's dark eyes widened in surprise as she spoke. He was visibly shocked to hear that the police suspected she had been deliberately murdered.

'But who would want to do that?' he asked.

'That's what we're trying to find out.'

39

Sam reported that Dirk had denied ever having even so much as a fling with Bethany.

'He said he fancied her all right, but it had just never happened. He'd been busy with Anna while Bethany was at the drama school and once they'd both left he never really saw Bethany to speak to again.'

Dirk's statement appeared to be borne out by the other students and staff at the college.

Sam wondered if Marco could be a suspect. Geraldine didn't think so, but they went through what they knew about him anyway. Whatever impression he had given, as Bethany's boyfriend they had to consider him seriously.

'Bear in mind that most of the people associated with the victims were trained and practised actors, skilled at dissembling. Don't take what any of them say at face value,' Reg had warned the team.

According to Lucy's statement, Marco and Bethany had recently split up. It sounded like their relationship had been a stormy one.

'Lucy reckoned Marco wanted Bethany to live with him but she refused,' Sam said. 'He must've cared more about her than she cared about him. He could have been jealous and possessive. We suspect she may have been seeing someone else, probably Piers. What if Marco found out? Lucy said he had a bad temper. Could he have killed her?'

'Lots of people have bad tempers. There's nothing to suggest he was violent. And why would he have killed Anna? And –'

Sam finished the question for her. 'How did he disappear from the crime scenes?'

Dinah Jedway was the theatrical agent who had represented Anna and Bethany. Given that her livelihood depended on her clients finding work, it seemed unlikely the agent would have wanted any harm to come to Anna who was by far her most lucrative client. All the same, it could be significant that she had represented both the dead actresses. At the very least, she might be able to shed some light on what had been going on in her clients' lives. Her office was located in an impressive address in Central London which turned out to be a room above a shop off Tottenham Court Road. At the top of a narrow staircase, Geraldine found the door with 'Dinah Jedway Theatrical Agent' emblazoned on a bronze sign. She knocked and opened the door without waiting for a reply.

In a small room, two women sat facing one another across a desk, one middle-aged with jet black hair, the other in her early twenties, blonde and slight. They both glanced up when Geraldine entered. The younger woman looked down at her keyboard again at once and continued typing, while the older woman stared shrewdly at Geraldine.

'I'm not taking on any clients,' she announced shortly. 'My PA will show you out.'

'Even though you've just lost two,' Geraldine replied, displaying her warrant card.

'Juniper, fetch us some tea, there's a dear,' the raven-haired woman said, turning to her young assistant.

The blonde girl scrambled to her feet and scurried out.

Geraldine took a seat and asked Dinah for information about the two dead women. The agent heaved a sigh.

'Where do I begin?'

'Let's start with Anna Porter.'

'It's a shocking business, deeply shocking,' the agent began in the rasping voice of a heavy smoker.

She told Geraldine she had represented Anna for eighteen months, since Anna had begun her final year at drama school. There had been no falling out, and no question of Anna quitting the agency. Dinah was effusive in her praise, and became tearful.

If she was right, Anna had been the most talented actress of her generation. Dinah was equally fulsome in her tribute to Bethany, who was apparently also destined for almost unprecedented success.

'I have an eye for talent,' Dinah went on, dabbing at her heavily made up eyes with a tissue. 'I know who has that special factor. I can sense it straight away. And they were both such lovely girls. They are a loss to the profession, a loss to the theatre, a loss to the world. Their death is a blow from which we can never recover.'

For all her eulogies, Dinah had little useful information to offer. She had seen both the girls in productions at the college and had invited them to her office where she had signed them both up.

'I knew I could help further their careers,' she explained, leaning forward and speaking earnestly. 'People think agents do the job for the money, but that's not it at all. You have no idea what a thrill it is to nurture young talent and watch it blossom into a successful career. I have a very close relationship with my clients. Anna had been with me for nearly two years. She was like a daughter to me –'

Dinah broke off, sobbing, and scrabbled in a large handbag for a packet of Menthol cigarettes. She offered one to Geraldine who refused.

When Geraldine asked her what she knew about Piers Trevelyan, Dinah pulled herself together at once.

'He was very good for Anna.'

'Good for her career, you mean?'

'No, no. That's not what I meant. I mean he was good to her. Piers is a wonderful man. He's a real charmer. He knows how to look after a woman. He's a gentleman. You know if I was ten years younger, I'd be after him myself. Anna was a lucky girl –' She broke down in tears and dabbed at her eyes again.

When Geraldine asked about Marco, Dinah's expression changed. She muttered darkly about his being totally unsuitable.

'With my help, Bethany was destined for a dazzling career. Marco would only have held her back. It's very difficult for these young talents to give a hundred per cent to their art while they're in a relationship. Bethany needed a special kind of partner. Actors can be called to work anywhere in the world. They can be on tour for months. Marco was no good for her. He's a selfish callow young man.'

'Have you met him?'

'No, but Bethany used to talk about him, and I saw his work.'

'His work?'

'His stage performances at the college. He's a good looking boy but he hasn't got what it takes. And he's only interested in himself. Bethany deserved better. She was a hard working girl. You know she had a job in the holidays to help finance her way through college? She was so dedicated.'

Dinah leaned back in her chair and inhaled deeply before taking a mirror from her bag and checking that her eye make-up was intact.

'Is there anything else you can tell me? Were you aware that Anna or Bethany was worried about anything?'

Dinah shook her head.

'They didn't say anything. They would have told me. My clients talk to me, Inspector, they trust me to take care of them. I look after every aspect of their careers, nurture them –'

'What about Dirk?'

'Who's Dirk?'

'Anna's ex, Dirk Goodbody.'

'He's nothing.' Dinah gave a dismissive shake of her head. 'No, Piers was the one.'

'Did you know Dirk? He's at the drama school.'

'There are so many of them. I've seen him in productions, but he hasn't got what it takes. I have an eye for talent.'

'Did either of the victims ever mention him?'

'No.'

The door flew open and Dinah's young assistant came in holding a tray of takeaway teas. After they had sorted out Dinah's decaff and Juniper's sugar, Geraldine questioned the young woman.

'She doesn't know anything,' Dinah interrupted. 'Juniper's invaluable,' she added with a sudden smile at her assistant, 'I'd be lost without her, but she focuses on the admin. I deal with my clients personally. That's my way.'

Juniper kept her eyes firmly on her tea.

'If anything occurs to you that could help us find out who might have wanted to harm Anna and Bethany, give me a call,' Geraldine said, handing Juniper her card.

'She sounds like a right drama queen,' Sam commented when Geraldine told her about the interview with Dinah Jedway. 'What about her assistant? Do you think she knew anything?'

Geraldine frowned.

'I don't think so. She kept very quiet. I'm not altogether sure if that's because she had nothing to say, or if she was intimidated in front of her boss. But I gave her a card, so she can call if she wants to speak to us.'

The two detectives exchanged a wordless glance. They each knew what was going through the other's mind. One phone call from a witness and the whole case might be resolved by the end of the day. Geraldine imagined Juniper arriving at the station to give a statement.

'I saw him, it was definitely Marco – or Piers – or Dirk –'

But that was an idle wish. In the absence of any unforeseen revelation, all they had to rely on was systematic detective work.

40

GERALDINE FELL INTO BED that night. After a sound sleep she woke feeling invigorated, and spent the morning catching up with her paper work, checking documents, bringing her decision log up to date and listing expenses. At lunch time she took the train to Goodge Street and walked along Charlotte Street to the bar where Bethany had worked over Christmas. Geraldine wasn't sure what she was going to learn there, but she had to find out as much as she could about the victims she was investigating. Such thoroughness might turn out to be a waste of time, but there were occasions when it proved invaluable.

A narrow entrance opened out to a bar area with benches along the walls. The dark wooden floor looked as though it hadn't been swept for a while. The furniture had been selected for its character rather than for comfort. When Geraldine arrived the place was almost empty, with just a few people sitting around chatting over a lunch time drink. After a quick look around, Geraldine spoke to a young man behind the bar. The manageress appeared promptly when Geraldine asked to see her. In a crisp white shirt and pin striped trouser suit, she looked out of place in the informal atmosphere of the bar. She frowned when Geraldine explained the reason for her visit.

'Yes, I heard about Bethany. It's hard to believe. I mean, I can't say I knew her well, but I interviewed her and knew her to speak to. She filled in during the holidays over the summer and Christmas and so on. It's useful to have people who know the ropes and can step in. But if you want to know about her in any detail, I'm not the best person to ask. All I can do is look up her details, address, phone number, the hours she's worked, and so on, nothing you won't already know. Thea would be able to tell you more.

She's behind the bar now. She worked with Bethany and I think they were friends. Wait here and I'll send her over.'

Geraldine sat down and waited. The bench was uncomfortably hard. She wondered why there were no cushions on the wooden seats. Meanwhile the manageress went to the bar and spoke to a young woman who glanced over at Geraldine. With a cursory nod at the manageress, the woman approached Geraldine and introduced herself. She was about thirty, short and thin, with ginger hair and a pointed face. She sat down beside Geraldine, gazing at her solemnly.

'I heard about Bethany,' she said in a low voice. 'What happened?'

'I'm afraid she was murdered. I'm sorry.'

'It's not like we were particularly close, I mean we never socialised, never saw each other away from here, but she was great fun to work with, you know. I really liked her. Who did it?'

Geraldine told her what little detail had already appeared in the papers, and then asked Thea if she could think of anything that might help them to trace who had killed Bethany.

'Did anything strike you as in any way out of the ordinary recently?'

Thea looked puzzled.

'I don't think so. I'm not sure what you mean.'

'Did her behaviour change at all? Did she mention anything or anyone she was worried about, or any trouble she was in?'

Thea didn't answer straight away but sat staring down at her hands. Geraldine waited. After a few minutes the barmaid looked up with a troubled expression.

'Well, yes and no.'

'What do you mean?' Geraldine prompted her after another pause. 'Do you think something was bothering her? Or someone?'

Thea shrugged.

'It was nothing new. She was worried about her boyfriend. I think his name's Mark.'

'Do you mean Marco?'

'Yes, that was it. Marco.'

'What about him?'

'You asked if she was worried about anyone. Well, she was always worrying about him. She had problems with him.'

'What sort of problems?'

'She said she wanted to leave him but he was really clingy, and that made it difficult. She was studying drama and she wanted to be in films or on the telly. She said she wanted to work in America when she finished at college. She said that's where the opportunities are. But she didn't think he'd ever let her go. He was possessive like that. To be honest, I think she was a bit scared of him, and what he might do.' She paused and leaned forward, lowering her voice. 'He beat some guy up one time, just for talking to her. He thought the other guy was pestering her. Anyway, I think she was a bit scared of Marco, although she wasn't the sort to be easily scared. She was tough.'

Thea stared at Geraldine, wide-eyed, clearly in awe of Bethany and the drama in her short life.

Although Geraldine was worn out, it was impossible to ignore a chorus of cheers as she walked past the visual images identification and detection office on returning to the police station. Officers who had been tasked with examining CCTV footage from the roads immediately surrounding the first crime scene were now scrutinising film recorded in the street leading up to the bridge where Bethany had been killed. Geraldine stuck her head round the door to see what the noise was about. Sam looked up and grinned at her, beckoning to her to join her.

'What's going on?'

The team were buzzing with excitement at having spotted a pedestrian who appeared to be following Bethany onto the bridge. Geraldine went over to look for herself.

A tall lanky figure in a dark coat was striding along the edge of the pavement. At times it disappeared off the edge of the screen into the shadow of a building before reappearing beneath a street lamp or lit up by the headlights of a passing vehicle.

'Look at that!' a constable crowed as Bethany paused and the figure did likewise. 'It happens again in a minute – look! There they go.'

Geraldine watched, mesmerised, as Bethany paused and looked around. At the same instant, the second figure halted and spun on its heel to face in the opposite direction. A moment later, the tall individual's head turned cautiously. There could be little doubt that Bethany was being followed. The victim resumed making her way along the street towards the bridge. After peeking round the tall figure set off in pursuit once more. It was an exciting interlude, but disappointing at the same time because there was no way of identifying the mysterious tall figure. They couldn't even be sure if it was a man or a woman. All they could tell by enhancing the image was that Bethany's pursuer was about six feet tall, wearing a long loose hooded coat, trousers, and flat shoes or boots.

Geraldine thought about what she had been told about Marco, and wondered if he could be the mysterious stranger who had followed Bethany minutes before she was murdered. He was quite tall. More than one witness had remarked on his violent temper, and now Thea had mentioned his jealousy. Remembering her meeting with him, she frowned. He was certainly volatile, yet she had the impression his passion was just so much hot air. Still, an impression wasn't evidence, and anyway she had to report what she had been told. She found Reg talking to Jayne, a psychological profiler. Reg's eyes lit up when Geraldine told them what Thea had said. He turned to the profiler.

'What do you think, Jayne?'

Geraldine did her best to hide her petty irritation when the detective chief inspector solicited Jayne's opinion first.

'It seems very likely,' Jayne replied.

She spoke slowly, as though considering what Thea had said. But she hadn't spoken to the witness herself, and she hadn't met Marco. Geraldine had. She couldn't control her irritation any longer.

'It's a bit of a coincidence, isn't it? First we suspect Piers of flying into a manic rage with Anna for seeing Dirk, and now Marco's apparently guilty of a similar motive for murdering his girlfriend who was seeing Piers. How convenient.'

'A coincidence, or a common motive for murder?' Jayne asked quietly.

'Murder isn't common,' Geraldine retorted.

She was no longer even trying to conceal her vexation with her superior officer and his tame profiler, neither of whom had even met the man they were glibly concluding had killed Bethany.

Her mood didn't improve when Reg raised his eyebrows on hearing that Geraldine hadn't asked Marco for an alibi when she had spoken to him.

'He's not – at least he wasn't – under investigation at that time.'

'He was her boyfriend,' Jayne interjected, as though that automatically made him a suspect. 'Statistically, the husband or the boyfriend is the most likely suspect in any murder case, Geraldine.'

'We're not dealing with statistics –' Geraldine began.

'Well, no harm done,' Reg interrupted. 'Let's bring the boyfriend in and see what he has to say for himself. I dare say he'll be more forthcoming when we put the pressure on him to tell us what really happened.'

'Yes, I'm dying to know how he managed to pull that disappearing act on the bridge,' Jayne agreed cheerfully.

'We'll find out soon enough,' Reg assured her.

Geraldine hoped his optimism wasn't misplaced.

41

NEXT TIME THEY MET, his uncle suggested a fashionable Italian restaurant off Regent Street. Zak went inside and looked around at white table cloths, white chairs, and waiters who hovered discreetly. The atmosphere was quietly busy. At first he didn't spot his uncle sitting in a dark corner where they were unlikely to be overheard. He felt like a spy as he sidled over and sat down, half hidden in the shadows. They had already agreed they would tell no one about their meetings. Zak didn't want his father crashing in on his relationship with his newly discovered uncle. Piers would want to take over. The secrecy of their liaison added to the thrill of meeting his uncle.

As they studied the menu, Zak started to relax. He selected dishes from the menu, reckless of expense. His uncle was footing the bill. His father rarely spent time with him like that, just the two of them. Whenever they went out it was always in a group. His father would make use of such outings to woo anyone supporting his latest production. When he wasn't courting people who could assist his career, he would be chatting up a young actress. Zak alone was never audience enough for his father. But his uncle seemed happy to pass an evening just with him.

'So, what's the latest with you?' Darius asked when they had placed their order.

He leaned his elbows on the table and smiled encouragingly at Zak who took a sip of wine and returned the smile. He was relieved to discover his uncle's interest in him hadn't diminished. On the contrary, he seemed eager to hear about his nephew's current project. Zak tried to explain the problems he was experiencing with his director.

'It's a great script,' he explained earnestly. 'There's so much we could do with it, but the director insists we stick to one stupid idea. It's not even his idea. Of course no one dares criticise him because everyone's scared of being kicked off the production. I'm supposed to work on his stupid design without making myself look pathetic. God, I could really do something with that set if I could just do it my own way. He's got no idea, but he thinks he's some kind of genius. He's as bad as my father.'

Darius frowned. 'What do you mean, as bad as your father?'

'He always has ideas – *his* ideas – about what I should do with my life. He's always trying to foist these stupid women on me, like he's doing me such a favour. They're all desperate to get off with me, because they think it's a way of getting to my father.'

'Getting to him?'

'Yes. I thought I told you, he's a casting director. He can influence their careers.'

'Of course.' Darius sipped his wine. 'But you're not interested in girls are you?'

Zak barely hesitated. 'No. But my father doesn't know that.'

'Really?' Darius sounded sceptical. 'Why not?'

Zak shrugged. 'Oh, I don't know. We've just never discussed it. I mean, it's pretty obvious, isn't it? You knew straight away. Do I really need to spell it out for him? I have tried to tell him, but he never listens. He's got his own ideas about me. What I want doesn't come into it.'

Zak drained his glass and Darius refilled it at once. He gave his nephew a sympathetic smile.

'It must be hard, having a father like that. So powerful, yet so blinkered. But you mustn't let it get to you. I'm sure he's very fond of you, in his own way.'

'Oh, I don't care. I'm used to it. I mean, he's fond of me, of course he is. He'd do anything to help me. But that's only because I'm his son. He's completely self-obsessed, sees everything in terms of himself.'

'At least he can help you in your career.'

'Only it doesn't help, not really.' Zak could feel himself growing angry. 'Everyone thinks I only got a place at a top drama school because of him, but it's not true. I wouldn't have got on the course if I wasn't good at what I do. It's a really difficult course to get on. There aren't many places, and lots of people want to study there. They don't give places out to just anyone.' He was close to tears. 'He's ruining my reputation, him and his bloody women. They all think they can take over my life, but I'm no pushover.'

On to his third large glass of wine and with some decent food inside him, Zak felt himself drifting beyond his agitation into recklessness. It wasn't just the food and alcohol. He had often drunk more than three glasses of wine, and eaten in smart restaurants. It had nothing to do with the time or the place. It was because of his uncle. There was something about him that loosened Zak's tongue. Although they had only recently met for the first time since Zak was a baby, he had felt a connection with the older man right from the start, perhaps because of their physical resemblance. Looking at his uncle he could have been watching himself in thirty years time. He suddenly felt an overwhelming desire to confide in his uncle who was listening to him so intently.

'I've got powers of my own,' Zak went on. He knew he had drunk too much, but he didn't care. 'They don't know what I'm capable of. No one does.'

He must have been talking too loudly, because a waiter came over.

'Is everything all right sir?'

Darius dismissed him with a wave of his hand but the mood had been broken. By the time the waiter had gone, Zak had recovered his self possession.

'You were telling me about your father,' Darius prompted him.

'I don't know what's happening to him. I don't know what's going to happen to me. You know he's been accused of murdering his girlfriend?'

'Tell me about it.'

'No, no, I don't want to talk about him any more. I'd rather hear about my mother.' He was feeling slightly dizzy.

'What do you want to know?'

'I just want to know what she was like. And don't say she was an angel. I want to know more than that.'

Zak tried to concentrate on what his uncle was saying about his sister: how good-natured she had been, the kind of woman who would do anything for anyone, as well as being beautiful.

'But what was she like?' Zak insisted. He had a feeling he was repeating himself, but he was too tipsy to care. 'My father never talks about her. He just says what's past is past and should stay there. You keep going on and on about how saintly she was. But what was she really like? Tell me the truth. You know, I don't even know what she looked like. He didn't keep anything that belonged to her.'

Darius looked surprised.

'You've never seen a photo of your own mother? That's shocking. Wait. I'll show you – you'll see, you look just like her.'

He took out his wallet and rummaged inside it.

'Here.'

He held out a small picture. Zak stared into the eyes of his dead mother, two dimensional, slightly faded, but still his mother. He had a few facial features in common with his father, but his resemblance to his mother was striking. They had the same large dark eyes and olive complexion, the same small straight nose and thin lips. He would have liked to see a picture of her smiling, but that was the only photograph Darius had.

'She looks sad,' he muttered. 'I'm not surprised, married to my father. But he'll get his comeuppance one day, and serve him bloody well right. You'll see.'

Darius put the photograph down next to Zak's plate. 'You can keep it.'

The room spun as Zak shook his head. 'What would I want that for?'

His uncle looked surprised. 'I thought you'd like to keep it.'

'I only wondered if I look like her, that's all.' He gave a wry smile. 'It's difficult enough keeping track of one parent. I don't need another one.'

With a cold smile, Darius replaced the photograph in his wallet.

42

IT WAS ONLY HALF past four but Geraldine didn't feel like going back to sleep. She lay in bed, musing over what they had learned. There wasn't much to go on, but what they had discovered was puzzling. A tall person had been seen following Bethany on to the bridge. Although the team had studied the tape for an hour after the time Bethany was killed, there was no sign of anyone, tall or otherwise, leaving the bridge. The person who had apparently been following Bethany had simply disappeared, just like the driver of the van. Suddenly Geraldine sat up, wide awake. The police constable who had been first on the scene of Anna's crash had sent a journalist packing, a tall woman with blonde hair. Geraldine wondered who she was, and whether she could have been the same tall person they had sighted following Bethany.

Arriving at the station she shared her idea with Sam. The sergeant didn't share Geraldine's interest in the two tall people who had been sighted immediately before and after the two murders.

'Lots of people are tall,' Sam said, 'it doesn't mean anything. We don't even know if there really were any such people there at all –'

'You saw the CCTV of someone following Bethany.'

'We don't know for sure she was being followed. It could've been a random pedestrian. What makes you think the person behind her on the pavement had anything to do with Bethany's death?'

'If they weren't implicated, they might at least have seen something. What happened to that pedestrian? People can't just vanish.'

It wouldn't take long to speak to the police constable who had been first on the scene of Anna's car accident. Questioning Marco might prove more time consuming, so Geraldine decided to see the constable first. He was easy enough to trace. Making sense of his testimony proved more of a challenge. He was in his late fifties, solidly built and square-faced, the picture of an honest copper. But he scratched his head in perplexity when Geraldine explained what she wanted.

'Yes, I was first on the scene,' he admitted. 'It was a bad business, a very bad business. The victim was an actress off Down and Out, wasn't she? My wife watches that programme, never misses. She was very cut up about the whole thing. It's a very sad affair. Such a young woman.'

'We're interested in tracing the journalist who was at the scene when you arrived.'

To begin with the constable didn't know what Geraldine was talking about.

'You reported seeing a journalist when you arrived. You said she had heard the crash and went to investigate. We caught a glimpse of her on the CCTV footage, hurrying out of Ashland Place on to Paddington Street, but after that we lost her. She was wearing a long coat, and we could see she had blonde hair but her face was hidden under a hood so there's no way we can identify her.'

Once Geraldine had jogged his memory, the constable's attitude altered and he bustled away to check his notebook. When he returned, he was apologetic. He had no record of the woman's name or what paper she had worked for. He could only confirm that she had been tall and he had sent her packing as soon as he saw her.

'We can't have reporters nosing around crime scenes, flashing cameras and trampling on the ground,' he said fussily.

'Could the reporter have been a man?'

'Well, she had long hair, but now you come to mention it she was unusually tall, and broad shouldered.' He screwed up his eyes then shook his head in regret. 'I can't recall her face at all, I'm afraid. I was distracted by the accident. Sorry, but I was there on my own and there was a lot to do.'

When they reached the college they found Marco chatting to a girl with white blonde hair and black rimmed eyes. Perched on a stool, he turned when Geraldine called his name and put his pint down with a belligerent expression.

'What do you want now?' he growled.

'We need to ask you a few questions about Bethany,' Geraldine said quietly.

Marco glanced back at the girl who appeared to be studying a script, putting on a show of not listening.

'It would be best if you came along to the station with us.'

Marco raised his glass. 'Do you mind if I finish my pint? Money doesn't grow on trees for some of us.'

Geraldine put a couple of quid on the table.

'Let's go, Marco. This won't take long,' she added although she had no idea whether that was true.

Marco didn't ask for a solicitor. He slouched sullenly in his chair like a sulky teenager, arms folded, head down, while Geraldine spoke.

'Where were you on Friday evening?'

'Why do you want to know?'

'Just answer the question, Marco. You know perfectly well what this is about. Where were you on Friday evening?'

He didn't answer straight away. Geraldine repeated the question.

'All right. Give me a chance. I'm thinking. I was going home.'

'Were you alone?'

'Me and half of London out on the streets in Camden.'

'How were you travelling?'

'I was on foot. I like to walk back to Camden. It's not far. And it saves the train fare.'

'Was anyone else with you?'

He shook his head. 'Not on the way, but I met a few other students in the Kings Head in Camden Road on my way home. You can check with them.'

'We will.' Geraldine took the names of the other students. 'What time did you meet them?'

He shrugged.

'So you were out walking the streets, two or three miles away from where your girlfriend was killed –'

Marco interrupted her irritably.

'You keep calling her my girlfriend but she isn't – she wasn't. Not any more.'

'She dumped you?'

Geraldine wasn't sure if he turned red with anger or embarrassment.

'It wasn't like that,' he muttered.

'What was it like? I'm trying to understand.'

'It was mutual. But we'd have got back together. We always did.'

'She'd left you before?'

'I told you, it wasn't like that.'

'Only this time it was different,' Geraldine continued, ignoring his interruption. 'This time she was serious about leaving you because she was seeing someone else, and you lost your temper with her.'

Marco scowled. 'I can see exactly what you're trying to do and believe me it's not going to work. God, you're transparent. You think you can provoke me into breaking down and confessing to something I didn't do? I've just lost someone I cared deeply about and that's all you have to say to me?' He stood up. 'I'd like to go now.'

Sam was convinced Marco was lying.

'He was her boyfriend, he was crazy about her, she dropped him for someone else – an older, successful man – and he lost it. Disguised as a woman, in a blonde wig, he followed her and there you have it, a crime of passion by a jealous ex-boyfriend. He would have had access to wigs and women's clothes, and he doesn't have an alibi!' she ended triumphantly.

Reg was inclined to agree but Geraldine wasn't sure.

'I know his alibi is a bit vague –'

'A bit vague?' Sam echoed. 'I'd say it was non-existent.'

Sam had been checking up on Marco's movements on Friday evening.

'He was seen in the college bar but he left by himself at about eight. He arrived at the pub in Camden at half past ten. There's at least an hour unaccounted for, if he did walk, and he could have taken a cab.' Her face fell as she realised what was coming. 'Oh God here we go, we need to check more bloody CCTV. I'll get the visual images identification and detection office on it.'

'Check his Oyster card and the CCTV at all the stations in walking distance of Holborn, and any buses that might have dropped him off in the area,' Geraldine said, 'and check all the London taxi drivers.'

'I'll need more officers.'

'Whatever you need to do a thorough job.'

Sam nodded. 'Leave it with me. We'll nail him.'

'If it was him,' Geraldine said.

She was thinking about Anna, and how this case looked more complicated than a simple crime of passion.

43

MEGAN DIDN'T LIKE going back to the flat by herself. It wasn't just the nagging worry about who Dirk might be with when she wasn't there to keep watch. She felt uneasy travelling in London by herself. Having grown up in a small village a half hour's bus ride from Norwich, she had found that while life in the metropolis was exciting, it could also be disturbing. When she was out on her own after dark the atmosphere felt positively menacing. She had heard terrible stories of women being mugged and worse. Dirk always laughed at her fears, assuring her nothing was going to happen. But since two girls she knew had been murdered on the streets, she had found it harder than ever to go home alone. This evening Dirk had gone out with the other lads in the cast. At least, that was what he had told her. If he was telling her the truth he would be back late, probably very drunk. If it was a lie, he might not come home at all that night.

The streets were well lit as she walked to Russell Square, from where she took the Piccadilly line eight stops to Wood Green. From the station it was only a five minute walk to the safety of her flat. The newsagents kiosk at the station was still open, as was the McDonald's takeaway restaurant by the cinema. She walked quickly past the closed metal shutters of the next few shops. Ignoring a few youths loitering at the bus stop, she hurried on. She glanced behind her as she turned off, past the pub on the corner. There was a constant stream of cars passing on the main road, plus the takeaway food shops were always open, however late it was when she went home. If there was any trouble on the street she could run into one of them, or into the pub, for help.

Leaving the main road, she walked quickly along a side street towards the turning where she lived. This was the creepiest part of her journey. Away from the bustle of the station and the main road she felt uneasy, vulnerable to attack. She tried to imagine Dirk was walking beside her. He would laugh at her for being afraid. 'Nothing's going to happen,' he would say, 'it's perfectly safe here.' But the pretence didn't help. If he had been with her, she wouldn't have been nervous. Anna and Bethany must have thought they were safe, out on the streets of London at night, all alone.

As though in response to her fears, she heard footsteps behind her. She didn't dare turn and look back. Instead she scurried on, walking as quickly as she could without actually breaking into a run. She didn't want to let on she knew she was being followed. Displaying her fear might provoke her pursuer into launching an attack straight away. If she could reach her front door while he was still a reasonable distance behind her, she would be able to dash inside before he could get to her. It was her only hope.

Her heart was pounding vigorously, blood pumping through her brain, pulsating inside her ears and behind her eyes. Gasping for breath, she stumbled on. Her legs ached but she didn't dare slow down. With all her strength she willed herself to keep moving, knowing that if she faltered now, her pursuer might pounce. She didn't care about losing her phone which had very little credit on it, or about her purse which was almost empty. Her credit card could be cancelled, her college swipe card blocked. None of those things mattered. But this would be no ordinary mugging. Because although no one had admitted as much in public, the truth was that a psychopath was targeting girls from her college.

The principal was busy playing down the connection between recent murders and the college, claiming it was an unfortunate coincidence two of his recent graduates had been killed in little more than a week. In a way his reaction was understandable. At the same time, it was recklessly irresponsible. He should have been taking steps to ensure the safety of his female students. It would be logistically difficult to protect them all as they lived in different areas of London, but they could at least have been warned against going out alone after dark. Dirk wouldn't have been able to leave her to make her way home by herself if the college staff had advised all the students to be extra vigilant until the killer was caught, and not to travel on their own.

She was close enough to her flat to see chipped black paint on the front door. Stumbling up the front path, she thrust her key in the lock. To her relief the key didn't stick and the door opened. As she turned to close it, she looked out into the street. There was no one there. She hoped desperately that whoever had been following her had packed it in and gone away. The thought that he might be prowling around outside the flat, looking for a way in, made her feel sick with fear. After a moment's hesitation, she pulled out her phone and called Dirk. There was no answer. Hearing his carefree voicemail message didn't make her feel any better. Although it was early, she went straight to bed with a mug of cocoa and her script. She hoped rehearsing her lines would take her mind off her Dirk, but she couldn't help wondering where he was.

Lying in bed, propped up against his pillow, she smelt traces of his sweat mingled with the familiar scent of his deodorant and struggled not to torment herself by speculating where he was spending the night. Eventually she slipped into an uneasy doze. She wasn't sure what woke her from an incoherent nightmare where footsteps echoed along deserted streets while Dirk stood laughing at her. The script was lying on the bed in front of her where it had fallen out of her hand. Half asleep, she heard footsteps shuffling around in the next room. There was someone else in the flat.

44

SAM WENT TO SET up the CCTV checks and Geraldine returned to her office. As she sat trawling through statements by Dirk, Megan, Marco, and all the other people associated with the drama school, Nick came in. He sat down at his desk but she knew he was looking at her. It was unnerving. She did her best to ignore him, gazing doggedly at her screen without acknowledging his presence.

'Always busy,' he remarked at last. 'You really need to make some time to relax, get away from the pressure for a few hours. You're not doing yourself any good carrying on like that. Get a life, for goodness sake.'

'I'm not sure what I do with my life outside work is any of your business.'

Once again she had retorted sharply when he was only being friendly.

'Look, Geraldine, I'm not being inquisitive about your private like, if that's what you think. We're colleagues and I don't think we want to confuse our roles here. We might be on a case together soon, and it's best to keep work and private lives separate.'

'I'm not confused,' she answered.

That wasn't strictly true. Nick was attractive. More importantly, he wouldn't be put off by her dedication to her work. He would understand her. She decided that if he asked her out again, she would say yes.

'How about a drink then, if you don't fancy supper? Just a drink, Geraldine. Look, I'll come clean, because we seem to have got off on the wrong foot, and maybe I've come across as a bit pushy. The truth is, I think you may need to talk to someone who's not working on your case, someone you can bounce ideas off. That's all. There's no shame in that. We all need some help with hard cases. And as luck would have it, I'm not actually snowed under right now – well, nothing pressing. Take advantage of my availability and spend a little time offloading. It might help you formulate your ideas if you talk about it. You can do the same for me when I'm on my next case, if it makes you feel any better.'

There was no reason to refuse to go for an occasional drink with a colleague.

As soon as she agreed, he turned away and busied himself with a report he was writing. Somehow Geraldine felt uneasy. He wasn't unattractive, and he was married. Unable to settle, she went to find Sam, keen to get to the bottom of the sergeant's hostility towards Nick. Sam was in the visual images identification and detection office chatting to a middle-aged constable. She looked up when Geraldine entered. 'We've seen Marco leaving Gower Street. Like he said, he was on foot. He didn't go into the station but crossed Euston Road and walked to Camden where he went straight to the pub.'

'There's no way he could have legged it over to Holborn, no time even to have taken a taxi there and back,' the constable confirmed.

Geraldine wanted to challenge Sam about her antagonism towards Nick but this wasn't the time. In any case, the squabble was between them and nothing to do with her, just as it was none of Sam's business if Geraldine chose to go for a drink with him. She left them to it.

After working late they drove in separate cars, north out of London. Geraldine followed Nick along the Edgware Road and on to the Watford bypass. They had been driving for over half an hour when they reached a country pub in a village, off the beaten track. Neither of them acknowledged out loud that Nick had chosen to bring her somewhere they wouldn't be recognised. The interior of the olde worlde black and white pub was dimly lit and quiet. Nick bought the first round, while Geraldine selected a table in as well lit a corner as she could find. When Nick sat down she shifted in her seat to avoid any contact with him.

They chatted idly about their colleagues for a few minutes. Nick described Sam as 'a fire cracker', but didn't volunteer any explanation for her animosity beyond what he had already offered. Geraldine didn't pursue the subject. He was more forthcoming about Reg, for whom he professed admiration.

'Don't you find him a bit heavy handed?' she probed cautiously.

'He's the boss. It's best to do things his way, and hope we get results.'

'And if we don't?'

He shrugged when Geraldine said she suspected Reg would never take the rap for failure.

'You can't blame a bloke for covering his own arse,' he said.

Respecting Nick's refusal to be drawn into any further discussion about their senior colleague, Geraldine muttered in agreement.

As soon as he raised the topic of her investigation, Geraldine launched into a detailed account of the disappearing killer. The case had been nicknamed Houdini by the team working on it.

'You keep talking about "him",' Nick pointed out, putting down his pint, 'when surely everything you've told me so far points to the killer being a woman?'

'You don't think the killer – or killers – were motivated by jealousy, because Piers was sleeping with the victims?'

'Quite possibly, yes. But doesn't that make it all the more likely the killer's a jealous woman, systematically eliminating her rivals for his attentions? Or else she's taking revenge on him. Using his own van suggests someone wanted to frame him, which all points to a jealous ex-lover hell bent on revenge.'

'When you put it like that, it sounds so obvious, I don't know why I never thought of that. The reporter who was first on the scene of Anna Porter's crash was a woman, and a woman was seen following Bethany shortly before she was killed.'

She turned to Nick, excited. Perhaps the reason they hadn't found the killer was because they had been looking in the wrong place all along.

'Nick, I don't know how to thank you –' she began, and broke off, flustered.

The last thing she wanted was to be in his debt, but despite her best intentions she felt herself warming to him. When he stood up, she felt a flicker of disappointment. She reminded herself fiercely that he had a wife waiting for him at home, estranged or otherwise.

'Same again?' he asked and she smiled, relieved.

She wasn't ready for the evening to end yet. 'It's just a casual drink,' she reminded herself, watching him going up to the bar.

The evening passed quickly. They were both hungry so they enquired about food. Nick grumbled at the limited menu and asked Geraldine if she wanted to go somewhere else, but she was content to stay. If they had been on a date, she might have expected something better, but what they ordered was entirely appropriate for an evening spent with a colleague discussing work. In any case she was too engrossed in discussing the investigation to pay much attention to the menu. Despite her preoccupation with the case – or perhaps because she was able to talk freely about it – she enjoyed Nick's company. All in all they spent a pleasant evening, and she told Nick as much when they were standing in the car park taking leave of each other.

'That was a very nice evening, thank you,' she said, suddenly rather formal. 'And thanks for listening. It was a great help.'

As he leaned forward she turned her head so that he kissed her softly on her cheek. If she hadn't moved, his dry warm lips would have met hers. She wasn't sure how she felt about that. Confused, certainly, and cautiously exhilarated. Given his marriage, it could be no more than a frivolous distraction from the case. But it would be foolish to embark on such an affair with a colleague. What was more important right now was that Nick had given her a new line of enquiry to consider. The killer might be a jealous woman, possessive about Piers. Focusing fiercely on that, Geraldine did her best to forget the memory of the soft touch of Nick's lips on her cheek.

While she was on her way home, her phone rang. Glancing down she saw Ian Peterson's number. Although she was on speakerphone, she preferred not to chat in the car and said she would call him back when she got home. Sitting on her sofa with a mug of chocolate she phoned him.

'You were working late,' he said.

'I wasn't working, actually.'

'Ha, a date?'

'No. Well, maybe.' She laughed. 'What's up?'

'Nothing's up.' He sounded slightly put out. 'I thought you'd like to know I got my promotion, that's all.'

'Ian, that's brilliant! Congratulations, Inspector!'

'Thanks. I thought you'd be pleased.'

'Are you sure nothing's wrong? You don't sound very happy about it.'

He didn't answer.

'Ian, what's wrong? How's Bev? How did she take the news?'

He didn't answer straight away. 'I'm not sure,' he said at last.

The pause told her more than his halting words.

'Ian, what's wrong? What's happened?'

'I'm not sure,' he repeated miserably. 'Oh, she was pleased about the promotion, of course, but she's not keen on moving.'

'Do you know where you're going?'

'York.'

'York? How exciting!'

Doing her best to sound pleased, she was glad he couldn't see her dismayed expression. York was a long way off. She had secretly been hoping he would move closer to London.

'I wish Bev thought so,' he was saying. 'She's pissed off at having to leave her job, and the house. She loves our house. She's worked really hard to get everything right.'

'But you both knew a move was on the cards. It can hardly have come as a surprise to her, after all your hard work.'

'She doesn't see it like that.'

The sudden rancour in his tone warned her to choose her words with more care.

'I'm sure she'll be fine once she gets used to the idea.'

'I hope you're right.'

It was a difficult conversation and for once Geraldine was relieved when he said he had to go. What with Nick and Ian, she wondered if anyone she knew was happily married. She fancied Nick, and was flattered by his attention, but she wasn't sure if she actually liked him. She certainly didn't trust him the way she trusted Ian. Not for the first time, she decided she was better off on her own. Relationships were too complicated.

45

MEGAN LET OUT AN involuntary whimper. Clapping one hand over her mouth she wriggled right down into the bed and pulled the covers over her head. She lay very still, alert to the slightest sound. With luck the intruder wouldn't realise there was anyone there, although if he looked in the room it would be pretty obvious someone was concealed under the duvet. It was stifling in the bed, yet she was shivering. She strained to listen through the bed covers. Someone was clattering about in the kitchen. Silence. All at once her heart began pounding as she heard the bedroom door creak open. Too late she realised she should have grabbed a weapon of some kind before hiding herself in the bed. As it was, she had nothing with which to try and defend herself against her attacker. Her worst fear was that he might slash her face. She wasn't as pretty as most of the other girls in her year yet Dirk still fancied her, and he wasn't the only one. If her face was disfigured, her career might be over before it had even begun.

She kept her eyes tightly closed, hardly daring to breathe as something thumped down hard on the bed.

'Megan! Are you asleep?'

She let out a sob of relief. Dirk pulled back the covers and leered down at her. His breath stank of beer and stale cigarette smoke. At least he had probably been telling her the truth about going to the pub.

'Lauren's here,' he announced very loudly.

'You're not going to throw up are you?' She scrambled over to the other side of the bed. 'Get into the bathroom, you stink.'

'Angela's here.'

'You said Lauren just now.'

'I know. That's what I'm telling you. Lauren's here.'

'Who's Lauren?'

'Listen.' He spoke very slowly, and his speech was slurred. 'I brought Lauren back here because she had nowhere to go. Missed her train, you see.'

'But who is she?'

'She's a girl. She's Lauren.'

Without any further explanation he fell back on the bed, laughing uncontrollably.

Megan didn't mind who was with him. He could have brought a whole harem of girls back to the flat for all she cared, she was so pleased to see him. Without warning she burst into tears.

'Oh for fuck's sake,' he grumbled, sitting up and scowling. 'She only came back with me because she missed her last train. What was I supposed to do? Leave her on her own in the middle of London? I was being chivalrous.' He stumbled over the word. 'You should be proud of me. I'm a gentleman.'

'I am proud of you.'

She flung her arms round his neck.

'So why are you crying?'

'I'm just happy to see you.'

'Well, make us a cup of tea then. It's freezing out there.' He leaned forward suddenly. 'Oh God, I'm going to hurl.'

Megan helped him to the bathroom and sat on the side of the bath while he threw up. She stared at her face in the mirror. Pasty-faced, with no make-up, her hair a mess from hiding under the bed covers, she hoped Dirk was too pissed to notice how awful she looked. At last he finished and followed her submissively back to the bedroom.

'I'll go and make the tea then.'

He grunted in reply. While the kettle was boiling, she went back to the bathroom and cleaned up. As she passed the living room she heard laughter.

Recovered from his bout of vomiting, Dirk was sitting on the sofa beside a girl who was laughing at something he was saying. Neither of them noticed Megan, standing in the doorway, watching them. She stared at the stranger. Lauren was very thin. Long skinny legs stuck out beneath her short skirt, and she waved her hands in the air when she spoke, displaying sparkly pink nails. Her blonde hair was dark at the roots, her huge blue eyes emphasised by thick black make-up. She looked like a cheap little tart, and worryingly young. Megan fought against her resentment. She gave Dirk somewhere to live, spent hours going through his lines with him, looked after him when he was sick and cleaned up after him, shopped and cooked for him, and he repaid her devotion by openly flirting with some skinny little bitch who was gagging to shag him.

'Here you are,' she said forcing herself to sound cheerful as she handed them their tea.

Lauren took a sip and screwed her face up in disgust. 'It's got sugar in it.'

Dirk gulped and grimaced. 'This one's yours. It's disgusting.' He and Lauren swapped mugs, laughing. 'Trust Megan to get it wrong,' he added.

Lauren looked up and met Megan's eye, seemingly noticing her for the first time.

'Thank you for the tea,' she said politely, as though Megan was Dirk's mother.

Megan wondered if she was even sixteen. One of these days, Dirk was going to get himself into a lot of trouble, and serve him right.

'I'm going to bed,' she announced. Turning to Dirk, she asked him if he was going to bring his tea with him. 'I'll find a sleeping bag for Lauren if she wants to stay on the sofa tonight.'

Lauren reached out a small hand and placed it on Dirk's arm. He didn't move.

'Good night,' Lauren said firmly, looking straight at Megan.

Without another word, Megan turned on her heel and left the room. Lying in bed, alone, she promised herself she would throw him out in the morning. He could find some other mug to put up with his selfish carrying on. But by the time he joined her in bed later, she had her jealousy fiercely back under control. However many girls he flirted with, Dirk invariably came back to her. She was going to make sure he always did.

46

'WE NEED TO LOOK at Piers' previous lovers – maybe his ex-wives,' Geraldine announced to the borough intelligence unit the next morning.

She sounded so enthusiastic that several officers looked up from their screens in surprise. Reg and Sam were both in the room and the detective chief inspector stopped what he was doing.

'What's your thinking, Geraldine?' he asked.

She explained the theory Nick had put forward. Sam raised her eyebrows. She looked narked.

'Nick suggested it? What's it got to do with him? He's not even on the case.'

'We were discussing it last night,' Geraldine answered shortly.

There was no reason why she shouldn't talk about the investigation with another officer, in general terms. He had been helpful, and his idea might even lead them to solve a case that had been going nowhere. The fact that Sam didn't like him was of no consequence. Reg was more positive.

'That makes sense. Come on, I'm meeting Jayne in my office in five minutes, we can see what she has to say about it.'

'This just gets better and better,' Sam muttered.

Geraldine didn't answer. Like Sam, she found the psychological profiler irritating, but any opinion could prove useful when they were floundering.

Jayne listened intently to Geraldine's theory. With her head tilted to one side, her long curly hair reached down to her waist. Dressed in her usual ankle length skirt and floaty scarf, the profiler reminded Geraldine of an art teacher she had at school. She struggled to understand how Reg could take her seriously.

'What do you think?' the detective chief inspector asked.

'It's possible,' Jayne agreed.

'Anything's possible,' Sam mumbled.

Geraldine glared at the sergeant, irritated that her colleague felt able to express the thought Geraldine had kept to herself. As an inspector, she felt obliged to conduct herself with some dignity and restraint. But if Sam ever intended to seek promotion, she needed to be more careful. Geraldine had already reprimanded her about her offhand attitude. Jayne scowled, clearly understanding that Sam was sniping at her. Geraldine suspected Sam was annoyed that Nick's idea was being taken seriously. Reg agreed they should investigate Piers' ex-wives, while Sam drew up a list of women with whom he had been involved.

'It's going to be a long list,' she pointed out, but she sounded more cheerful now she had something to do.

'What is it about Nick?' Geraldine asked Sam as they walked down the corridor, away from Reg's office.

'What about him?'

'What's between the two of you?'

'Nothing at all.'

'Why the constant bitching about him then?'

'You know why I don't like him.'

Geraldine nodded. Sam had told her about a stupid sexist remark Nick had once made about an alleged rape victim. But anyone could blunder. Now that she knew him better, Geraldine genuinely believed he had been thoughtless rather than nasty. The comment might have been unforgivable at the time, but Sam couldn't hold it against him forever.

Sam followed Geraldine into her office, where Nick was seated at his desk fiddling with a pen. He looked up and smiled.

'Fancy a drink after work, ladies?'

'No thank you. As if we'd want to,' Sam added to Geraldine, lowering her voice, yet making sure Nick could still hear her.

'I think you'll find Geraldine already has,' he retorted. 'In fact, it was more than a drink. How about supper again tonight,

Geraldine? My treat.'

Sam stalked off without a word. Geraldine watched her go but didn't follow or call after her. She had no time for the sergeant's immature antics.

Sam caught up with Geraldine in the canteen at lunch time.

'Mind if I sit here, or is this seat taken?'

Geraldine gave a wary smile and gestured to her colleague to join her.

'You went out with him?' Sam hissed, leaning over the table so Geraldine could catch her whispered question.

'It was just a drink.'

'That's not what he said.'

'We were in a pub, we were hungry, and we ordered some crap bar food, as if it's any of your business. What the hell's got into you?'

'Be careful, Geraldine.'

'What?'

Sam hesitated for a second. 'You know he's married.'

'He and his wife have separated. And we didn't go on a date. We went for a drink and discussed the case.'

'Separated? Is that what he told you? Listen, Geraldine, he's a lowlife. He's slept his way round half the station – it's a standing joke. He's always sniffing round the new recruits. He's married and he's a –'

'That's enough,' Geraldine interrupted gently. 'You know you're raising your voice? I don't want to hear you gossiping about your superiors, or about any of your fellow officers if it comes to that. If you get a name for being indiscreet it could affect your chances of promotion. Seriously.'

Telling herself she was concerned for Sam's reputation, Geraldine tried not to feel disappointed at what she had heard. After all, Nick's affairs had nothing to do with her. She wasn't interested in him romantically. He was simply a colleague who had given her a helpful insight into the investigation, that was all.

Sam suspected that wasn't the whole picture, and was still talking.

'He leads his wife a dog's life by all accounts.'

'Whose accounts?'

'Everyone says it. He's always chasing after someone or other, and now it's your turn. I don't get what women see in him. I mean, he's OK, but he's no pin up, is he?'

'I said that's enough.'

'This isn't just gossip, Geraldine. Ask any of the female officers. And as for telling you he's separated from his wife, that's a barefaced lie. I'm not telling you all this to be mean about him, Geraldine. You went out with him –'

'For a drink after work –'

'And you ought to know what he's like. What sort of a friend would I be if I sat back and watched you make a fool of yourself, and maybe get hurt into the bargain, without trying to warn you what he's like? He's bad news.'

Sam looked so earnest, Geraldine couldn't resent her interference. Instead, she thanked Sam for the caution and promised to keep Nick at arm's length.

'It's not as if I fancy him,' she lied. 'You've got it all wrong if that's what you think.'

She wasn't exactly lying, because she wasn't sure herself how she felt about Nick. But in any case, her feelings were not Sam's business, however well intentioned the sergeant's concern might be.

47

GERALDINE WASN'T SURE why she had been asked to interview a young woman who had come to the station to report an assault, but she responded to the summons promptly. It would be a welcome distraction from the monotony of filling in time, waiting for something to advance the investigation into the deaths of Anna and Bethany. The girl didn't stop crying when Geraldine entered the room. Geraldine watched her narrow shoulders shuddering as she sobbed. The female constable introduced her as Cheryl. Geraldine waited another moment and then called the girl's name. Cheryl looked up, dabbing at her eyes with a damp tissue. Her pale complexion formed a stark contrast to her jet black hair which Geraldine guessed had been dyed, because the girl's large eyes were blue.

'Cheryl, I'm DI Geraldine Steel.'

The girl nodded and reached for another tissue from the box someone had thoughtfully placed on the table. She blew her nose very loudly.

'Let's start from the beginning,' Geraldine coaxed her. 'What happened?'

Cheryl sat up straight. As she moved her head she flicked her hair back off her face, exposing a large bruise on her left temple. Geraldine waited but the girl just stared, wide-eyed, like a frightened mouse. Now that Geraldine could see her face, she realised she had seen the girl before, quite recently, although she couldn't remember where. She had encountered a number of pretty young women in the course of the investigation so far.

'I remembered your name,' Cheryl said, giving Geraldine a weak smile. 'You came to arrest him, didn't you?'

Geraldine nodded as she recalled where they had met before.

Cheryl had been keeping Piers company after Anna's death.

'You shouldn't have let him go,' Cheryl cried out suddenly. She glared accusingly at Geraldine. 'Why didn't you lock him up when you had the chance? Look what he did to me.' Angrily she pointed at her bruised face. 'He nearly killed me.'

Geraldine nodded to indicate she was listening.

'Tell me what happened,' she said gently.

'I never did anything. He just flipped. He's a fucking head case. He went mental and started yelling at me. I hadn't done anything.'

'Did something cause him to lose his temper like that? What set him off?'

The girl shrugged and looked away.

'Cheryl, unless you're going to be honest with me, you might as well not bother talking to me at all. You're just wasting time for both of us.'

Geraldine stood up signalling that the interview was over.

Cheryl looked crushed.

'Don't go,' she muttered, very quietly. 'I'll tell you what happened. He was drinking whisky when I got there. I'm not supposed to tell anyone. I don't suppose it matters now.'

'So he was drinking whisky. Was he drunk?'

'I don't know. Yes. He was completely plastered and he just went for me. He was like a wild animal. First of all he was just shouting at me, then he forced me to drink his stinking whisky.' Her eyes flicked nervously to Geraldine and slid away again. 'Then he threw the bottle at me and did this.' She pointed to her bruises. 'If I hadn't ducked he could've killed me. He nearly did.'

Geraldine had been making notes. When Cheryl stopped talking, she looked up.

'Do you want to press charges?'

'I want him locked up. Lock him up and throw away the key!'

When Geraldine didn't respond, the girl continued.

'Yes, I want to do that thing you said. He's dangerous. He's going to kill someone if he carries on like that.'

Geraldine wondered if he already had.

An hour later, Geraldine was back in the same chair. This time Piers faced her across the table.

'I've got nothing to say to you,' he announced pompously.

He spoke like a man used to giving commands, leaning back, arms crossed, his face a mask of contempt.

'We've received a complaint against you,' Geraldine said. She tried to hide her satisfaction.

'What sort of complaint?'

'Cheryl's been talking to us.'

Hearing the name he abandoned his sneer and lowered his eyelids until his eyes were barely open. Although he made no comment, Geraldine was sure she had his full attention. She didn't speak again straight away, and they sat watching each other in silence for a few minutes. He kept very still but she had the impression he was nervous. His narrowed eyes were glued to hers, waiting.

Geraldine broke first, but only because she didn't want to spend any more time on the interview than was necessary.

'Cheryl came here to complain about you,' she said at last. 'She's filed a formal complaint against you.'

'Complaining about what, exactly?'

'A violent physical assault.'

'That's bollocks.'

'Do you deny attacking her in your home a week ago?'

'Of course I do.'

Piers' account of the incident was simple. Cheryl had drunk too much.

'So you don't deny that you invited a twenty-year-old girl to your flat, with the purpose of getting her drunk?'

'On the contrary, I absolutely deny it. First off, I never invited her round, she came of her own accord. The whole thing was her idea. I didn't want her in my house at all, but she turned up anyway. And secondly, how was I to know she can't hold her drink? What was she doing drinking whisky if she can't take it? It didn't take much, I can tell you. She was completely off her trolley.'

Geraldine sniffed sceptically. 'Why?'

'Why what?'

'Why did she come to visit you at home?'

'She wanted to consult me.'

'Consult how?'

'Anna had asked me to advise Cheryl about her career, tell her which agents to trust, how to set about finding the right one for her, that sort of thing. Anyway, she got horribly drunk and threw herself at me. When I rejected her advances she went for me and then rushed off, walking slap bang into the door on her way out, no doubt giving herself a really nasty bruise.'

He had hardly finished speaking when Geraldine asked if that was the first time Cheryl had turned up at his house. Piers stared at her, his penetrating eyes still half-closed. She hoped he had forgotten that Geraldine and Sam had seen Cheryl at his house.

'No,' he replied carefully. 'She's been to my house before. She was friends with Anna,' he added.

Geraldine did her best to conceal her disappointment. If she had caught him out in such an awkward lie, she could have put pressure on him to tell the truth. But he was too wily for that.

'So she continued to visit you after Anna was dead?'

'Once or twice, just to see if I was all right.'

Geraldine sat forward suddenly.

'I don't believe you.'

'I'm not sure I care for your good opinion,' he replied with studied nonchalance.

Once again Geraldine was reminded that she was dealing with a suspect accustomed to acting roles.

'Cheryl claims you beat her, and caused her an injury by throwing an empty whisky bottle at her head.'

'If you want to believe the twisted lies of a disappointed girl rather than me, there's nothing I can do about it, is there?'

He must have known she had no proof, only Cheryl's word against his.

'In what way disappointed?'

'Rejected, disappointed, she thought she could persuade me to cast her in Anna's part by throwing herself at me. It didn't work so she's seeking some sort of petty revenge by accusing me of hitting her. It's a lie, a damned lie.'

'You seem very relaxed about being accused of assault, given your recent history.'

'My history?' He knew very well what she meant but he put on a transparent act of being perplexed, all wide-eyed innocence and raised eyebrows.

'First your live-in girlfriend, Anna, was murdered, then another of your girlfriends, Bethany. Was Cheryl next on your list of unfortunate girlfriends? '

'I wondered how long it would be before you brought all that up. Well, you can't pin any of that on me. And Bethany wasn't my girlfriend, Anna was. It's malicious, unsubstantiated lies trying to link my name with Bethany. You don't have a shred of evidence, or you would have locked me up by now. So, if that's all, I'd like to go home now.'

'Bethany said –'

'Yes, well, I'm afraid Bethany was a silly deluded girl.'

'Like Cheryl?'

Piers heaved an exaggerated sigh.

'Inspector, you wouldn't believe how many young actresses try to get their names linked with men like me. It's just another stupid lie the media love to get hold of. I daresay Bethany was paid a fat fee for spinning a yarn. No one even cares if these stories are true or not. No one takes them seriously. Cheryl was probably playing the same game.'

He stood up, clearly agitated. Some part of what she had said had upset him. She wished she knew what it was.

48

ZAK HAD ONLY A hazy memory of his mother's face: large dark eyes, like his own, framed by short dark hair, peering down at him. He wasn't sure if he was recalling a dream, or an old photograph, or a false memory based on scraps of information he had heard. After he had been cared for by a succession of women, when he was nine his father had remarried, only to get divorced after three years. At least between the ages of nine and twelve Zak had enjoyed the benefits of a relatively stable home, despite the constant bickering between his father and his stepmother. She had made little effort to befriend Zak once she had married his father, and he had been relieved when she had finally moved out. When his father had asked him how he felt about her leaving, Zak had just shrugged. He didn't really care. He soon grew accustomed to his father bringing a succession of different women home with him. Sometimes Zak recognised their faces from television but most of them were just starting out on their careers. He still remembered his recent shock on discovering that one of his father's girlfriends was the same age as him. He wondered if she knew how old his father was, and guessed that his father probably didn't care if she did.

The next time they met, Darius asked if he remembered his mother. Zak wasn't sure what to say. He thought about the photograph that his uncle had shown him.

'I think so,' he mumbled.

'You know she really loved you.'

Privately Zak thought that was fair enough. After all, she was his mother. It was a pity his father never wanted to talk about her.

'She's dead,' was all Piers ever said, 'let sleeping dogs lie.'

Darius, on the other hand, seemed to like talking about his dead sister. He encouraged Zak to question him freely about her.

'What do you want to know?'

Zak hesitated. He really wasn't bothered.

It was different for his uncle. He had grown up with her.

'Anything you want to tell me. I mean, I don't know, do I? I never met her.'

'But there must be lots of things about her you want to know.'

Zak shook his head and then wished he hadn't. After drinking too much far too quickly, he felt as though he might be sick.

'How did you feel when you saw her picture?' Darius pressed him. 'Don't you think she was beautiful?'

Zak thought about it. He wasn't sure what his uncle expected him to say.

'I didn't feel anything really.'

He could tell Darius was disappointed. A faint frown creased his uncle's face. He had the same high cheekbones as his nephew, and the same very dark eyes. But where Zak looked physically delicate, his uncle was wiry and muscular, without being bulky, like Zak might look in thirty years' time if he worked out every day.

'I tried to feel something, some sort of connection,' Zak blundered on, aware that he had let his uncle down. 'I know she was my mother. But I never really met her, not so I can remember,' he concluded lamely, 'so I don't feel anything about her. How can I?'

Darius stared coldly at him.

'You're her flesh and blood,' he exclaimed loudly.

A woman at the next table looked round.

Zak was mortified. 'It's not my fault. I never asked her to die, did I?'

His uncle looked shocked.

'I mean, I'm the one who lost his mother.'

'I lost my sister,' Darius reminded him softly. 'But let's not dwell on the past right now. Tell me how it's all going with this new production you're designing.'

Zak was relieved to be back on a safe topic. He knocked back the rest of his glass of wine and refilled it himself. It was nice being taken out for a good meal. His uncle knew how to select a decent wine, not like the rubbish his father offered his guests, at least when Zak was there. He was always pleading poverty, but Zak didn't believe a word of it. He just put on a show of being short to make the point that he wasn't going to bankroll his son forever. As though Zak wanted to have to rely on his old man for support. But even given the excellent food and wine, once he was over the novelty of meeting his dead mother's brother, Zak found his uncle quite boring.

'There's nothing very interesting to tell,' he replied, when Zak asked his uncle about his own life. 'Not like you, Zak. You've got everything to look forward to. I'm retired and all I do these days is potter about.'

'Retired? Already? What did you do?'

'I was in films.'

Zak sat forward. This promised to be more interesting than he had expected. He wondered if his uncle might still have any contacts in the industry who could be useful. An up and coming theatre designer couldn't have too many contacts.

'I don't know anyone in theatre,' his uncle said apologetically. 'I'd help you if I could.'

When Zak said he would jump at the chance to get some experience in films, his uncle insisted he knew no one who might possibly be able to help his nephew.

'It's not that I want to pump you for contacts,' Zak lied. 'Nothing like that. But I'm really interested to hear about you. What did you do? I really want to know. Were you a cameraman or something?'

Darius smiled. 'No, I was in front of the camera. You've probably seen me in lots of films, though you wouldn't know it.'

'An extra?'

His uncle laughed. 'Yes, something like that. It really isn't very interesting.'

He refused to say anything else, however hard Zak tried to wheedle more information out of him.

The evening was turning out to be more fun than Zak had anticipated.

'I'm on form tonight,' he said more than once as he told another joke. He was dimly aware that he was repeating the same jokes, but it didn't matter because they grew more amusing with each retelling. His uncle kept laughing with him. Zak hadn't appreciated what a brilliant comedian he was. Only when his companion insisted they leave did he realise that he couldn't walk straight, and that was funny too.

'I've had a great time,' he told Darius.

'Good. I've enjoyed the evening too. Now, are you in a fit state to get yourself home, or shall we get you a taxi?'

His uncle took Zak by the elbow and steered him towards the door with a firm strong grip.

49

GERALDINE STOOD IN THE corridor watching Piers stalk out of the police station. Tall and slender, he walked with the dynamic stride of a much younger man. If it weren't for his greying hair, it would have been difficult to believe he was in his sixties. Only his slightly bowed shoulders gave a hint of physical ageing. He must have been devastatingly attractive when he was younger. Even now, it wasn't hard to understand his appeal. With the power to boost their careers, actresses might well find him irresistible. What puzzled Geraldine was that after he had spent so many years loving women, there seemed no reason for him to suddenly start killing them.

Jealousy could be a compelling motive but even apart from his narcissism, Piers was too experienced to become seriously attached to one woman. Despite his denials, she suspected he had been having a fling with Bethany while living with Anna. He had quite possibly been sleeping with other women at the same time. But he wouldn't have cared enough about any one woman to kill her for being unfaithful. That didn't mean he had a forgiving nature. If he wanted to be revenged on a woman who had spurned him, he might well set about destroying her career, but Geraldine couldn't imagine he would commit murder. However unpleasant a character he was, they had no evidence to place him at either crime scene, and Geraldine didn't believe he had killed either Anna or Bethany. He hadn't cared enough about either of them to commit a crime of passion.

A taxi was waiting to take him home. He had declined the offer of a lift, claiming he had spent enough time in the back of a police car for one lifetime.

'Was that an innocent man wrongly accused, or a serial killer escaping justice?' a voice muttered in Geraldine's ear. 'How the hell can we be expected to judge? We're not mind readers.'

She turned round and smiled at Nick. 'That's just what I was wondering.'

'It's never easy letting go of a suspect. You can never be sure if you've done the right thing by an innocent man, or let some evil slime bag slip through your fingers. Should he face prosecution for murder, or be allowed to return to his ordinary life? The truth can be so difficult to get at.'

'I don't think his life's what you could call ordinary.'

She watched Nick's reaction closely as she added, 'Glamorous young women were throwing themselves at him all the time.'

She wished Sam was there. According to the sergeant, Nick never missed an opportunity to make a sexist quip. Geraldine had fully expected him to say he wished glamorous young women would throw themselves at him, or something along those lines. Instead he remarked blandly that Piers' attractions doubtless had something to do with his influential position.

'I've been reading up on him, in case you wanted to discuss the investigation again. You know I'm around if you need someone to bounce ideas off. You'll do the same for me if I'm ever in need of help with a tricky case.'

With a nod and a grin, he walked away, the perfect example of a supportive colleague.

'Of course he wasn't going to say anything offensive in front of you,' Sam countered when Geraldine explained how she had tried to provoke Nick into revealing a patronising attitude to women. 'He's doing his best to impress you. Besides, you work with me, and he knows what I think of him.'

It was clear that Sam was determined to think badly of Nick.

'Right then, let's stop wasting time on idle gossip about colleagues and get back to work,' Geraldine said. 'We can start by going over what we know.'

It was depressing. There was little point in going over old ground again, but they had nothing else to do. They decided to tackle the most confusing aspect of the case head on. The crucial missing information about the killers – apart from their identities – was how they had escaped from the crime scenes undetected.

'It doesn't make sense,' Sam complained, for the hundredth time. 'People don't just vanish. They must have gone somewhere.'

They went back to the visual images identification and detection office and chatted to Bill, the constable who was looking after the CCTV surveillance. There was no sign of anyone leaving the scene of the car crash, apart from the reporter who had been sent packing by the first officer to arrive on the scene. They couldn't find any sign of her arriving.

'But even if this mysterious reporter was somehow involved,' Sam said, 'there's no way she – or he – could have got out of the van, if she was at the wheel. It's impossible at that speed.'

Geraldine frowned. 'Almost impossible,' she said.

Sam and Bill both turned expectantly to her.

She shrugged helplessly.

'Don't look at me. I don't understand it any more than you do. But if this reporter was the only person at the scene, then he or she must have been driving the van. Just don't ask me how.'

They checked the CCTV film again and caught a glimpse of the reporter hurrying away from the crash. Tall and broad-shouldered, just as the first constable at the scene of the crash had described her, her face was hidden from the camera by her hood.

'Was it raining?' Bill asked. He was shrewd for all his good-natured easy manner.

'It was drizzling,' Sam replied.

The camera picked up someone who could have been their target, striding along Marylebone High Street. In jeans and flat shoes, the figure might have been a man.

'Her walk reminds me of Piers,' Geraldine said quietly. 'But then lots of people walk like that. It's not conclusive. Still, if that's a woman, she walks very like a man.'

Glued to the screen, they observed their possible suspect arrive at Baker Street station where they lost her in the throng of jostling travellers. A similar figure went into the Ladies toilet, but they didn't see her emerge. Bill spotted a tall blonde woman in a hood travelling down one escalator, Sam saw another one walking out of the station. The longer they stared at the moving crowd the more tall people they noticed, with blonde hair, or wearing hoods. Any one of them could have been the killer. Or none of them.

50

THE REHEARSALS WERE PROGRESSING slowly. They were using Zak's set for the first time. Several members of the cast were in a muddle about their entrances, although Zak had gone over the script with them, one at a time.

'It's not the same when you're actually on stage with it,' one of the actors grumbled.

'It's so unnecessarily complicated,' someone else said.

Zak couldn't see the problem but he kept his cool. The set wasn't exactly how he had envisaged it anyway. The final word lay with the professional designer who was on board as a mentor for Zak.

'Think of me as a consultant you can ask if you have any queries,' he had told Zak before they started work on the production. 'It's your set.'

As it turned out, the professional had dominated the whole design process, using Zak as a runner and general dogsbody.

'It's a great opportunity to learn from a successful theatre designer,' was all Zak's tutor had said when he protested.

After that he had kept his frustrations to himself, only sharing them in private with a few sympathetic students on the design course, and his uncle. There was no point in complaining again. No one took any notice of students. Once he graduated, everything would be different. He intended to milk all of his father's contacts. Armed with a growing list of directors and producers he had met, and his own creative talent, Zak wouldn't need to rely on his father's help for long.

Near the end of the rehearsal a clumsy actor stumbled and fell against one of the flats, putting his boot right through it. No one seemed to take any notice of the damage to the set. They all clustered around the boy who had tripped.

'Are you all right?'

'Is he OK?'

The girls in particular were making a ridiculous fuss. The student hadn't even hurt himself. Of course it was left to Zak to mend the flat.

'It shouldn't take long,' the visiting designer said glibly. 'It just needs some tape and a touch of paint.'

The next rehearsal was at half past nine the following morning.

'You'd better do it now so it can dry overnight,' his so-called mentor added, handing Zak a key. 'Well, I'd best be off. Don't forget to lock the room when you leave. You can let me have the key back tomorrow.'

Alone, Zak taped and painted, cursing the stupid oaf who had fallen over, the designer who had left him to sort out the mess, as usual, and the director who had left early and knew nothing about the extra time Zak was putting in after everyone else had gone. No one would thank him for staying late. The moron who had knocked over the flat hadn't even stopped to apologise. It took the best part of an hour to complete the job. At last he was finished. He left the paint and other gear neatly in a corner of the room. That at least could wait until the morning to be returned to the store. With a last look around, he switched off the lights and closed the door, locking it carefully behind him.

It was dark in the corridor. As Zak felt around for the light switch there was a faint sound, like a soft sigh. The sudden glare was blinding. Before he could turn round something walloped him hard on the back of his knees. He cried out in pain and shock. His bag slipped from his shoulder as his legs buckled under him.

'That's not funny!' he yelped. 'That hurt!'

His attacker spun round and turned the light off. Zak barely had time to glimpse the back of a hooded figure before his assailant vanished into the shadows.

'What the hell are you playing at?' he cried out. 'Put the light on at once!'

For answer, he felt a second whack. This one caught him a glancing blow on the side of the head. If it had made direct contact, it could have cracked his skull. As it was, he pitched forward, stunned, jarring his shoulder against the wall. He yelled out in fear. This was no accidental injury. It was a deliberate attack.

'Put the light on! Put the light on!'

He was begging now, afraid he would be badly hurt. He wondered who might want to beat him up, but his mind was too fuddled with fear and pain to think clearly. Still his assailant didn't speak. The silence was terrifying. An agonising throbbing started in his head, sending splinters darting through his brain. Gingerly he fingered the side of his head. His hair was wet. He put his hand to his lips and the tip of his tongue explored a warm salty taste mingled with the acrid tang of paint. It took a few seconds before he realised he was bleeding. Petrified, he felt himself breathe in staccato bursts.

'You've really hurt me,' he gasped. 'I've got a head wound for fuck's sake.'

Everyone knew that head injuries must be taken seriously.

'I need a doctor. I'm going to be sick. Stop mucking about and put the light on.'

But he knew this wasn't a fellow student playing a stupid prank to frighten him.

Desperately he stretched out his arm, his fingers feeling for his bag. There was a window in the door at the far end of the corridor. In the light from the stair well he could dimly see the outline of his bag lying just out of reach, where it had slid along the floor when he fell. He hadn't switched his phone on after the rehearsal, but if he could just get to it he could try to turn it on and call for help, even though the signal wasn't strong in the rehearsal block.

'Listen,' he gabbled, as he groped forwards. 'There's no point mugging me, all I've got is a crappy old phone. Actually, it's not crappy, it's almost brand new and it's in my bag. You can have it. I'll give you the password. And I've got a bit of cash. Not much, but you can have it. Only please let me call for help first. I need a doctor. You never meant to hurt me, I know. This is all a mistake. Just take my bag and go, please.'

He heard footsteps shuffle towards him before darkness flooded his mind.

51

THE TEAM INVESTIGATING THE murders of Anna and Bethany were stunned to learn there was a third victim associated with the college, and with Piers.

Sam was aghast. 'Does this mean his father's no longer a suspect? I mean, he's hardly likely to have killed his own son, is he?'

She had voiced the exasperation of most of her colleagues working on the case. Geraldine remembered what Nick had said, 'It's never easy letting go of a suspect.' Even though she hadn't really believed Piers was guilty of murdering Anna and Bethany, it was still disturbing to hear that the third victim was Piers' son.

She thought back to her few meetings with Zak. He had seemed very young, barely out of adolescence. He hadn't yet escaped his father's influence to begin a life of his own.

'He was only a kid,' she said aloud.

Reg threw her an inquisitive glance. 'Your point?'

'I mean, of course his age makes no difference, but –' she shrugged helplessly, struggling to express her feelings, 'he was just very young, that's all.'

'All the victims were young,' someone else responded.

'But he was Pier's *son*,' Sam bleated.

'We don't know they were all killed by the same person,' Reg pointed out.

'Is it possible he was responsible for the deaths of Anna and Bethany because he was insanely jealous of his father's attention?' Jayne suggested. 'His death could be a revenge killing by someone who cared for one or other of his victims and discovered he was the killer.'

'That makes sense,' Reg agreed, 'but we need to gather some evidence about this third death before we start putting forward too many theories. Let's hope we're looking for one killer who's slipped up and left us some incontrovertible proof of his identity this time.'

The top corridor of the rehearsal block was closed. The building remained open, with the staircase and lift that led to the top corridor out of bounds. By using a staircase in an adjoining theatre building, the students were able to access the lower storeys and continue their work. It was inconvenient for them not being able to use the upper floor at all but no one raised any objections. The college principal assured the police they could take all the time they needed to examine the crime scene free of interruption. By the time Geraldine and Sam arrived, scene of crime officers were at work on the stairs and along the corridor. The identity of the victim was known from the outset. Apart from the fact that everyone in the building knew him, his bag was found a foot or so away from the body with his wallet, phone and student card.

There was no need for a forensic tent in the enclosed space of the narrow corridor, which was closed off by a fire door at one end, and an outside wall at the other. Several doors leading to rehearsal rooms were locked. So far nothing had been found on the stairs. Each step was being examined for traces of blood or any other evidence that the killer had escaped down them. CCTV film from surveillance cameras on the stairs and in the lift had been sent to Hendon for scrutiny. It was fortunate that the college took security very seriously, to protect expensive equipment kept on the premises.

'The cameras here are state of the art,' Sam said admiringly. 'At last we'll be able to get a close up view of the killer as he's leaving.'

'Unless he's done another vanishing act.'

'Don't joke about it!'

Geraldine didn't say that she hadn't been joking.

Miles arrived soon after Geraldine and her sergeant. They waited anxiously for his report. It wasn't long before he straightened up and turned to them with a grin. Geraldine returned his smile. She liked the brisk young pathologist. He was obliging and relatively quick at his work. Some doctors she had worked with were more measured in their approach, reluctant to voice any opinion before conducting a thorough post mortem. Either Miles understood her impatience, or else he wasn't so punctilious in his approach to his work. Whatever the reason, he was willing to offer an unsubstantiated opinion straight away. 'Don't quote me on this,' was a refrain he often repeated, in case he later had cause to revise his first impression. He hadn't misled them so far.

'What do you want first, the good news or the bad news?' he asked.

Geraldine stifled a groan. Miles liked to crack immature jokes.

'Go on then, surprise us,' she answered.

'The bad news is – he's dead.'

'OK. And the good news?'

'The good news is it all looks pretty straightforward. I'll be able to tell you more once I've had a chance to take a proper look, but he's been badly beaten with some hard object – a metal pole or something.'

'A pole?'

'I can't be specific, I'm afraid. A stick, a pole, something along those lines.'

'How do you know it was metal?'

'I don't. It could have been wood, or plastic, anything very hard, long and rounded, with very smooth surfaces. He was beaten on the back of the legs while still alive. Look.'

He pointed to bruising on the back of the dead man's knees.

'To knock him down?'

The pathologist grunted.

'He bruised his shoulder, probably against the wall as he fell. It looks as though he crashed into it.'

Scene of crime officers had already marked an indentation on the plaster of the wall. Geraldine stared at it, then at the position of the body. Although the victim had been turned over, she could see he might have fallen against the wall at that point. The size of the bruise, depth of indentation on the wall, height of both from the floor, everything would be meticulously photographed, measured and compared. Meanwhile, as far as they could tell by simply looking, the injury matched the damage to the wall. She nodded then turned back to Miles who had resumed reporting on his initial findings.

'There are two head wounds,' he said. 'They could have been inflicted with the end of the weapon that was used on the back of his legs, but that's just more speculation. The first blow caused a relatively superficial injury, enough to break the skin and do some damage. It might have caused internal bleeding so could be more serious than at first appears, but I can't confirm that until I've had a look inside. Anyway, his assailant missed. Perhaps the victim saw it coming and rolled out of the way, because he was on the ground by then. The second blow – probably with the same weapon – that one did for him straight away.'

'Did for him?' Geraldine queried.

'It smashed his skull. That tells us his killer was strong. You can quote me on that.' He looked thoughtful. 'Unless the victim had osteogenesis imperfect – a brittle skull.'

'What are the chances of that?'

'It's very unlikely, but we can't rule it out completely yet.'

'So you think we're probably looking for a man then?'

Miles shrugged. 'You said it, not me. Although you can't rule out a female killer. There are some strong women around,' he added, a hint of bitterness in his voice.

Geraldine wondered what lay behind that comment, but there was no time to dwell on it. She and Miles both had work to do.

52

REG WAS LOOKING SERIOUS, reflecting the mood in the room. For the third time in the investigation they were facing a conundrum. There was no way Zak's fatal injuries could possibly have been self inflicted. Apart from any other consideration, there was no weapon anywhere along the top corridor or on the ground outside. Once again the killer had vanished impossibly, and without trace. The security guard couldn't be everywhere at once. His brief was to patrol the premises. Not only was there more than one exit from the building where the murder had been committed, but the college had more than one building.

The top corridor where Zak had been discovered early on Saturday morning was protected by electronic surveillance equipment. A team of constables was watching film of the lift and the staircase leading down to the ground floor. At ten o'clock the previous evening the cast and crew had left their rehearsal room. Only Zak had remained behind to fix some damage to the scenery. The others could be seen trooping along the corridor where someone had turned out the light before they all descended the stairs together. No one had returned upstairs. Reaching the ground floor, most of them had headed straight for the exit. A few had gone back into the main building, to the toilets or the bar. No one had gone back up to the top floor where Zak was working alone.

For nearly an hour the corridor had remained dark and empty. Two constables were watching the film in real time in case they missed anything by speeding it up. So far nothing had happened until shortly before eleven, when the door to the end rehearsal room opened. Zak appeared, silhouetted in the doorway. Then darkness returned. Suddenly the corridor was brightly illuminated showing

Zak standing by the light switch, his back to the camera. Before he could make his way to the door, a figure leapt out of the shadows and hit him on the back of his legs, felling him. The light flicked off. It was difficult to work out exactly what happened next. Even with the image enhanced, they could see only vague shapes moving around. Zak appeared as a dense patch on the floor, while a second figure bent over him.

'That's the killer,' Geraldine whispered.

They watched in horror as the hazy image hovered over Zak, waving its arms and striking down twice.

'Two blows to the head,' someone said as the figure turned and ran down the corridor, away from the camera. A second later they saw an outline in the doorway, lit up by light from the stairs. Then the figure disappeared.

'Rewind,' Geraldine said, 'and freeze the frame so we can examine it.'

The figure was visible briefly in the doorway. They could only see it from behind, shrouded in a long hooded coat.

'It's hopeless,' Bill said wearily. 'We've tried everything possible to enhance the image sufficiently to get a look at his face, but the only time we got him in enough light to see anything, all we can see is the back of his hood. There's no reflection in a window, nothing.'

'What happened after he reached the stairs? And why didn't he turn the lights out there as well?'

'The lights on the stairs can only be switched off by the maintenance staff.'

'So you must have got a good view of him on the stairs?'

Bill shook his head. 'No, I'm afraid not, because he didn't go down the stairs.'

'Well, the lift then?'

'No. The lift wasn't used.'

'I don't understand,' Geraldine said. She had a horrible feeling she already knew exactly what Bill was going to say next.

'No one used the lift and no one went down the stairs,' was how he put it.

'But there was no one there when the cleaners went in the next morning.'

'No one used the lift or left by the stairs this morning either.'

'So you're telling me the killer just vanished?'

Bill shrugged his shoulders. 'That seems to be what happened, yes ma'am.'

A team had been sent to search Zak's flat looking for names of contacts in whom he might have confided, drugs, or large sums of money, anything that looked irregular. A constable had returned from the search team to report back to the detective chief inspector. The momentary frisson of excitement faded as soon as she began to speak.

'All we could find was a load of rehearsal schedules and lists of props, paints, colours, scraps of fabric, his room was littered with them,' she said. 'But we did find this.'

She held up an envelope.

'What is it?' Reg asked.

Carefully removing a sheet of paper in her gloved fingers, the constable unfolded it and read aloud.

'"Hello Zak, It's a long time since we met. You won't remember me. You were just a baby when I saw you last. Your late mother was my sister. Perhaps I can take you out for dinner? Please give me a call on the number below and I hope we can spend some time together soon. And it's signed, Darius (your uncle)".'

'OK, follow that up,' Reg said, 'although it sounds innocuous enough. Is that what you came all the way back here to show us?'

'So far that's all we've found. He doesn't seem to have kept a personal diary, or a record of friends' names or anything like that. No phone either, so we reckon the killer must have taken it because he didn't have one on him, did he?'

'Still nothing to help us find his killer then,' Reg said miserably.

'Oh for crying out loud, this is getting ridiculous,' Sam burst out. 'What are we dealing with here? The invisible man?'

No one answered. Somehow Sam's outburst didn't sound as far-fetched as it should have done.

Only one thing was clear. All the victims had been directly involved with Piers. Sam insisted he couldn't have killed his own son, but Reg wasn't so sure.

'I think that's crazy!' Sam insisted.

'Let's not be under any illusion that this killer is sane,' Jayne said.

She smiled at Reg like an indulgent mother amused by something her child had said. Geraldine could see Sam bristling with irritation at the profiler's patronising tone.

'I agree with Sam,' Geraldine said firmly. 'This was a vicious brutal murder. The victim was beaten to death. And it was carefully planned. The killer knew where Zak would be –'

'Unless he stumbled on him by chance,' someone said.

For a moment no one spoke. They really had no idea why any of the victims had been killed.

'No,' Geraldine said firmly. 'The killer must have worked out in advance how to get in and out of the building. That couldn't have happened by chance. So he was familiar with the set up there. He would have needed a swipe card to get in, and he'd worked out his escape route, whatever it was.'

Jayne stepped forward to stand at Reg's side. He shifted to make room for her, as though they were joint senior investigation officers.

'It's quite feasible for a man to kill his own son. There are plenty of precedents –'

'Please don't quote them all at us,' Sam muttered under breath.

Jayne ignored the muted interruption and continued. 'It's not unknown. Remember we're dealing with someone who is seriously unbalanced.'

'I wish she'd lose her balance and fall flat on her face,' Sam whispered in Geraldine's ear.

Geraldine couldn't help smiling. When she had first arrived in London, alone, she had been grateful to Sam who had been kind enough to befriend her although they had only just met. After an initial misunderstanding, the acquaintance had developed into a genuine friendship. Geraldine really liked her colleague, although recently she had begun to see a different side to the sergeant. Sam had been quite vindictive in her remarks about Nick. She would have to be careful. One day Geraldine might have to write a reference for her, if Sam went chasing after promotion. There was now a question mark in Geraldine's mind about Sam's ability to get on with her colleagues. She hoped it wouldn't become a problem.

53

BUOYED UP BY JAYNE'S confident assertion that other men had been known to kill their own children, Reg remained convinced that Piers was guilty. When Geraldine challenged him for his evidence he looked irritated, although claiming to welcome her scepticism.

'That's your job, to challenge theories, Geraldine, and you do it very well. I'm impressed with your doggedness in questioning everything, but there's really no need to carry on now we know what's what. Once we've picked him up, I want to get inside his mind, find out what makes him tick, and Jayne will be able to help us with that.'

Sam threw her a sympathetic grimace. Geraldine knew straight away what the sergeant was thinking: Reg was a patronising moron.

Trying to ignore her superior officer's annoying manner, Geraldine wondered if Reg might actually be right. He was the senior investigating officer on the case, after all, and a chief inspector. An experienced detective, he must know that he was putting his reputation on the line by insisting Piers was guilty. If he was wrong, he would have to answer for it to those in authority further up the chain of command. All the same, she struggled to believe the arrogant director was capable of resorting to acts of such crass brutality, and he had appeared to care about his son.

Reg began listing his reasons for believing Piers was guilty. He finished by reminding Geraldine about the accusation that the suspect was dangerous.

'A girl came to the station to accuse him of violent assault,' he reminded her. 'She warned us he was going to kill someone, and now look what's happened.'

'The girl was frightened by a drunken brawl,' Geraldine replied. She had interviewed the girl. Reg hadn't even seen her. 'She was an aggrieved girlfriend. No, she wasn't even a girlfriend. It was nothing more than a casual relationship, but I dare say she was expecting more than that and came here out of spite when he dumped her. That's all it was. And we still haven't explained his disappearing acts from the crime scenes.'

Reg grinned. 'We're about to find out exactly how he managed that.'

He was excited and insisted on accompanying Geraldine to arrest Piers.

'It's about time we wrapped this up,' he said.

Geraldine kept her reservations to herself for now. She wasn't happy about the way things were developing, but she remembered her own conclusions about Sam and was reluctant to encourage her own detective chief inspector to write her off as a trouble maker who didn't support her senior investigating officer. And there was still the chance he might be right.

Geraldine thought Piers looked surprised to see her back on his doorstep. He maintained his outward composure until he saw Reg. Then he swore aggressively. He must have realised the presence of the detective chief inspector signalled that the visit had a serious import.

'We are here with a dual purpose,' Reg began in his high-handed way. 'May we come in?'

'You can say what you have to say here.'

Piers crossed his arms, adopting a belligerent pose as though to prevent Reg from entering the house.

'I'm afraid we have some bad news, Mr Trevelyan.'

Piers frowned. He hadn't expected that.

'It concerns your son.'

'Zak?' Piers started forward. 'Zak? What's the stupid boy done now?'

When he heard the news that his son was dead his expression didn't alter, but all the colour drained from his face. He stood absolutely still. With his pale face and rigid figure he could have been turned to stone.

'Zak dead?' he repeated at last. 'No, I don't believe it.'

'I'm afraid so.'

Piers seemed to crumple.

'He was all I had. He was my son.'

With a curious animalistic wail he doubled over suddenly as though he had been kicked in the guts. He didn't even remonstrate when Reg arrested him on suspicion of murder. Geraldine felt a rush of pity for this man who was accustomed to being in control.

Reg ushered his suspect down the path towards the car. Piers' hands were visibly trembling, and he walked with a shaky gait. He seemed to want to talk about Zak, but his words were incoherent.

'We didn't always see eye to eye. But we were – we had a strong relationship. Our bond – Oh God, my son, my son –'

Reg gazed speculatively at the bereaved father as though calculating how genuine his reaction was. Geraldine saw the anguish in his eyes and felt like crying herself. She wondered if anyone could be that good an actor.

'He was my son,' he repeated then went on with a sudden burst of energy, 'Who did this? Who?' He gasped like a man drowning. 'Where is he? Where is my son? I want to see my son.'

'Of course. We'll take you to him now. We need a formal identification.'

'Identification?'

'Mind your head, sir,' Reg said, gesturing for Piers to climb into the car.

By the time they reached the mortuary, Piers had recovered his outward equanimity, his face had regained its natural hue, and he had stopped shaking.

'You need someone to identify the body?' he asked with a return of his characteristic authority. 'So you're not even certain it's my son. This could be a mistake. It might not be him at all.'

All at once he grew talkative, and slightly hysterical. He didn't once refer to Zak by name, as though keeping his name out of the discussion might somehow protect the boy.

The visit to the mortuary was painful as such visits usually were. Reg had returned to work leaving Geraldine to make the arrangements. By the time they reached the viewing room, Piers had persuaded himself the body couldn't possibly be his son. Even Geraldine's gentle reminder that she had met Zak didn't shake his conviction.

'You didn't know him, not really. You'd only met him briefly a couple of times. It's easy to be mistaken. It could be anyone,' he insisted, with unnatural composure. 'No one could want to harm Zak, unless –'

'Unless?'

He turned troubled eyes to Geraldine. 'Unless someone wanted to hurt me.'

Geraldine shook her head, astonished by his narcissism. He really seemed to believe the world revolved around him.

Piers didn't speak. There was no need. As soon as he caught sight of his dead son his mask of control dissolved, every muscle taut as he struggled not to break down completely. He nodded once and turned away, unable to look at the body. He didn't cry, but tears slid down his cheeks. Zak was covered up to his chin. Only his face had been uncovered for the identification. He had been cleaned up but his head was shaved, exposing ghastly bruising and pulpy skin where he had been beaten to death. Piers didn't say a word as she led him back to the waiting car. He didn't protest when she handcuffed him before manoeuvring him into the back seat. He seemed completely stunned.

As they drove back to the station, Geraldine pondered over what Piers had said earlier. She had dismissed it as narcissistic fantasy. But if anyone had wanted to hurt Piers, they couldn't have achieved their objective with greater success. Anna, Bethany, and now Zak – was it possible they had been killed in a macabre crusade against the one man who had cared for them all? The shattered man in handcuffs might not be the killer as Reg believed. He might be the victim.

54

Geraldine was surprised to see Piers' solicitor was a young blonde who looked as though she had just stepped off a film set. A closer look revealed a sharpness in her expression that put Geraldine on her guard. She explained that Piers' solicitor had sent her.

'Terry is away,' she explained.

The lawyer was docile enough while Reg began to question her client. His initial shock had quickly given way to anger.

'I'll say it again, Inspector. If you really think I killed my son, you must be completely barking. It's a monstrous suggestion. He was my son.'

Despite the circumstances, Geraldine felt a flutter of excitement as she gazed into his compelling eyes. Notwithstanding his age, there was something undeniably seductive about him.

'Let's go over this one more time,' Reg said, firmly stepping in to assert his authority over the situation.

'My client isn't going to repeat himself interminably,' the solicitor announced in a penetrating, nasal voice.

Reg ignored her. 'Last night,' he said. 'Between ten and twelve. Tell me again where you were.'

'I was at home and before you ask again, I wasn't alone. I've already told you Gemma was with me. We were going through an audition piece she's preparing. You can ask her.'

'We intend to. Where can we find her?'

Like all the girls involved with Piers, Gemma was young and pretty. It didn't take Geraldine long to confirm that she had spent Friday evening with him, 'rehearsing a speech'. She had arrived at his house shortly before eight. When Geraldine asked what time she had left, the girl coloured slightly.

'I stayed there.'

'All night?'

'Yes. It was a long script –'

'I'm sure it was. Now think carefully before you answer, Gemma. Did Piers leave the house at any time during the evening?'

'No.'

'Are you quite sure?'

'Yes.'

'There's no possibility he could have slipped out without you noticing?'

But Geraldine knew it was hopeless.

Back at the station, she reported back to Reg.

'Was she lying, do you think?'

Geraldine shrugged. 'I don't think so, but who knows? It's impossible to say for certain. I mean, I could imagine him being very persuasive, and doubtless he can pick a young woman who's easy to manipulate from his army of hangers on.'

Reg nodded. 'Yes he seems to have no problem attracting women.'

The unexpected bitterness in his voice startled Geraldine. She wondered whether his opinion of Piers might subconsciously be influenced by envy. A rumour had been circulating that Reg's wife had left him. Geraldine didn't know if there was any substance to the claim. If it was true, it might account for the detective chief inspector's angry insistence that Piers was guilty. More likely, he was under pressure from his boss to sort out the high profile murder case.

Certainly Piers had been closely associated with all three victims. Geraldine wondered if Gemma might be next.

'Would you like me to talk to him? He might be more open when he's talking to a woman.'

'Go on then. See what you can find out. I didn't get anywhere with him.' Reg glanced at his watch. 'That bloody brief of his has gone so now would be a good time.'

With a nod to show she understood, Geraldine hurried away to speak to Piers. She found him slumped on the bench in his cell. He appeared to be dozing as she went in and didn't stir when she made no attempt to close the door quietly so as not to disturb him.

She called his name and he opened one eye a slit.

'Mmm?'

There was something reptilian about him as he stared at her.

'Mr Trevelyan,' she repeated, leaning forward confidentially. 'You mentioned you thought your girlfriends and your son might have been murdered as a way of getting at you.'

'Bethany wasn't my girlfriend,' he protested wearily, but Geraldine took no notice.

'Can you think of anyone who might have wanted to hurt you?'

He shook his head and closed his eyes again, leaning his head right back so that he was facing the ceiling.

'You must have rivals who are jealous of your brilliant talent and success.'

Geraldine forced herself to appear enthusiastic, as though meeting Piers was the highlight of her life. If it would help her to worm the truth out of him, she was happy to toady to his huge ego. She hoped she hadn't laid it on too thick, but he was accustomed to adulation and took her flattery at face value.

His shoulders relaxed slightly as he said, 'The women who imagine they have a grievance against me are legion.' He sat up and gave a resigned smile. 'There's not a great deal I can do about it. When you have talent like mine, you have to pay the price.'

Geraldine ignored that and pressed on, reminding Piers that he had suspected the killings might actually be veiled attacks against him.

'Yes,' he agreed. 'That's possible. Especially now.'

She understood he was referring to the death of his son.

'Does that mean you have an idea who might be carrying out these attacks?'

He looked thoughtfully at her for a second, holding her gaze, before answering.

'If I had the faintest idea who was responsible for the deaths of my son, and of a woman I loved, do you really think I would hesitate for one moment to tell you everything I could? I wonder what you people think of me, really I do. You must think I'm some kind of monster.'

'Mr Trevelyan, if you didn't kill them, we need your help to try and figure out who did.'

'You really have no idea who's responsible?'

'Honestly? No. Do you?'

He shook his head. 'How can I help?'

'There must be a reason why someone has suddenly started targeting people close to you. We need a list of anyone who might have held a grudge against you, particularly anyone who might have felt slighted recently. We're already checking those with a history of violence lately released from prison who might have had contact with you in the past.'

He nodded. 'I understand. I'll let you have a list of names as soon as I can come up with one, although I might need to go home to check.'

'Did Zak have any particular friends he might have confided in? A favourite tutor perhaps? Or an old school friend?'

Piers thought for a moment. 'Not that I'm aware of. He didn't really confide in me. You know what teenagers are like.'

When Geraldine asked him what he knew about Darius Cooper he blinked in surprise.

'Cooper?' he repeated with a puzzled frown. 'I haven't heard that name in a long time. Darius was my second wife's brother. He's Zak's uncle. We lost touch a long time ago, when Ella died.' He sighed, and repeated sadly, 'a long time ago.'

'What can you tell me about him?'

'Why do you want to know?'

Geraldine repeated her question and he shook his head.

'To be honest, I can't remember him that well. I couldn't even tell you if he's still alive. He probably died during a stunt. But like I said, I haven't seen him for about fifteen years. So, what can I tell you about him? Well, I remember he was very protective of Ella, my second wife.' A wistful expression crossed his face, softening the shrewdness in his eyes. 'Not that I blamed him for that. Ella was – special.' He sighed. 'After she died we never saw him again. He didn't even turn up to her funeral.'

'One last question. Is there anyone you can think of who has unexpectedly appeared, or reappeared, in your life recently? Anyone from the past who might have been harbouring a grudge against you for some reason?'

He shook his head. 'A few young girls.'

'We're ruling out anyone below about five foot ten. We believe the killer is around six foot, though that's not definite, but we think it's someone fairly tall which suggests we may be looking for a man.' She wasn't sure if she was giving too much away but continued anyway. 'If you've upset a tall woman in the last few weeks –'

'I'll add her name to the list,' he agreed thoughtfully.

55

DARIUS COOPER LOOKED REMARKABLY like his nephew. He had the same olive complexion, dark hair and beautiful black eyes, very like Geraldine's own. But where Zak had been slim and delicate, his uncle was slender yet muscular. Despite this, there was something effeminate about him that she couldn't quite identify. Wiry and lithe, he moved with the grace of a dancer. He described himself as retired, so she was surprised to see how young he looked. He couldn't have been much over forty.

'I'm sorry to tell you I have some bad news,' she said, after introducing herself.

'Do come in, Inspector.'

'It's about your nephew.'

'Zak? What's happened? Is he in trouble?'

Piers had asked a similar question. It was a natural enough reaction on learning the police were involved with a nineteen-year-old boy.

'There's really no easy way to say this. I'm sorry to tell you he's dead.'

'Dead? I don't understand. I saw him the other day and he was fine –' He broke off, frowning. 'How did it happen?'

Geraldine explained.

Darius looked shocked. 'And all this took place at his drama school, you say?'

'Yes.'

'That's terrible.'

'Terrible anywhere.'

'Of course, of course. What I meant was that his drama school should have been a safe place. I mean, you hear of young men being mugged on the streets but inside the drama school – I can't believe it. Zak wasn't the sort of boy to get into fights.'

'It doesn't appear to have started as a fight. He was attacked as he was leaving a rehearsal.'

'Why didn't anyone stop it?'

'He was alone at the time. The rest of the cast had left.'

'But why would anyone do such a thing? What motive could they possibly have? Was it a robbery?'

'We don't know.'

'But you must know who did it?'

Geraldine shook her head. 'Not yet. But we will.'

'Of course, of course. If there's anything I can do to help, although I didn't know anyone at the drama school.'

Geraldine was relieved to see he was taking the news calmly, because she wanted to question him further. If Zak had confided in him, Darius might be able to pass on useful information.

She followed him into a small poorly lit dining room, sparsely furnished with pine seats and matching table. The windows were covered with slatted blinds instead of curtains, which added to the bare appearance of the room. It was more like an office than a home, but not without a functional attraction of its own. She wondered whether to put up similar blinds in her own spare room at home, as they took their seats facing one another across the table.

'Were you close to your nephew?'

'Close? No, I can't say we were close, not really. I was a regular visitor to the house when he was a baby, but after my sister died I lost touch with his father and didn't see the boy again until recently. I was hoping we might build a relationship, for my dead sister's sake. She would have liked me to make an effort with him. But we'd only just met up again.'

'Did you and his father fall out over something? Mr Trevelyan can be quite overbearing,' she added, aware that she was being deliberately provocative.

'No, it was nothing like that. It was just that there was no particular reason why Piers and I *should* see each other. We never fell out, but we weren't particularly friendly either. It was my sister who used to invite me over, and when she died – well, I just never went round there any more. You know how it is.'

Geraldine nodded. She was thinking about her own sister. It would be so easy for them to drift apart without Geraldine ever building a meaningful relationship with her niece. It was bound to become more difficult as the years passed. She asked what had prompted Darius to contact his nephew after so many years. It must have taken a certain amount of determination to risk the humiliation of a rebuff after so long an estrangement.

'I read about that poor girl, Anna Porter, in the papers.'

As the star of a popular television series, Anna's death had been all over the news.

'When I saw Piers' name linked to the case, I couldn't help wondering if my nephew needed help. The poor boy had already lost his mother when he was still just a baby.' Zak sighed. 'I felt I owed it to my sister to check he was all right. I read somewhere in one of the papers that Piers had a son called Zak who was studying at a drama school in Gower Street. You know how the papers love to publish everything they can discover about people, even when it's not true. Anyway, I wrote to Zak care of the drama school, on the off chance the paper had actually got it right. He'd be the sort of age to be studying there, so it wasn't that much of a long shot. And if I'd got it wrong, well, my note would end up in the bin and I'd hear no more about it. But it ended up at the right address. My note reached him and he got in touch. He was really keen to meet me. I think he wanted to ask me about his mother.' He smiled. 'It was simple really. We hit it off straight away. He was a great kid.' His smile disappeared abruptly. 'First the mother, then the son. What a waste. You know, he wasn't that much younger than Ella was when she died. She was only twenty-two.'

Geraldine stayed sitting in Darius's living room for a while, listening to him reminisce about his dead nephew. While he couldn't speak highly enough of Zak and his artistic talent, he was dismissive of Piers as a father.

'Don't get me wrong,' he added hurriedly, after he had laid into Piers for neglecting his son. 'Piers has worked damn hard to get where he is –'

'Where is that, exactly?'

'He's right at the top in the world of theatre, controlling budgets that would make your eyes water. And he's made a name for himself. Everyone's heard of Piers Trevelyan, in film and theatre at least. Any time they want to cast an English actor in a Hollywood films or series, he's the one they call on to find the actors they want. That's how big he is. You have to admire the guy. Credit where it's due.'

When Geraldine asked how he knew so much about his ex-brother-in-law if they had lost contact, Darius explained that he was 'in the business' as well.

'Are you an actor?'

He smiled weakly. 'I used to do jobs for actors, as a kind of extra.'

When Geraldine asked him to explain, he became irritatingly self-effacing.

'It's not that interesting,' he replied, 'and anyway, I've retired. Look, I'm sorry if that sounds rude but you have just told me that my nephew's been murdered. It's not an easy thing to hear. So if you don't mind, I'd rather not answer any more questions.'

Disappointed, Geraldine could only thank him for his time and leave.

56

AFTER WRITING UP HER report on her meeting with Darius, Geraldine had a meeting with Reg and then went home. It was early but she was feeling tired, and there was nothing urgent waiting for her attention. The CCTV footage of all three crime scenes was being watched once again by teams of officers. She could have joined them, but she wouldn't notice anything they couldn't observe for themselves. They didn't need her looking over their shoulders. Sam had warned her before that she was gaining a reputation for refusing to delegate. At first Geraldine had been taken aback by her sergeant's allegation. She had never realised how controlling she could be. But when she had thought about it, she had to acknowledge the justice of the accusation.

Ever since Sam had pointed it out, Geraldine had been making a conscious effort to be more relaxed about trusting her colleagues, recognising that she didn't need to do everything herself. It wasn't easy to admit that she wasn't indispensable. Still, sharing responsibility certainly made her life easier, and allowed her to step away from the case and think clearly. A few years ago she wouldn't have considered taking an evening off in mid-investigation. Even now she wasn't sure she would have relaxed her attitude, if Sam hadn't spoken so frankly. There were two sides to Sam's outspokenness. While she risked getting herself into trouble, at least she dared to tell Geraldine the truth.

She had just climbed out of the bath when her phone rang. Feeling unusually relaxed she was tempted to ignore it, which was strange because they were halfway through an investigation and getting nowhere. She should have been tearing her hair out in frustration.

Instead she felt curiously calm. She recognised the voice on the phone at once.

'How about next weekend?' Celia asked.

'What?'

'Next weekend. Say yes, please, Geraldine, it would mean so much to her.'

'Hang on,' she interrupted with a nervous laugh. 'What's that about next weekend?'

Celia joined in the laughter, but Geraldine could hear exasperation in her voice when she spoke again.

'You keep promising to have Chloe to stay and you keep on letting her down.'

Since the death of their mother – Celia's birth mother and Geraldine's adoptive mother – Celia had been desperate to persuade Geraldine to spend time with her niece.

'I can't fill mum's place,' Geraldine had said, but Celia insisted it was important for Geraldine to develop a relationship with Chloe.

Geraldine was about to protest that the following weekend was impossible. She was in the middle of an investigation and couldn't even consider inviting Chloe to stay. She might be called into work at any time.

'You're entitled to some time off,' Celia was saying, 'and Chloe's growing up so fast. It won't be long before she doesn't even want to come and stay with you. Right now she's so excited at the idea, but soon she won't want to spend a weekend with an old aunt. You'll be asking her to come and see you and she'll be busy with her own social arrangements. You need to establish a relationship with her while you can, but you hardly ever see her any more. You're like a stranger.'

It was true. Geraldine had never spent much time with her sister and niece, but at least until recently they had all lived in Kent, not too far apart. She had been able to pop over and see them for quick visits when she was busy at work, taking Chloe to the shops or the cinema. Since her move to London she had seen even less of them than before.

Celia wasn't the only person to accuse Geraldine of being a workaholic. Sam had remonstrated with her more than once for spending too much time at her desk.

'The reports will still be there in the morning,' she had said. 'You don't have to dot every I and cross every T before you go home today.'

'You don't know what else might come in tomorrow,' Geraldine had pointed out. 'It's always best to keep on top of things.'

'Not if you end up so knackered you can't think straight.'

Irritated, Geraldine had mocked Sam's advice about developing a sensible work-life balance.

'So now you're a life coach, are you? Going around telling other people how to live their lives?'

Geraldine wished she hadn't been so harsh with Sam. The sergeant was only trying to be helpful. Geraldine remembered her former detective chief inspector, who had devoted her life to the job. She had been a first rate detective, and a brilliant senior officer. Focusing on her work to the exclusion of anything else had been fine – until the day she had to retire. Geraldine had seen her a few months after she left the force and had been shocked at the change in her former colleague. She seemed to have aged decades in a few months, as though she had nothing to live for any more.

'OK,' she said, surprising herself, 'next weekend it is.'

'I won't tell Chloe yet, in case you cancel again.'

'I won't,' Geraldine promised. 'That is, not unless it's unavoidable.'

'At least you're making an effort,' Celia conceded. 'That's something, I suppose.'

She didn't sound entirely convinced.

57

EVEN SUPPOSING CHERYL'S ACCUSATION against Piers was true, it was no proof that he had murdered two other girls, not to mention his own son. At most he might be charged with assault in the course of a drunken row with a girlfriend, but even that came down to her word against his. It would never reach court. Her allegation that he had thrown a bottle at her in a drunken rage was credible, but so was his rebuttal. He claimed she had been so drunk she had walked into a door and was set on revenge for his rejecting her advances. Maybe she was deliberately lying. It was possible she had persuaded herself it had really happened. It could equally well be true. Still, as far as the murder investigation was concerned, it was all just so much hot air.

Piers was at home when Geraldine called round to go through his list of possible enemies. At first she was encouraged to find he had come up with a few people he thought might have a grievance against him. Most were women and it didn't take long to rule a number of them out on the grounds of height. That left three women and two men who had worked with Piers, all of whom were over five foot ten.

'There could be hundreds more,' he added unhelpfully, 'maybe thousands. I come across a hell of a lot of people in my line of work, and they're not all what you might class as normal. These are just the first names I thought of, off the top of my head. But I can't believe any of them would have gone to such lengths,' he added, shaking his head. 'People in the entertainment industry might be unconventional, by your standards, but they're not bad people. To kill Anna and Bethany, and my son –'

She returned to the station with his revised list. A team of sergeants was despatched to investigate them, and establish their whereabouts at the time of the murders.

Geraldine would have preferred to be out questioning potential suspects herself, but as an inspector running a team she had to allocate some of her time to dealing with tedious paperwork.

'How's it all going?' Nick asked her as soon as she sat down. 'You look a bit low.'

'It's going slowly. And now I've got all this lot to sort out.'

Thumping a pile of papers with the flat of her hand, she couldn't help smiling at his comical grimace.

'Fancy a drink tonight to mull it over?'

'I would have loved to, but I've arranged to see a friend tonight. Maybe another time?'

She hoped she hadn't sounded too keen about accepting an invitation for a casual drink in order to talk about work.

'How about tomorrow then?'

She nodded, turning away so he wouldn't see how pleased she was.

'OK. Tomorrow it is.'

Geraldine settled down to work, feeling happier. That evening she had arranged to meet with her former sergeant, Ian Peterson, who was coming to see her flat for the first time. So far only her sister and niece had seen her new home. Now she was quietly excited about showing the place off to her friend. She had spent a couple of hours tidying up especially, shoving clothes into her wardrobe, and cleaning the kitchen. Then the following evening she was going out with Nick. Life was looking up.

She had no intention of telling Sam about her plans to go out with Nick again. There was no point in provoking another tirade from her touchy sergeant. Usually good-humoured, there was something about Nick that put Sam in a temper. They were sitting in the canteen together having a break for tea, when, as luck would have it, Nick passed right by their table. He paused. Sam looked away pointedly as Geraldine smiled at him.

'Where do you fancy going tomorrow night?' he asked, casting a sly glance at the sergeant.

Geraldine sensed Sam bristle as she replied, 'I don't mind.'

'Same place then?'

'That sounds fine to me.'

He sauntered off, whistling.

'What was that all about?'

Even though she was aware that Sam detested Nick, Geraldine was taken aback by the anger in her voice. Sam was leaning forward, her shoulders raised, her voice tense with emotion.

Geraldine put down her tea.

'Leave it, Sam. This isn't something we're going to discuss.'

Sam glared at her, but she spoke gently. 'I'm just worried about you, Geraldine. I'm only trying to look out for you.'

'Yes, I appreciate that, but I'm not some naïve teenager in need of advice, thank you.'

Sam heaved a sigh. 'We all need advice sometimes.'

Geraldine frowned, vexed that Sam had made her feel like an arrogant idiot who thought she always knew best.

'Yes, that's very true. I know we all need advice at times. This just isn't one of those times.'

'I think it is.'

'And I think it's time for you to mind your own bloody business.'

With that, Geraldine stood up and strode out of the canteen.

Ian arrived so promptly she thought he must have been waiting outside in the car. She buzzed him in and took a couple of beers from the fridge while he was making his way up to her flat. As they exchanged greetings, she was relieved to see that he looked like the Ian she remembered, animated and cheerful. It didn't take long to give him a tour of her new home: kitchen, bathroom, living room, bedroom and spare room.

'That's it,' she concluded as they returned to the living room and she poured beer into two glasses and handed him one.

'It's really nice here,' he said.

She knew him well enough to recognise his praise was genuine.

'Thank you.'

'I mean it, Geraldine, I'm really pleased for you. It's great. And

I'll tell you something else. You don't know how lucky you are to have a place like this to yourself.'

'I'd rather have someone to share it with.'

He raised his eyebrows and she felt herself blush.

'I mean, living on your own, it's not ideal, is it?'

He sighed and put down his glass. 'The alternative can be a whole lot worse.'

'Yes, of course, I know it could be worse. I wouldn't want to be stuck with the wrong person –' Too late she broke off, afraid she had put her foot in it.

'Let's not talk about personal stuff tonight,' he said. 'I don't want to spoil the evening boring you with my problems.'

She nodded. 'I'm here if you ever want to talk about it –'

'I know, but there's nothing to talk about. What I mean is, sometimes talking doesn't help.'

'OK, let's eat then. Are you hungry?'

'Starving, and something smells good.'

She smiled. 'Spaghetti carbonara,' she said. 'Home made.'

'My God, that's my favourite. How did you know?'

'I have met you before.'

They exchanged a smile.

While they were eating, they talked about her new life in London, and the colleagues they had both worked with in Kent. They discussed his promotion and exchanged views on the cases they were both working on. Ian's investigation sounded fairly straightforward, although he confessed to Geraldine that he had his reservations about the guilt of their main suspect. He was fascinated to hear about her current case.

'It sounds like a Sherlock Holmes mystery,' he said, his eyes alight with excitement. 'The Case of the Vanishing Murderer! What fun!'

Laughing, she scolded him for joking about it. 'This is serious, Ian. It's no laughing matter. Three people are dead and we've still not got the foggiest idea who's responsible, and the crime scenes make no sense. How is he getting away?'

'That's certainly some stunt,' he agreed.

They passed a pleasant evening. Ian left early to drive back to Kent and Geraldine cleared up and went to bed. She was tired and thought an early night would do her good, but she couldn't sleep. Not knowing what was making her jittery wound her up even more. First she decided she must be feeling nervous about seeing Nick outside of work again, and wondered if Sam knew more about him than she was letting on. Then she had an uneasy feeling she had missed something in Piers' list. A team of sergeants was checking through the names, but she decided to take a look at it herself in the morning. Under pressure, she could no longer contain her need to control the investigation. Almost a month into the case, the mystery had grown more baffling at every turn. With three people murdered, it was anyone's guess when another victim might be discovered.

58

GERALDINE WOKE EARLY THE next morning. Having lain in bed worrying about the investigation for what felt like hours, but was in reality only about forty minutes, she got up and made herself an unusually large breakfast. It was too much for her so she ended up throwing half of it away, which didn't improve her mood. She would have liked to look her best that day as she was planning to spend time with Nick later on, but instead she looked dreadful; tired and wan with grey circles under her eyes. Too late she regretted having spent the previous evening with Ian, although she knew that wasn't the reason for her looking and feeling so lousy. They hadn't drunk much because Ian had a long drive home, and he had left her quite early. The problem was that she had passed a disturbed night. She felt as though she could do with a good sleep but there was a day's work to get through before she went out with Nick. It was only a casual drink, she reminded herself. But it was a long time since she had spent time with an eligible man – if he really was unattached. Sam had implied he was still married and regularly unfaithful to his wife, the most despicable kind of womaniser.

She was pleased Nick wasn't in the office when she arrived that morning. Geraldine usually arrived first as she liked to get in early to beat the rush hour. Her journey time could easily double if she left the flat after seven thirty. This morning she was at her desk by seven, starting to trawl through the statements made by the people named on Piers' list. It made tedious reading.

'On Friday evening I was babysitting for my sister's twins.'

'On Friday evening I was out for a drink with my mates.'

'On Friday evening I was running over lines with a friend.'

'On Saturday evening I was visiting my parents.'

'On Saturday night I was staying with a friend… out clubbing… at a hen night… at the theatre… at the cinema… at home with my flatmates.'

She yawned, struggling to focus on the screen. So far the sergeants who had been asking the questions had not stumbled on anything even vaguely curious. All the accounts had been verified with other witnesses. Not a single person was without an alibi for at least two of the evenings when Anna, Bethany and Zak had been killed. It had been a necessary but fruitless task for the sergeants to carry out in the first place, and completely pointless for Geraldine to double check.

Glancing over at his empty chair and untidy desk, her thoughts wandered to Nick. She wasn't sure she would want to embark on a serious relationship with him, and a casual fling with a colleague was never a good idea. There was far too much potential for disastrous consequences. The only reason she had even considered seeing him was that he was there and had professed to be interested in her. She wouldn't have picked him out in a crowd as particularly attractive, and she wasn't sure she trusted him, or even liked him. She turned her attention resolutely back to her work. By the time Nick arrived she was already tired of reading fatuous statements. Welcoming the distraction, she greeted him eagerly and was dismayed when he merely grunted in reply without even bothering to look up. Evidently he wasn't that interested in her after all. It wouldn't be the first time she had misread the signs, but it would be particularly galling to discover she had fallen out with Sam over nothing.

'Are we still on for tonight?' she asked.

He turned to face her and she was shocked to see that one half of his face was bruised and swollen.

'God, what happened to you?'

'Nothing,' he mumbled, adding after a brief awkward pause, 'I broke up a fight and got this for my pains.'

He gave a short angry laugh.

'What happened?'

Reluctantly, he explained that on his way home the previous

evening he had passed a group of teenage boys brawling in the street. He had stopped his car and gone to intervene, and one of the boys had socked him.

'Didn't you arrest him? Assaulting a police officer –'

'No. It wasn't like that. This,' he pointed to his injury, 'was an accident. He took a swing at the other boy and I got in the way. They were only about thirteen.'

'Even so.'

'They were just kids. When they realised what they'd done, they were so scared they were almost crying. I took the names of the two who had been fighting – the rest had scarpered as soon as they knew who I was. I scared the hell out of them, and then I let them go. There was no harm done.'

'Except to you. That's a nasty black eye you've got.'

'It's not the first time,' he told her with another laugh, 'these things happen. It could've been worse. Now, I don't know about you but I've got work to do.'

With that, he turned back to his desk and began typing furiously.

Nick was beginning his day's work while Geraldine was ready for a break. She went to see what Sam was doing and they went out to a nearby café together. Sometimes it was good to get away from the station, and Geraldine wanted to avoid Sam seeing Nick in his present state. Seated in a corner they discussed Piers' list of possible enemies. So far none of them was even a potential suspect as they each had a solid alibi for the times of at least two of the murders. Sam was sceptical about the whole idea.

'Three people killed just to punish one man?' she scoffed. 'Piers Trevelyan has got to be the most self-centred man ever, and that's saying something. Talk about thinking the world revolves around you. I see your precious Nick had another bust up with his wife,' she added, taking a sip of coffee, her eyes fixed on Geraldine.

Geraldine put her straight about the cause of Nick's black eye.

'He was only doing what any self-respecting officer should do.'

Sam rolled her eyes then leaned forward and spoke in a quiet, urgent tone.

'You know he hits his wife,' she said.

'No, I don't know that, and nor do you. Have you ever seen him hit her?'

'No, but –'

'Have you even met his wife?'

'No, but –'

'It's just idle chatter then.'

'Everyone knows it.'

'If you will listen to unsubstantiated rumours –'

'I'm telling you –'

'Come on, I've told you before, it's not appropriate to talk about colleagues behind their backs like this, spreading malicious gossip. And anyway, it's time we got back to work.'

'But I haven't finished –' Sam gestured at her plate.

'I'll see you later then.'

Inwardly fuming, Geraldine stood up and left.

59

FROM THE RIGHT, AND the front, Nick was virtually unrecognisable. His right eye was usually slightly closed in a permanent mischievous wink. Now it was swollen completely shut, and hideously discoloured with black and purple bruising. The suggestion of violence about his injury made him look vicious, so that it was suddenly easy to believe he was a wife beater. Geraldine was shocked to realise how far her impression of people was influenced by their appearance. She knew Nick. He was a decent officer who dedicated his life to supporting his fellow man, protecting the innocent, preserving law and order, and serving justice, like almost every other officer she had ever known. But if she had passed him on the street right now, without having met him before, she would have assumed he was a thug who went around getting into fights.

'You sure you don't mind going out with me looking like this?' Nick asked her when it was time to leave.

'Don't be daft. Shall I drive?'

He nodded his thanks then winced when the movement hurt his eye.

As they walked down the corridor together to the exit, several male colleagues called out to Nick, trying to wind him up, ribbing him about his face. Nick smiled in resignation. A bit of good-natured banter was inevitable, once he had gone into work with a black eye. Geraldine couldn't help noticing that a couple of female officers averted their eyes, as though they were embarrassed to be caught looking at him. They neither teased him nor expressed sympathy, but pointedly ignored him. Presumably they had been taken in by the rumours about Nick beating his wife. But they didn't know him. Geraldine glared at them but they weren't looking at her.

'You'll have to direct me,' she said as they set off. 'I can remember the general direction but not the last bit, after we turned off the A road.'

Nick leaned back and closed his eyes. He looked pale.

'Are you sure you're up for this?' she asked. 'I can easily turn round, or drop you home, if you're feeling rough. We can do this another time.'

'I'm fine,' he assured her. 'Just fine.'

They drove on in silence. Geraldine regretted not having insisted they postpone the outing. Nick was feeling rotten, she was preoccupied with the case she was working on, and it was going to turn into a dreary evening.

'Are you sure you're feeling up to it?'

'I thought we were just going for a drink,' he said, laughing. 'What else did you have in mind, Inspector?'

She relaxed when he started flirting with her. Perhaps it was just as well she hadn't insisted they cancel their date. He was an adult, after all. If he wasn't feeling well enough to go out, he would have said so. No one was holding a gun to his head. Even though nothing serious was likely to develop between them, at least they could pass a pleasant evening in one another's company. Besides, he was the ideal person for her to share her thoughts about her current investigation, which had hit a brick wall. As a fellow inspector, he understood her frustrations and anxieties, without her having to explain what she was going through. He had already come up with one helpful insight.

Comfortably settled in a corner of the pub, Nick quizzed her about her companion of the previous evening.

'He's just an old friend,' she said.

She felt a twinge of guilt. Ian's friendship deserved more than such a dismissive comment.

'Just an old friend? Why don't I like the sound of that?'

Geraldine laughed, ignoring a passing irritation. Her friendship with Ian was none of Nick's business. She wondered if he was signalling that he was interested in moving their relationship to a new level. She brushed off his questions and the conversation moved on to the fight he had dealt with.

They talked for a while about young people and what society had to offer them, disagreeing just enough to make for a stimulating debate.

'I know some people are dealt a lousy hand from birth,' Geraldine said. 'Of course it's not fair. As a society, we have a duty to try and give everyone a chance in life – an equal chance – but that's not going to happen, is it? Some people are born intelligent, or beautiful, or well off, and others aren't dealt any cards at all. But that doesn't mean people don't have to take responsibility for their own actions. Otherwise, what's our whole justice system about? You can't punish someone for committing a crime at the same time as claiming they're not responsible for their own actions.'

'I can see I'm never going to convince you,' he said at last.

'No.'

'But we've got time for another drink?'

'I'll agree to that. I've got all evening.'

They smiled at one another and he went off to the bar, bringing back a menu.

As they were eating, Nick returned to the subject of the friend Geraldine had seen the previous evening. His interest had been flattering to begin with, but his questioning was becoming intrusive.

'Where did he take you?'

'We went to my flat.'

Nick raised his eyebrows as though she had admitted something shocking.

'He's an old friend, a colleague I worked with in Kent.'

She was about to add that her friend was married. Just in time she remembered that Nick was too. 'It's really none of your business who I see, so can we drop it? There are more interesting things to talk about than my cooking.'

She tried to make light of it, but she was growing angry.

When they left, a light snow was falling for the first time that year, leaving a dusting of white on the roadside verges. The trees looked ethereal and the scene was magical. Her good temper restored, Geraldine drove slowly along the slippery country lane until they reached the main road. Nick leaned back, eyes closed, and appeared to fall asleep. She realised he was probably in some pain and felt guilty about being fractious with him. Overall she had enjoyed the evening and hoped he had too. She smiled to herself. Socialising for two evenings in a row was unusual for her. It was just a pity that both of her male companions were married. She glanced sideways at Nick, wondering about the nature of his relationship with his wife. He had asked about her friendship with Ian, but she hadn't felt confident enough to challenge him about his wife in return. She wondered if she already knew the answer, but didn't want to hear her suspicions confirmed. Sam's words raced around in her head: 'Nick had another bust up with his wife… he hits his wife… everyone knows… '

In many ways, she was better off being single. Relationships only caused problems. Nick claimed to be separated from his wife, and Ian didn't seem to be happy in his marriage. She was genuinely fond of Ian, and concerned that he was miserable. He hadn't wanted to talk about Bev which meant she had more time to tell him about the investigation into Anna, Bethany and Zak. He had listened intently, keen to help her make sense of the Case of the Vanishing Murderer. During the course of the evening, she had a feeling he had said something significant, if she could only remember what it was. At her side, Nick began snoring gently.

60

HAVING DROPPED NICK BACK at the station to collect his car she set off back to her flat. She was slightly put out by his insisting he was fine to drive, although his bruised face was clearly bothering him. As he drove away she realised she didn't even know where he lived. The more evasive he was about his situation at home, the more Sam's accusation bothered her. But she had only been out for a casual drink with him. He hadn't even stopped to kiss her goodbye, had barely thanked her for the lift, before he had sloped off. With a shrug, she spun her wheel and drove away. Right now she had something more important to think about than Nick. As soon as she reached home, she brewed a pot of tea and sat down at the table in her living room. She hadn't yet decided whether to buy a desk for her spare room. Using it as an office was the obvious way to make use of the space, but at the moment she was keeping a camp bed made up in there for when Chloe came to stay. Meanwhile, the only place she could work comfortably was on her living room table.

The trouble was that now she was ready to start, she wasn't sure what she was looking for. All she knew was that Ian had made a comment that had reminded her of something. Not having written a report on the evening she had spent with her friend, of course, she had no record of their conversation. However hard she tried, she couldn't remember what he had said. If she thought he might know what she was talking about, she would have called him, but she didn't even know what it was she wanted to ask. Yet she couldn't shake off the feeling that if she could only recall one random remark of his, she might be able to find a lead to unravelling the mystery. It would most likely turn out to be a wild goose chase, and was certainly too vague a hunch to share with anyone else, but she was at home on her own and unable to sleep. She had nothing better to do but hunt for this elusive lead. As long as she was looking, there was a chance she might stumble on something that would help them solve the mystery. So far they were casting about in the dark, hunting desperately for clues. This was as good a place to start as any.

Suspecting it might have something to do with Piers, she began by scanning through all of his statements. Nothing jumped out at her so she turned to Cheryl's accusation, and from there went on to read what Darius had said about his former brother-in-law. It had struck her as odd that Darius was so well-informed about Piers, but when she had pressed him he had admitted to being 'in the business.' He wasn't an actor but said he used to 'do jobs for actors.' She wondered if he had worked with Piers, perhaps without the knowledge of the casting director who wouldn't know the name of every member of the stage crew. He might have been stalking Piers behind the scenes for years, for some unknown reason. But that still didn't solve the problem of how the killer had disappeared from the crime scenes. She couldn't find Darius Cooper listed in any stage or film production, but it was possible he had never been credited, or he could have worked under a different name.

By now she was tired. She brewed herself a fresh pot of tea and made some toast, ready to continue searching. Having spent half the night poring over statements, pushing herself to keep going in case the next page might contain some dramatic revelation, her eyes kept closing. Once or twice she caught herself leaning forward in her chair, dozing. It was a struggle to focus on the screen. In the end she gave up and closed her screen. In the morning she would pick up where she had left off. Reluctantly she went to bed, leaving her tray of tea things on the table. She could clear that away in the morning. For now it was effort enough to get undressed and clean her teeth before she fell into bed. As soon as she pulled her duvet up to her chin, she felt herself drifting into a welcoming sleep.

Arriving at the office early next day, she had been looking through statements for two hours by the time Nick arrived. His black eye looked no better and he was clearly in a foul mood.

'Sorry to be uncommunicative, but I've got the mother of a headache,' were the only words he said to her all morning.

Preoccupied with work, Geraldine hardly noticed him. At lunch time Reg summoned her, demanding to know what she was doing. When she tried to explain, he complained she was wasting time going over old statements.

'I just get the feeling we're missing something,' she protested.

'Like the killer's name?'

'There's something staring us in the face, we've just got to find it,' she insisted.

He scowled at her. Like Nick, he seemed determined to be irascible. Even Sam was crabby, pointedly asking about her evening out with Nick, and commenting on his black eye.

Having looked through all of Piers' statements without finding what she was looking for, Geraldine resolved to go and see him again. After so many questions and interviews, it seemed unlikely she would learn anything new from him, but she couldn't think what else to do. Sam wanted to accompany her, but Geraldine couldn't face any more of the sergeant's snide remarks about Nick. Instead, she directed Sam to go and talk to Darius. There wasn't much point but it would give Sam something to do. Geraldine hoped it would take her mind off Nick and the gossip that surrounded him.

'Ask him what he knows about his brother-in-law, and find out what you can about his sister, and her marriage. Perhaps he'll say something that will help us nail Piers.'

'You said you thought Piers was innocent,' Sam pointed out.

'To be honest, I don't know what to think any more. I'll see you later.'

With any luck, by the time they met up again, Sam would have stopped griping about Nick.

Piers didn't seem to mind Geraldine calling on him again.

'You must be as keen as I am to find out who's behind all this insanity,' he said.

Geraldine went through the names he had given her, but it was a futile exercise. He had just come up with a list of people he thought might have a grudge against him. It soon became apparent why he had invited her in so readily. He wanted to talk to someone about his son. Geraldine listened patiently while he spoke of his pride in all that Zak had achieved, and his regret that they hadn't spent more time together.

'I suppose every parent feels this,' he said, 'but my work always got in the way. I never gave him the time he should have had with me, and now there's no more time to give him – it went by so quickly and now –' His voice shook and he broke off.

Geraldine thought about how quickly Chloe was growing up, and resolved that nothing would stop her seeing her niece at the weekend.

Piers was surprised when Geraldine told him Zak had been in contact with his uncle. He began to reminisce about Zak's mother, Ella, and her brother Darius. He spoke slowly, choosing his words with care. As she listened, Geraldine felt a growing sense of unease.

'It's not an easy thing to talk about, but it was all a long time ago.'

'What was?'

'Darius and Ella.'

'What about them?'

'Well, they had an odd sort of relationship, really. They'd lost their parents when they were children, and perhaps as a result of that they had become very close. But it was more than that, really.'

'What do you mean, more?'

'He was overly protective of her. I always thought there was something unnatural in the way he doted on her. Don't get me wrong, I'm not saying there was anything inappropriate going on. There was nothing sexual in their relationship, nothing like that. At least, I don't think there was. Ella was – pure – and anyway I had the impression he wasn't interested in women in that way. But he was obsessed with her. And then, after she died, we never saw him again. He didn't even come to her funeral. But I thought I'd already told you all this. '

'Can you tell me anything else about him?'

'What would you like to know?'

She shrugged. 'What did he do?'

'I thought I told you, he was a stunt man.'

All at once, a mist lifted in Geraldine's mind. Piers had unwittingly exposed the killer to her. He might have revealed the truth before, only the first time he had told her she hadn't been listening. That was what she had half-remembered, Ian's comment that it had been 'some stunt' for the killer to vanish from the scene of the crime. While they had been wracking their brains to discover how the killer had managed to get away from the crime scenes, the answer had been staring them in the face all the time. The one aspect of the case that had been a constant source of discussion and speculation had been telling them the killer's identity right from the start.

Only a stunt man could escape alive from a speeding car, climb safely off a bridge and out of a third floor window. And Darius was a retired stunt man nursing an insane hatred of Piers.

'How did Ella die?'

'She drowned in the bath.'

'At home?'

'Of course.'

'Were you in the house at the time?'

He frowned. 'Yes, I was, but if you think –'

Geraldine didn't wait to hear any more of his protestation. The important issue wasn't her conclusions, but those of Ella's brother. She ran from the room, grabbing at her phone. With trembling fingers she dialled Sam's number. There was no reply.

61

SAM FOUND A PARKING space opposite a school, several doors along from her destination. A light sleet was falling as she stepped out of the car and made her way towards the converted house where Darius occupied the first floor. Freezing droplets splashed around her. A few hit her face like icy prickles. Although it was only four o'clock, it was overcast and murky as she hurried along the wet pavement. Reaching her destination, she paused with unexpected misgiving. The house seemed to loom darkly over her. She shivered and hurried up to the front door. At first no one answered. Just as she was about to turn away, she heard footsteps and the door swung open.

A tall, willowy man stared coldly at her as she introduced herself.

'I've already spoken to your people.'

There was something forbidding in his voice, but Sam was used to encountering all sorts of reactions from the public when she went calling. Reminding herself he might have useful information about Piers' past, she adopted a conciliatory tone.

'I know, and we're very grateful for your co-operation, Mr Cooper. I'm really sorry to trouble you again, but I'm here to ask you a few questions about your former brother-in-law, if that's all right with you.'

He was alert now, leaning forward, his black eyes alive with interest. A faint smile curled the corners of his thin lips.

'You're investigating Piers Trevelyan? Well, come in, come in.'

He stepped to one side so she could enter. Gratefully she went in.

'It's cold out there,' he said, with a nod towards the street.

'Freezing,' she agreed, rubbing her hands together as she

followed him past an internal door and up a narrow carpeted staircase.

They sat down in a sparsely furnished dining room. Darius faced her across the table, leaning on his elbows and watching her as she took out her notebook. There was an air of expectation about his demeanour that would have been surprising, considering he claimed not to have seen his former brother-in-law for over fifteen years, but she understood he was keen to discover who had murdered his nephew. Nevertheless, the intensity of his gaze unnerved her as she fumbled with her pen; her notebook slipped from her lap and fell to the floor with a muffled slap. Retrieving it, she mumbled an apology for keeping him waiting. He nodded with more than a hint of impatience.

'What do you want to know? I'll help you if I can.'

She began by offering him an open invitation to share his recollections of his former brother-in-law. To her relief he needed little prompting to talk about Piers, allowing her to focus on listening while discreetly jotting down notes. Initially reserved in his comments, he grew increasingly animated as he warmed to his topic, while his face contorted with misery.

'He was a vicious brute. It was positively criminal, the way he treated my sister. A decent person wouldn't treat a dog the way he treated her. Men like that shouldn't be allowed to marry. Believe me, you'd never guess what he was like from meeting him. All of you detectives, with all your insights, probably had him down as civilised. Certainly he gives that impression. That's how he wormed his way into my poor sister's affections. But once they were married, he showed his true colours.'

He heaved a deep sigh and rubbed his eyes with the back of his hand. Recovering, he continued his recitation.

'He was constantly running after other women – young girls, some of them. He used to bring them into the house while she was there, even when she was pregnant with his son. Can you believe that?'

Sam sympathised with the sad-eyed man facing her across the table who had been so attached to his sister. He had surely been devastated when she died.

'Your sister must have been very unhappy,' she said gently. 'But it must have helped her to know you cared about her. And her son would have been a comfort to her.'

He nodded without answering, too overcome with emotion to speak for a moment. Sam waited.

'I'm sorry,' he said. 'My sister was a beautiful woman, an angel. She didn't deserve what happened to her.'

Sam pressed him to explain what he meant by that.

'I don't want to talk about it.' He shook his head, and heaved another sigh. 'There was an inquest. But –'

Sam sat forward intrigued.

'An inquest into what?'

Darius looked surprised.

'I'm talking about Ella's death.'

'Go on,' she urged, wondering where this was going.

His voice rose in agitation. 'The fools said otherwise, but I know what happened.'

'Wasn't it an accident? I thought she drowned in the bath.'

'How many people drown in the bath?'

She pressed him to tell her how he knew, but he became increasingly hysterical and less and less coherent.

'He's evil. She was an angel, and he destroyed her. He took all the joy out of her life, and he destroyed her with his own hands.'

'Are you saying you think he *killed* your sister?'

Hearing disbelief in her voice, he sprang from his chair. 'You're like all the rest of them. I'll show you!' he cried.

Assuming he was leaving the room to fetch some photographs of his sister, Sam bent her head and began adding to her notes while he disappeared from view behind her.

A powerful arm pressed against her throat. Hard as metal, it constricted her breathing until she could no longer gasp for air. It was too late to fight against her assailant. Her arms flailed helplessly in the air, straining to make contact with any part of him. Vainly she tried to grab hold of him and scratch his skin while she still had any strength left. Her last thought before she hit the floor was that he had never even been a suspect.

62

GERALDINE STRUGGLED AGAINST A feeling of panic that threatened to overwhelm her ability to think clearly. She knew she would never forgive herself if anything happened to Sam as a consequence of her instructions. She reminded herself there was no proof that Darius had killed anyone. Summoning back up might turn out to be an embarrassing overreaction. But if her instinct was right then she had sent Sam to the killer's home, alone, and oblivious to the danger she might face when she arrived. Assuming Piers' account was trustworthy, Darius had been excessively attached to his sister. In her ignorance, Sam might follow Geraldine's instructions and enquire about Ella. As a rule the sergeant was able to take care of herself. Supple and strong, she was an expert in martial arts. But as far as she was aware, Darius wasn't even a suspect. He just happened to have known Piers in the past, so was in a position to offer helpful information. Sam might press him to talk about his sister's marriage, without suspecting her questions could provoke a violent reaction. Even someone skilled in self defence was at risk when an attack was unexpected.

Her mobile in her hand, Geraldine was on the point of contacting the station when her phone rang. Expecting to hear it was Sam returning her call, she was startled to recognise Nick's voice on the line.

'How's it all going?' he asked easily. 'Look, I just wanted to explain why I was a bit short with you earlier –'

'What?'

'This morning, when you wanted to have a chat –'

Geraldine interrupted him impatiently.

'Nick, I've got a bit of a situation here.'

She bit her lip, hearing her voice wobble. She had faced death several times in the course of her career, and not once had she faltered or given way to panic. After all, she was trained to maintain her composure under pressure. But this was different. In despatching Sam to question Darius, Geraldine had quite possibly sent the sergeant to her death.

'What's wrong? Is there anything I can do?' Nick asked.

Reaching a decision, Geraldine spoke rapidly. 'Sam Haley's gone to question a possible witness, Darius Cooper. I think he's our killer.'

She hoped desperately that she was wrong.

'What?'

'Don't talk, just listen. Meet me outside Cooper's flat in Frognal as soon as you can, and arrange for urgent back up. Tell them to wait nearby. No one's to do anything until I get there. He could be dangerous.'

She hung up without waiting for a reply.

There were no missed calls on her phone, which remained obstinately silent. If Sam was fine, she was certainly keeping quiet. The one hope was that there was no signal in Darius' flat. Geraldine imagined the conversation in Reg's office if that turned out to be the case.

'You summoned back up, and took another inspector off his case, because a possible witness from years ago had no phone signal in his flat?'

All the same, he would approve her decision. He might grumble about wasteful deployment of limited resources, but he would understand that she had no choice, faced with a potential threat to the safety of a fellow officer.

The traffic moved painfully slowly up Highgate Hill. Past The Gatehouse pub on the corner, Geraldine put her foot down and sped west along Hampstead Lane, north to Arkwright Road where she turned left into Frognal. Several police cars were already waiting. Although he had travelled further, Nick arrived only a moment after Geraldine drew up.

'I'll go in first,' she said. 'He's seen me with Sam and might not realise anything's going on if I show up.'

'Is that sensible, given that you think he's dangerous?'

'It's better to have two of us in there when we make the arrest.'

'Why don't I go in? Surely this is a job for a man. You said yourself he could be dangerous –'

Geraldine was glad Sam wasn't there to witness his blatant sexism, but there was no time to protest.

'He's not going to murder police officers in his flat, is he? The danger is that he might get away. He's a dab hand at that. Get uniform in position front and back. Surround the place. Remember, he can vanish through a crack in the wall.'

Nick winced as his inflamed eye hurt when he frowned.

'Are you sure you know what you're doing? It doesn't sound very safe and, if you don't mind my saying, you sound a bit emotional.'

'Can you think of a better plan?' She took a deep breath. 'Look, I'm fine. I'm just going in there to arrest him. He's not going to kick off with two of us in there, is he? We've only got back up here because he's such a slippery customer. He's extricated himself from tighter spots than this. Watch all the exits – including upstairs windows, and the roof. You'll need to check for fire escapes and be ready to alert the neighbours. He might try to get out of the building at any point, however unlikely. He's like spider man.'

'Let's not allow our imaginations to run away with us. Now, there's one piece of advice you really ought to listen to before you go haring off. The main drawback to allowing two women in there unaccompanied –'

Geraldine had no time to listen to any more of his advice. Nick might be under the impression that he was the superior officer present by virtue of his gender and experience, but this was her call to make. It was her investigation. Her sergeant was inside the flat with Darius. The longer they waited, the more chance there was that Sam would say something to provoke him.

'Get uniform in place now. I'm going in.'

63

KEEPING HER EXPRESSION IMPASSIVE, Geraldine rang the bell. She had been here before, but on her first visit had paid no attention to the property. Now she registered the old-fashioned sash windows which would be relatively easy to climb through. A drainpipe ran down the length of the house right beside one of the first floor windows. Apart from the internal stairs, there was likely to be either a permanent metal fire escape out of sight at the back of the property, or a ladder of some sort that could be lowered in case of fire. Moreover, an athletic man could slip out through a skylight in the roof and effect an escape that way. All this passed through her mind as she stood on the step, waiting for Darius to open the door. She hoped Nick would give the uniformed officers sufficiently detailed instructions to prevent anyone leaving the property undetected.

After a few minutes, she rang the bell again. This time Darius opened the door. He smiled easily at her.

'Inspector. What a surprise, seeing you again. How can I help you?'

'I've come to join my colleague.'

She succeeded in keeping her voice level, her tone relaxed, although her heart was beating so fast she could scarcely breathe. She could feel the muscles in her shoulders and back stiffen with tension.

Darius frowned. 'Your colleague?' he repeated. He shook his head and looked perplexed. Then his refined features softened again. 'You're not talking about the sergeant who was here, are you? I've answered all her questions.'

As he made a move to close the door Geraldine stepped smartly across the threshold, preventing him from shutting her out. He raised his fine eyebrows but shuffled aside to make room for her in the narrow hall.

'Where is she?'

He shook his head, still smiling at her.

'I'm not sure who you're supposed to be looking for, but whoever it is you won't find her in my flat. I live here all alone.'

'I'm here to join my colleague,' she repeated quietly. 'Where is she?'

He shrugged. 'I told you, she's not here. No one's here but me – and now you.'

She wasn't sure why his words sounded like a threat.

He folded his arms, considering.

'She was here, but then she left.'

'When?'

'I'm afraid I didn't make a note of the time. I can't be expected to keep track of your sergeant. Now, if that's all, I'd like you to leave.'

Geraldine hesitated, momentarily nonplussed. No one had left the building since the police had arrived in the street, and Darius himself had admitted Sam had been there. The likelihood was that she was still in the building, and Darius was lying. Geraldine knew she could summon the team waiting outside, but first she wanted to get Darius out of the way. If he realised what was happening, he might easily dart through the door to his flat and slam it shut. They would waste valuable time gaining access, by which time he could have made his escape. Not only would they risk losing him, but if a serious crime *had* been committed, the scene would be hopelessly contaminated if they were forced to break in before scene of crime officers arrived. Somehow Geraldine had to get him away from the flat without arousing his suspicion. With a shudder, she realised she was approaching the place as a crime scene. It might already be too late to save Sam.

Darius stood perfectly still, his expression bland. If anything, he looked bored. Yet his eyes never left her face. He seemed to be watching her, catlike, waiting for her next move, calculating his response. She felt as though she had been standing in that narrow hallway for hours, although in reality it was just a few minutes. Too long, if Sam was lying flat on her back injured, unconscious, or possibly dying. Every second counted. Geraldine contemplated abandoning caution and hitting the button on her phone as a signal to Nick that she was in need of urgent assistance. One tap of her finger and a small crowd of bulky constables would come crashing through the door. But she hesitated, wanting to make sure she hadn't got this completely wrong.

'There are a few more questions I'd like to ask you before I go,' she said gently, doing her best to adopt a conversational tone. 'It's just routine. I'm sure you'd like to help us find whoever killed your nephew, wouldn't you?'

Her instincts told her not to trust him; Sam was upstairs. But she had no proof. She couldn't be certain until the flat had been searched. If her suspicions proved unfounded, Darius need never know the street outside his home had been crawling with police, watching every possible means of exit from his flat.

'We're investigating your former brother-in-law,' she announced firmly.

'I know. Your sergeant told me. You seem very keen to tell me about your suspicions. First her, now you.'

'Zak was your nephew. You have a right to know what's going on. And, to be honest, we're hoping you can help us establish his guilt.'

'What can I do?'

This was her chance.

'It would be best if you came with me so we can talk about this somewhere more suitable.'

It seemed a fair enough request, on the face of it, but he looked uneasy. She waited, trying to hide her impatience.

'So,' he replied, moving nearer to her as he spoke, 'you're looking for your colleague and you thought she might be here?'

He was so close he was almost touching her. The front door was shut. She had already considered the possibility that Darius had succeeded in overpowering Sam. The sergeant was a tough, strong woman, trained in self defence and a martial arts expert. For the first time it occurred to Geraldine that in her eagerness to protect Sam, she might have put herself at risk. She had been so wrapped up in worrying about Sam's safety, she hadn't paused to consider her own. Meanwhile, the minutes were ticking by and she had to acknowledge that she couldn't manage the situation by herself.

As she reached for her phone Darius lunged forward to seize both her wrists in a grip like a vice.

'What have you got in your pocket?'

'I was going to blow my nose.'

He tightened his hold. She couldn't move. She squirmed in pain but she couldn't break free of his powerful grip. Suddenly he yanked one of her arms across her chest so he could clutch both her wrists in one hand. At the same time, he thrust his other hand into her pocket. His action was so swift, he had tossed her phone away before she could react. Watching it slide across the floor, she struggled to control her fear.

She had been a fool to go in alone. She had allowed her judgement to be clouded by guilt at having sent Sam to speak to Darius alone, and by her own pride in the face of Nick's patronising tone.

'You said you wanted to join your colleague, didn't you?' Darius hissed, leaning forward until she felt his warm breath on her ear. 'So let's go and see her.'

'The longer this goes on, the worse you're making it for yourself. I suggest you start co-operating, because she will have called for help by now –'

In the poorly lit hall she saw Darius grin.

'She'll be exactly where I left her.'

64

NICK PACED UP AND down watching Geraldine as she strode away. After a moment she disappeared from view and he returned to the car. It was too cold to stand around outside for long.

'Freezing my bollocks off out there,' he muttered to the sergeant who had driven him there. 'Might as well be stuck behind a desk as stuck in here.'

The sergeant grunted. Nick was in a foul mood. It was nearly twenty-four hours since the fight. His face had settled into a steady ache that sent a stabbing pain through his head every time he moved or spoke. All he had planned to do that day was sit quietly at his desk, not talking to anyone, because that only made it hurt more. But he had been dragged away on this crazy chase after a possible suspect.

Normally he would have been pleased to help at a stake out. He hadn't joined the force to sit at a desk all day, like a bloody civil servant. He wanted to be out on the streets, preferably in a speeding car. The rush of adrenaline was what made the job worthwhile. He loved racing through the streets while other vehicles pulled over to let him pass. Nothing matched the exhilaration of a chase on blues and twos, sirens screaming above the roar of the engine, voices barking out orders and tyres squealing. Sitting in a car waiting for a signal from a colleague was less thrilling. The chances were she would reappear and they would return to the station, and that would be the end of it. Another bloody waste of time. If he hadn't been keen to curry favour with Geraldine, he might not have responded to her request in person.

He checked his phone. It was switched on, battery full, with a good signal. He placed it on the dashboard where he could see as well as hear if it rang. There was nothing else he could do but wait. After fifteen minutes, he snatched up his phone and called her. If she didn't need him any more, the least she could do was tell him. He realised she must be busy, questioning Cooper, but he was put out when she didn't answer. He waited a few moments then phoned her again. Still there was no answer.

'Do you think they're all right in there?' his sergeant asked.

'How the hell should I know?' he snapped, irritably.

The situation was out of control, his head ached, and sitting kicking his heels in a cold car wasn't helping anyone.

'Turn the heating up for Christ's sake.'

After ten minutes, he tried her phone again. The fact that she still didn't answer wasn't merely annoying; he was beginning to worry about her. He decided to go in and take a look. If she didn't appreciate him barging in before she'd requested back up, it was her own stupid fault for not communicating with him. She had been in there long enough. His sergeant at his heels, he marched up to the front door. Two uniformed officers accompanied them. The back door was covered, as were the side windows, and more officers were watching the roof. There was no way Cooper could leave unseen. If he really was the invisible killer Geraldine had been looking for, he wasn't going to get past Nick. With a grim smile, he rang the bell.

A dark-haired man came to the door.

'Darius Cooper?'

'Yes.'

The two men sized each other up. Cooper was thin, but he looked strong. His black eyes flicked from Nick to the sergeant at his side, and beyond to the two constables in uniform standing behind him. Nick had his foot over the doorstep but before he could move closer to the suspect, Cooper turned and dashed back along the corridor to disappear up the stairs. He moved like a panther. A second later they heard a door slam upstairs. The four police officers sprinted after him. Nick turned to the constables.

'One of you stay here and watch the street door,' he said. 'There might be another way down. Radio through to the others to watch all the windows. He's on the first floor. He's probably going to try and make a run for it.'

He turned and raced up the stairs after the sergeant and the second constable, his aching head forgotten in the rush of the chase.

'Which door?' the sergeant panted.

There were two doors off the first floor landing. Nick jerked his head, indicating one of them to the sergeant. He ran to the other door himself and began thumping noisily.

'Open up! Police! We've got the building surrounded.'

The door the sergeant was knocking at opened and a wizened face peered up at him.

'Is anyone else in there with you?' the sergeant asked.

'What? Who are you? What do you want?'

'Don't be alarmed. We're the police. We're looking for Darius Cooper. Have you seen him?'

As the sergeant displayed his warrant card, the uniformed constable went over to stand at his side. The elderly man in the flat shook his head.

'Check inside,' Nick instructed the sergeant. 'You –' he nodded at the other constable, 'come with me.'

Nick banged on the door to the next flat but no one answered. He stood back with a nod at the constable.

'Open it.'

Inside it was eerily quiet. Flicking on his torch he found the light switch and looked around at a small square hallway. They split up to search. A quick glance in the first room revealed a sparsely furnished dining room. There was nowhere anyone could be hiding. Torch in hand he went into the bedroom and put the light on. With a swift lunge he dragged the duvet off the bed. It was empty. He approached the wardrobe and flung it open to reveal several pairs of jeans, shirts and a shelf of T-shirts, but no sign of a demented killer and no cowering women. The only other place where someone could be concealed was behind the curtains. They hung a couple of feet off the floor and he could see there was no one there. All the same he checked, just in case. The bedroom was empty. He met the constable in the hall. The kitchen and bathroom were also empty. This time the suspected killer hadn't vanished alone. He had taken two detectives with him.

65

A BRIGHT LIGHT PENETRATED her consciousness. Groggily, she forced her eyes open. Before she had a chance to look around, the bright light disappeared, leaving her in darkness. She hadn't the faintest idea where she was, or how she had arrived in this cold dusty place. She blinked repeatedly. It didn't make much difference. She still couldn't see anything. When she closed her eyes, dazzling neon arrows darted across her field of vision making her feel sick. All she knew for certain was that she was lying on a hard surface, in complete darkness. Her head was pounding, her throat burned, and her arms ached from shoulder to wrist as though they had been twisted fiercely after almost being pulled out of their sockets. She thought she must have been the victim of an attack. Gingerly she turned her head. Raising it from the floor, she was relieved to find she could move normally without any stabbing pains.

Taking a deep breath she sat up. The movement made her feel dizzy. Afraid she might not regain consciousness again, she resisted the temptation to lie down and go back to sleep. Instead she forced herself to sit upright while she tried to collect her thoughts. Everything was hazy. She spoke out loud, encouraging herself, hoping the sound of her own voice would jog her memory. It didn't. Her voice sounded dry and unfamiliar. Ignorant of where she was, or even who she was, it was hard not to panic. Not being able to see anything didn't help her efforts to stay calm. In an attempt to ease the stiffness in her back she shifted her weight, leaning on one elbow, so that she was half sitting up. The floor boards beneath her creaked quietly. Somewhere nearby pipes gurgled softly. As her eyes became accustomed to the darkness, she could see a faint square glow above her head which she thought must be a skylight, and guessed she was in an attic.

Feeling around in the darkness, she worked out that she was lying on bare wooden floorboards. There was nothing in reach of her groping fingers, no phone, no purse, no bag. A slight indentation on her wrist suggested she had recently been wearing a watch. It was unsettling, not knowing what time it was. She hadn't a clue how long she had been lying there when all of a sudden she was bathed in a cold light. The moon was shining through a skylight overhead. Quickly she looked around, eager to learn as much as possible before the darkness returned. A very low sloping ceiling confirmed that she was in a loft, empty apart from a large irregularly shaped bundle of sacking lying on the far side of the room. She wondered what was beneath it. She almost wept when darkness engulfed her once more, before she had time to discover a means of escape. If she was in a loft, there had to be trap door somewhere.

Doing her best to ignore her throbbing head and aching shoulders, she began to make plans. Whoever had brought her here was intending to harm her. Of that she was certain. Before he returned, she had to locate the trap door. When he opened it she would be kneeling behind it, poised to whack him on the head. For her plan to succeed, she needed a weapon. At worst, she would have to beat him off with her bare fists. She tried to ignore the possibility that he might never come back, but in any event that danger was less urgent. If he did return, she would have only one opportunity to take him by surprise. Apart from the large bundle of sacking she had seen, the floor was bare. She began to edge towards it, feeling around in the darkness for something to use as a weapon. There might be a tool box, or at the very least a hammer, concealed under the sacking. Cautiously she crawled forwards on her hands and knees, feeling around for any irregularity in the floor that might indicate a door. Splinters stung her hands and knees. Resolutely she inched her way forwards in the direction of the pile of sacking. It couldn't be far away, but crossing the floor seemed to take hours in the dark.

Dragging herself across the floor boards disturbed the dust, making her sneeze. At last her groping fingers found what she was hunting for. Any desperate hope there might be a box of tools, or an object she could use as a weapon, vanished as her fingers explored the bundle. A shock of adrenaline flooded her body. Her mind cleared. She wasn't alone. All the time someone else had been lying in the loft with her, concealed beneath the sacking. Feeling her way along the other person's back, her fingers found a shoulder and moved past it to bare skin. Whoever was lying there didn't stir, but wasn't cold. Just then the room was suddenly lit up once again. In the moonlight she saw a face.

Memory hit Geraldine like a slap, winding her. She recalled precisely who she was and what she was doing there. It felt like weeks since she had entered the building looking for Sam. Now she had found her, but she might already be too late. Her escape plans forgotten, she leaned over Sam checking for signs of life. Finding a faint pulse, she gave a cry of relief. All the same, Sam was unconscious and in need of urgent medical attention. Not knowing the extent of her injuries, Geraldine didn't dare move her. As darkness enveloped them once more, she heard muffled footsteps below her. Instinctively she hauled herself around to the other side of the inert sergeant. Lying flat on the floor between the body and the wall she listened to a door creaking open. With a sudden crash the trap door fell back, causing the floor to vibrate. The flickering beam of a torch waved around the walls. Over the top of the sacking, Geraldine saw a man's head and shoulders appear. She watched him heave himself up through the trap door. He had to stoop to avoid hitting his head on the sloping roof as he shone the torch around, following it with his head. Behind the beam of light his silhouette loomed. Geraldine held her breath.

66

ONE SNEEZE, ONE INVOLUNTARY movement, and it would all be over. She thought about her sister, and young Chloe, excited about her imminent visit to London. Geraldine had barely considered what they were going to do. London had so much to offer: museums, galleries, shops – she hadn't even asked Celia what Chloe would enjoy. There was still time to plan a few outings. It must be Wednesday night, or possibly Thursday. She had lost track of time. Celia was bringing Chloe round on Friday evening, by which time Geraldine would be either free, or dead. She tried to picture her sister and niece ringing her bell and trying her phone without success. Celia would be furious. She would drive back to Kent fuming at Geraldine for letting Chloe down again.

It was hard to decide who else would care if she died in this cold dark place, beside the sergeant who had spent her final moments carrying out Geraldine's orders. She tried to remember the wording used on such occasions: 'They died in the course of their duty,' or some such stock phrase. Whatever it was would make no difference. Sam would have mourned for her, but she was going to die too. Geraldine's oldest friend, Hannah, would be deeply upset. Other colleagues would be shocked by the fact of her death, but no one else would be personally bereft. Ian Peterson would miss her. Tears threatened at the thought that she might never see him again. With an effort she controlled her emotions and focused her attention on her situation. She wasn't ready to give up yet. With luck and a cool head she might survive.

Even with so many thoughts and emotions spinning in her head, she had been constantly aware of him moving around. The light from his torch wobbled up and down, round and round, searching the shadows, looking for her. Fear threatened to sap her remaining energy. Only her desire to protect Sam drove her to control her physical trembling. If she could manage to stay out of sight until he reached Sam, she might be able to take him down. He was stronger than her, and possibly armed. Nevertheless, she could be in with a chance if she managed to surprise him. Sufficiently startled, he might drop his torch and lose his balance. Lying motionless, straining to hear the slightest sound, she played through possible successful outcomes in her mind. Tripping him up was her best chance, especially if he hit his head in falling and knocked himself out. Realistically, she might at least cause him to stumble and lose focus, buying her enough time to hit him anywhere she could hurt him. If she managed to grab his torch, she could use that as a weapon. Otherwise, she would have only her hands and feet. The prospect made her tremble with terrible anticipation. Kicking a stranger might be the last action she ever carried out.

Shielded by Sam's body, she tensed her muscles, preparing to leap. It sounded as though his shuffling footsteps were creeping closer. If she waited much longer he might hear the pounding of her heart.

When he spoke, she almost yelled aloud, she was so startled.

'Over here!' he shouted. 'More light! Get the paramedics up here now. Holy shit, they're both here.'

Trembling, Geraldine hauled herself off the floor.

'She's in a bad way,' she said, indicating the body lying on the floor between her and Nick.

'You're not looking so hot yourself.'

He shone the torch in her face, making her squint. 'What the hell happened here?'

'Where's Darius? Have you got him?'

'He won't get far. We've got the whole area covered, two choppers sweeping the streets, every road blocked off, armed response unit, half the Met forming a cordon, the streets are being cleared. Nothing moves out there without our say so. There's been a bit of flack from local residents, but we're not taking any chances this time.'

Geraldine frowned. She wouldn't feel safe until Darius was locked up.

Paramedics appeared, accompanied by a couple of constables carrying a strong light. One by one they emerged through the trap door. A doctor examined Geraldine despite her assurances she was fine.

'With respect, you don't look great,' he replied. 'I can't find anything too worrying, but I'd like you to go along to the hospital for a check up.'

'It's nothing a shower and night's sleep won't sort out.'

The doctor insisted, and she was too tired to argue. As she walked over to the door, Nick caught up with her.

'It's over, Geraldine,' he said gently. 'It's all over.'

She glanced at Sam and hoped his reassuring words wouldn't prove to have another meaning altogether for Sam.

'Here,' he went on, handing her the phone and purse Darius had taken from her. 'And mind you don't lose them again.' He grinned, as though he had cracked a joke, before he turned away.

A police constable took Geraldine's elbow to steady her as she climbed into the ambulance.

'Are you all right now?' he asked.

'Yes, thank you,' she answered brusquely, embarrassed at needing help to climb the ramp, but shaking too violently to manage unaided.

Inside the ambulance a nurse was tucking a cover onto the bed. She slipped smartly to one side to allow her patient to pass. Geraldine sat down and fell backwards onto the pillow. Her eyes closed gratefully. She was dimly aware of the nurse gently lifting her legs onto the bed to make her more comfortable, and a blanket being tucked in tightly around her so she could hardly move. A moment later she heard the door click shut, and the vehicle jolted into motion. Geraldine wanted to sleep but every inch of her body ached. When she swallowed, it felt as though she had sand in the back of her throat. She asked for a drink of water and heard the nurse moving quietly beside the bed. She opened her eyes.

Darius was leaning over her, wearing an ill-fitting nurse's uniform and a blonde wig. Thinking she must be dreaming, Geraldine closed her eyes. When she opened them again, he was still there.

'It's not a terribly good disguise, is it?' he said, with an apologetic shrug, 'but it did the trick. Got me out of there. That's all that matters in the end. The place was crawling with filth. Of course they couldn't catch me.' He grinned.

Without answering, Geraldine rolled onto her side. Lying with her back to Darius, she struggled to move her arm beneath the blanket. At last she succeeded in slipping her hand into her pocket, tensing with anticipation as her fingers rummaged under the blanket for the phone Nick had given her.

'I'm not boasting,' Darius went on. 'I'm just saying it how it is. I really do have a gift for theatre. No one ever appreciated it, of course.'

She found the phone and fumbled with it, trying to switch it on. She hoped there would be a signal in the ambulance.

'Well, I suppose I'd better sort you out before we get there.' Darius' voice had lost its conversational tone and become sharp. 'I should have dealt with you when I had the chance,' he added under his breath.

'Wait,' Geraldine said, turning to face him.

He was holding a pillow in both hands. She felt pathetically vulnerable, lying down. Once he had the pillow over her face, she might not stand a chance, however hard she hit out. Desperately she tried to free her arms from the bed cover.

'You might need my help to get away.'

'Why would you want to help me?'

'Look,' she said, staring intensely over his shoulder.

She scarcely dared hope he would fall for such a childish trick and look round. He didn't turn his head, but he hesitated. It only gave her a second. In one rapid lunge, she flung the blanket from her and hurled herself from the bed. The pillow dropped from his hands as he staggered backwards in surprise, hitting his head on the side of the vehicle as they fell to the floor in a heap. She was on top of him, pummelling his face. Snarling, bloodied and enraged, he gripped her under her arms, lifting her up with an almost irresistible strength.

Shrieking with terror, she looked around frantically for something she could use as a weapon while her arms thrashed wildly at him. Summoning the last vestiges of her energy, she swiped at his face with her left hand. Her nails ripped through his skin. Momentarily distracted by the pain, he didn't notice her reach for an oxygen cylinder. He was yelling, 'Not my face!' She was aware of the danger the cylinder might explode, possibly engulfing them both in flames, but there was no time to stop and assess the risk. With a final burst of energy, she brought the cylinder down on his head. Thinking of Sam, she hoped she would crush his skull. As she rammed the cylinder down as forcefully as she could, the ambulance braked. Instead of hitting him directly from above, the blow glanced off the side of his head.

His hold on her loosened, his eyes glazed over and he went limp, but he was still breathing. She raised herself cautiously, observing the gentle rise and fall of his chest, afraid this was another performance. Apart from his bleeding nose and battered face, he could have been asleep. A single thread of blood trickled down his temple from where the edge of the cylinder had caught him. She held his wrists to the floor, leaning on them with all her might, praying that he wouldn't stir before the ambulance reached its destination.

She didn't register when the engine stopped, or hear the door open behind her. She clung on to Darius' wrists, even when a voice cut through her whimpering.

'What the hell's going on?'

67

APART FROM SOME NASTY bruises and a mild shoulder sprain, Geraldine was unharmed. As she had promised, she looked a whole lot better after taking a shower. An amazing quantity of dirt washed off her. The water literally flowed black down the plug hole. Standing in the hot shower, her muscles relaxed for the first time in hours. It felt as though she had spent weeks keeping still, crawling awkwardly, crouching out of sight, or tensed to pounce. In fact only a few hours had passed since she had walked into Darius' flat. Her skin stung where she had grazed herself or been pierced by splinters, and her shoulder ached, but such minor scrapes and bruises would soon heal. Meanwhile, the severity of Sam's injuries was still under investigation, her recovery uncertain.

Despite her anxiety about Sam, Geraldine slept well on Thursday night. On Friday morning she discharged herself from the hospital with the doctor's guarded approval. First she had to give an undertaking that she would visit her own GP the following day, and go straight back to the hospital if she felt at all unwell. After a shower, a thorough examination to confirm that she hadn't suffered any serious injury, and a night's sleep, she felt almost back to normal. Only her aching shoulder and her constant worry about Sam reminded her of her ordeal. As soon as she had checked out, she went to see how Sam was doing. The sergeant was stable and making progress, whatever that meant, but she hadn't yet regained consciousness. There was nothing Geraldine could do for her friend, so she left.

She was relieved to discover that Reg was out. If he had been there, he would probably have insisted on questioning Darius himself. Not only was Geraldine keen to see the investigation through, she had to make sure nothing could possibly go wrong. Whatever else happened, Darius had to pay for what he had done to Sam.

'Are you sure you should be conducting the interview, after what he did to you?' Nick asked. 'Can't it wait till Reg is back tomorrow? Or I could talk to him if you like. I don't mind.'

Briskly Geraldine dismissed both his suggestions.

Darius had killed three innocent people, endangering the life of a young police sergeant in the course of his killing spree. Geraldine wasn't interested in finding out why he had done it. Her sole reason for wanting to question him was so she could make sure he went down. He might be a master of escape, but he wasn't going to get away this time. And she was determined to be there to nail him. For now, he was merely a suspect. Even the charge of assaulting two police officers could be mitigated by a spurious defence about temporary derangement. With a clever barrister, he might even convince a jury that he had mistaken Sam and Geraldine for intruders. She had to make sure he was convicted.

Darius acknowledged her entrance with a nod. When the preliminaries were over, Geraldine began to ask her questions. He didn't need prompting. On the contrary, he was eager to boast about his exploits, his attempt on his interlocutor's life apparently forgotten.

'So you admit you killed Anna Porter, Bethany Marsden, and Zak Trevelyan?'

He didn't flinch at the mention of his nephew's name. 'It was the only way,' he said softly.

'I don't follow. What had any of them done to you? Help me out here. I really don't understand why you killed them.'

'He had to pay for what he did.'

'Who had to pay?'

'My brother-in-law.'

'Piers Trevelyan?'

'Yes, Piers Trevelyan.' He screwed his face into a grimace of disgust as he said the name.

'What did he have to be punished for?'

'For Ella's death.'

'Ella, your sister?'

'Yes, my sister.'

'She died nearly twenty years ago.'

'It's not as long as that. And in any case, time makes no difference. She deserves justice.'

He leaned forward, and his voice grew urgent.

'You can't depend on the law to do anything. I tried.' He shook his head, his expression solemn. 'God knows, I tried. I told them over and over again, but they wouldn't listen.'

'Who wouldn't listen?'

'The police. I told them he did it. She never should have married him. I did my best to warn her, but she wouldn't listen to me either. He had a hold on her. She would have done anything for that man.'

'She was in love with him.'

He glared at her. Geraldine wondered if that was what Darius had been unable to forgive.

'Ella loved everyone,' he replied sourly. 'She was an angel.'

Geraldine nodded. He had told her that before. She wanted to talk to him about Piers.

'Piers must have loved her very much –'

'Love? Huh. There was only one person he ever loved. Himself. He was selfish and cruel. She should never have married him. He was always running after other women when he could have been with her. She was so miserable. I would have killed him myself, right there and then, but I didn't want to see her any more upset. I wish I had done afterwards, because he grew tired of her and that's why he killed her, so he could be free of her.'

Geraldine wasn't sure she had understood him correctly.

'Are you telling me he made her so unhappy that he drove her to suicide?'

'No!' His voice rose hysterically. 'Why won't anyone believe me? He killed her. He held her head under and drowned her. He wanted to be rid of her.'

'Why didn't he divorce her?'

He shrugged. 'Because of his son. He didn't want to lose control of her child.'

Darius could offer no evidence to support his accusation.

'When did you ever hear of someone drowning in a bath by accident?' was all he would say in defence of his claim.

Carefully Geraldine steered the conversation back to the recent deaths. Off the subject of his sister, Darius cheerfully described in detail how he had carried out the murders disguised as a woman. He had worn the same blonde wig to escape from each of the three crime scenes, and had been wearing it again when he had been apprehended in the ambulance.

'It's not the best wig,' he added apologetically.

He confessed he had been shaken by the car crash, but had managed to jump from the van virtually unscathed.

'It's what I do,' he added airily.

Miraculously, Anna had survived the crash. Within seconds he had discovered she was still alive, and had inflicted a fatal wound on the back of her neck. Those few seconds had nearly cost him his freedom, because a policeman arrived before Darius had a chance to slip away.

'That stupid plod.' He grinned at the memory. 'He didn't have a clue! I didn't have to do anything. He sent me away himself.' He laughed out loud. 'I spun him a yarn about being a reporter, the public have a right to know and all that claptrap, and he told me to sling my hook. He said the public had a right to be protected from people like me. It wasn't perfect. I would have liked her to drown. I should have drowned her –'

He broke off with a far away look in his eyes.

With the right preparation, it had been easy for a stunt man of Darius' experience to climb off a road bridge, and out of a third floor window. He boasted that he had escaped from all three crime scenes with very little trouble.

'Impressive, eh?'

Geraldine listened impassively. Inwardly she was shocked by

his cavalier attitude to human life. Unhinged by his sister's death, he had ended the lives of three innocent people – including Ella's own son – without any compunction. Geraldine should have been satisfied with his full confession. But there were still unanswered questions.

'I don't understand why you killed Anna, and Bethany, and Zak. Your anger was directed against Piers. Why didn't you kill him?'

'Death would have been too easy for him. He had to be made to suffer, just like he made her suffer. I wanted to break his heart. He would have had his turn, only you stopped me before I'd had a chance,' he added with a spark of anger.

'What do you mean? A chance to do what?'

'Don't you see? When I'd made him suffer enough, broken him down to nothing, I was going to drown him in the bath.'

Geraldine frowned. 'I still don't understand. Why did you want to persecute him after all this time? Ella's been dead for nearly twenty years.'

'Yes, she's dead, and he gets an award for lifetime services to the industry. You must have seen it in the news. *She's* forgotten, and *he* gets a lifetime of achievement.' He sat forward, with sudden energy. 'Do you know what happens to a stunt man when he reaches forty-five? He's finished. I tried, but no one would give me work. So I went to Piers, God forgive me. I knew what he'd done but I went to him for help. And you know what? He didn't remember me! His own wife's brother! When I told him who I was, he said "Ella's history." His own wife!'

He shrugged and leaned back in his chair. 'That's when I knew what I had to do. All these years I'd imagined him riddled with guilt and grief, and he'd moved on as though she'd never even existed. She had to be avenged. I did it for her. A life for a life.'

'Three lives,' she corrected him.

It could be four. At the thought of Sam, her head seemed to fill with blood pumping with such force it felt as though her skull would burst. She paused in her interrogation, shocked by the power of her feelings. In that instant, her will was almost swept aside by an urge to kill Darius, squeeze the breath out of his lungs with her bare hands. But between desire and action lay an unshakable belief in the right to life.

'You killed Ella's son,' she said, trying to put Sam out of her mind.

'Her son, huh! He, of all people, should have wanted to avenge her death, but when I offered him a picture of her, he threw it back in my face. Oh come on,' he added, noticing her frown, 'it's not as if I was doing anything wrong. Quite the opposite, wouldn't you say?'

'What do you mean?'

'I was putting things right. He drowned Ella. She was mine and he took her away from me, held her head under the water and watched her struggle. In the end only her legs were kicking, because he was holding both her wrists as he pushed her head, pushed it and pushed it until even her legs stopped moving.' His eyes were still, looking inward. 'He sat with her until all the bubbles had gone and the water was cold.'

Geraldine stared at him, aghast.

'It was you,' she whispered. 'You drowned your sister.'

'No, I wasn't there when they found her.'

He gave a cunning smile. His eyes glittered.

'There was a window in the bathroom,' Geraldine said.

'They said it was an accident,' he repeated. 'I told them he did it. Why didn't anyone listen to me?'

'You killed Ella.'

'No, no, it wasn't like that. I loved Ella. I loved her.'

68

GERALDINE WENT ALONG TO the hospital early on Saturday morning. She sat by her colleague's bed, trying to feel reassured by the steady rhythm of the heart monitor. After a while she dozed off and missed the moment Sam's eyes flickered open. A faint mutter alerted her to the patient's return to consciousness.

'Is that you? Mum?'

Geraldine sprang to her feet. 'It's Geraldine. Your mother will be here soon. I'm going to call a nurse.'

'Wait.'

Geraldine hesitated at the curtain while Sam mumbled incoherently under her breath. All Geraldine could make out was 'I'll try to be there next Christmas.'

Seriously worried, Geraldine hurried off. Before she reached the desk she met a nurse who was on her way to check on Sam.

'She's awake but she's rambling, talking about Christmas. Is she – will she be – She thought I was her mother.'

'Don't worry. It's perfectly normal. She's been sedated for hours, and even when she wakes up properly she's going to be confused for a while.'

Sam had been moved out of intensive care so Geraldine went back to the ward and sat at her bedside. She would have stayed there all day on the off chance Sam would wake up again.

Sam's parents arrived shortly before midday. Without directing her recriminations at Geraldine specifically, Sam's mother made it clear she blamed her daughter's senior officers for her condition.

'I don't understand it,' she said, glaring at Geraldine. 'Sam would never have put herself at risk like that, going to question a dangerous suspect all by herself. Someone must have sent her there. Whoever it was should at least have gone with her. But I suppose senior officers know better than to endanger their own lives.'

'Now, now, Alice,' Sam's father said, 'don't go upsetting yourself all over again.'

'My daughter's lying here in a coma and you're telling me I shouldn't be upset.'

After an awkward exchange of greetings, Geraldine took her leave. There was nothing she could do for Sam, and she felt as though she was in the way at the hospital, so she arranged for a lift to Hendon where her own car was parked. After checking in at work, she intended driving back to the hospital, and then home in time for Chloe's arrival at seven.

It felt weird rapping on the familiar door to check in with Reg. Outwardly nothing had changed, but Sam was lying in a hospital bed, drifting in and out of consciousness. Geraldine had managed to have a word with a doctor that morning. He had confirmed that Sam didn't appear to have suffered any brain damage. But he admitted that was a clinical judgement, not a certainty.

'How is she?' Reg asked without any preamble. He knew Geraldine had come straight from the hospital.

Only after she had brought him up to speed on Sam's condition did he enquire about her own state.

'You're looking rough,' he added, gazing at her with such genuine concern that she felt her eyes water.

'I'm fine,' she answered gruffly. 'Just a few scrapes and bruises, that's all.'

Naively expecting him to send her home, she was unprepared for his censure as he rounded on her for placing Sam in danger.

'What the hell were you playing at?'

Dismayed at the turn things were taking, and vexed with herself for failing to see this coming, she explained how no one had known the truth about Darius at that time. Sam had simply gone to ask him about Piers' past. As soon as Geraldine suspected Darius himself might be the killer, she had gone straight to Frognal, arranging for Nick and a back up team to join her as quickly as possible. Reg was remorseless as he challenged her decision to send Sam alone in the first place, and asked her to justify why she had summoned Nick, who wasn't even on the case, and how she had selected the back up team.

'More important than all of that, it beggars belief that you never once thought to consult me while all this was going on. I had to find out from another officer, who shouldn't even have been involved in the first place.'

'I know I should have called you, but it all happened so fast. There wasn't time –'

'There wasn't time? Yet you had time to phone Nick. The fact is, you took it on yourself to make a decision that risked the life of an officer.'

'Nick happened to call me so I asked him for help.'

'He *happened* to call you? Is that how we operate here, on the basis of random phone calls? What would you have done if he hadn't happened to call you when he did?'

Geraldine understood Reg was covering his own back. If Sam was seriously injured, he had no intention of being held accountable. It was fair enough. After all, it had been Geraldine's decision to send Sam to Darius' flat. Reg had nothing to do with it. Not so long ago she would have been angered that his priority was to keep himself out of trouble. As her senior officer, he expected her loyalty and unquestioning obedience, yet was prepared to abandon her at the first sign of trouble. Intent on promotion, she wondered if his cavalier attitude to others would prove his downfall. More likely it would protect him from blame when anything went wrong. But it had been her call, and she was prepared to shoulder the blame. She didn't care any more. If her blunder led to demotion, she would live with that. All that mattered to her right now was that Sam recovered.

Shocked by the dressing down Reg had meted out, Geraldine drove back to the hospital. There was still time to visit Sam before Chloe was due to arrive. It meant she wouldn't have time to prepare anything for them to eat, but she was sure Chloe would be happy to be taken out. To her relief, Sam's parents had gone to the canteen. She sat down and noticed Sam's eyelids flicker.

'Mum?' she muttered.

'It's me, Geraldine.'

Sam's eyes flew open. 'I hope my mum didn't give you a hard time over this.'

A weight that seemed to have been pressing down on Geraldine's head lifted suddenly.

Sam opened her eyes and stared at Geraldine with an anxious expression.

'What is it, Sam? What's up?'

'Apart from all this, you mean?' Sam indicated her hospital bed. 'Oh, don't you ever just want to stuff the job, and all the protocols and regulations in PACE, and just go out and get the evil bastard you're after, and beat the crap out of him?'

Having wanted to strangle Darius with her bare hands, Geraldine knew exactly what Sam meant. 'Take the law into your own hands, you mean?'

Sam sighed. 'I know,' she agreed, misinterpreting Geraldine's question as an expression of disapproval. 'We're the ones who are supposed to uphold the law, maintain some sort of order in society. We're the bastion against lawlessness and rioting and lynching. Without us there'd be a bloodbath. Armageddon. I just find it hard sometimes, always playing by the rules.'

'It is hard. That's why there have to be rules.'

Ashamed at not having the courage to admit to her own violent impulse, Geraldine forced what she hoped was a reassuring smile.

'Don't look so smug,' Sam scolded her. 'You know I'm never going to forgive you for what happened.'

Geraldine started forward. Exhausted, she struggled to blink back tears of disappointment.

'I'll never forgive myself. I shouldn't have sent you there alone –'

'Oh, I'm not talking about *that*,' Sam interrupted her. 'You weren't to know he was a psychopath. In fact, if it wasn't for you, we still wouldn't have worked out who killed Anna, Bethany and

Zak, and he'd probably still be at it, plotting his next murder.'

Geraldine didn't pause to reveal that Darius had admitted he had been planning at least one more death. She had a more immediate question on her mind.

'I don't understand. What won't you forgive me for then?'

'For letting that tosser Nick Williams act like some bloody knight in shining armour. Christ, Geraldine, of all people, how could you let *him* save my life? As if he's not insufferable enough already. He'll be impossible now.'

Seeing Geraldine's expression Sam laughed, then stopped abruptly. 'Ow. It hurts my neck when I laugh.'

'Serves you right!'

They smiled at one another.

'Don't go yet,' Sam said as Geraldine stood up.

'I've got to. My niece is coming to stay and I need to get back for her.'

'Do me a favour?'

'Anything.'

'If you see my mother, don't tell her I'm awake. The nurse told her I shouldn't be disturbed when I'm asleep. It just means I'll get a bit of peace. She's on at me to leave the force. She won't shut up about it.'

Geraldine carefully kept her feelings to herself as she asked, 'Are you going to quit?'

'You think I'd be here now if I listened to my mother?' Sam smiled. 'She'll get over it. She's not so bad really.'

'But what about you?' Geraldine asked. 'Are you sure you're going to be all right?'

'Yes. There's nothing wrong with me. They might send me home tomorrow. I'll probably go and stay with my parents for a few days, but the doctor said I could be back at work in a couple of weeks.'

'I'll see you soon then.'

'Geraldine?'

'Yes?'

'Thank you.'

'What for?'

'For always showing me how we should be.'

Geraldine hesitated, wondering whether to come clean about her own dark urges, but Sam's eyes had closed and she was snoring gently. The opportunity had passed. Uncertain whether to feel ashamed or relieved, Geraldine turned and made her way out of the ward.

A LETTER FROM LEIGH

Dear Reader,

I hope you enjoyed reading this book in my Geraldine Steel series. Readers are the key to the writing process, so I'm thrilled that you've joined me on my writing journey.

You might not want to meet some of my characters on a dark night – I know I wouldn't! – but hopefully you want to read about Geraldine's other investigations. Her work is always her priority because she cares deeply about justice, but she also has her own life. Many readers care about what happens to her. I hope you join them, and become a fan of Geraldine Steel, and her colleague Ian Peterson.

If you follow me on Facebook or Twitter, you'll know that I love to hear from readers. I always respond to comments from fans, and hope you will follow me on **@LeighRussell** and **fb.me/leigh.russell.50** or drop me an email via my website **leighrussell.co.uk**.

That way you can be sure to get news of the latest offers on my books. You might also like to sign up for my newsletter on **leighrussell.co.uk/news** to make sure you're one of the first to know when a new book is coming out. We'll be running competitions, and I'll also notify you of any events where I'll be appearing.

Finally, if you enjoyed this story, I'd be really grateful if you would post a brief review on Amazon or Goodreads. A few sentences to say you enjoyed the book would be wonderful. And of course it would be brilliant if you would consider recommending my books to anyone who is a fan of crime fiction.

I hope to meet you at a literary festival or a book signing soon!

Thank you again for choosing to read my book.

With very best wishes,

Leigh Russell

noexit.co.uk/leighrussell

About Us

In addition to No Exit Press, Oldcastle Books has a number of other imprints, including Kamera Books, Creative Essentials, Pulp! The Classics, Pocket Essentials and High Stakes Publishing > oldcastlebooks.co.uk

For more information about Crime Books > crimetime.co.uk

Check out the kamera film salon for independent, arthouse and world cinema > kamera.co.uk

For more information, media enquiries and review copies please contact marketing > marketing@oldcastlebooks.com